BOOKS BY CECELIA HOLLAND

The Serpent Dreamer
The Witches' Kitchen
The Soul Thief
The Angel and the Sword
Lily Nevada
An Ordinary Woman
Railroad Schemes
Valley of the Kings
Jerusalem
Pacific Street
The Bear Flag
The Lords of Vaumartin
Pillar of the Sky
The Belt of Gold
The Sea Beggars
Home Ground
City of God
Two Ravens
Floating Worlds
Great Maria
The Death of Attila
The Earl
Antichrist
Until the Sun Falls
The Kings in Winter
Rakóssy
The Firedrake
Varanger
The High City

FOR CHILDREN

The King's Road
Ghost on the Steppe

A TOM DOHERTY ASSOCIATES BOOK

New York

KINGS
of the
NORTH

CECELIA HOLLAND

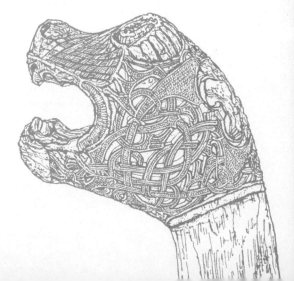

This is a work of fiction. All of the characters, organizations, and events portrayed in this novel are either products of the author's imagination or are used fictitiously.

KINGS OF THE NORTH

A Forge Book
Published by Tom Doherty Associates, LLC
175 Fifth Avenue
New York, NY 10010

www.tor-forge.com

Forge® is a registered trademark of Tom Doherty Associates, LLC.

ISBN 978-0-7653-2192-3

First Edition: July 2010

Printed in the United States of America

0 9 8 7 6 5 4 3 2 1

for CHARLES BROWN

KINGS
of the
NORTH

CHAPTER ONE

The two men were tending to the horses, Raef drawing up water from the well, Leif stooping to run his hand along the black mare's foreleg. Neither of them was paying any attention to Laissa, and she slipped away from them into the market.

The wide village common boomed with people, haggling with the fishmongers and piemen, calling wares, arguing and yelling and laughing—crowds of children and animals. A pig had gotten loose, and two boys were whooping after it in and out of the packed shoppers. On the far side of the common, a stone church stood, and along its front porch a line of women sat with baskets of bread for sale.

She went that way. She had to find her mother; as if some blood memory warmed in her she knew she was near. For over a year now she had been hearing French spoken but never before with this accent, and this accent rang in her ears like silver bells. She had heard these voices before, a long time ago. Her heart was pounding. She was close, close, after all the years of searching she was very close.

She spoke French badly, but she had memorized the words she needed and knew from experience to ask women. She went toward the church and the women with their bread, waited until a girl only a little older than she caught her eye, and smiled.

The girl smiled back. Laissa sank down beside her. "Please. Maybe you can help me?"

The girl gave her a puzzled look. "I must have money for my bread."

"No, I am not begging. I want—I look for my family, my home. I think I am from here, when a little child, very little.

Somehow I am—was lost. I was found alone in Constantinople, many years ago."

"Constantinople!" the girl gasped, cast a look around her at the other women, who were turning to listen. "How could this be? That's the far side of the world. Why do you think you are from here?" Her gaze searched Laissa's face. "But yes, I see it. You are like us, your hair, your eyes. You look Norman."

Laissa gripped her hands together. It was all she could do to keep from throwing her arms around the other girl. "I am. I recognize the way you speak. He called me ma p'te chérie—"

"Ma chérie," the girl repeated. All the other women were crowding around her now. Laissa's head reeled. When the girl spoke, for the first time she heard a woman's voice in her memory.

One of the other women murmured, "What a sad story this is! And you've come all this way alone?"

She slipped over that. She did not want to explain about Raef and Leif. She said, "Do you know of anyone—around the time your King Hugh is crowned—." She had practiced this much; she knew what would fix the time for them. "Anyone who went eastward, on the pilgrimage to Jerusalem, maybe."

They bloomed with sympathy; they gathered her in, womanly, motherlike. Someone pressed a piece of bread into her hand. "Poor thing!" Their gazes on her were lively with curiosity. "Poor girl! No mother?"

"Constantinople!" said an old woman. "The city of gold! Why did she ever leave?"

"What is your name?" someone said.

"She's not that old," said another. "King Hugh was long ago."

"I was very young. My name is Laissa."

The girl she had spoken to first was shaking her head, her brow furrowed, her eyes soft with feeling. "But this is so sad. You remember nothing?"

"I remember some words," Laissa said. "Ma petite. Ma chérie. Sacre cœur. Rawn."

The others sighed. "Laissa. How strange. That's not French, surely. Would that we could help you."

"Rawn," said a man's voice, behind her. "That could be Rouen."

At that a quiver went down her back; she wheeled toward him. "Rouen. Rouen." She strained to make it sound familiar.

He smiled at her, a fair young man with red cheeks. He said, "They keep records in the church. Let's go find the priest. Maybe we could find something there."

"Oh," she said, almost breathless. "Would you help me?"

"Yes, of course. Come with me."

He started off toward the church, and she followed. The women turned at once to one another, their voices rising, excited at new gossip. The young man led her down a lane beside the church, away from the market. The lane turned, following the church wall, a graveyard on the other side.

Over her head, a hawk screamed, and she looked up, startled. It was Raef's hawk. She seldom followed them into towns. Laissa's hands prickled up with warning, but she thrust that away. She was finding her mother. The young man ahead of her led her on. Records, names and places, written in the church, at last something solid. He turned another corner, so they were behind the church, and wheeled and grabbed her arm.

"Now," he said, "be good to me, and then I will help you."

She went stiff with fear. His high-colored face had changed, not smiling now, not kind, and she wrenched at his grip. "No—"

He wrapped his free arm around her and clapped his hand over her mouth. "Do as I say. If you fight I'll tell them you came lewdly to me. They'll have no mercy on you for that."

She thrashed in his grasp; he shoved her against the wall, trying to hold her and at the same time get her skirts up, and then from the sky the hawk stooped at him.

He screamed. In a wild flapping of wings the hawk thrust her talons at his face, and he let go of Laissa to strike at the bird. Laissa turned and ran. At the corner of the church she glanced back and saw the hawk beating her wings, climbing up and away, and the young man swaying, dazed, his red cheeks streaming blood.

He lurched after Laissa, screaming. "Liar—Stop her—she's a whore—she's a witch! She did this to me—"

"No," she cried, but she ran down the lane toward the market. Before she reached it Raef burst into the narrow way toward her, his face wild, and she flung herself into his arms.

"I didn't—"

The young man was still coming after her. "She attacked me—" His voice high, panting—"when I took her to the church—when she stepped on holy ground she turned into a demon—"

"No," she cried, again. Raef spun around and thrust her ahead of him toward the market.

"Don't talk. Run!"

"Pagans!" the bleeding man cried. "Stop them—they are devil spawn—"

Laissa burst out into the market, past the women selling bread, their heads all swiveling at once toward her, open-mouthed. Around the market everybody was looking toward her. After her came the shriek of the bloody man.

"Get them! Stone them! For Jesus's sake, fight the evil!"

Leif surged up before her, mounted on the bay horse, leading the mare by the bridle. Half a step behind her, Raef got her arm and boosted her onto the black mare's saddle. "Go!" A stone caromed off the horse's flank, and it bolted.

Laissa almost fell off. She dug her fingers into the mane, her feet kicking frantically for the stirrups. Leif had her reins. He led her at a gallop across the crowded market. People scattered out of their way, but now the cry came from all sides.

"Pagans! Stone them—"

She clutched the mane, her breath sobbing through her teeth, and Leif led her at a dead gallop out of the village.

⟿

The road led them northwest, and, only a few miles later, they reached the edge of the sea.

Leif wrestled the horses to a stop at the lip of a little grassy bluff. The pale sandy beach swept away down to the water. The wind blew the tang of salt and seaweed straight into their faces. Raef jogged up beside them, panting from the hard run. When he saw the water he cried out and went down onto the beach and stood there, staring out to sea, the wind lashing his cloak and his long hair.

Leif twisted to look behind them. "They're still coming."

Laissa glanced over her shoulder. A crowd of men was struggling along the road half a mile behind them. Even from here she could see the blood on the face of the man leading them. Her heart hammered. He had turned the sin on her. To save himself he was damning her. Overhead the hawk screamed again.

Laissa looked up. In the sky the hawk was struggling to reach them, fighting the wind, circling higher and then tumbling down the wild air. On the beach, Raef turned and held up his arms, and the hawk fell toward him. As she fell she seemed to stretch, a long ragged russet robe of feathers.

Leif said, "We have to get out of here." But he dismounted and helped Laissa slide off her saddle so they stood in the lee of the bluff. He put his arm around her. Raef came toward them, his cloak folded around the hawk.

He came in among them and drew the cloak back. Where the hawk had been was an old, old woman in a russet gown, her eyes huge and fierce, her nose like a beak.

She was tired. There was blood on her mouth, and she

leaned on Raef as if she could not stand without him. Laissa had seldom seen her in this, her real form; the girl lowered her eyes, shy, murmured "my lady," and bowed. Leif backed away and went down on one knee.

"Raef," he said, "they are still after us."

"They don't matter." Raef drew the cloak around the old woman again, holding her against him. "Gunnhild. England is just beyond this water. We are almost there."

Gunnhild laid her head against his chest and shut her eyes. "You must go on without me. I am done."

"Did he hurt you? I'll kill him."

"No, no," the old woman said. "This is my ending, long foretold. I dare go no closer to her. Already I can feel her power."

Raef said, "Who? Whose power? You only said we had to go to England."

"You must. Because of her, the other, the enemy. The thief of souls. Who has no name in this world or maybe anywhere else." Her eyes closed. "You know who she is. You were born in her house."

Raef let go an explosion of breath. "The Lady of Hedeby." Beside Laissa, Leif shaped his fingers into a sign against evil. Raef said, "But Corban destroyed her."

"No—Corban and his sister and his wife only bound her. This is my fault, son of my soul, curse me for it if you want, but you must make it right."

"What?"

"I have never told you this—I feared your anger. I deserve it. You remember when I left you years ago in Denmark, after King Bluetooth died. I went to Hedeby, where she was bound, and I freed her. She must have a woman's body to inhabit, and I gave her mine. I thought to hitch her power to me, you see, and become great again thereby. But I miscalculated. She is much greater than I, and she would have consumed me. She may consume the world. This much I know—you can stop her. Somehow, if you can get to Jorvik, you can defeat her. And so I went and found you and brought you this far. But now I am done."

Laissa turned her head; even with the wind in her face she could hear now the cry of the mob. She turned back toward Gunnhild, who mattered more than that. Leif tightened his arm around her. "We've got to get moving, Raef."

Gunnhild said, "One last thing I can do. Howe me."

Raef leaned over her, sheltering her in the hollow of his arm, his cheek against her hair. "I won't let you die."

"Obey me, damn you, Raef!" Her face quivered. She seemed thinner, as if she were fading into the air. Laissa whimpered. Gunnhild said, "Remember what I taught you. Howe me here, now."

He lifted his head, his gaze on Laissa and Leif, standing there, watching him. The grief harrowed his face. He said, "Help me." He bent and lifted the old woman's body in his arms, carrying her like a child down onto the beach.

⸻◦⸺

He wrapped Gunnhild in his cloak. He laid her on her back on the sand, with her head toward the north—where the North Star would shine when the night came—and drew the edge of the cloak over her face. He put his long knife at her right hand, because she was a warrior. He set the last of his money at her feet, a cup and a hunk of bread there also, to keep her on her journey. Finally, he cut off a piece of his hair and twisted it into a knot and put it inside the cloak above her breast.

Laissa and Leif brought the horses down after him and helped him gather stones, and quickly they laid them around her in lines that came to a point at each end, the bow and stern of the ship that would carry her home. As they finished this the fair young man and his mob panted up onto the edge of the sea bluff behind them.

Laissa and Leif shrank back away from the mob, almost to the water's edge. The sun was setting. Raef kneeled by the old woman's body. He could not bear to cover her. The young man was shouting at him. Raef ignored this; with his hands he began to heap the sand onto Gunnhild's body.

The bleeding man cried, triumphant, "You see—I told you—see what they do? They are evil—stone them to death!"

Raef ignored him, piling the sand up into a mound over her. Down, at the edge of the shore, the sea growled up a white froth. He knew this was not the broad ocean, but it was close enough. If he stopped working even a moment, his grief and terror drove sharp into the center of him.

"God, strike them down. God, give us the honor of killing them in your name!"

Someone in the crowd had cobbled together a torch and lit it as the darkness fell, and the light flickered out over the beach, cast Raef's shadow down toward the sea. He put stones onto the howe. He set them down gently, to keep from hurting her. He wished he could cut out the stone of his heart and lay it there with her. He went down toward the beach, looking for more rocks.

The mob rushed forward toward the mound. The young man cried, "Get them—as we are Christians, we must stand for our faith—God will not forgive us if we let them go!"

Leif called, "Raef, someone else is coming."

From the mob came a pelting of stones. Raef faced them, angry, getting between them and the howe; a rock glanced off his shoulder. Several horsemen were galloping down the beach from the north. The mob swarmed toward Raef, the torch blazing overhead, the young man howling as he came in an ecstasy of righteousness.

"Heretic! Devil's spawn—"

"This is no matter of yours, or your god's," Raef said. "Why don't you leave us alone?"

"You admit it," the young man cried. The crowd gave up a huge yell.

"Kill them! Kill them all!" The young man lifted his two hands and formed a cross of his forefingers and thrust them toward Raef, and the torchlight cast the shape out over the howe.

The howe exploded. For an instant it shone bright as the sun. Raef felt the blast against his back and saw the white blaze glare across the beach; he felt the fire pierce him through and through. The young man tumbled backward, his arms over his face. The rest lurched away, screaming, and many ran and many fell down and all prayed. Down the beach, the oncoming horses skidded to a stop, neighing and rearing.

As the light faded, one rider forced his frenzied mount up toward Raef. His voice thundered with authority. "What is this? What just happened? Who are you?"

The dark closed down on them. Raef could make out the big man's form, the horse still jumping and snorting under him, its eyes white. "I am Raef Corbansson. Who are you?"

"My lord." The young man struggled up to his feet, his gaze on the first horseman. "Thank God you have come. These are heretics—they have made this heathen altar—" He staggered forward, his arm thrust toward Raef. "Take them!"

Raef folded his arms over his chest, looking up at the horseman. The rider glanced at the young man, took his foot from his stirrup, put it on the man's chest, and kicked him flat to the sand. To Raef, he said, "I am the Duke of Normandy, and nothing happens here save I permit it." He turned his gaze on the howe. "This is a grave. A Viking grave. Whom have you buried?"

"The Queen of Norway," Raef said. "I obeyed her wish, which is higher to me than anything of yours."

The horseman stared at him a moment, silent. The mob had mostly vanished. The young man crawled off into the grass on the bluff. Finally the Norman lord said, "I have never heard of you." He turned, waving toward his horsemen, clustered a good distance away down the beach. "Come with me while I think about this."

Raef glanced at Leif and Laissa, off by the surf. The mob was gone. Gunnhild had saved them again, one last time. He looked back at the man looming over him and shrugged one shoulder.

"Very well. There's nothing more to do here. I will go with you."

⸙

Richard FitzRichard liked to call himself the Duke of Normandy, which sounded loftier than just count. He had some vague idea it was Latin. He would have preferred to call himself king, but the French king claimed suzerainty over Normandy from old times, and Richard could not deny what had been sworn, even though this king was not the man or even the grandson of the man it had been sworn to.

In fact Richard was master over all Normandy, and no one was master over him, no matter what had just happened on his beach. The Queen of Norway, he thought, and some words of an old tale rose into his mind. He had heard the name Corbansson before too, with a different forename.

What this Corbansson had done, back there on the beach, the old Normans would have understood. Richard's father would have understood, who had favored Vikings above all others. The present Richard rode over the bluff, his men coming after him, and the tall stranger with the long white hair walking beside him, his two followers on their horses just behind.

Nonetheless, Richard was supposed to be a Christian, and this would not sit well with the Christians, especially the King of France. He said, "You are not staying here within my country."

The tall man walked beside him, keeping up effortlessly with the long-striding horse. "I am going to England."

"Ah." Suddenly Richard's interest sharpened. He glanced

at the man beside him, the homely face, the pale hair hanging in its matted braids almost to his waist. "Why?"

The tall man shrugged and said nothing. They were riding away from the beach, along the road that wound north. In the dark the broad country spread around them, picked out here and there with the faint lights of home fires. Richard said, "You are Ethelred's man?"

Corbansson gave him a brief sideways glance. "I am no one's man. Is Ethelred Edgarsson then still King of the English?"

"Yes. My sister is his queen." Richard remembered something else. "I have heard this name before—Corbansson. Together with Sweyn Forkbeard's."

"I pulled an oar once for Sweyn Tjugas," the tall man said. "I have not seen him in a dozen years or more."

Richard frowned. He wondered if mere chance brought this Viking with the strange name here now, on his way to England. For a long time Richard had been playing his own game in England, in which marrying his sister Emma to Ethelred had been a key move. Between him and Sweyn Forkbeard, the King of Denmark, and Ethelred, the King of the English, there had grown a dense, constantly shifting web of ambition that many would-be spiders danced upon. Emma had been more use in this than he had expected. He wondered if the white-haired stranger was a spider or a fly.

In any case it did no harm to help him along. He lifted one arm and pointed.

"Yonder is my hall, where I am stopping now. You are going on your way. Here." He took a ring from his finger and held it out. "Show this to anyone who bars you or anywhere you need help. Go north on this road and in three days' time you will come to Sainte-Valerie. There you will likely find a ship to take you to England."

The tall man took the ring, "Thank you." Even in the dark Richard saw the piercing attention of his look. He had the sudden sensation that the tall man was looking straight through his eyes into his mind.

"I need no thanks. I am getting you out of here. Give the ring to the priest at the Church of the Sacred Heart in Sainte-Valerie." Richard lifted his arm. "Farewell." He swung his horse around and galloped off toward a distant cluster of lights, glad to be getting away from this.

⎯⎯⎯⎯⎯

They walked along the road awhile, in the dark, until they came to a stone barn. There was nothing inside but old straw, and Leif and Laissa flopped down on that and were asleep almost at once. Raef went to the other side of the barn and sat down.

Remember what I taught you.

Nothing. A handful of chants and phrases. "You won't need these after a while," she had said. "When you're used to it." He had never gotten used to it.

Part of it was the way he had always been. He had always felt laid open, exposed, as if his body were inside out, his nerves on the outside, stretching into the world. He had always known more than he should. Often he could tell what the people near him were thinking, what the land around him was shaped like. Gunnhild had said, "Yes. You have your mother's gift, her wide-mindedness. And you were born of an act that shattered her body, so you were more of her mind than her body." Then she taught him another mysterious rhyme, which did nothing.

She had tried over and over to teach him how to leave his body behind, to follow his nerves outward into the world. "You can do this!" He couldn't. Finally she slapped him, shouted, "You are such a coward, Raef!" and walked off. A moment later, astonished, he found himself floating along beside her, in a strange blue twilight where she seemed almost transparent, his own body lying slack and empty on the floor behind him.

Now she would teach him nothing more.

He sat in the dark, longing for her. Across the wide barn Leif began his whistling snore. Raef thought of going over there and rolling the fat man over or stuffing something into his mouth. Instead he closed his eyes and let his mind drift.

He could stretch out some little way without even leaving his body. His senses grazed over Laissa; he had wanted to lay her under him for a long while now, but he had known her first as a child, and she had grown up day by day before him, so he still thought of her as a child. In the past sometimes when he dealt with women that way, they gained some momentary power over him, and he was wary of that also. When she was deep in sleep he spread his mind down on her, covering her from head to foot, and she moved, opening, her lips parting. She did not waken, but her hand slid down between her legs. He felt, in her belly, a rising lust.

Let her dream. He let go, his mind drifting past her, his body behind him now. Across the cold meadow and the horses grazing, through rows of trees and another hall, where men lay sleeping, mounds of dense, bloody, sweating flesh. The cold air was blue under the rising moon. The air tasted of grapes and lime. Like a wave in an ocean of light he flowed on past the wall, in all directions, through peasants in their huts with their sheep and goats beside them, their heads on their pigs, past haywains, sleeping cattle, a fox trotting down a road with a chicken in its jaws. A monk praying among monks sleeping. In the other direction, he lapped up against the rock mound, where he had left Gunnhild.

She was gone. He knew that at once, drifting through the piled stones. But even as he knew that, he felt something coming over the misty sea toward him, and he caught a stiff of something more horrible even than the stink of death.

The reek panicked him; instead of pulling his mind back into his body he let his whole awareness flow to that one place, beside Gunnhild's empty grave. Like a child running to its mother. As if she could still help him. Out over the sea, through the milky moonlight, rushed something churning and filthy like a foul smoke. He could not make it out. It seemed either to have no form or size or to be many forms and sizes, changing faster than he could see. Yet he could see it even in the dark, somehow.

He turned and fled in a blind terror, trying to get out of her way. She stopped behind him at the grave. The rocks and sand flew up and around in a fury, a whirling wind in the center. She was looking for Gunnhild. He forced himself to face her.

Before him was only a prickling in the air, a whirling, and then a shriek so loud it pierced his head like a lance. He shouted back to make another noise, to be there. He shouted his name at her. She swarmed at him, a swirling filthy mist with claws.

She needs a female body. He thought, Maybe she cannot hurt a man. Testing this he ran straight ahead, into the choking awful crackling miasma.

The thick gritty air battered him from all sides, up and down, like huge fists. He whirled helplessly in a black and terrible mist; his mind stretched toward some limit, some safety, and found nothing, nothing.

"Raef!"

The call came from somewhere outside and roused him. He clutched at that, who he was: himself.

All around the mist burned, hotter than fire, searing his lungs, his eyes boiling.

He had failed already.

"Raef!"

raef, he thought, raef, raef, raef

he held to that last flicker

⸺⸱⸺

The sun was rising. Leif got up; they had brought in their saddles and packs and he got some bread, drank from the rain barrel at the corner of the barn, and sat down on the threshold. The horses were grazing nearby. The new sun felt good. Across the stretch of grass a strange man was walking toward him.

"You!" this stranger called. "What are you doing here?" He spoke a kind of Frenchified dansker, like many of the Normans.

Leif did not stand up. He knew of the duke's ring, and he had no fear of this farmer. He said, "We're only passing the night. We'll be gone as soon as my friends wake up."

The farmer stuck his hands on his hips. "Be gone now, or I'll call my men."

Leif suspected there weren't too many of these men. He said, "The Duke of Normandy gave us word. I can fetch the ring he gave us, if you want."

The farmer's face altered slightly at the name of his lord. His eyes pushed past Leif into the barn; he started forward, and Leif swung his arm out to bar him.

"They're still asleep." This was true of Laissa, but he wasn't sure what to call what Raef was doing. He could see Raef from here, sitting on the straw, staring into space, as if he had gone somewhere else entirely. Leif had called to him, when he himself woke up, and had gotten not a flicker of attention, and he knew better than to press it. The farmer's mouth was working, uncertain.

"We'll start on the road before too long," Leif said to him. "We've done nothing to harm you."

"My lord the duke sent you?" The farmer crossed himself.

"He gave us a token, if you need to see it." Leif glanced over his shoulder. Laissa was awake, was rising up from the packed straw in the dim space and stretching her arms. Leif stood up, to keep the Norman farmer from being able to see her; as she grew and her body rounded, he imagined that every man wanted her. He saw them all seizing her, and he remembered what she had been, before. He looked back over his shoulder again, wondering where the ring was. The new sunlight spilled into the room behind him, and Laissa turned toward him and smiled. Raef still sat motionless on the other side of the room. Probably he had the ring. Laissa turned toward him. "Raef."

"Leave him be," Leif said. "He's dreaming again. He hates being wakened."

The farmer said, "These are your horses? Only two?"

"My friend prefers to walk."

Laissa stood, her head turning toward the door, and then looked back at Raef. Leif said, "Don't worry, he'll come to soon; he doesn't do this much in the daytime. Laissa, come on and eat something."

She was standing there, but she was looking at Raef, not at him. She went across the room to the other bench, sat before Raef, and looked into his blue eyes.

"Raef," she said, again, and leaning forward gripped his shoulders, and then she cocked one arm back and slapped him.

Leif gave a startled grunt. The farmer signed himself again. Raef jumped almost clear off the bench, still cross-legged, his skin flushing all over, his whole body knotting up, and his long arms reached out and caught hold of her. He was jerking and thrashing, as if in some kind of fit, and Laissa in a panic clawed at his hands on her arms, trying to fight out of his grasp. Leif rushed to help her, but before he reached her the fit suddenly ended, and Raef sat still on the straw, his hands biting Laissa's arms, his wide blue eyes blinking, his breath sobbing in his throat.

His hands opened. She reeled backward from him, her hands on her upper arms where he had held her. Leif took a step and was between them, a hot churning anger in his liver.

Raef put his hand to his face. He said, "We have to get out of here."

Leif said, his voice stiff, "Then let's go."

Raef rose and went out the door; he gave the farmer an

incurious glance and went to the rain barrel at the corner. Leif saw the farmer's eyes slide down to Raef's hand, to the heavy ring on his finger, and again the Norman signed himself, and he backed away. Raef scooped cold water into his hands and splashed it over his face.

Laissa came out, and Leif turned toward her. She stood there, her jaw hanging open, her eyes stunned. Her hands lay on her arms, but he could see the bruises already darkening her skin. Over by the wall Raef bent to drink from the barrel, ignoring them, as if he had not just savaged her. A hot reproach bubbled up in Leif's throat, but he could not bring it out. The farmer turned suddenly and went away. Leif went out to catch the horses.

CHAPTER TWO

They went off into the north, following the road, Leif and Laissa on their horses and Raef walking along. A girl with Laissa's yellow hair passed them, driving a cow to pasture, the tether rope wrapped like a crown around her horns. In a long narrow field people gathered onions. The weeds were already standing high in the fields on either side, leathery leaves, gross hairy stalks and pods with thorns. Just across the ditch a brown goat was eating brambles, its sides swelled out unevenly wide. The road led up onto the bluff, into sight of the sea, blue under the sun, the wind curling the waves over into whitecaps.

Although he could not see it, Raef knew there was land close beyond the horizon, breaking the sea's surge: the southern coast of England. Where the Lady was. His mind cringed from even the memory. He thought he knew why Gunnhild never told her purpose in leading him here; it was not because of his anger, but because she was afraid he might shirk the task.

Beside him, Leif said, "You hurt her."

Raef felt a surge of rage. He throttled down the will to knock Leif off his horse. On the Icelander's far side, Laissa turned to look at him. His hand fisted, the Norman duke's ring heavy on his finger. He lowered his eyes from the mottled bruises on her arms.

He said, "I couldn't help that. I couldn't stop it."

He bit his lips together, fighting down his temper, which he knew was mostly fear. There was no way to tell them what had happened. He said, clipped, "From here on, until we get to Jorvik, things could get dangerous. Maybe I won't even make it that far. If you want you can take your own road. You and her."

Laissa looked from one of them to the other. Leif rubbed

briefly at his face. He said, "When you get to Jorvik—what's there?"

Raef shook his head. "I don't know."

"Ah, so much you don't know."

He knew nothing, except that his enemy was stronger than he in every way. He had no idea even what she was. He avoided Laissa's questioning gaze.

Now that he could lose Leif, he saw the good friend the fat Icelander had been all this time, how he had rowed them out of danger in Thessaloniki with three Imperial dromons after them and Raef himself unconscious in the hold. How he had forced the gate in Rome, heaved the rocks down to block the trail in the mountains, found horses for them outside Rheims when Laissa was too sick to walk at all. Mostly, in spite of Leif's whining and fussing, his jealousy over Laissa, Raef did not want to be alone again.

He thought of losing her too, and his heart clenched.

But he feared to take the others into what he saw before him. He told himself it was better if they left. He thought then at least no one would see him fail. They continued on.

⸺⸺

Toward evening the duke's ring got them a place at an inn beside the road. While the men went off to put up the horses, Laissa went around the yard until she found the kitchen house.

Through the open door came a clamor, voices shouting, and she went to the threshold. Inside the cook was beating a scullion with his iron spoon and the kitchen maids were clustered by the table laughing and calling out advice.

"Please," Laissa said. "Please, I'm hungry."

The uproar faded a moment; the girls swung toward her, wide-eyed, and the cook paused a moment, his head turned toward her. He went back to smacking the scullion. One of the women called, "Come here, child, come eat."

She went in toward the table, where there was a pile of bread and several cheeses still in their wraps. One of the women came over and broke off a piece of a loaf for her.

"Are you alone? That's very dangerous. Who are you?"

Laissa began her well-practiced explanations. "I am a stranger. But I think my family must be from here. I think I was taken away when I was a baby. I think my father may have taken me away, maybe on a pilgrimage to the Holy Sepulcher. When Hugh was your king. My father died on the way. Now I look for my mother."

Like the women at the last place, they gathered her in like a baby, fed her more bread and some cheese and a cup of small beer, cooed and sighed at her. "What is your name?" someone said.

Around a mouthful of good sharp cheese she said her name, hopeful. But already their heads were shaking, their mouths sad, their eyes soft on her. "That is not a French name."

She said, low, "But I hear this French. I understand—more than I say. I must go everywhere—someone will know—"

"Alais," someone cried out, in the crowd of women.

There was a sudden hush. A little girl tittered. The old woman said, "Oh, Hawisse, shut up." She bent toward Laissa, confiding. "She's a little off, Hawisse. She churns the butter." Her finger made a wheeling by her ear.

"Alais," Laissa said, softly, her eyes lowered, as if she tasted the name. "Alais."

"There's nobody named Alais here," the old woman said.

"It's her name backward," called the woman in the crowd.

Everybody gasped. The old woman said sharply, "Hawisse, that's witchcraft. I told you, shut up." She turned to Laissa. "We can't help you, dear. We'd like to, it's a sad story, but nobody remembers anything."

The little girl said, "Nobody here ever goes anywhere."

"It's all right," Laissa said. "I'm sorry. It's all right." She walked out into the courtyard again.

Alais, she thought. Alais. Her heart leapt in a wild excitement. That was her real name. She knew that was her real name.

⎯⎯⎯⎯

They slept in the inn's common room; there were some other travelers, but they found a big bench to themselves. As the night deepened Raef told himself he needed rest, not to roam the light field, and he lay down in the rugs as if to sleep. But he knew it was fear of the Lady that kept his mind inside his skull. If he was too afraid to roam he was too afraid to do anything; she had beaten him already.

He had been lucky to get away the first time. He willed himself to sleep. But the rugs itched. The hall whispered with rats, with birds in the rafters, with strange people sleeping, the dark air murmurous. Leif lay next to him, Leif whom he misused and took for granted and might now lose; Laissa, whom he loved, snuggled against the Icelander's far side. He could not let go of himself.

Yet the great ocean of light drew him, irresistible now, his mind slipping out beyond the barrier of his skin. He shut his eyes. He let go, and he drifted out upon the world.

At first he stayed very close. He felt the familiar bodies around him as thicknesses in one great wheeling and stirring field of subtle color. Sometimes he thought he could hear music in its turning. Sometimes he thought it gleamed of its own, but other times he thought a greater light suffused it. He struggled with his fear, with his need to sleep and his longing for the light. Finally the shell of fear cracked, and he let his mind stream out, rippling wide.

Drifting by Leif and Laissa and outward, past people

throughout the inn, slaves asleep in the kitchen hearth, grooms yawning in the stable, he spread in a circle, one hand toward the sea, the other inland. There seemed nothing else moving in the blue moonlight. Cold and quiet, the countryside smoothed itself through him. He heard, or felt, a low trill, like the wind singing.

A smell reached him that frightened him so that before he even put a name to it he plunged back to his body in a great rush. The light vanished. He opened his eyes in the dark and for a swirling drunken moment he felt seasick.

A fluty whistle came to his ears. Leif was snoring. But he was far away now, and it was a much larger room. The barn. Raef had come back, not to the inn hall, but to the old barn where they had slept the night before.

Even as he knew this he felt something drawing hard on him, like a current, and he slid backward again into the light, helpless and confused. Fumbling as a baby must fumble in the womb, his mind sank down, contracting, folding into himself, into his body, nesting behind his eyes, looking out, Leif next to him, Laissa beyond that, the big hall full of other snoring people.

He lay quietly breathing. Somehow for an instant he had jumped backward a day. He wondered what would have happened had he stayed there—could he have stayed there? What would happen if he were stuck somehow out of his right time? He remembered the tidal current pulling him out again, like wrack drawn irresistibly back into the sea.

He was suddenly very tired. In his mind there was a long stream of music, deep and dark and sweet. He shut his eyes and went to sleep.

⸺◦⸺

By midmorning the next day they were riding over the south rim of a river valley that was like a vast wedge driven into the plain. Below them the river wound its way out of the east through drifts and bars of white sand, lines of drifted leaves and spiky brown reeds, down to the sea. Thirty houses, shops, huts, a stone church, and a squat little wooden tower clustered along the southern high side of the riverbank. The narrow course of the water ran along the front of the town, and a fringe of wharfs reached out into it.

They rode down off the south rim, and the road bent to follow the river inland; the wide white riverbed stretched out before them. They came to the city gate, where they had to pay a toll. As they stood there, Leif fingering the money, Raef looked down through a lane to the river and saw three big sow-bellied cargo ships moored at the bottom of the hill.

They went on down to the river street and found the church where the duke had told them to leave the ring. The old priest who came out to meet them on the porch had one eye looking straight and one aimed out to the side. His sparse hair was wispy and grey over his spotted scalp; whiskers framed his humorous mouth. He took the ring, looked curiously from one to the other, and thanked them.

"We have to find a ship," Raef said. He started off, Leif on his heels.

Laissa said, "I'm going to stay here and pray."

Leif wheeled, his gaze going to the priest, who said, "She will be safe here, in Jesus's name." Laissa went past him into the church.

The priest came after her. She said, "This is the Church of the Sacred Heart?"

"Yes, it is." He made the sign of the cross over her. "Are you troubled, daughter? Please, let Christ our Lord help you find your way." He smiled and went on past her, toward the altar.

At the front of the church she kneeled down. On the wall behind the altar a wooden Jesus hung on his cross. She lifted her eyes to the carved face and crossed herself, remembering to do it the right way. Then she covered her face with her hands.

Raef was looking for a ship to take them to England. He

was taking them away from here, before she had found her mother, before she had found out who she was. She bent forward, curling over her pain.

"Daughter." The old priest sank down beside her. His voice was mild as milk and the kindness of his smile warmed her. "Tell me why you are suffering."

She raised her head, looking into his face—into his good eye. Once again, she told her story. He listened, his patient face puzzled; she told him the name she had just found, Alais, and he gave a little shake of his head. She told him the pitiful handful of words she remembered, and then his one eye narrowed with recognition.

"Rawn," he repeated.

"Rouen, I think," she said, but remembered where she had heard that and shivered.

He laid his hands together over his belly. His hands were small and plump, with well-kept nails. "Maybe not Rouen, but Ranuld?"

She stared at him, her jaw falling open, and a wild hope rising. He said, "Long ago a man named Ranuld stole a child from a woman here and went away and never came back. For years we prayed every Saint Nicholas Day for her, until—"

Laissa reached out her hands to him, suddenly afraid. "She hasn't died? Is she still here?"

"You can find her in the last house on the river street." He gave a shake of his head. "But wait, my daughter, you may not—"

She heard none of that. She whirled up and ran out of the church.

⚊⚬⚊

"What if she does find her mother?" Leif said. They had taken the horses to the market and sold them; he carried the pack on his shoulder and his hand ax hung from his belt. Raef wore his old cloak in spite of the day's heat. "We'll never see her again."

Raef walked a stride ahead of him. All this way he had thought, In the end, she would not leave them, whatever happened, but now he was not so sure. He went down a narrow cobbled way where the houses crowded close along the street and the roofs tilted toward him, penning down the dank stinks. Ahead the water glinted. He stood on the edge of the river before the cargo ships.

Two were clunky French scows, but one was a dansker knarr, thirty feet long, half-decked, her mast stepped and her single sail furled neatly on the yard. She was foul bottomed and leaky, but she could carry them to England, with the wind or on oars. A steady line of shoremen was packing casks and bales of cargo into her hold. Raef weighed the purse in his hand. He passed up the French barges and went straight to the knarr, whose captain was sitting on an upturned barrel on the beach, paring his nails with a fish knife.

"I want to go to England," Raef said. "I'll pay well. Three of us."

The captain stuck the knife into its sheath on his belt, his gaze going past him to Leif. He shook his head. "Not this time of the year. The narrow sea's full of gales, fog, pirates—plus there's the wind, dead foul for Portsmouth, say."

"Anywhere in England," Raef said. He tossed the purse in his hand, so that the coins jangled. "You could run before the wind up the narrows and, with just a little luck, get across where the two coasts are so close there." He knew no names for these places, but he saw them in his mind.

The captain's eyes followed the purse, up and down. But then he shook his head. "Not me. Not this time of the year."

Raef glanced at the French barges; he turned his head and looked up the river bar. There were two more ships beyond, neither of them particularly seaworthy. He fixed his gaze on the dansker captain, sitting on his barrel, supervising the shoremen loading his ship.

Raef tossed the purse up and down again, and the captain brought his gaze back to him. "I said no." His voice was curt. But he watched the purse. Raef opened it and turned it over and poured a stream of silver money out onto the sand in front of the barrel.

The captain looked down at the pile, and his lower lip thrust out. He nudged it with his shoe.

"Go on," Raef said. "Count it."

"It's a hard crossing this time of the year," the captain said. "Any time of the year, actually, east to west." But he got off the barrel and kneeled on the sand and began to gather up the money, counting as he did.

Raef watched him patiently; when he got to thirty pence, which was about half, Raef said, "Keep that. The rest when you get us to England."

The captain's fist was full of money. He looked longingly at the heap still on the sand. Raef squatted down on his heels and shoveled the coins back into the purse. The captain's gaze followed the purse as Raef stood up.

"I'll take you out," he said. "No promise I can get you across."

"Good enough," Raef said. "No more money unless you do, though." He reached out his hand, and the captain shook it.

"The tide ebbs in an hour. Don't make me wait, you understand." The fistful of coins disappeared into a pouch on his belt.

"Yes," Raef said.

"No promise I'll get you to England."

"Yes," Raef said, and went back up to the street that ran along the riverbank.

"Now we have to find Laissa," Leif said, looking all around.

"That won't be hard," Raef said. "It's a small town." He turned onto the river street, walking east.

⸺⸺

Laissa had seen them going down toward the ships and circled well away from them. Raef sometimes seemed to know even out of sight where she was. She ran on down the street, dodging through the market, where their horses stood in a line with a dozen others, and onto the last stretch of the white-pebbled street.

At first she passed houses on both sides of the street, but ahead, at the end, there was the last house. She slowed. It was a long, low shack with a stone wall around the front. Her stomach tied into a knot. Up and down in the street in front of the house, women walked, their hips swaying, their long hair uncovered. Laissa stopped still.

She knew what this was. She had seen houses like this from Constantinople to Rheims, the women strolling back and forth, and now, from the enclosed garden, she heard the sound of laughter and loud voices and music. This was a tunnel back to a life she had escaped.

She crept closer. She felt sick to her stomach. At the corner, she slipped into the cover of the garden wall and went along it, away from the street. The wall was only a little taller than she was, and near where it met the house she came across a rock she could stand on to peep over.

The garden was full of people, men and women, some sitting on benches and some standing. Some standing together, their arms around each other. Kissing. Their hands on each other. Their hands in each other's clothes. Going in and coming out of the low building, their faces smeared and slack. In one corner, even, two men had a woman between them, their leggings down around their ankles.

She slid down behind the wall, unable to catch her breath. The lewd laughter and the babble of voices pressed around her, forced itself over her, as if it would drown her. She heard a roared oath, someone howling for more wine, a woman shrieking with excitement. She made herself climb up onto the rock again and peer over the wall.

Most of the women were young, her age. One walked close by her, the front of her bodice open and her breasts hanging out. The men were all kinds, old and young, many of them also half-undressed. She made herself look from one face to the next, until, on a bench by the door, she saw an old woman shelling nuts.

She wore no coif, her hair straggling down over her shoulders. Fair hair, like Laissa's, streaked with grey. She dumped a handful of nuts into her mouth and chewed, then reached down by her feet and took up a jug and drank.

Laissa slid down into the shelter of the wall again. She could not breathe; her heart beat so hard it shook her. She shut her eyes. Jesus, she thought. Jesus help me. With all her will she forced herself to look over the wall again.

The old woman saw her. Their eyes met. In that face Laissa saw her own face, seen half a dozen times in water and in glass: the shape of her eyes, her cheekbones, her nose, old, raddled and foolish with drink.

The priest had tried to warn her. Her chest clenched, her guts churning. The old woman stared at her a moment, spat, and reached down for her jug again, looking away, uninterested. Laissa backed away from the wall, swaying, caught between terror and pity, all her love and longing like a bloody stump. She went back out to the street and trudged back into the town again, her body rigid.

Raef moved over to the side of the street to avoid a wagon trundling toward them. They were nearly to the end of the town and had not found Laissa yet, and he could feel the tide in the river beside them starting to yield toward the sea. He began to regret giving the ship captain so much of the silver. He said, "What will you do, Leif?"

"What?"

"Are you coming with me? There are three places on the knarr to England. Fat as you are I think one of them will still be enough for you."

Leif gave him an evil look. "Sometimes I believe you're mad."

"Maybe."

"But I have come so far with you, how could I stop now?"

Raef bobbed his head. "Good."

"But we have to find Laissa."

Then as if the mention of her name had brought her into being she was coming toward them. Raef swore under his breath. She was walking stiffly, blindly down the center of the road. He got Leif by the arm. "There."

Leif cried, "Laissa!" and ran toward her. She lifted her head, and her face was streaming tears. She raised her arms and the Icelander gathered her up.

"I'm sorry," she said, and wept. "I'm sorry."

"Come on," Raef said. "You'll be more than sorry if we miss that ship." In spite of the girl's wretched looks, he could not keep from smiling. Laissa buried her face against Leif's shoulder. They went quickly back up the street.

CHAPTER THREE

Laissa alternately wept in Leif's arms and vomited over the lee side of the ship. They were sitting on the half deck in the stern of the knarr, bundled in their fur cloaks and sheltered somewhat by a canvas awning. The captain had been right about the weather. They had rowed on the tide down the river, and as soon as they were out of the lee of the coast the south wind hit them like a fist. They raised the sail, and the knarr began to lumber and roll along into the north.

Raef stood up in the prow, his face wet with spray. He had not sailed these seas in fifteen years. He had tasted the salt tang on his lips now the first time he left the shore, at the far side of this ocean. The harsh edge in the wind made his blood race.

On the water he always knew where he was. The sway and heave of the sea tumbled through the narrows like a great dance. The bottom rose here, even as the shorelines pinched together toward the north and the wind blew hard from the south-southwest as if into a giant funnel, piling the water up over itself in crosscurrents and rips. The ship skidded across the steep, hard-running seas, the stays groaning and water shipping in green over the gunwales. Amidships in the hold, two of the crewmen were bailing steadily, to their ankles in slop.

The ship swooped along the slope of a wave, heavy with her cargo, and wallowed on. Raef went along the ship, past the other crewmen huddled down against the sides, and climbed over the casks that filled the hold, back to where the captain stood at the helm.

On the steerboard side the coast of France faded down to a blue line on the horizon. The sun shone some of the time. As the day went by the wind was backing around into the east, Raef saw, glad; if they got a little farther north they could run to England on this wind. He leaned against the gunwale, content to do nothing. But as the day wore on, more clouds shut out the sky, and the mast creaked and the stays sang, and finally the captain said, "I'm bringing in the sail. We can row in to Normandy from here."

Raef said, "This wind will take us to England. Keep going."

The captain grunted at him. "I'm not losing my ship for your sake. I'm putting in for the night. Maybe tomorrow—"

Raef pulled out his knife and put the tip against the captain's belly. "Or I could just throw you overboard and go myself."

The captain let out an explosion of breath. Raef could tell Leif was watching this from the shelter of the half deck; Laissa had fallen asleep. None of the oarsmen had noticed. Raef was watching the captain's eyes. He put a little pressure on the knife.

"How far can you swim?"

The captain said nothing. His mouth tightened, and he swallowed. Raef said, "I'll take the helm. You stay right where you are." He slid past the captain and pulled the tiller bar out of his slackening grip. "Tell them to ease the sheets."

The captain said, "This wind will tear the sail to shreds."

Raef stuck the knife hard into the gunwale by his elbow. "Tell them to ease the sheets."

The captain swallowed again and called to the crew. Two of them crawled out of the shelter of the half deck and over the cargo to let the sail out; Raef leaned on the tiller a little, following the wind northwest.

⁓

The sun sank. The coast of France slid over the horizon. The captain said, "If we're stuck out here at night—"

Raef said, "We'll be there by moonrise." If there was a moon. With the coming of the night the wind lightened, the knarr steadier, slower. On the water ahead of them patches of fog were appearing, sea smoke, salt cloud, breath of the ocean. The English coast, he knew, was still miles away.

Then, from the bow, one of the crew shouted, "Captain, sail! Sail to the south—"

The captain wrenched around, peering down to the south. "Damn you," he said to Raef.

Raef stood up on the gunwale to see. Far down there in the fading light a blotch of red showed. He stepped back down onto the stern deck. "Tell them to get the oars out and ready."

The captain snarled at him, his face dark. "You see the color of that sail? That's a Jomsviking. They owned this sea all last year. We can't outrun them."

"Right. Get the oars ready."

The captain swore at him awhile, but he shouted the orders. The wind was failing fast. The knarr rowed from the bow end because of her cargo piled in amidships and aft: four oars on either side. Raef glanced south again. The wind was still gusting, down there, and the red sail was flying toward them, the dragon ship beneath already hull up. Leif rose, leaving Laissa bundled in their cloaks on the half deck, and went forward, in among the crewmen.

Raef lifted a hand to him. "Oars out," he said to the captain.

The man hesitated, glaring at him, and Raef reached for the knife. "I'll kill you before the Jomsvikings do."

The captain turned stiffly forward. "Oars out!"

The oars rattled out, and Leif got the men rowing together. He walked back and forth between them, his feet widespread on the ship's tilting floor. Raef put the knife back into its sheath on his belt. The captain sat down suddenly, his head in his hands. Raef looked back over his shoulder. The Jomsviking was under oars now too, striding after them.

His heart rose at the sight of the dragon. Not even the

dromons of the Imperial fleet were as beautiful as these ships. But he had no inclination to meet the crew of this one. He slid the helm over slightly, heading for the nearest fog bank.

Night was falling, the sea and the darkening air mingling together in feathers and sheets of mist. The crewmen bent to the oars. Leif went along between the rows of benches, keeping the stroke. The knarr lumbered along through patches of fog, stretches of open water, more fog, thicker, like cold fleece.

"They're still coming," Laissa said. She had wakened; she stood up and leaned on the gunwale, looking behind them.

The captain said, "Why shouldn't they—we can't go much farther." He rocked his head in his hands. "He'll wreck my ship and kill us all."

The ship creaked along, the oars rumbling in their tholes. Raef's beard was wet from the fog. In the dark he could barely see the rowers; he left that work to Leif. They were still a long way from the shore. The tide was at its height, but the tides here were very strange. The mist made the dark impenetrable. He could barely see the knarr's mast, and he touched Laissa's shoulder.

"Go up there and tell him I'm laying her over to steerboard, and then oars up."

The girl slid out of her cloak and went nimbly up the ship, leaping from cask to cask. In the thick fog, in the dark, Raef put the helm over. The oars stroked once to make the turn and rose, and the ship came neatly around and glided to a stop.

The captain lifted his face out of his hands but said nothing. In the silence, Raef looked behind them. In the night soup of the fog he could feel the Jomsviking back there, the great dragon groping after them like a monster in a cave. Then even the captain could hear the splashing of oars.

"They're—"

Raef kicked him to quiet him. He glanced quickly forward, where he could see nothing. The ship rolled slightly in the waves. The sound of the Jomsviking's oars ground steadily closer. They were at half beat; he could hear someone calling the pace. The captain was looking up at Raef, his forehead wrinkled. He opened his mouth and Raef nudged him with his foot again, and the captain said nothing.

The Jomsviking was almost on them. The rhythmic grinding of her oars came through the fog like dragging footsteps. Laissa appeared beside Raef, and he put his hand on her shoulder. Out there, in the dense clammy blackness, someone called, "No bottom." The Jomsvikings were sounding as they went. He could see something moving, in the dark, not the form, only the movement, rising and falling, and hear the creak of the oars, less than a bowshot away.

The sound drew closer, closer. Under his hand Laissa was taut as a harp string. The creak and rattle of the oars seemed almost upon them. Now he could hear the whisper of the sea past her hull. Then the rhythmic thunking grew fainter. The dragon was moving on by. The same voice called, but Raef could not make out the words. He squeezed Laissa's shoulder.

She needed no directions; she raced off down the ship. A moment later, the knarr's oars went out with a rattle that seemed loud as thunder, and the ship began to move again, slow, clumsy, but heading dead away from the Jomsviking.

Back there, in the dark, somebody yelled. Raef held the knarr on course. On the backboard side, the coast was still a way off, but a mile or so west of where they were, a flat cape curved out into the sea. The tide was starting to ebb, dragging them back toward France again. Then abruptly the fog gave way and the knarr rowed out into a patch of moonlight bright as a lantern.

"Pull!" Leif roared up among the rowers, and a hundred feet behind them, in the dark, a long jubilant howl rose, like that of a hunting pack on its prey.

"We're dead," the captain said. "We're dead." Laissa was

bounding back up the knarr to the stern; she came in beside Raef and leaned on him.

"Good girl," he said. He glanced over his shoulder.

The moonlight shone white on the fogbank, and for a moment he saw nothing. Then the great fierce head of the dragon burst into the moonlight, and her breast split the fog. The men crowded around her prow let out a scream of bloodlust. Raef thrust the tiller bar into Laissa's hands.

"Hold this! Leif! Make them pull!" He leapt down from the sterncastle, in among the casks and bales, and began heaving them overboard.

Under him the knarr shuddered; the rowers were thrashing forward at their work, shouting one another on. The captain jumped down beside Raef and grabbed his arm.

"That's my—" He looked astern, saw the Jomsviking dragon bearing down on them, and seized the nearest cask and flung it into the sea. Raef raced back up to the helm.

Laissa was clinging to the tiller bar, leaning hard against the drag of the ship, which wanted to keep on straight. He got the bar away from her and put it over. The ship curved into the turn, sliding into the fog again. The moonlight faded. Dark settled over them like a lid.

He heard a thunk behind him as the Jomsviking hit one of the floating casks. He doubted it would hurt the ship, but he thought they might slow to pick it up. When he looked back he saw nothing but the dull black of the night curtain. The crew was still pulling frantically at the oars, Leif yelling them on. Laissa was clinging to his sleeve. The captain was huddled down among the last of his cargo.

Ahead of them, he knew, was the flat stony cape. "Leif," he called. "Steerboard. Steerboard—" He leaned hard on the bar, and Leif bellowed, and between them they bent the ship out to sea again. The tide was slacking, somehow; where before it had been ebbing now it seemed to rise again. He could hear the distant growl of surf. The captain came up beside him.

"What are you doing?"

"Going to England," Raef said. "Go down there and row." The rising tide was hauling them inshore. Now they were wearing the tip of the cape, and he felt the water under them smack and surge together, the sea floor only a few feet beneath the keel. Beyond the cape the stony bottom rose up, shelving to the beach.

Then, behind him, he heard the grating crash of the Jomsviking running aground.

"Leif," he shouted. "Leif, oars up." He whirled toward Laissa. "Get your cloak."

Leif called out hoarsely, "What are we doing?"

"Follow me!" He turned to the captain and thrust the purse into his hands. "Get back to the tiller. Keep going. They'll be after you as soon as they rock off that bar." He jumped down to the floor amidships, among the few remaining casks. Leif was already there, his cloak over his arm. Raef put one hand on the gunwale and vaulted over the side.

He went up to his waist in the icy sea. A wave carried the ship up and flooded over him almost to his chin, lifted him a moment off the bottom, and rushed on by. He got his feet on the ground again, stretched his arms up, and shouted, "Laissa! Jump!"

Without hesitation she leaped into his arms, her cloak bundled in her grip. Holding her up out of the water he staggered in toward the shore. Leif splashed in after him. Another wave struck Raef from behind and almost knocked him down. He held Laissa up over his shoulders, paddling desperately with his feet, and plowed on through the rushing water, slipping and stumbling on the tilted bottom. The next wave rose up only to his waist. The girl was safe and almost dry in his arms.

The moon shone white on the surf ahead of them. He waded up out of the fog, out of the sea. The breaking wave almost knocked him down. Then he was staggering up onto the land. Leif panted up beside him. They stood on the beach and looked back and saw the stern of the knarr vanishing into the fog. He put Laissa down on her feet; she still clutched her cloak in her arms, and he took it and swung it around her. Her teeth rattled together. She gripped the cloak closed with both hands. Raef was soaked to the skin. Leif was already ahead of them, walking fast inland, and Raef took Laissa by the hand and followed.

CHAPTER FOUR

The beach was a stretch of shingles, clicking and turning in the rush of the surf. The wind swept in across the flat open ground. Raef was shivering, his feet squelching in his boots. They walked on inland, looking for some shelter, some place to rest and build a fire, but for a long way from the shore the land was all rock and marsh, without even a tree. They left the fog behind and walked in the cold moonlight. The night stretched away before them, barren and empty. The wind rose, knife edged.

At sunrise they were still walking; Laissa was exhausted, and the two men half carried her between them. The sun came up behind them and cast their shadows across the barren land, and now at last they found a human place. It was two sides of a house, the rest burned to the ground.

This was shelter enough. They got out of the wind and broke wood out of the ruin to build a fire. Raef's and Leif's cloaks were still soaked, and the men hung them to dry on the wall, and all bundled together under Laissa's, between the wall and the fire, and slept.

—◦—

Later in the morning they set off again, following the road across the barrens. Soon Laissa began to cry, the tears slick on her face. "We're always going to be walking. We'll walk until we die."

Raef said nothing. Leif said, "We'll come to somewhere soon." His voice sounded flat with disbelief.

"No, we won't," Laissa said. "I came all this way, all across the world, to find my mother. I found her, and it made no difference. I'm still walking; I still have nobody." She sobbed. Leif put his arm around her.

"That's all right. Don't cry, Laissa."

She flung his arm off, tipped her head back, her cheeks glittering with her tears. "I have no home. No family. My mother is a drunken whore. My whole life is over."

"I will be your father," Leif said. "Haven't I been so, all these years? What matters, if not the doing?"

Raef said, "Which matters, the name of the thing or the thing itself? You could marry me, and then you'd have a husband."

She lowered her head and barked an astonished, scornful laugh. Leif turned and glared at him. Raef said nothing more; he felt the idea strike her mind like a dart and for a moment regretted saying it. Rain was starting to fall. He thought, At least we'll have something to drink.

All the rest of the day, savagely hungry, they trudged inland through the driving rain. The country they walked over had once been farmland, but now the people were gone, the fields and pastures overgrown with weeds, trampled and burned out. Raef remembered the captain saying that the Jomsvikings had been raiding this coast for years. Clearly they had taken everything useful and destroyed the rest.

A wolf trailed along after them awhile, its ribs like hoops under its hide. The road was a stream of mud. Raef could sense how the people had fled along it, their footprints still warm somewhere under the icy muck. Here and there they found some relic of those people, an old broken shoe, a piece of a basket. Laissa took the shoe and chewed on the leather. Then, around sundown, with the rain pouring down, they walked into the ruins of a farmstead.

Where there had been a dozen buildings only a few walls stood in masses of dead weeds. The place had been abandoned awhile, over a year. In the center was a fire-scarred oak tree, bones hanging from the branches.

Laissa said, "Who did this?" She drew back, her arms folded up over her chest. Raef went toward the tree, where bones lay scattered everywhere on the charred ground, blackened and split. Broken skulls and fingers.

Leif said, "It's Danish work. Sweyn Tjugas. Or the Jomsvikings."

Raef said, "There's nobody left here. There's nobody for miles." He went up past Laissa, toward the ruined hall.

The walls had been made of stones and mud; with the thatch burned off the rain had melted them down to waist high. Inside the door the spined burrs of teasels stood up over his head. Behind him, Laissa said, "They killed all these people?"

Leif said, "Most of them probably just ran off."

"Afraid to come back," Raef said. "They've been gone awhile. But look here." Behind the hall was a walled garden. He pushed open a battered wooden gate and went inside.

They pulled old onions and woody turnips out of the mud, gnawing into them before they washed the dirt off. A crooked apple tree grew in the corner, and the ground under it was covered with tiny red apples. In the angle of the wall and the remains of the roof, out of the wind and the worst of the rain, they built a fire and roasted turnips and onions, ate the apples, and threw the cores out to the garden. After dark the rain stopped at last, and the wind blew colder and stars glinted in the sky. They sat there in the shelter of the wall, stupid from gorging themselves, the fire warm on their faces.

Presently Laissa said, "What you said before, you meant it?"

Raef put another piece of wood into the fire. "About marrying you? Yes."

Leif said, harshly, "There's danger in this, Laissa—he is not telling you everything." He gave Raef a stinging look.

She said, "Not in a church. Not you."

"No, no. Handfast. How we have done this forever. We need only the two witnesses, and then to agree."

She turned away and said nothing more. Leif said, "You are not fit for her, Raef."

"So all fathers have said since Adam."

Laissa said, "Adam had no daughters." She was drawing her cloak around her, settling down, ready for sleep.

"He must have had some," Raef said. "How would we be here?" But he was tired, and they were nestling together, ignoring him, unwilling to argue. He stood up and shook his cloak out. Under the soaked fur the good wool lining was warm yet, and he wrapped himself in it and lay down.

⸻

Laissa thought, He would belong to me then. Whatever he was, she would have someone, at last, someone of her own. She knew Leif was furious, jealous, afraid, but Leif was old and fatherly. Her heart pounded when she thought of Raef, of touching him like that, but most of all of owning him.

⸻

Raef dreamed he dropped into a great well and went down and down, floating, not toward darkness but into light. The well was made of bricks, and soon he was descending a staircase that spiraled down the circular brickwork, walking it seemed for hours, until he reached the round room at the bottom.

There was a door, and he opened it and looked out at nothing—neither the sky nor stars nor even emptiness but nothing at all.

"You came to me." The voice sounded around him, as if it came from everywhere. "You see this. You are coming to me because you have always belonged to me. You are my slave. I owned your mother. You were born in my house! If your mother and her brother had been wiser she would have reigned with me into eternity and you would have been fed to the dogs. Instead the Twins betrayed me. You'll pay for that."

He was stiff with fear, his tongue stuck between his teeth and his hands trembling. But he made himself think: Why is she trying to frighten me like this? Why not just kill me? Then suddenly, without willing it, he was awake, lying on the ground beside Laissa, his feet cold.

He shuddered with relief. The dream clutched him hard still. He lay breathing deeply, trying to fathom what had happened.

He remembered the door into nothing. He ran his mind over the idea that she did not belong here, but then he had to try to think where she had come from, and he had no way to imagine that. He wondered if she had even been in the dream—if he had not made her up, out of what he already knew about her.

The dawn was breaking. Somewhere nearby a raven barked. He thought of Conn, his heart's brother, asleep under the mountain in Kiev. Of Corban, who had hated kings. His memory skipped to the false prophetess in Chersonese who had said that he, Raef, would be a king and that his son would be a king. His true father, Eric Bloodaxe, had been King of Jorvik. Gunnhild had said that was why he had to go to Jorvik.

Now he was remembering something else, which was that it was in Jorvik that the Lady had bought his mother from Eric Bloodaxe, with Raef himself only a seed in her belly. They had first crossed paths there, he and she.

He could not push his mind past that thought to see what it meant. If it meant anything. If he wasn't just making it up, a patch of words over his ignorance. The day was coming on, and

he had to get up and get going again. The dream slid into the
back of his mind. More important was finding something to
eat. He pushed his cloak aside and stood up.

⸺⸺

With the last two onions and a turnip, they went up along the
overgrown road that led north. The land was better here. As they
left the last of the farmstead behind, a dozen hares leaped away
across the open ground before them. Quickly they ate up the
food. Laissa found some mushrooms; she saw wolf scat when
she squatted in the bushes. The land was rising, and stands of
trees grew up alongside the road, many standards, but new
sprouting saplings too, the copses thick with dropped leaves and
branches. Dense and dripping, these woods gave way suddenly to
broad brown meadows. Deer grazed along the margins, and once
they saw a flock of white sheep scattered across an open hillside.

"Maybe there are people," Laissa said, pointing. "Tending
the sheep."

Raef shook his head. "There's nobody for miles. Something
up ahead, but days away." But he stood staring at the sheep, and
a strange look came over his face. He turned and looked widely
all around them.

"We need something to eat," Leif said. "Before then."

Laissa's stomach growled at the idea of food. The road led
across the shoulder of a low hill, and as they reached the crest,
the wintry trees and meadow beyond opened up before them.
Rain began to fall, light at first. They went off the road, looking
for shelter. There were more sheep at the far side of the meadows. Somewhere in the distance a wolf howled.

⸺⸺

Night was coming. They went downhill into a little copse of trees near a trickle of a stream. They put branches up against the widest trunk, and laid their cloaks over the cone shape. Leif cleared out the wet leaves and built a little fire ring. Under the soaked fallen drift in the woods he found bits of dry wood, shaved it with his axe for tinder, got that lit, and carefully fed bigger wood into the flames until they had a fire going.

Raef sat down with his back to the tree; the other two worked on their fire, ignoring him. He shut his eyes. After a moment his mind began to drift out across the light field.

He widened, as he always had, like the ripple of a wave, but now he tried to pull his mind tight together, into a point that rode along the front of the wave. That was easier than he expected. He ranged across the rainy meadows, the bogs, and came on the sheep, huddled in a tight flock with their backs to the wind. A little way on, he found the wolf, stalking the sheep.

The great light field spread all around him, singing with its wild music, but he tightened his interest on the wolf. For a while, with the beast moving, he could not separate it from the field around it, but then the wolf lay down, its tongue lolling out, and Raef sank into it.

The warmth shocked him. The bloody tangle of muscle and bone, the gnawing appetite. He looked out through eyes that saw only grey and white and black, but that very well; the dark was like daylight. A growl curled his lips. He stood, stretched long from front to back, and trotted down closer to the sheep.

—❖—

Leif said, "Is he out again? Damn him."

Laissa hunched her knees against her chest. Beside her Raef leaned against the tree, his eyes half-open, his hands slack. The little light of the fire flickered over them all. Out the narrow gap between the cloak wall and the tree she could see across the meadow, streaming rain. She said, "Leave him alone." She was afraid to touch him. "I'm so hungry."

Leif said, "What if he doesn't wake up this time? We have to go on, soon. We can't carry him."

She hugged her knees to her chest and stared at him. Raef wasn't asleep. Somehow, he wasn't even there. "He'll come back."

"What if he doesn't?" Leif's wide honest face turned toward her. His face seemed graven with the dust of every road they had walked together. He said, "We're going farther and farther into this country none of us knows. He says he's going to Jorvik, but he has no notion what he will do there. And this place is full of enemies—Sweyn Tjugas is not his friend, certainly the Jomsvikings are not, and the English, who knows? and there's something worse."

Swiftly, Laissa said, "What?"

"I don't know. But he is afraid of something, and he is afraid neither of Sweyn nor the Jomsvikings nor the English. I have known him long enough to know that."

"Wait," she said. "He'll come back. He says he will marry me." She glanced at the inert body beside her, the half-open, sightless eyes. "He'll come back."

Leif's face twisted, fretful, jealous, desperate. "Why should you marry him—you'll be—we'll all be wrecked together. One of us should live—"

She turned her eyes out toward the meadow, not wanting to talk about this, and gave a startled yell. "Leif, look!" She pointed out the gap between the tree trunk and the cloak's edge. "What's that?"

Down the meadow, streaming in the rain, a big white wolf trotted toward them, dragging something heavy in its jaws. Leif swore, grabbed his axe, and got between Laissa and the opening in the lean-to. The wolf stopped, out there, and Leif pushed out the opening and shouted and waved his axe.

Beside Laissa, suddenly, Raef stirred. Leif went out into the rain; the wolf was running off.

It had dropped what it was carrying. Raef said quietly, "Go get that," and rose and went out, brushing by the Icelander.

Leif grunted. His hand with the axe dropped to his side. Raef came back into the lean-to, carrying a dead lamb. One foreleg and the head and most of the lights were missing. He dumped the carcass on the ground and said, "Let's eat."

They roasted the meat and ate it, saying little, tossing bones and pieces of wool out into the rain. Afterward, Laissa looked over at Raef, and said, "Your hair needs combing."

"Comb it, then," he said.

She took the comb she had brought along with her all the way from Constantinople and crept in behind him, between him and the tree trunk. With the comb and her fingers she began to untangle his hair. His hair was thick and wiry and some of the braids so old they had matted. The rain slackened a little. Inside the lean-to the fire burned down to coals. Leif slumped in the gloom, grim faced.

She paid no heed to him. She heeded only Raef. She worked each hank of hair gently into its straight, separate strands. As she did she could feel Raef soften under her touch, as if she gathered him into her grasp. A thrill of excitement shook her. She realized she had some power over him.

She said, "Were you the wolf?"

His shoulders moved, putting that off. He made no answer. She stroked the comb through his hair, dividing it into parts. She remembered when she first met him. He had been strange then, but not like this. Something wild in him, deep and dark. Gunnhild had taught him, but she must have found something in him to start with. He had grown since she died, as if she had somehow laid her mantle on him. Or, alone, he had needed more and found it.

She divided one long tress of his hair in three and began to braid them together. She said, "Where are we going now?"

His head tilted slightly under her hands, following her touch. "There's a city up ahead of us. I have kindred there."

"Who?"

"My cousin's aunt. My foster mother's sister. Arre is her name; she is married to a merchant named Euan Woodwrightsson."

In her fingers the long thin plait came to an end; she wished she had a bead to hold it, but she could only twist it together. He sprawled back, almost lying upon her, his shoulders against her legs, his head in her hands. She knew she could ask him anything. Under her hands he felt yielding, submissive. She could not think how to ask the right questions: What would happen next? What should she do?

Instead, she said, "When will we be married?"

Through her arms a little tingle of warmth surged up from his body. "When you agree. When we have two witnesses."

"Not me," Leif said harshly. "I would not marry a wolf and a lamb."

Laissa had finished another braid. She said, "I have not agreed yet." She twisted the ends of the long white hair together to hold her work.

⸻

They walked all the next day, slogging through the mud and puddles, eating the remains of the lamb and whatever they could find on the road. They came on two men hauling along a cart full of split wood, and Raef and Leif helped them in return for some bread. The rain had stopped. They slept that night bundled together in a field. In the morning, moving on, they were part of a little stream of people on the road, most moving north, a boy herding pigs, and now and again a man carrying a basket on his back.

The road was better, broader, and in some places hardened with logs of wood laid across it. Toward the middle of the afternoon they reached a village, a thick crust of hovels and stables and houses around a marketplace, itself packed with people and wagons, barrels, strings of horses, and screaming pigs.

Raef pulled them to the biggest building. This was an inn, Laissa saw, as she followed the two men into the yard. Behind the great front building was an open space and then a low kitchen house. Between was a huge stack of unsplit logs.

She hung back; sometimes people drove them off when they wanted work. Leif went to the kitchen house and banged on the door and tried to talk, gesturing, with the man who came out, whose blood-splattered filthy apron made him out for a cook. Behind him through the door the light of the hearth shone red on the kitchen wall.

This man spoke no French, no dansker, only an odd gabble Laissa had not heard before. After a few moments the cook came out of the kitchen, went by Leif and by her and Raef standing there, and climbed three steps into the big front house. Leif turned, his hands spread.

"I can't talk to him."

Raef cleared his throat. In a few moments the cook came back out with a spry, spindle-legged man in a fine hat, who stayed in the doorway behind Raef at the top of the steps. The cook left at once for his kitchen. Raef stared at the newcomer as if he could see into his skull, but he said nothing.

Leif tried out his feeble French again, and then his dansker, and the man in the hat said some feeble French and shook off the dansker. Then Raef, suddenly, spoke in some new tongue.

The man in the hat straightened and answered him. Raef spoke slowly, halting over the words, but the man in the hat understood him and nodded, agreeing. Raef turned to Leif and switched to dansker.

"If we split all the wood we get fed."

Leif's lips were pinched together. "Show me the axe."

Laissa followed them and stood by the foot of the steps. They had been doing this all along the road, and they had made it a practice; it was fun to watch. They moved together, one man setting and the other splitting. When the one turned for the next log the other stacked the split stuff, so they were always moving and the wood flew into its orderly pile.

They switched places every fifteen or twenty strokes, so smoothly they kept the rhythm constant. Laissa heard a soft grunt behind her and turned and saw the innkeeper in the fine hat on the step above her, watching.

He spoke to her in the other language, and she shook her head. Turning, he went inside, and soon kitchen boys set out a jug and a wooden board with a loaf and some cheese and a sausage on the lower step. The innkeeper came back and stood in the doorway watching the men work. Some other people had come in from the street to watch too.

Leif split the last log, and Raef tossed the pieces on the top of the stack. They turned at once toward the food. The innkeeper called out something in his tongue, and Raef shrugged and answered, slow but sure with the words.

He sat down on the step, reached for the bread, and broke off a piece. Turning to Laissa, he handed it to her. She took it, sitting down beside him, and said, "What language is this?"

Raef waggled his head. "I don't know. Theirs."

"How do you speak it?"

He was chewing bread and cheese; his eyes looked at her through their corners. "They speak it," he said, sounding surprised, as if she had to ask this.

She gave up. She wondered again if she wanted to do what

had come into her mind. She said, "What is the word for married?"

His gaze flattened, seeing what she intended, and then swiftly he looked around at the small crowd still watching them. He swallowed the mouthful of food and said the word clearly, precisely, so she would remember it, although she did not understand it: *mund—waed*—something.

She seized hold of his hand at once, before she forgot it, and cried, "I call you all to witness, we are married now."

She led up to the strange new word with dansker, but the onlookers understood at once. Already good humored, they threw up a ragged whoop of a cheer and began to clap. On Raef's far side Leif's jaw dropped, his eyes astonished. Raef smiled at Laissa. He rose to his feet, his wrist still in her grasp, and bent down and kissed her. More people were pushing into the wood yard, drawn by the excitement, hooting and chanting and yelling and kissing at them. Laissa kept her eyes down, her ears red; she heard the lewdness in their voices even without knowing the words.

The kitchen boys came running out with a jug, which they passed around, and the innkeeper shouted something from the door of his hall. Raef turned to her.

"He's saying we can stay in a room in his inn. For the wedding night."

Leif said, "Do we have to cut more wood for it? Or does he just get to watch?"

Raef gave him half a glance. Leif's head sank down into his shoulders. Laissa had kept her hold of Raef since the beginning, and now she tugged on him.

"Take me to it, then."

⇒

Raef was jittery, climbing the ladder, Laissa just ahead of him with the lamp. She was so eager, she who he had thought would need coaxing, leading him up the narrow rungs to the top, under the eave, where a little door opened.

The space behind was just big enough to lie down in. There was a fresh pallet laid down on it, sprinkled with herbs. At the foot of the stair the innkeeper was leading a wedding song full of explicit advice. Laissa crept into the space, set the lamp in the niche, and turned toward him. She was joyous as an angel, as if some dream had come true. He felt suddenly shy, left behind, confused. He followed her on hands and knees into the chamber and closed the door.

Mine, she thought. Mine now. She faced him, whom she had known so long, and now saw all new: hers.

In his long bony face the blue eyes were wary. He said, "Do you wish this?"

"Yes," she said, "very much." She unclasped her tunic; under the eave there was no room to stand, and he, being so tall, had to kneel and stoop to fit, but she pulled off her clothes, wanting him to see her. He looked down at her breasts, her belly, and she spread her knees apart to show him her hot part. His face sharpened with lust. She crept to him and straddled his thighs, put her arms around him, and kissed him.

She had been with men when she was much younger but not in many years—not since they fled from the burning city, at the beginning of the long journey west. She knew what to do. But first she wanted to kiss him. A sudden tenderness welled up in her. It seemed she had wanted to kiss him for years. She put her mouth against his and shut her eyes.

At first his mouth would not yield. She felt in this kiss the long hard habit of aloneness, his inwardness, his resistance to any power save his own, his bone-deep doubt of his own. She put her hands against his cheeks above his beard and tried to kiss him soft, open him to her. She felt him tremble against her. His hands stroked down over her buttocks and gripped her and she felt the sword of his cock against her thigh, but he did nothing to join them. He was heeding the kiss.

She stroked his lips with her tongue, and a shudder went through him; he turned toward her, helpless as a child, toward what he had forgotten he needed or had never known. She put her tongue deep in his mouth, to be to him as he would be to her, and reaching down drew his cock into her body.

She sobbed. She had forgotten how deep the penetration was, how gross and thick. His arms tightened around her. She turned again to the kiss, clung mouth to mouth with him while he rolled her down on her back. He knew exactly where to touch her. She yielded to him, trembled on the brink of a swollen desire; he held her there a moment and then took her with him in a hot mingling flood.

He moved a little, withdrawing. She kept one arm around his neck. He gave her a sudden, shy look, and she smiled at him, pleased. Hers. She said, "Are you hungry? I brought some bread."

CHAPTER FIVE

Raef lay with his eyes closed, pretending to sleep. He let his mind drift just a little way, enough to cover Laissa beside him.

This was not what he had expected. He had thought to lead her, to master her, to have the use of her body, but he had not foreseen that anything else would change. But something had changed. None of his other women had lasted for more than a moment, not even Merike, in Rus. His hated father dead, his mother mad and strange to him. Conn he had loved as simply as a brother. Corban, always, a borrowed father. Then Conn died. Raef had grown cold, except for the chilly witch love of Gunnhild, steel and ice, justice and magic, all mind and no heart.

Laissa was so soft. Aware, young, and sweet. And she loved him. The shock of this still sang in him. For all she knew of him she loved him. He drew himself back into his body and kissed her awake, to have her again in his arms.

—◦—

Long before they came to the city they could see it ahead of them, crowds boiling along the road, buildings, walls, and side streets, brooks with little bridges and lowland swamps with boardwalks, a bustling, coming and going, everybody moving faster now, horses running along, people running, shouting, the rattle and bang of wheels. A wagon full of turnips had over-turned in the middle of the road, and people were stealing them as fast as they could while the cursing drover cracked his whip helplessly at them. They passed by a shambles, yards and hang-ing sheds on either side of the road, pits of stinking offal, the stench of blood everywhere. As they got closer to the bridge over the river, both sides of the street were crowded with shops, people swarming around them trying to buy. Two men on blinkered, terrified horses and three others on foot carrying spears were dragging along a half-choked black bear by a rope around its neck. The bear's claws left long furrows on the street. A dozen men jogged past on big muscular horses; they wore mail, these men, and their hair was cut short and they were clean shaven, like Richard of Normandy. On the south side of the river, houses stood thick along either side of the road to the bridge. At the foot of the bridge half a dozen beggars in rags were calling for mercy.

The bridge looked new, with big timbers lashed in clusters sunk down into the riverbed and layers of planks set across to make the road. All along the rails on either side people stood calling out wares, baskets at their feet full of nuts and apples. The bridge went flat across the river, which boiled through the narrow gaps between the posts: Raef thought it was here as much to stop ships going upstream as to let people get across. He led the others across the long span and into the swarming heart of the city.

"What's the name of this place?" Leif asked.

Raef was looking around them. "London." He was trying to feel his way through the tumult of the city. He had met Euan Woodwrightsson long before, and given this connection he thought he should be able to feel out his house, but the space around him seemed packed, airless, deafening. His nerves itched. "Come on."

They went off along the road that led by the riverbank. Stubs of old piers stood in the water, boats moored among them. A brook came down into the river, stinking of offal and carrying garbage, and Raef turned to go up alongside it toward a bridge on the higher ground. He was still struggling just to keep the city's chaos from flooding in on him when he realized Euan Woodwrightsson's house was off to his right. In his mind it stood like a big yellow beacon in a churning of vapors and screams. He led the other two up through narrow lanes.

Laissa said, "What are we doing here?"

Raef stood looking up at the tall house, the bottom section made of stone, the upper story of wood, the massive roof of slates; as if they hung like beans in a soup of wood and stones and air, he could feel the people inside, the servants and slaves and hangers-on, and at the center of them Euan Woodwrightsson, the very rich man.

Now also he was beginning to make out something larger, a spinning top of power, a furious, enormous motion. Euan Woodwrightsson was part of it, Richard of Normandy another part, and he himself, entwined around and around some terrible purpose. He looked around him. The itching along his nerves was getting stronger.

He led the others around to the back of Euan's house. The claim of kinship should get them at least some place to stay the night. They waited in the wood yard until someone came in, and in his newfound Saxon he sent that someone for someone else in the big house, who came back to the yard and took a message: Your kinsman Raef Corbansson is outside.

They waited awhile. A man carried a sack of cabbages into the kitchen, and another came by with a basket of bread. The sun was going down. Raef fretted; Laissa needed a place to stay, and the porch of a church wasn't good enough anymore. He could feel Leif's gaze on him, the Icelander wondering what he was doing.

Then a kitchen boy came out from the backdoor and stood on the step above him and said, "My master commands you leave at once, or he will attack you with dogs."

Raef turned and walked off, his teeth gritted together. He burned with humiliation, but he should have foreseen this. Laissa said, "Where are we going?"

They went back down the slope toward the busy part of the

city. "I'm hungry," Leif said. "Let's go spend those farthings." Raef said nothing, his head down; he wanted to go back to throttle Euan. The deeper they went into the churning city, the more edgy he was, confused, angry.

The Lady of Hedeby was somewhere nearby. That was the itch. And if he could sense her even within the barricades of his body, then she was very close. She could be anybody. His gaze swept the crowd around him. Any woman. Corban had seen her as a merchant woman, old but strong. She could be any of the women in the street, with their white coifs wrapped around their hair and their broad-brimmed hats and long dark skirts, although it was hard to see how a woman carrying a basket of bread could overturn the world. Then suddenly someone came up and caught hold of his arm and said, "Let me see you."

He wheeled, his arm cocked back ready to strike, the heat of her touch like a brand. She stepped away, saying, "Hold. Hold, Raef, do you not know me?" She laughed.

He lowered his fist. The laugh resounded in his memory. She was a big woman, round and well plumped, her red-brown hair escaping from the confines of a crumpled white coif. She wore big wooden clogs like a peasant, but she was no peasant; she gave off a shine of strength, and, poor as she wore them, her clothes were richly made.

She had direct, dark brown eyes, and it was the eyes that brought her name to him. "Arre," he said. "Arre."

She laid her hands on his arm. "Yes, I am your aunt, somehow, close to, anyway. It is you, Raef; you have come back." Then she lowered her hands and cast her gaze swiftly around her, almost furtively. "And none too soon. Now, listen. I know you tried to get help from Euan, but he is a lost fish here. Trust me. We must meet. There is—something you must see. Tomorrow, the King and Queen will ride out, after Mass. They go to the minster, down around the curve of the river to the south. The

King has a hall there. Here." She was going. Now he saw a servant hovering a little way down the street, his hat pulled down, waiting for her. Looking back over her shoulder, she held something out to Raef. "Tomorrow." She ran off. The servant scuttled along with her.

Raef looked down; she had given him a little leather purse, which jingled. He turned to Leif and said, "Do you think we can find an inn?"

"The city is packed," Leif said. "They're having some festival. Those farthings won't be enough."

"This is enough," Raef said, hefting the purse.

━━◦━━

Yet in the end all they could find for any price was a storeroom in a stable behind an inn. The straw was warm, and the space dry, but the dark and the reek of horses drove them out again before they slept, into the boisterous city.

With the feast day almost on them, the city was filled with people there to celebrate. Torches burned on posts at every corner, and crowds milled through the streets, drinking and singing and calling out. Laissa clung close to Raef, unused to all these strangers. Across the crowd they saw a parade of horsemen going by—six men wearing fine dark coats and peaked hats and riding fine, prancing horses.

As they went, the people shouted and called, and one of the men turned, sweeping off his cap in response. His long blond hair tumbled over his shoulders. The call rose again: "Aethelstan! Aethelstan!"

Laissa stood on her toes to watch them ride by. They were her age, all but one younger boy. Her gaze fell on the handsome blond-haired Aethelstan. *I am married now.* She took hold of Raef's arm.

Leif said, "Who are those lordlings?"

"Aethelstan," Raef said. "The King's eldest son. From the old wife, the Saxon, not the Norman duke's sister." He glanced around him; he was hot, his cheeks ruddy, his eyes piercing. Laissa could feel the surge of his blood through his wrist, where she held him.

"So the new wife is a Norman," Leif said. "Maybe she can help us."

"I don't think so."

"He did."

"He got us out of his way." Under his breath, Raef said, "But it's all connected. I just don't see how."

They went on down the broad street along the river, where the vendors were selling food and drink, charcoal and candles. Eating sausage and cheese, they went by the young English princes again, clustered at a tavern doorway, lesser men around them in a ring. At their center the handsome fair-headed Aethelstan was laughing, his head thrown back.

They came to the filthy stream, winding down toward the mucky bank of the river, and went to the bridge and crossed, crowding through a constant stream of people coming the other way. Just beyond that was the bear pit. The torchlight did not quite reach into the bottom, and she knew the bear was there only by the restless stirring and rumbling of the shadows.

Leif stood watching the bear, and Raef pulled Laissa off and down below the shoulder of the bridge, by the brook, where nobody could see them, and leaned her against the pier. She put her hands behind her, arching her body toward him. She loved this attention, this homage. He pulled her skirts up and rubbed his hands over her, holding her close against him, filling her crevices with his heat. She coiled her arms around his neck.

"Not here." She licked the skin above his collarbone.

"Everybody can see us. Let's go back to the stable. Leif can catch up." She led him back toward the quiet and the straw.

———

Edmund Aetheling followed his older brother Aethelstan into the tavern. After the quiet of his grandmother's house in Wessex, the noise and confusion of London was overwhelming. He was fourteen, almost grown up, and now he was to attend his father's court, but in this strange place he felt like a child again, and he stayed close to his big brother. He loved Aethelstan best, anyway, and always had, golden Aethelstan, one day to be his king, deserving of all his loyalty.

Inside the crowded tavern, at the sight of them, a cheer went up; but he knew it was for Aethelstan.

Aethelstan's carls went ahead of them, clearing the way. Then another man came up through the crowd.

"Prince Aethelstan. Thank you for coming. Will you join us in the back room?"

Aethelstan swept his hat off. He was taller than anyone else in the common room and drew all eyes to him, handsome and high headed. "What's this about, my lord Morcar?" His clear voice sounded through the sudden hush.

"Please," the other man said. He was in middle age, with a long face, a bulbous nose, eyelids that drooped at the corners like a hound's. "We should talk out of the common earshot."

Aethelstan looked around. His gaze lighted on Edmund, and he said, "Come on, little brother. The rest of you stay here."

Edmund was glad to be chosen. He followed Aethelstan into the back of the tavern, to a door that opened into a small room with no windows. Here at a table sat four other men, who leaped to their feet when the princes came in. The hound-faced Morcar, who Edmund remembered was a thegn of the Five Burhs, shut the door behind them. His seat was Derby, north somewhere, in Mercia. Edmund was pleased with himself for knowing that.

He wondered what this was about. Something to do with the Martinmas feast, probably, everything else was.

The other men around the room were also high Saxon lords. He recognized them from the court, but he did not remember their names. This must be some part of the court festival. Nobody told him anything.

"You know my brother Edmund," Aethelstan said.

These men only glanced at Edmund, muttered greetings, and turned back to the crown prince. "My lord," Morcar said. "I pray you, sit down with us. We have heavy words to say."

Aethelstan folded his arms across his chest. "I'll stand. What's this about?"

The other men glanced at one another, shifting their feet. They could not sit while the prince stood, and they seemed uncertain now how to begin. Edmund saw how his brother had taken control of this. The other men hemmed, their eyes lowered. Finally Morcar said, "You know that Aweard of Bath was murdered last summer. Stabbed to death in his own dooryard."

Edmund licked his lips. This was not about Martinmas. This was something bad. He glanced at his brother and saw Aethelstan frowning.

"Yes. An old feud caught up to him. I don't know what it has to do with us."

"And Maer Longnose, of Avon, before that," another man said. "Drowned crossing a river, they said." He gave a humorless harrumph of disbelief. The others growled.

Aethelstan said sharply, "What are you getting at?"

"My lord," Morcar said, "I will say it bluntly. It is the King."

"What!"

"The King is killing us all off, one at a time, and now there

is a rumor going around that he means to sweep England free
of all his enemies at one stroke. Every man here fears for his
life."

Edmund froze. He switched his astonished gaze to Aethelstan.

"The King." Aethelstan's jaw was set like a ledge. His glittering eyes turned from one to the other. "You blame this on the
King. You think you see some great scheme of Ethelred's in
this."

"Not by his own hand," said another man, balding, heavy-
set. "It is Eadric Streona who carries out his will. The King sets
this upstart and the Normans against his own countrymen.
Everybody knows Streona wields the axe for the King."

Aethelstan said, "This is foul and fearful gossip. You start
at shadows. Nightmares. You can prove nothing of this. My father is no such man as that, much less such a king as would do
that. I will hear no talk against him, do you understand me?"
He turned to Edmund. "Go on out, little brother—I would not
have brought you if I knew they meant to say this."

Edmund said, "I—"

Aethelstan said, harshly, "Edmund, go."

Edmund turned and went out the door, his hands shaking. In
the big, crowded room beyond, stinking of ale and bodies, alone,
he stood with his heart hammering, wondering what to do. These
men were speaking treason against his father. They were trying
to turn his brother against their father. This was what it meant to
come to court, he thought, to learn such things. Then the door behind him opened, and the big, balding man he had seen inside
came out and took him by the arm and led him to a quieter
corner.

"Now, boy," he said, "you should not have heard that. Put it
from your mind."

"Put it from my mind!" Edmund said. He kept his voice

low; he was shaking. "Everybody always blames my father for everything." He was still shocked, and now he was angry.

"Well," the older man said, "Aethelstan does not. Even now he is ripping Morcar up and down like a hung deer." He lifted his hand, and an alewife came toward them with cups. "You must keep this secret, Edmund."

Edmund swallowed. If he said nothing, was that not a kind of treason? The other man was watching him narrowly. In the silence, the alewife held out a cup to him, and he shook his head.

The balding man took the cup and waved the woman away. When she was gone, he said, "I am Sigeferth, Morcar's brother, and thegn of the Burhs." He held his hand out.

Edmund ignored it, and after a moment Sigeferth lowered his hand. The prince wondered what to do. He knew who Sigeferth was: Like Morcar, his holding was in Mercia, and this Streona whom they had called the King's henchman had lately become overlord of Mercia.

He clutched at that. That must be what was going on here. The feuding of the Saxon lords was legendary. They would say anything in pursuit of their interests.

He said, "I have to do what is right." That sounded stupid.

The big man watched him cooly. He said, "If word of this meeting gets out, it will look bad for Aethelstan, you see. You see?"

Edmund did not see it. He did not know what to think. Before he could speak, the door in the back opened, and Aethelstan came out again. He was not smiling. He clapped his hat on his head. With a wave he summoned his carls to him. "Edmund," he called. "Let's go." He shot a fierce glare at Sigeferth. Edmund went gratefully after him, into the street.

There Aethelstan turned to him. "What did he say to you?"

Edmund shook his head. There was no use in telling him. It was all surely lies. But his spine tingled. "Nothing," he said, and followed Aethelstan down the street.

In the corner the little man saw them go and wondered who was in the back room. He didn't bother to find out. Streona would pay him for this news, and he would pay more if the men in the back room were Danes, so they were Danes. He hurried out to the street, down toward the King's hall, to find his master, Streona.

CHAPTER SIX

The next day, Raef and Laissa and Leif went down the road out of London to the new minster, around the southern bend in the river and across another bridge, to meet Arre. Hundreds of other people had also come and lined the road all the way to the porch of the low wooden church. The day was bright and the sun warmed them; they had left their fur cloaks hidden in the stable. Leif beside him, Raef let Laissa stand in front so she could see, and they could protect her from the buffets of the crowd.

He laid his hands on her shoulders, though; he had noticed how she had looked at Prince Aethelstan.

Now the doors of the church cracked open, and out came a steady parade of people. First were men with long brass-bound horns, all dressed in bright tunics, who blew shrieking blasts on their instruments as if the noise would open a corridor ahead of them. Raef shook himself; his body was crazed, as if every nerve stirred, and an icy panic went through him in waves. He wondered if it was only the huge city around them, overwhelming his senses. He was drowning in noise and color.

After the horn players, half a dozen children in very rich clothes ran by, casting bits of money and nutmeats to either side. Meanwhile, as the poor scrabbled for these alms, grooms were leading horses to the porch. First mounted up were the royal princes; Raef recognized Aethelstan again, with his long fair hair. When the princes came down the road, the crowd cheered them so loudly that Aethelstan stopped his horse and swept his hat off and saluted them. He had done this the night before, Raef remembered. He was their favorite, and he meant to stay so.

Aethelstan was part of it too, this spinning, this quickening whirl of power, around a center he could not see.

Some other men followed them, a few in mail but most in rich fur-trimmed coats. The Saxons were as clothes proud, he thought, as the Greeks. People around Raef were saying names— *Sigeferth*, *Uhtred*, *Morcar*—but he knew nothing of them: Saxon lords. Then came a dozen men who were clearly Normans, beardless, their hair close cropped to fit under their helmets, many in mail coats. Their horses were strapping southern stock. The crowd subsided as they approached and was quiet, even sullen, while watching them pass.

Then another cheer went up; the King was coming. Suddenly through all the buffeting racket of the city, the itchiness and the panic, an unforgettable stench reached Raef's nose, and the hair stood up on the back of his neck, and his tongue stuck to the roof of his mouth.

The King of the English was riding toward him, a broad, handsome man of middle age, dressed in sumptuous dark velvet trimmed with spotted fur. His horse was black with white socks, gold threads braided into its mane and forelock. Beside him on a little dun mule rode his new Queen, the Norman girl, Emma. As Raef looked at her she turned her gaze on him, and from her there went out a blast of power that he felt down to his heels.

It was she, the Lady, inhabiting the Queen.

He backed away, stunned. The King and Queen rode by him, the King booming loud and massive, the girl short and plump. Her coif and her gown were white with gold laces, her furs white. Her face inside the hood of fur trembled and glimmered in a chaos of change. She went by him without turning, smiling straight ahead, small beside her great boar of a King. Raef realized he was holding his breath.

He lowered his gaze. He came back to himself. Beside him, a woman stood, her head wrapped in a dirty coif. It was Arre, wearing the same long stained apron and clog shoes as the night before. He wondered how long she had been there, watching him. He lifted his head, the shock of seeing the Lady still rippling through him.

Arre said, "You saw the Queen? She makes my blood bubble."

Raef laughed, shaky. He thought, That is the center, and in his mind he saw the mill storm of war and murder spreading out around her, England already caught; Denmark, Norway, and the rest of the North beginning to fall, as well as Normandy now; everything sucked into destruction in a whirling chaos. The last of the royal retainers were swarming by, and the crowd was hurrying to follow, leaving him and Arre behind.

He realized that Arre was talking to him. She was apologizing for the way her husband had treated him the night before. "The King suspects everybody. He's threatened to charge Euan with some made-up crime and throw him into a dungeon, and Euan's out of his mind with worry."

Raef said, "What you did made it right. We are in your debt." He had seen she was wary, even out here, of being seen. The crowd was boisterous, many drunken, and it was shoving out onto the road to follow the King and Queen and their retainers up to the hall. Up there a line of Norman knights swung out behind the royal party to hold the crowd back.

Laissa still stood by the road with Leif, watching the procession but not following the crowd. Raef called to them. From the crowd in the road there went up a loud, angry bellow at the Normans holding them back.

Arre said, "This would not be Martinmas in London without one good street fight." She brushed back a tendril of her hair that had escaped her coif. "We cannot do more than talk, and that only a few moments. I only wish you good journey. You are on your way to Jorvik?"

"Yes." He was in a fever to get away. He had to protect Laissa, whom he had drawn into this. He had to get out of London, find somewhere he could collect himself.

Arre said, "Uhtred of Bamburgh thinks he rules Jorvik. But the place is ruined, hardly anyone lives there anymore." Her broad, shrewd face was seamed with worry; her eyes darted from side to side, keeping watch. Her voice tightened like a drawn wire. "Here comes a page. Take care."

A boy in royal colors trotted up to them, his long hair in his eyes. Two knights on horseback followed. The page bowed down before Raef and said, "The King and Queen request your presence before them at court. You and your wife."

Raef straightened, his eyes going toward the noisy swarm growing smaller in the distance. "I am unknown to them."

"You are known; your name goes on before you, they say."

He raised his eyes to the two knights who had come with the page. It was in his mind to run, but there was Laissa. He looked over his shoulder at Arre, who made the sign of the cross at him and slipped away, looking like a peasant wife in her dirty apron. He turned to Laissa and Leif. "Come with me."

"Just two of you," the page said. "My lady the Queen bade me that expressly, only you and your wife."

Leif took a step back, looking relieved. He said, "I'll meet you in London," and went off down the road. Raef took hold of Laissa's hand, and they followed the page.

⸻

Emma sat beside her King, smiling, her eyes forward. Inside this shell the Lady churned with rage.

She had long known Raef was coming, and she had recognized him at once there in the crowd, even in his manifest body, tall, stooped, his white-yellow hair in braids down his back. At least, she thought, he no longer had the hawk to guide him.

She should have known what he was years before, when he was only a worm in his mother's belly.

She had suspected when Gunnhild escaped that the Danish

witch intended to thwart her. Gunnhild had freed her of the
loathsome imprisonment in Hedeby, and the Lady would have
absorbed her, but, before she could turn, something warned
Gunnhild, who broke loose and fled, and the Lady had had to
leap quickly into another, lesser body.

Since then the Lady had gathered in many souls, but none
so strong and broad as Gunnhild's. Many Christian souls had
no power at all of their own, having given it to their god. Emma
was only just satisfactory, pliant and stupid, and inhabiting her
meant putting up with Ethelred.

Now the loss of Gunnhild had turned back on her, and the
Lady had come face-to-face with the one creature who could
do her damage.

She should have killed him when his mother had been in
her hands. She had tried. She had given Mav powerful drinks to
wash him early from the womb, plotted to seize him when he
came out, to drown him before he drew breath. Mav had forestalled it all, loving her son, in her greatness of soul loving even
the product of a rape.

The Lady did not know exactly how he could harm her, but
the urgency grew in her steadily to get rid of him.

He was still only a man, ignorant, bumbling. He hardly knew
more of himself than he had in the womb. If she killed him now,
he would crumble away like a dry leaf. She had to keep him out
of Jorvik, where he would be strong even beyond her reach, and
where he would grow. But keeping him from Jorvik seemed easy
enough. And there was the wife, the pretty little wife. The Lady
coiled herself in Emma's body, waiting.

—⧫—

Only a narrow creek separated the minster's island from the
hall of the King of the English. It was a well-built wooden hall
with a roof of slates; the walls were hung with weavings, and

the floor covered with rushes scented with rosemary. Crowds of men in fur-trimmed coats stood around talking, as at any court; Raef had seen half the courts in Christendom, and they all reminded him of swarms of flies buzzing over a pile of shit. He followed the page up before the raised platform at the end. On the wall behind it was a broad red banner, figured with a golden serpent, and in front of it two thrones stood.

On one was the King of the English, bluff and massive. The red banner behind them on the wall was his, blazoned with the winged dragon of his house. On the other throne was a swirling, stinking madness wrapped in a plump whey-faced girl-child. Raef faced the King.

He said, "I greet the King of the English, whose name is known as far as Freising and even Rome."

He did not bow. Behind Ethelred stood a row of men with swords, and Raef kept part of his attention always on them.

Ethelred said, "You have heard me spoken of in Rome." He turned to look behind him, to make sure everybody else was as impressed with this as he was. He leaned on the great carved arm of his throne. His wide face was dark from the sun, his beard sun crisped. The skin over his cheekbones was coarse and pocked. When he smiled it was only with his mouth, a twitch of his meaty lips.

Half Raef's mind was bent to hold off the blast of rage from his right hand; he spoke to Ethelred in a clumsy voice, halting.

"It is known what enemies you face. And England is far famous for her wealth."

Ethelred beat his fist once on the arm of the throne. "I am glad to hear it. You have come recently from lands to the east, I have heard."

"Yes," he said. He was burning with a horrible itch. His gaze flicked toward the Queen, sitting among her waiting women. Emma had called Laissa up before her, first in Saxon and then in French. "Yes." He cast another instant's glance that way and saw Laissa kneel, her eyes turned down, at the Queen's feet.

"Is it true that the emperor is dead?"

"The true Emperor, in New Rome, he may live forever. The Emperor of the West is truly dead, Otto the Saxon." Laissa, he thought, Be careful. His mind roiled, trying to pitch his thoughts into the girl. Tell her nothing. Do not touch her. "I have heard his cousin will be emperor, but they are still fighting over it." When the Queen beckoned to a page to offer Laissa something to eat, Raef had to grip his hands together to keep from reaching out and knocking the dish away.

Laissa shook her head at the food. Ethelred was saying, "And the Pope."

"Sylvester is dead. There's another pope, but he belongs to the Roman strongman." Glad, he saw through the corner of his eye that Laissa was too frightened even to look at the Queen. The other waiting women, all dressed in white, had drawn back behind the throne, leaving Laissa alone at Emma's feet. Emma leaned toward her, but Laissa would not even lift her eyes.

To Ethelred, Raef said, "And the new pope anyway is hardly what Sylvester was." He had liked Gerbert d'Aurillac.

"What happened to Sylvester's brazen head?" Ethelred said. "Was that not some instrument of the devil?"

Raef laughed. He had heard this before, and since he had seen the actual head and heard wise, mad Gerbert talk to it, a deep place formed in his mind, and for an instant, sinking down into memory, he was beyond the reach of dread. He saw, for an instant, Laissa white as a candle flame before the Queen, and the swirling black lust of the Queen, and the women behind her like candles with their flames blown out.

Then he rose to the surface, and the commonplace shuffling and stink and noise of the court around him flooded in again. The dread came back, a cramping nausea in his guts. Other people were pushing up closer around him, trying to catch Ethelred's eye. Raef backed up into their midst. "It was just a piece of brass. I think it was buried with him." He let a burly man with a thick black beard shove by him. "My lord," he said to the King, "my wife is ill. I would have leave to get her somewhere quieter."

Ethelred waved his hand. "Go. I see no harm in you."

⟶

"They have heard of me in Rome," Ethelred said to his wife.

The Queen was staring after the tall stranger and his wife. She turned to him and gave him her pretty smile. His heart swelled with love; he bent and kissed her cheek.

She said, "You are the greatest king in Christendom, my lord."

He laughed. This he knew was not true, but her adoration of him was delightful, and he meant to keep it. He had few such pure pleasures. He had foreign enemies on all sides, and, even in his own kingdom, men conspired against him. They always had, since he was only a little boy, the junior King. He still remembered when his older brother was murdered. He had thought then, This will happen to me, someday, and since then he had been working to prevent that.

Now again the evil of conspiracy was coiling around his court. The kingdom was infested with Danes and half Danes and even some Saxons and Angles who preferred the Danes, and until they were gone he would not be the true King even here. He glanced over his shoulder at the men standing behind him, his guards. Eadric Streona stood among them, clean shaven and close cropped, and the King met his eyes. Streona smiled at him. He shared his mind on this. Streona would be his sword. They had made plans. They had talked through everything, and now the moment was coming; at Ethelred's word, Streona would lead Ethelred's men against all his enemies. Wipe the kingdom clean. He looked down the hall for the tall white-haired wanderer. He was likely a Dane too somehow. If not, better to be sure. He took Emma's hand in his.

"My dear lord." She lifted her eyes to him. "The girl who was just here—she seemed so sweet to me; I would see her again."

He lifted her fingers to his lips and kissed them and, turning, beckoned Streona to him. "It shall be done, my dear child." All would soon be done.

CHAPTER SEVEN

Outside the hall, Raef said, "You did that very well."

"I did nothing."

"Yes, very well."

"She scares me."

"She should." He towed her on through the thick of the people waiting at the cold end of the hall, going toward the door where they had come in. Mailed knights stood all along the walls. Normans. He twisted his head once to look back over his shoulder, toward the Queen. He wondered how far he had to run to get away from this creeping, stinking heat, the scum of fear she cast over him. He turned to Laissa.

"Do you feel that?"

She looked wildly at him. "What's the matter? You look so strange." She clutched him. "What is it?"

"Where's Leif?" He realized he was panicking, spreading the dislocated terror the Lady bred in him. "We have to find Leif and get out of here."

They went out the door and through a busy dooryard, where horses stamped and an important-looking man stood by the hall step keeping people out, and through the broad, open gate onto the road. Leif had gone toward London. Raef could find him there easily enough. Laissa cried, breathless, "Don't go so fast—I can't keep up," and he slowed down, the road hard under his feet.

He had Laissa by one hand, and she took his arm with the other and said, "Tell me what's wrong."

"Be careful," he said. "The Queen—Don't let her near you. Don't let her touch you—" Then the long-haired page who had brought them there in the first place ran up, out of breath.

Panting, he bowed down before Raef, again; the passersby divided to walk around them. A few men on horseback were coming slowly up from the direction of the hall. The boy said, "My lady the Queen would have the wife of Raef Corbansson attend her in her bower."

Raef gripped Laissa and pulled her behind him. "No. She is not well—"

Laissa cried, "I have no fit gown, don't make me," and then from either side horsemen were lunging at them.

Raef wheeled, dodging a blow from behind that whistled over his head, and banged up against the horse there; he got the man in the saddle by the arm, on the swordsman's return stroke, and yanked him off the skittering horse. Laissa was screaming. They were hauling Laissa away. He shouted her name and lunged after her. Another horse smashed into him from the side, and something struck him on the head. He went down on hands and knees on the road. For an instant he could see nothing. But he could feel the sword coming, and he lurched up. Weaving under the swing he got the man by the wrist and twisted the blade from his grip. The sword clanged on the road.

The knight shouted a French oath, grabbing for something else to kill him with. Raef reached for the sword on the ground and stuck upward, taking the Norman through the skirt of the hauberk. He hauled the blade free, and the body fell.

People were yelling. He wheeled around. On the ground, the other man was getting to his feet, and Raef kicked him down again. There had been more than two. They were gone now, and they had taken Laissa. People were watching, were gathering; soon another crew of knights would come.

He knew where they had taken her. He knew what he had to do now. He sprinted down the crowded road toward London.

—◦—

Leif sat outside the tavern in the sun, a can of ale on the table at his elbow, watching a juggler flipping a stream of colored balls through the air. The juggler was not as good as he could have been, and, when he dropped a ball, Leif joined the other men around the front of the tavern hooting at him and throwing whatever came to hand. A few people threw stones. The juggler hurried off, leaving a red ball behind on the pavement before the tavern. Leif sat back, reaching for his ale.

Someone had come up beside him and was standing there, and now, turning, Leif saw him and recognized him for one of the Saxon lords from the court. He wore the gold-trimmed and fur-lined fancy Saxon clothes, but he was short haired and clean shaven, like a Norman. A little crinkle of alarm went down Leif's back. He took the can of ale and found it had been filled up again.

"Good day to you," said the Saxon. First he used his own language, which Leif waved off; and then French, which Leif also refused; and finally dansker, with a look on his face as if he knew all along it would come to this.

"Good day," Leif said. The ale was crisp and bright, and he drank the whole can down. "So," he said. "You are Eadric Streona."

The Saxon looked surprised. He was younger than Raef, square headed, with thick curly brown hair; the hood of his black cloak was down like a big cowl around his shoulders. He said, "You know me."

Leif said, "I have heard of you. You are the King's axeman. What do you want with me?"

The Saxon turned and signaled for more ale. He sat on the bench beside Leif. When the alewife came to fill his can and Leif's, Streona looked down the front of her bodice. She was used to this and gave him a little flirt with her tits.

Leif took his can, reassured. People didn't buy drinks for people they were about to arrest. He looked Streona over again, a handsome young man, a ready smile.

The Saxon faced him, solemn. "You know, you yourself, Leif whoever you are, we would let you walk on anywhere you wish."

"Yes," Leif said, his gut tightening. "But it's somebody else, isn't it? What's he got himself into this time?"

"Do you know where he is?"

"As far as I know, he's at the court. The King summoned him this morning. You've lost him so soon? What about Laissa?"

"Laissa. The girl? We have her." Streona shrugged that off as unimportant. Leif lifted the can of ale, giving himself a chance to think about this. They had her. He wondered what that meant.

"But you've misplaced Raef." He cursed Raef silently for abandoning Laissa to them. "Where is she?"

Streona turned, sharp eyed, and said, again, "We have her. Nice tender bit."

"Leave her alone," Leif said roughly and at once regretted it.

Streona's teeth showed. "So. It's her, is it. Not so happy with him, but you'd do a lot for her, wouldn't you?"

Leif lifted his head, silent, wishing he had been silent sooner. He met the Saxon's pale, clever, mirthless eyes.

"Tell us where he is," Streona said. "We were supposed to kill him, but we missed. Tougher than he looks. Just take us to him, and we'll let you and the girl go free."

———

In the Queen's bower Laissa sat up, panting, her hair all in her face, and looked around her; she was alone here. The place was pretty, with flowers of silk and jewels, painted jugs, and cushions and stools. The walls were covered with rugs. She thrust at the air with her hands, trying to get away.

"Why am I here? Who brought me here? Where is my husband?"

The door opened and the English Queen came in. The door swung shut behind her.

Laissa fell still, wary. The Queen was young, roundly made, with fine little hands and a pretty smile, pretty like this room, but Laissa felt in her something else, something she had no name for and no way to see, but which she could barely resist, somehow, as if a flood pressed against her. She bent down, bowing.

Emma said, "No, sit, my dear. Let me speak French to you. Do you speak French?"

Laissa understood it, but her uncertain skill at speaking it abruptly vanished. "I—Me—I—"

Emma laughed, sat on the soft cushions, and, reaching out, drew Laissa down beside her.

"No need to talk. I knew when I first saw you we should be friends. I so need a friend here, you cannot know." Suddenly her huge dark eyes quivered full of tears. Laissa shrank away. The pressure on her was like something crushing against her, all around, and yet she saw nothing but this innocent, eager child.

"Please be my friend. My lord the King will give your husband all the preferment he wants." Emma caught at Laissa's hand. Her eyes were hot, still damp with tears, but the tears forgotten now. "Kiss me, let us be sisters."

"My lady." Laissa twisted away. "I—Me—worthless. Me unworth."

Emma laughed again, a sound like birds or bells or breaking glass. "Let me determine that. I knew at once how good you are, how true and kind. Come, give me a kiss, to bind us together as sisters. Friends."

"No." Laissa stood, trying to twist her arm out of the Queen's grasp; how could so small a girl be so strong? "I go— My husband—"

"I am telling you your husband will be great in the King's eyes from this day on, if you will but grant me this one boon."

Laissa turned and looked at her, confused; the girl's round face, with her milk-white skin, her deep dark eyes, seemed so innocent. Maybe Raef was wrong, she thought. Why should she fear such a gentle girl? She could make Raef a great man here, just for a little kiss. Slowly she drew nearer, her face uplifted to the Queen.

⟞§⟝

Raef reached the stable where they had spent the night; for their coupling he had taken Laissa deep into the low narrow back of the barn where the straw was high and nobody could see, and he went in there now behind the bales of hay and sat down. It was dim and shadowy here even in the middle of the day. He settled himself and shut his eyes, but for a moment his body was rigid as iron, would not let his mind out, a shrieking warning all along his nerves.

He gathered himself; he made his mind creep out onto the field of light and time.

Here in the city the field was no smooth circling glow but a fire heap of hot and dark, lights flashing and leaping in arcs, the seething and spinning of the hundreds and thousands of people all going different ways, all up or down or sideways with their thoughts; he flew through it like a bird through a thick, burning forest, weaving and soaring and diving.

Yet he saw Laissa at once, far away, the bright golden light of her, all his love in one moment. Around her, swirling thick and black and stinking, was his enemy, about to surround her, envelope her, consume her entirely.

He saw not a thing but a hole in the light field, trying to draw Laissa into the abyss.

He flung himself across the space between them, banging and scraping around the upheaving light field like a bird through a burning forest, and dove headlong into the filthy stench and the howling. He screamed, although the roar around him soaked up the sound entirely. All around him was the smoke, heavy, full of grit, choking. He thrashed at it, trying to scatter it. The Lady had hold of Laissa. He knew that even as his mind began to shiver and shake and crumple. That made her weaker against him, having to keep hold of Laissa. He was falling into shreds. Scraps of color flew by. He saw Merike's hands; he heard Conn's voice. For an instant, he was on the island, carrying fish. Each swift piercing instant flew away empty. He thrust forward what of his mind he still controlled, into the stench and the heat and smoke, screaming his name so he could remember who he was.

—⚬—

Laissa bit her lip so hard the blood ran on her chin; she cast a quick look at the gate into the bower. There were men outside, the Queen's knights. What they would do if they found her this way she dared not risk finding out.

The Queen had frozen, was still as ice, not even breathing, her eyes wide. Her grip on Laissa's hand was like a steel ring. There was no one else in the bower, and yet all around the air had gone suddenly dark and dirty, with a horrible stench, and it whirled around her like a storm wind. In the middle of it Emma sat like a stone.

Laissa pulled at the Queen's hand on her wrist, made claws of her fingernails and ripped at the white skin of Emma's arm. Nothing moved the grip on her. Then she remembered finding Raef this way, and she swung her arm and hit Emma as hard as she could on the face.

The girl startled all over. For a moment her white-brown eyes turned on Laissa, soft, confused. Laissa pulled free of her slackening grasp. Then the brown eyes dissolved into a wild spinning fire, and Laissa lunged for the door.

⟶⟵

Raef felt Laissa break free and gave a yell of joy. The Lady boiled around him, a fury hotter than the clearest flame, iron smoke, hideous deafening screams in his ears, encompassing him, a smothering of shit, of offal, a twist of pain all through him like a wire through his spine. Then abruptly she released him. He hung an instant in the bower, Emma before him, the filthy smoke seeping back into her through every pore.

He held there only a moment. He knew he had not beaten the Lady. She had gone to do something else. He had to get out of here. Wheeling, he followed Laissa.

⟶⟵

Laissa ran all the way to London, through the crowds of people on the river street, to the stable where they had spent the night. She called his name, but he was not there. She went back past the stalled horses, a line of rumps hipshot in the dark. Where they had slept on the comfortable straw was empty, cool, and dim. Their cloaks and packs were still buried in the straw under the rick. She stood, panting, her mind numb. Then she remembered lying wrapped around him in the dark.

She crawled around behind the rick, pushing on her hands and knees through the heaped straw at the back, where he had hollowed out the space for them, safe from other eyes and ears. It was dark there, even now, and close.

He sat at the back end of the hollow.

She said his name. She went up before him. He did not move. Like the Queen he was stone still, his eyes stared, and his mouth hung open. Then, before she could cry out, she saw him come back.

His eyes widened, and his skin flushed. He lifted his head and looked at her and smiled. She went slack with relief. He leaned forward and kissed her. "Come on. We have to find Leif and get the hell out of London."

—✦—

Emma lay sobbing on the cushions, and Ethelred rushed in ahead of the guards who had come and gotten him when the girl fled. The King sank down on the cushions by his wife and caught her in his arms.

"Now, child. Oh, Emma. Hush. Hush. I'm here." He held her against him, her body trembling. "What happened?"

She raised her head, her face all sick with tears. "Someone— someone came at me—" She put her hand to her face. "Hit me—"

Ethelred gasped; he saw the bruise growing on the side of her head and laid his hands on her cheeks and pressed his lips to her forehead. "Oh, child. Who? Who?"

"I don't know who—a Dane—"

"A Dane."

He spat an oath in his guttural language. He set her gently down on the cushions and sent one of the guards for her maids. It did not occur to him to ask why she was here anyway without her maids. To the other guard, he said, "Go find Streona. Tell him now it begins. Tell him the word—*Strike.*" In the corner of her eye she saw him swell with the power of saying this. She gave another shuddering sob.

"I will kill every Dane and every half Dane in my king-dom," the King said. He bent down and laid his hand on his sobbing wife. His voice was slick with a strange kind of lust. "There, there, cry no more. I shall avenge you."

Leif came out of the alehouse onto the street. "Well, I guess he's not there either." The afternoon sun was bright and low, and he shaded his eyes.

Streona came up beside him. Two mailed men, Normans, walked behind them, muttering to each other in French. Streona wasn't smiling anymore, his thick brows folded over his nose. He said, "You have any more ideas where he could be? I thought you knew him well."

"I thought he was at the court," Leif said, looking away. He wanted to know where to run when Streona finally turned on him. Off down there was a market, where the people were beginning to pack up their stalls for the day; at the edge of the street some baskets of unsold nuts and bruised cabbages stood beside a furled awning.

Then a Norman on a big horse galloped up from the other direction. Streona at once stiffened, alert, and the other knights stood sharp. The horse slid to a stop on the muddy street. Still in the saddle, the Norman raised his fist.

"The filthy dogs attacked the Queen! The King has ordered them all slain!" He spoke French. "Today we get rid of all the Danes and their friends!"

Streona yelled, "Starting with this one," and turned toward Leif, drawing his sword. But Leif, understanding the French well enough, was already running into the market.

He vaulted over the stacks of cabbages and nuts, into a street where people were packing up their goods on mules and into wagons, but, before he had wound his way through the wagons, he could hear screams in the next street. Streona bellowed behind him. He ducked into a lane down between two withy fences, panting. He was too old for this. He had always preferred anyway to think of a way through things rather than fight.

He watched the street he had just left until he saw Streona and his men pushing their way through the crowded market, shouting, striking at people to get them out of the way. Still after him. He sprang over a low fence and went through an orchard of bent, gnarled trees, going toward the stable where they had spent the night before.

He had to find Laissa. Raef could take care of himself, damn him. Laissa needed him.

The sun was going down. The streets streamed with a raw red light. He came out on the high street and saw a mob of armed men on foot surrounding a house, and, even as he stood there in the alley getting his breath, he saw them drag two men out of the house and hack their heads off.

Inside, women were shrieking, and on the thatch there grew up a tree of fire.

He went down the street on the side away from the mob; there was smoke now rolling up from the center of the city too, and a howl rose somewhere nearby like the baying of some vengeful animal. Two men ran by him, looking back, and plunged away down the street, and then almost at once after them came a stream of horsemen. Leif shrank against a wall. The horsemen caught up with the two running men, and the first rider leaned out from his saddle and slashed them down with his sword like a boy knocking the heads off daisies with a stick. The horses galloped on; the two bodies lay in the street. Leif hurried on, looking all around now, his palms clammy.

Kill all the King's enemies. Someone had attacked the Queen. They had Laissa—they had taken Laissa. He turned a corner and saw two more houses burning and a pile of bodies in front of them, and, as he watched, two men hurled another body on top, a child, a little child, all bloody.

He reeled away from that, fumbling his way blindly downhill, and then someone called his name.

"Leif!"

He wheeled, and Laissa ran into his arms.

"Oh, girl," he said. "Oh, girl." He hugged her tightly. Raef stood behind her, his eyes half-closed, his face drawn and worn.

"We have to get out of here," Raef said. He thrust Leif's fur cloak and the pack at him.

"You found her," Leif said. "Eadric Streona said—"

"Come on. They're after us."

Raef led them back up toward the high street, following the narrow lanes through the gathering dark. Leif swung the pack over his shoulder; the last of the money jingled softly in there. He clutched Raef's arm, trying to turn him off this path.

"Not that way. They're killing people up there."

"They're killing people everywhere," Raef said. "We have to warn Arre."

"Why would they go after her? She's just a woman."

Raef said, "They're from Jorvik. They're half Danes."

He led them swiftly, certainly across another wide street, where down a hundred yards a house burned and men ran back and forth shouting. Leif kept hold of Laissa by the hand. He thought, We have to get out of here. He almost stepped on a body. The thick smoke rolled down the street, and he stooped a little to breathe. Suddenly in the street ahead of them, the ground collapsed into a pit the size of a grave.

Raef, in the lead, muttered, grabbed Laissa's free hand, and towed her off down a lane; Leif followed. They were still going away from the river. He kept hold of Laissa, his breath short.

They went almost running along the bank of the dirty little brook, past the bridge. As they went by the bridge, a sudden fierce gust of wind knocked Laissa down. Raef scooped her up, her knees over one arm and her shoulders over the other. Turning, he caught Leif's eye.

"She's chasing us," he shouted. His blue eyes were wild.

"Who?"

"Keep moving," Raef said. He was still carrying Laissa in his arms. "We have to keep moving. There's—" He pointed ahead with his chin.

Across the narrow square Euan Woodwrightsson's great house stood two stories high behind its fence. Lights gleamed in the yard. The gate of the fence was locked. Leif said, "Are you sure we should—" and then the house burst into flame from top to bottom, all at once.

Raef stopped still, the ruddy light like paint on his face. Laissa, in her husband's arms, whimpered against his chest. Raef said, "Too late. They're all dead now."

"Let's go," Leif said.

They hurried on. Behind them a stone wall collapsed on the street where they had been, and Raef glanced back and began to run, Laissa in his arms with her arms tight around his neck. Leif ran with him. They came to the old stone wall of the city, and Raef led them along it. They came to a main gate, crowded with shouting people, and turned back the other way.

Steps led up the wall to the rampart. Crouching in the cover of the notched battlement, they looked south over the city. Flames and smoke rose from down near the river, in patches from their left and right. Leif looked over the edge of the wall. He could not see the bottom.

They made a rope of their belts and cloaks and Raef's dalmatic. Leif climbed down first; the rope ended in midair, and he dropped into the dark.

He hit the ground only a few feet below. Laissa shinned down the makeshift rope after him, and Raef drew it up, lodged it against the battlement, and swung down after her. From the bottom, he twisted and shook and swung the rope until it came loose. Beyond the wall came the muffled screams and cries of the city. Off in the east, beyond a line of trees, the late moon was rising. They strapped their belts on, and Raef put his shirt back on; they swung their cloaks around them and ran off into the dark.

—=§=—

Aethelstan stood boldly there before the King, where none of the others dared even speak a word, and said, "This will be our doom, my lord. You have stained your name forever with this bloodshed. You killed your own people today, as well as Danes. This will only give Sweyn Forkbeard another excuse to come down on us."

Ethelred sat on his throne, one leg cocked up. He had just eaten. His beard was scattered with crumbs. The boy Edmund, standing shyly behind his brother, thought Aethelstan the bravest man in all the world to confront his father, the King, like this. His younger brothers had not come at all, hiding behind their nurses.

Ethelred did not seem angry. His broad face, meat red above the greying wire of his beard, was unconcerned.

"It will make fewer enemies to stab us when our backs are turned, when we are fighting Sweyn and his Danes. I'm not a fool. Whatever you think."

"Sir," Aethelstan said, steadfastly. "I don't think—"

"No. You are the fool; you think not at all. You should mind who you talk to, boy. Go, you bore me." The King glanced toward the empty throne beside him.

Edmund saw this and wondered where the Queen was. There had been a whisper, before, that she was taken with some woman's ill at the beginning of the massacre and gone into her chamber. Aethelstan was saying, stubbornly, "My lord, the people already hate the Normans."

"The people," Ethelred said, with a snort. His fingers pawed briefly at his face, his eyes dark with bad temper. "What people? There are no people. No English. Only Wessex men, Essex men, Angles, Mercians, half Danes, and true Danes, and all of them—" He hitched himself around in the throne, staring at Aethelstan, his head forward. "All of them would sell my kingdom for a silver penny to anybody who had one." He smiled, his temper fading. "Why should I not then have the Normans?"

Edmund thought, The Normans take his penny, but they heed the Queen.

In the short while he had been in his father's court he had come to hate the Queen. She made fun of him and had gotten his father to call him stupid names. He hoped she was sick. He wished she would go home.

Someone came in the door behind them; someone else called out sharply, "How many? Who?"

Edmund shivered. He thought he could hear people screaming in the distance, and then Aethelstan turned, his face stiff with anger, and marched out, with Edmund following him.

In the little hall, outside the throne room, Aethelstan wheeled. "This is crazy," he said. Two of his chief carls came to him, saluting, and he spoke to them. "The King is tearing the kingdom apart when we most need to be together." He paid no heed to Edmund, who was too young to matter. "He can't kill everyone in England who disagrees with him."

"He will surely deal with anybody he can catch," said one of the carls. "Meanwhile—"

"Meanwhile," Aethelstan said, "we go to Mass, like good Christians." At last he noticed his little brother. "Edmund. You shouldn't have come." But he smiled, clapped him on the shoulder. "You're a brave boy, though, for doing it."

Edmund swelled, warming in the glow of that smile. Aethelstan ruffled his hair. "Come on, now, let's go hear a song and get drunk. And hope nobody takes us for Danes." He shepherded Edmund along beside him, the two carls walking just behind.

As they went out of the hall, Edmund marked a woman coming in. He did not know at first what he thought was strange about her. She was a big, well-fleshed woman, of some age, in a dirty coif, her clothes rumpled. She wore wooden clogs. She walked past him as if she would go straight into the King's hall, and to his surprise no one stopped her. He followed after Aethelstan, and his skin crept. He could not say what it was that was strange about her. When he glanced back over his shoulder, he could not see her. He wondered for an instant if he had imagined her.

Aethelstan was hustling them out the door. In the yard, a dozen Normans were mounting their horses, shouting back and forth; they ignored the Aetheling princes. Aethelstan ignored them as well. He led his men and his brother off to a hall nearby, and Edmund followed in his steps. If one thing in the world were noble and true, it was his brother. Gratefully, he let Aethelstan lead him into the warmth of the hall.

CHAPTER EIGHT

From London Raef drove himself and Leif and Laissa to walk that night and most of the next day before they could stop. North of London the open land, scattered with farms and villages hedged around with new walls, gave way soon to stands of trees, bogs, meadows, and then to forest. Old snow covered the ground and splattered the trees, a white crust poked with stalks of dead grass and patches of stony earth, everything brown and grey— the sky, the hillsides under their grey icy ridgelines. At a cross-roads they bought bread and cheese from a woman going to market. Weary to the bone, they trudged along the road into the North, eyes downcast, stumbling over pebbles. In the mid-afternoon Raef hustled them down into the ditch, and a moment later a stream of horsemen galloped by, the heavy hoofs jarring the ground.

After that they moved away from the road, into the forest, until with the sun going down they came out of the trees to the bank above a river, and there they finally slept.

In the morning, nobody said much. Laissa sat with her legs drawn up and watched Raef steadily. They ate the last of the cheese and bread. When they were done she came to him and sat behind him and began to comb his hair.

She said, "In London, they were killing people."

"The King was killing everybody he thought was his enemy."

"You aren't his enemy. He said so. No harm in you."

"No, but I am the Queen's."

"Yes. When I was with the Queen, what happened? She turned to stone. There was something going on, but I couldn't see it."

Leif watched them, lounging on his elbow in the sun-dappled shade. He said nothing but his eyes were sharp.

Raef said, "There is a power in the Queen—not in Emma; Emma may not even know it's there."

Laissa stroked the comb through his hair. "A—a demon?"

"I don't know. Maybe." A demon was as good a way as any to tell them. He was imagining the great field of light and time and the hole in it that she boiled up through. From somewhere else he could not imagine. He said, "Anyway, the Lady. She steals souls. She binds women's souls to her somehow. Men, I think, she just devours."

He stopped. It came to him that what she took of her victims was their place in the light field. His heart shrank. Now he could get some reckoning of what she was doing, what was to come. He remembered the crushed bones in the southern village, where he had felt not one soul left. In such chaos as the massacre in London, she could feed like a shark in a shipwreck.

"What can she do to us?"

"What happened to Arre Woodwrightsson's house."

Leif growled, stirring, his shoulders hunched. Raef said, "But I think to do things like that she must be in her host body, and her range is small. I don't think she can hurt us now, so far from London, not like that. She has other means. And she grows with every soul she eats."

"And we grow less?" Laissa said.

"The world grows less," he said. He leaned his head back into her hands. He turned his gaze on Leif, fat and balding, his forehead rumpled with doubt. They were all part of the field of light, one flawless sheet of being, flowing on and on, ever changing and never dying, world without end. Except that the Lady would destroy it all.

Gunnhild had said he could defeat her, but he had found no way to combat her. Nothing he did against her worked.

Laissa said, "What's the matter?"

He shook himself. He had been a long time silent.

Laissa said, "You . . . went somewhere else."

"No," he said. "I was here."

"This demon, then. It isn't Emma."

"No. Emma is only her . . . vessel."

"Why is she after us?" Leif said.

"I don't know." Raef put his fists to his face. "There's nothing I can do to her. She will eat up the world, Gunnhild said, beginning with England. Gunnhild said I could stop her, and she tried to teach me, but I didn't understand it then, and I still don't. I've never been able even to hamper her."

"You got me free of her," Laissa said. She leaned into his back, her face against his shoulder.

"You got yourself free. You freed us both, when you woke her body up—she had to get back into her host."

"Oh," Laissa cried. "Poor Emma."

Leif said, "She's making a nice job of tearing the place up already here in England."

"Yes."

"Where does she fit with Sweyn Tjugas and the Norman duke?"

"They know nothing of her. She will eat them too when she chooses. She's come very close to eating me."

Leif's face was seamed with frets. He looked away, and then angrily back at Raef. "You have a knack for getting us into trouble."

"You've chosen this," Raef said. "Every time you could have turned aside you came on. There is the great heart in you that knows the challenge here somehow. And you have stood fast with me. I will not forget that, ever. But it's not for my sake. Even if I were not here, she would be, and she is the evil, not me."

Leif grumbled, frowning. Laissa said, "Who are you?"

Raef turned and gave her a long look over his shoulder. The question startled him. Finally, he said, "I don't know."

—⁂—

In the days that followed, they went on, steadily north, along the road through forest and bog. When they cut back to the road, within a day a band of armed men passed them again, and Raef led them across the country.

They stopped for the night by a ruined wall. When the others were asleep, Raef got up and went off a little, restless, thinking of the Normans on the road. He remembered when he was a wolf. He thought he could drive these men away, if he were a wolf.

He walked back to their camp, and lay down on the ground beside Laissa. The moon was rising. The wind rose, tumbling down the hillside, deeply scented. He shut his eyes and let himself roam out into the luminous dark.

—⁂—

Laissa huddled under her cloak, not asleep, and felt him leave. His body slackened when he left it, cooled, and quieted, a stillness deeper than sleep. She held her cloak tightly around her and wrapped one arm around her waist, thinking about what lay within and what might become of it. What it might become. She had been walking for years, and now she was with child and needed to go home, and she had no home. She prayed, but it did not calm her. She squeezed her eyes shut and sobbed. On her other side, Leif heard her, and wordlessly his arm rose and wrapped around her, and she turned her face into his shoulder and wept.

—⁂—

After some searching Raef came on a big white wolf and sank into it, crowding the wolf's own small mind out of the way. He spent most of the night harassing the little band of Normans; their horses sensed him and were restless and loud the whole time, so that the sentries were always jumpy, and once or twice the whole camp came awake, shouting and running around and cursing one another. He enjoyed this. He strolled in almost to the fire once, before they saw him, and the yell was pleasing to him, although he barely got away.

Their leader was Eadric Streona, the sharp-eyed, tallow-voiced, clean-shaven Saxon who made himself so useful to the Queen.

In the dark, he caught something small and soft that squeaked when he bit it. Warm in his jaws as he ate it. The tiny brain like a gobbet of thick, rich blood. Toward dawn, he howled and howled, but nobody answered him.

Then he went back and returned to his camp and was Raef again. The others said nothing. They did not mind staying there another day to rest; Laissa was worn and lean and footsore, and even Leif had a pinched-in look. But there were nuts under the trees, and even now mushrooms, and Leif caught fish in the river as Raef slept.

—·—

Leif said, "What do you make of what he said about the Queen?"

Laissa shrugged. She was picking bits of fish from the flat rock he had cooked it on. She said, watching her hands, "She is—I know she is bewitched. In Constantinople I heard stories of people demons took. When she was with me, I know she was possessed. But what Raef said about her—I don't understand that." She lifted her gaze to him. "Do you think he is mad?"

Leif's pale eyes narrowed, nestled in wrinkles. His mouth

performed a slow smile. "Oh, probably. Hasn't he always been? You married him."

She licked her lips. The fish's empty skin and bones lay there on the rock. She said, "He would let us go, if we wanted."

"Do you want to leave him?"

"Where is he taking us?"

The man before her shrugged. Even after all the walking he was round bellied. He was losing the hair at the top of his head, his stubbly beard greying. She remembered what Raef had said, that he had chosen, every time, to follow him. He was a hero, Leif, without any of the hero's shine. She loved him; she almost said so.

But Raef, surely, was mad.

She said, "Maybe it's better to be wrong for the right reasons than right for the wrong reasons."

Leif shook his head. "I don't understand you either." He stood up, shaking his cloak out, and hung it on a branch. "All I understand is that I have come this far and will not stop now." His head turned, aiming his eyes toward Raef, who was lying asleep under the trees. "Call me when he wakes up." He went down toward the river to catch more fish.

———

They went on the next day. They were moving along the foot of the hills now, the villages and farms farther apart, and some abandoned, burned, the fields fallow. They passed a dozen bones strewn around the road, as if animals had dragged pieces of bodies there. They stopped in an empty village, where they managed to catch a pig that had gone wild but still lived in its old muck-hole. Roasting joints of it in the fire they stuffed themselves, and Leif and Laissa slept at once.

Raef was restless and could not sleep. He got up and walked around the old village. He knew the white wolf was close by. It had been following them all day, since he had used its body against the Normans, as if he had left some knowledge of himself in it. The urge grew strong in him to be the wolf once more.

He could see no harm in it. They never had to know about it. He could look around and see if there were enemies nearby. He could scout the way forward. The moon shone above the hill. The long wind rustled through the grass. He went back to their camp, lay down, and yearned himself into that body.

He loped away across the hills, looking for something to chase and kill. At the crest of the slope he stopped to howl, calling out into the dark; wherever this howl reached, now, was his country. Being a wolf was much easier than being a man, only running and sniffing and chasing and eating, and the howling felt good, better than any man talk, the rising call into the wind for the rest of his kind. Come run with me.

As he loped along that idea grew in him: To be with others like him would feel so good, so exciting.

Then, from the near distance, an answering howl.

He stopped trying to do whatever it was he had set out to do and ran at once toward this sound. Something all through him responded to it. When he came on her, lean and dark in the moonlight, his body went stiff all over, his tail straight up and his fur on end down his back.

He strode around her prancing on his toes. She was beautiful, slim and dark as he was big and white, and she circled toward him, her head down, her ears flat. He minced closer, her odor delicious in his nostrils, rich and promising. She let him sniff her there, and he found her warm and moist and swollen, ready.

He climbed onto her, his forelegs over her shoulders, and coupled with her. This was not as good as with human beings, over in a moment, just a hot piping. But then as he slid down, disappointed, she nipped his ear and ran off, and he chased her, and they ran and chased, back and forth, until he caught her, and again he mounted her.

They ran shoulder to shoulder, the black wolf, the white wolf, and he wondered why he should ever go back to the human life.

There was something he should be thinking about. Instead he put all his power into running. They hunted together, catching hares in the moonlight. She licked the blood from his face.

At last, near dawn, after they had played and coupled a third time, he grew tired. If he fell asleep, he might turn back into a man. Even now he saw that doing so was dangerous, and he trotted back toward the human beings. The black wolf went part of the way and then veered off and was gone. He wished he could go with her. It seemed so easy, a good life, to run, to couple, to hunt and kill and eat, no more. But he thought of Laissa, and suddenly he remembered something about Laissa he had forgotten.

The wolf slowed, reluctant to go near the people, and he left it and drew across the twilight back into his body.

She and Leif were awake. He had been lying on the ground; he sat up and went down by the fire, looking into the flames, frowning. There was something he should be thinking about. He felt different, his body strange, like a loose sack all around him. He poked at the fire with a stick.

"What's wrong with your ear?" Laissa said, kneeling down beside him.

He put his hand up, only now realizing that his ear hurt; there was a great scab on it. He said, "I don't know. I hurt it somehow." He glanced at her, remembering the wolf, and felt a little guilty. He had betrayed her. His gaze fell to her middle, and once again, he felt the stir in there, the life spark.

She was grinning broadly at him. He flushed; he realized she knew, of course, better than he did. He leaned down and pressed his mouth against her clothes over her belly. She laid her hands on his hair. Silently he promised her he would not go back to the wolf.

They went on. The snow was deeper, the nights colder, and the wind blew harsh from the northwest. He stayed with Laissa during the nights. He wanted to go run as a wolf, but he stayed with Laissa. His ear itched and swelled, oozing under the scab, and sometimes the whole side of his head felt hot.

He heard the black wolf howl, calling him, and he shivered all over. Laissa grabbed him by the hair.

"Stay here," she said, and he knew that she knew. He shut his eyes, unwilling to look at her, humiliated. All this time he had thought he hid it from her. The wolf's howl shuddered in his mind. He had to go out running again. But she knew; she would know.

They trudged up through a fold of the hills. Snow had fallen during the night, and the land was white and featureless around them, the sky grey as wool. He was tired, and his mind seemed clogged; he would not think of the wolf, and so he could think of nothing else. He would go back again, just once. Just once.

So, his senses stuffed with dreams, he led them stupidly into the ambush.

―――

The cold was piercing and there was no sun. Laissa had her cloak bundled tightly around her, walking along in Raef's track through the snow. The road took them along a crease beneath a hill, and, as they came around the curve of the hill, the men on foot rushed at her and she screamed.

Raef lurched back, almost stepping on her. Down from the hillside came more Normans, with the Saxon Eadric Streona first. Streona shouted, "I knew you'd have to come this way!" He was swinging a sword as he ran.

Laissa backed up rapidly, trying to find some place to hide, her arms wrapped around her belly. Out there on the road Raef was dodging and lunging among five or six men, but Leif had drawn his axe out of his belt and hammered one before they turned on him.

Raef went sprawling. In a wild tangle of men, Streona hoisted up his sword into the air to drive it into Raef's body. Leif jumped on Streona from behind, and then the other two rushed on Leif, and he fell on his back.

The Normans closed on Raef, who still lay motionless on the road. Laissa pressed herself to a tree, stuck her fist into her teeth and whined. Streona raised his sword again, and from the far side of the road a huge white wolf leaped on him.

The Norman screamed. He flailed with his sword at the wolf, and his men scattered, yelling, stumbling over one another. The sword went spinning off into the ditch. In the midst of the Normans, the great white beast dodged their blows, slashed and snapped among them. One fell limp to the ground before the others wheeled and ran, shrieking. The wolf charged after them.

Leif was struggling to rise. He was bleeding from his side. He was saying, "Not bad, not bad," but he sank down again, groaning. Raef still lay on the road, and Laissa went to him and put her hands on him.

He was gone. She knew that at once, not dead, but gone.

There before her lay a dead Norman, face down on the road in a puddle of blood. Beyond him Streona struggled onto his feet, one arm dangling. His face was covered with dust and blood, and his eyes stared wildly from this mask like shining stones. He got his feet under him and stood, and then the white wolf hurtled up from behind him and smashed him down again.

Streona screeched and rolled, his arms flailing. The wolf lunged for his throat. Laissa flung herself at it.

"No—he's helpless—Raef! Raef!"

The wolf spun around and knocked her flat and stood over

her, and for an instant the savage blue eyes glared into her face as if she were a stranger, as if she were only prey, something to kill, and the bloody jaws reached for her throat.

She whined. She gripped both arms tight over the baby in her belly. The white teeth snapped shut an inch from her. The wolf backed off, its head low, turned, and fled.

On the road where he had been lying, Raef rolled over and stood up. He looked at her a moment, lowered his head, as the wolf had, and walked up the hill.

Streona was scrambling away along the ground, using his feet and his good hand, getting some distance between him and them. Now he got up and shambled off, his arm flopping at his side, down the road after the others. Somebody down there shouted. A horse neighed.

Leif sat up, breathing in sighs. He said, "Laissa, are you all right?"

"Yes," she said. Her lips were stiff. She was cold, not just because she had dropped her cloak. She got up, looking around. Down the road the Normans and Streona were hurrying away. They would not come back.

In the other direction, Raef was still walking up the road away from them.

Leif said, "I won't let him hurt you; I won't let him hurt you." But he could barely stand. She went to help him, and, while he leaned on her and she leaned on him, somehow they went back to where her cloak lay.

⚯

Raef walked a long while before he stopped, stood, and thought about what had happened.

He remembered the urge to kill. He had not thought, Laissa. He had thought only, Kill.

He remembered the black wolf and put his hand to his ear.

The wound there still festered. Half his ear was chewed up. When his fingers touched it a thin flick of pain ran down his arm all the way to his elbow.

He drew in a long shuddering breath. The Lady had tricked him. She had heard him howling, and she had sent him what he wanted. He had done with her as a wolf what he would never have dared do as a man. And she had poisoned him, as surely as he had sown his seed in Laissa.

⸻

Leif's wound was just a scrape, but Laissa made him lie down with his cloak and hers and went for wood to make a fire. She was not good at this, and she was still trying to get the wet, rotten wood to burn when Raef came walking back.

She stood up, and, before she had thought of it, she had backed away several steps. He bowed his head. He went down on his knees by her miserable fire.

But he spoke to Leif. "Take your axe," he said, "and cut off my ear."

Leif threw the cloaks off and sat up. He seemed suddenly purposeful. He got onto his feet. "You were going to kill her." He drew his axe.

Laissa sat down on the ground, breathless.

Still on his knees, Raef said, "Help me. While I was a wolf—something happened, and now she has—she—has—somehow—swarmed in my ear. I could do it myself, but it would be a botched job—help me!"

Laissa rose. Leif took his axe in both hands and glanced at her.

"Hold his ear away from his head."

She pulled her sleeve down over her hand and cautiously drew next to her husband, where he kneeled. His ear stuck out through his long white hair.

She gulped to see it. The whole outer edge of his ear was raw, eaten away and oozing purple and green. She took hold of the poisoned edge with her covered hand, and Leif hoisted his axe.

"Stand back."

In his face she saw as plain as if he spoke that he thought of splitting Raef's skull instead of his ear. Raef, kneeling at his feet, looked up and said, "Strike."

Leif brought the axe down. The blade passed cleanly between Laissa's hand and Raef's head and cleaved off the rotting ear.

Raef yelled. Laissa still gripped the severed ear, and she flung it away, tore off her sleeve, and hurled the smoking cloth as far as she could. Raef kneeled there, the blood flowing from the gash along his head.

She took her undersleeve, wadded up the cuff, and held it against his wound. They were all watching the ear, where it lay on the road, steaming.

Laissa whispered, "God have mercy."

The shapeless flesh was bubbling, red and purple and green and blue; then the whole mass writhed up, clenching together like a hand gathering into a fist, only smaller and smaller, until with a burst of fire it disappeared.

Raef put one hand against the wad over his wound. He turned and kissed Laissa's hand, and then, still on his knees, put out his hand to Leif.

Leif clasped it, hard.

"You try a man. It went through my mind, what you know."

Raef said, "I knew you better." He took Laissa by the wrist and drew her hand down from where his ear had been. The wound had already begun to heal. He said, "Let's go find somewhere to spend the night."

Up in the pass, a mile or so on, was an old rock house. Some earlier traveler had left wood under cover, and they built a fire and huddled together under their cloaks.

Raef, after a while, said, "The hanged god gave an eye for wisdom. I can give up an ear."

Laissa said, "Are you wiser for it?"

"I know I will not be a wolf again. I think that's wisdom."

Beside them, Leif was sleeping. Laissa was hungry; they had eaten nothing since around noon. She dozed, but she kept her arms around Raef, as if she could somehow keep him from leaving.

⟶⊱

He did not leave. But he dreamed.

He went down and down, along the spiral of steps, deeper and deeper. He had been here before. He knew what he would find at the end.

At the bottom of the well he came to the door and opened it, looking out at the end of everything, the finish. The blank black collapse.

A dread seized him: He felt drawn into it, felt himself leaning forward, falling, willing himself to fall, to be nothing.

He said, "Face me. Are you afraid to face me?" while the hair on his head stood on end and his flesh turned rough as oak bark.

A sizzle of light ran up and down around him, and there was a clash of filthy sound. A voice spoke inside his head. Do you think you force anything? You have done only what was intended. Take Jorvik. Stay in Jorvik until your doom comes.

He said, "Under your roof I was born. You bought me in my mother's womb. You and I are bound. I want to know—"

A surge of electric fire went through him, an instant's furious pain. Nothing is bound. You misunderstand. You cannot compel me.

The dark stirred, streaming wraiths of smoke. Eyes in it. Faces rose and disappeared. Suddenly he saw Corban's face, floating in the dark; Mav's, the same face, torn to pieces and gathering again; Benna's; and a flash that emptied out the inside of his head like an eggshell.

Raef cried out, blind and thoughtless. The voice sounded again. They broke their promise: They bound me. Nothing is bound. They bound—they bound. Nothing is bound—

Then the darkness was a wild stinking uproar, shredded light and rasping shrieks, hot against his face, and the voice blasted from all around him, outside and inside. You will die for me! You will die of me! You will die—

He woke startled, lying in the moonlight, his ears ringing. He remembered Gunnhild saying, She is mad. When they struck her down in Hedeby, they took away whatever was good in her. Then Gunnhild let loose the evil and came to him to make it better. A spurt of fear and rage and resentment went through him. He put his head in his hands. You will die for me. He shut his eyes but did not sleep.

CHAPTER NINE

Aethelstan said, "London is the finest city in England. Even better than Winchester." The hawk stretched out one wing and a talon and settled again on his wrist. All morning they had been down on the marshes east of Southwark, on the other side of the river, hunting hares. He loved the long gallops by the river; the clean, rushing air; the stoop of the hawk. "Look, there, you see that? That was a Roman palace once."

"Roman," Edmund said. "You mean—the pope?"

"No." Aethelstan laughed and turned and cuffed his little brother's arm, companionably. Edmund delighted him. "The pagan Romans. They were here once. A long time ago. Caesar and Claudius. Don't you remember old Bede? A very long time ago." He remembered mostly trying to avoid reading old Bede's endless Latin.

Edmund turned to stare at the ruined building. It was only three irregular walls, the stones black with age, but Aethelstan had no trouble envisioning something much larger, vague in his mind but grand. His brother said, "How do you know?"

"You can tell Roman work," Aethelstan said. He did not want to say that he had actually heard this from someone else. He liked Edmund's awed looks at his knowledge. "The roads. That's an old bath, up there."

"A bath?"

"Like a sweathouse but fancier."

Edmund looked obediently where he pointed. Aethelstan searched around for something else to impress him with. Ahead of them was a burned-out house. He turned quickly away from that; Edmund already knew too much about how that had happened.

Yellow flowers sprouted in among the char. Spring was coming. The wooden bridge carried them up and over the deep narrow trench of the Wall Brook.

"There is the King," said Aethelstan and lifted his horse into a canter down to the river street.

Edmund loped beside him. He was a fair rider, and Aethelstan considered finding him a better horse than his placid little gelding. By the side of the street, Aethelstan reined around and took off his hat, and Edmund imitated him exactly.

The King was coming toward them on his black horse. Obviously he was just down from Bishopsgate. Eadric Streona, Uhtred of Bamburgh, and a few other lords rode behind him, all in a cloud of pages and knights and hangers-on. Aethelstan and Edmund bowed, and their father lifted his hand to them.

"Come with me! I would not have you idle—attend me now and I will find tasks to your hands." The King's voice boomed out. Ethelred was in a fine mood, his cheeks glowing red, and his eyes snapping.

Aethelstan said, "Father, just command us."

"Yes," Ethelred said, "better me than somebody else, anyway. Come on, then."

They rode after him, part of the loose mob of men who were riding and on foot around the King. The herald and some pages ran along ahead of everybody, calling the way. The river curved to the left, and the road followed the bank toward the King's hall. The long ridgeline of the roof cut straight across the upright of the minster tower just beyond it.

Another bridge crossed the ditch there. The herald and the pages went clattering over it; horns blew, announcing the coming of the King.

A shriek rang out. Hoofs clattered, and Ethelred's horse stood straight up on its hind legs, neighing. The King himself was hanging half out of the saddle. The men behind him scattered away. Shouts rose. The King stayed on his horse, but his face was twisted and his eyes bulged. He it was who had screamed first. He screamed again. He was staring at the bridge, and then his horse bounded backward as if something rushed at him from the bridge.

"Get rid of her! Can no one get rid of her—Kill her—Kill her—"

He lashed his horse around as if circling some obstacle and galloped over the bridge and on toward his hall. The other horsemen were strewn across the road, shouting out, and looking all around. A horse bucked, and somebody went flying off.

Aethelstan said, "Come on," and trotted his horse after his father. Edmund followed, but he was twisted in his saddle, looking back over the bridge at the confusion there. His face was white.

"Who was that woman?"

Aethelstan swiveled his head toward him, keen. "You saw her?"

"Yes—I have—I've seen her once before, I think." Edmund looked up at him, his face worried. "She must be mad, to run at him like that. Why was he so frightened? He won't kill her, will he?" His face altered. "Didn't you see her?"

They rode into the stable yard of the King's hall, where grooms waited to take their horses. Aethelstan gave the hawk to a servant and dismounted.

"No. I have never seen her. And he did kill her," he said, looking across the saddle at Edmund. "On Saint Brice's Day. Come inside, he said he wanted to talk to us."

⇒⚬⇐

Ethelred's face was spangled with sweat. He sat in his high seat and shouted at them, "Don't get yourselves involved in the feuds of this kingdom, I warn you. Make sure you know who your friends are. And they're not always who claim to be your friends, boy." He banged his fist on the arm of the chair. He drank more ale.

Aethelstan said, "My lord, we are loyal. We serve only you."

Edmund lowered his eyes, remembering the meeting in the inn with Morcar and his fat, balding brother Sigeferth. His father knew everything, and he was glad of Aethelstan's honor. He thought of the woman he had seen, rushing at him there by the bridge, her coif half off and her eyes dark with rage. She had shouted something. He caught himself making the sign of the cross on his chest. They said that on Saint Brice's Day hundreds of people had died, all over England.

Ethelred was still hammering at them, the same thing about making sure of their friends. He did this sometimes, went on and on, just to keep them standing there. Aethelstan had stopped trying to talk to him. They both bowed whenever the King paused for breath, and finally he waved at them.

"Go away. I have some charters to write tomorrow and I'll need you both to witness."

Aethelstan's face was white, his cheeks stiff. He said, "I'm going to tend to my hawk. I'll see you at dinner," and went off. Edmund drifted toward the far end of the hall.

He thought about the woman in the messy coif. Slowly he made himself admit that she was a ghost, one of Ethelred's victims. Why had he seen her, and Aethelstan not? He wondered what it meant to be good and honorable, in a place where such things happened as Saint Brice's Day. If obeying Ethelred meant agreeing to murder, what was the right thing to do? His gaze moved around the room, taking in the other men around him, in their fine coats, their sleekly combed beards, the rings on their fingers and arms, all very polished. On the wall, the great banner of the House of Wessex floated in the drafts, the golden dragon writhing on its red field, the pride of Alfred, the hope of England.

All this elegance meant nothing, a gilded lid above a cesspit. The world was evil, he thought. He wondered if he was evil. Maybe that was why he had seen the ghost. Unhappily, he went off to find something to do.

—◦—

Aethelstan said, "This happens often?"

"More and more," said the physician. The King was still screaming but muffling his own voice with a pillow stuffed into his mouth. He sat in his nightshirt on the side of his great bed, shaking so hard the whole bed trembled.

Aethelstan said, "He seemed very well yesterday."

"The Queen's news cheered him. But then he had a dream, a terrible dream," said the physician. "And he saw the ghost again yesterday."

"Where is the Queen?"

"She has left; she cannot endure this—it is most harmful to her condition."

Aethelstan went to his father and kneeled at his knee. "Papa," he said, and Ethelred turned toward him.

His eyes stared from a face white as lard. His voice was hoarse from the screaming. "I knew they meant to kill Edward. My mother meant to have him killed."

Aethelstan realized, startled, that he meant his half brother, murdered thirty years before to make the boy Ethelred sole King. The first taint on him, when he was only ten years old: where his life had twisted out of true. "That was so long ago. You were a child, sir."

"I knew she meant to do it."

"Papa—" Aethelstan laid his hand on his father's knee. The older man's suffering moved him to tenderness. He said, "Think of the baby, Papa. You'll be a father again."

"I can't sleep," Ethelred said. He picked up the pillow,

started it toward his mouth, and lowered it to his knees. His eyes were bleary with exhaustion. "Every time I sleep—"

Aethelstan rose, turned, and waved to the physician to leave. Three of his father's house carls stood by the door, armed and mailed, as if they could drive their swords through a ghost or a nightmare.

"Get me the highest priest in the minster. Bring him here."

"My lord." One of the Normans left. That, they were good for: They took orders well. He paced across the room, uneasy. His father had been ailing, off and on, since Saint Brice's Day. Haunted. The door opened, and the priest came in.

This was no mere priest but Alphege, the archbishop of Canterbury, his robes splendid, immaculate; his gold and ivory crozier in his hand; his miter looming up like a church steeple. He was a tall, fleshy man with a constant sniffing frown on his face, as if all he saw was sin, all he expected to see was sin everywhere, and it gave him a certain satisfaction. There was a council in Westminster, which was why he was here.

He came into the room, glanced once at Aethelstan, and turned to the King.

"My lord King." His voice was clear and strong. "God be thanked I am here. Tell me what befalls you."

Ethelred barely mumbled something, his eyelids sagging, and sleep coming on him against his will. Alphege walked around his bed, the staff tapping the floor. Aethelstan watched his father's head nod, fall to his breast, and then jerk up again, the eyes bulging like knobs from his skull, his hair bristling.

The archbishop came around before him. "The room is full of demons. And who knows but you deserve them, my lord King."

Ethelred reached out toward him with both hands, the pillow on his knees. "Help me. For God's sake, Father, for the love of sweet Jesus Christ—"

"As you helped the pleading victims of your soldiers?"

Alphege said. "Say your prayers. Beg God's forgiveness. And leave London."

He went around the bed again, murmuring under his breath and making signs with his hands. Aethelstan stepped back; the air around him felt busy. He glanced at the Normans. Alphege went to the window and pushed the shutter wider.

He came back toward Ethelred. "Out of pity I have asked our Lord Jesus Christ to dispel the demons. But they will come back, because you are a fertile ground for them, Ethelred, and you have no true faith in God. You should keep moving. Because it will not stay peaceful wherever you are."

He turned and went to the door; he paused, before Aethelstan, and the prince thought for a moment that the archbishop would speak to him or at least give him a blessing, but Alphege only shook his head and went on. Aethelstan cast another look at his father, who had curled up on the bed, fast asleep and snoring, and Aethelstan left.

⟶⟵

The court moved down to Winchester. Aethelstan went to see that his horses were stabled, and in the dusty lane outside the barn he found Morcar of Derby waiting for him.

Morcar's long, sad face was intent. He said, "I understand the Queen is with child."

Aethelstan nodded. He looked around them, to see who was watching. The sun came through the leaves of the trees along the lane, dappling the ground.

Morcar said, "Have you thought about what this means for you and your brothers, if she bears a male child?"

Aethelstan turned to him, angry. "I am my father's heir. Do you think he would throw me over for an infant?"

Morcar's hound face watched him steadily. The moving

shadows of the leaves dappled him. "Not Ethelred, perhaps. The Queen is another matter."

"The Queen does not rule my father," Aethelstan said sharply. He was taking a strong dislike to Morcar.

"Does your father rule himself?"

The prince reared back and cocked his arm, as if to strike. Morcar stood solidly where he was, his drooping eyes steady. Aethelstan lowered his hand to his side.

"The King is better now that we are gone from London."

"A man who sees ghosts everywhere."

"I will not hear this, my lord. The kingdom is wracked enough with troubles."

Morcar shrugged one shoulder. "You are a noble son, my prince. But they say that Jomsvikings have been seen off the coast. And now Sweyn Forkbeard has made peace with the Trondejarl in Sweden and is ready to come at us again. Can your father lead his army into war?"

"We shall be ready for Sweyn Forkbeard," Aethelstan said. "The King has a pact with Normandy, which will keep the Danes out of the narrow sea. And the Norman duke has sent him more soldiers. If Sweyn tries to take a bite of England, he may find too much in his mouth to swallow." He fixed the thegn of Derby with a hard look. "Will you fight for England, Morcar?"

"I will fight for my lands," Morcar said. "For the Five Burhs. And for my life. Against any who threaten us." His lips twitched in a bad smile. "That includes your father, sir. Good day."

—⊷—

Emma said, "You are sleeping without dreams, my husband."

"Soundly as a corpse," he said. He smoothed her cheek with his fingers. She had come down to Winchester at last, with two midwives to attend her and a pile of new clothes. She was the prettiest little thing in his kingdom, and he could not wait to get her into bed. "We shall feast tonight. I shall raise cup after cup to my new prince."

She let him fondle her belly, which was beginning to swell beneath her belt. She said, "He is only a little prince. Aethelstan is the true prince. We know our place. My little prince and I." She simpered.

Ethelred kissed her ear, thinking he knew her place also, and there was all the rest of the morning to have her there before the feast began. He felt airy, almost breathless, with relief; he had not seen the ghost for almost a week now. Perhaps she only haunted London. He would never go to London again. He gathered his wife into his arms.

"Come," he said. "Let us make merry while we can."

The Queen came into the hall on the arm of the King, and all through the vast, drafty space the crowds of people bowed in a noisy fluttering of sleeves and doffed hats. The men peered at her, their noses ruffled. It was not common for a Saxon to have his wife beside him, and some were put off.

The air was already warm. Smoke wreathed the beams of the ceiling. She let Ethelred settle her in the left side of the high seat, with some jokes that soon she would be too large for that, and bring her a cup of wine. Her thighs were still slippery with his seed. She glanced quickly around the room.

She was hoping the ghost Arre would appear. Shorn of her body, Arre would be easy prey, even in a crowd. An interesting woman, a great soul—although, since she was dead, much weaker than she would have been, had she been taken alive.

The Queen sat at the high end, and on either side down the hall were long, stout tables. Ethelred's court stood behind them, waiting for its signal to sit down on the benches. Eadric Streona was at the very top of the long table to the right, his hands clasped behind his back, shorn like a Norman with clipped hair and no beard. Down beyond them, others of Ethelred's lords, Uhtred, Morcar, Sigeferth, Leofwine, Eadwy, Alfgar, on and on, still wore their hair long and flowing, their beards combed smooth on their chests. She caught them looking at her disapprovingly and laughed, scornful.

Ethelred settled himself beside her in the high seat, and she bent to let him kiss her cheek. Looking past him, she saw the prince Aethelstan behind the front table, waiting with his carls for permission to sit, and young Edmund.

Flanked by musicians with drums and horns, three men in fantastic hats were marching up the center of the hall to deliver a speech of welcome to the King. She had to seem interested, which meant giving the stupid girl Emma more room than was comfortable. Ethelred spoke to Emma, and she gave her husband a beaming look.

"I am so glad you're sleeping well again. I missed you so much."

Ethelred kissed her. The Lady let this continue a while. Idle, she turned inward. She was still annoyed that Raef had escaped her on his way to Jorvik. Biting him had not worked as it usually did. Then in his more straightforward effort Streona had failed. She was tempted to get rid of him. But Raef was far away now, out of her reach, still a stupid man, still afraid of his power, and slow to use it, and so she need not fear him.

She would get the war going and feast again.

More gaudy people were coming up before the King to do a display of welcome. Emma could sit there and smile; the Lady was going from fret to fret.

Emma chafed her like a coat too small. She would make the best of that, and the best would be good enough. Anyway, now she had captured dozens of useful souls, and she could not easily abandon Emma without losing them.

There were benefits in Emma. However cramped the space, she had maneuvered the silly girl into a good position. Queen of England, now pregnant, she had Ethelred befuddled and malleable. He rejoiced at the prospect of another Aetheling. He had several heirs already, but they would present no problem to Emma's son. Aethelstan was the most dangerous, not least because he refused to turn against his father.

There might not even be an England anyway after another war.

She looked around the hall at the boisterous men now crowding the benches, so brawny and stout and loud with their own importance. It was the women they disdained whose souls she craved, deeper, more subtle than any man's, the women's souls whose inchoate vital force gave her power. The men she only destroyed.

They had betrayed her, every man she had ever trusted: Bluetooth, Corban, Eadric Streona, on and on. Ethelred would betray her in time. The fury boiled up in her, jumbling everything out of order, out of control, the souls within her stirring and slipping. The will rose in her to align them all at once and blast this place. Combined, so close, she could burn the whole hall back to its fundament, turn wood and stone, flesh and bone to ash in an instant.

But that would likely mean Emma's death also, and she would have to start over.

Ethelred was stroking Emma's thigh, and the silly girl leaned toward him, giggling, and rubbed her cheek on his. She knew how to beguile him. As she did during the ugly coupling, the Lady turned away. The air of the hall was thick with smoke and the smell of bloody meat. On her left side there sat Uhtred, lord of Bamburgh, whose brawny body had once attracted Emma. Now he watched the Queen with a dour dislike from beneath his shaggy brows. Emma smiled vacantly at him, as if she had forgotten who he was.

"Here, ducky." Ethelred held out a bit of roasted lamb on his fingertips, and Emma obediently opened her mouth for the greasy morsel. Streona was chewing on some big bone. Aethelstan frowned down at his hands on the table, Edmund silent behind him, and Uhtred was glaring at Emma, trying to catch her eye. Perhaps he regretted now that he had not smiled back that time. Then a horn blared down by the door.

Everybody fell still, all at once, and swung that way. Into the crackling silence walked a single man, tall and lean as a lance, with a great hooked nose. Golden rings circled his upper arms and hung from his ears, and a gold clasp held his heavy red cloak fast at his shoulder. At his side hung a long-handled, double-bladed axe. Aethelstan had stood up, in his place, and now Uhtred of Bamburgh rose too, although neither of them were armed.

The Lady laid her hand on Ethelred's arm and turned Emma's wide pleading glance on him. "Who is this?"

"Thorkel the Tall," Ethelred said, tautly. "Chief of the Jomsvikings."

"Ethelred Edgarsson," the Viking shouted. He stamped his foot hard on the floor. "I come from the King of the Danes, to tell you you will not wait long for retribution for your wicked murder of the innocent on Saint Brice's Day."

The crowd buzzed with whisperings. Streona leaped up from his place on the bench and came over beside Ethelred, the arm of the high seat between them. He whispered something, and Ethelred pushed at him. The Lady still had her grip on his sleeve; she saw Streona wanted the King to make some show of force, but Ethelred, even without her advice, was refusing that. At least he had some sense.

He leaned forward.

"Thorkel Strutharaldsson," he said, "when will the Danes pay retribution for the innocents they have killed since they first struck at England, long ago?"

The Queen beamed at him, glad of this war talk. Eadric Streona stood back, his face dark, his eyes shifty, his lips grim.

The tall Viking before them curled his lip into a sneer. Behind the bone arch of his nose his small eyes were buried deep in their pits. "So it is, Englishman. You have brought the wolf time on you. Know now that Sweyn is released from his oaths to you over the last Danegeld." He turned and walked out the door.

The whole hall buzzed; Streona had gone to sit down again, and on the other side Aethelstan was leaning down, talking fiercely to his younger brother Edmund, his face flushed. The Queen turned to Ethelred.

"So the war will begin again?" She kept her voice small, worried.

"Don't fear." He clapped his big rough hand over hers. "I have done much to prepare for this. Marrying you—" he kissed her forehead, a loud smack—"keeps your brother Normandy on my side. And I have throttled Jor'ck and wasted Man and Wales—"

She said, "Jor'ck. Wasn't that Jorvik a Danish kingdom?"

"Yes, I told you, I have crushed it; no one lives there anymore. It is a habitation for owls."

"As long as there's anything there, it's a threat to you," she said. "Did you not tell me how they could winter over there and attack all of East Anglia and the coast—"

"I've blocked up the river," he said. "I've taxed them until they fled. There is no more market, no harbor."

"You could send Uhtred up to Northumberland. He could finish Jorvik off on the way."

He blinked at her. It was hard sometimes to move him, and since the Arre haunting had begun, harder, as if the ghost had deadened part of his mind. Remorse, thinking backward, the curse of memory, the part of him beyond her reach. She said, slowly, "Send Uhtred to wipe out Jorvik."

Ethelred wiped his hand across his mouth. His eyes looked unfocused. "I trust Uhtred," he said. "Rather I would keep him by me."

"My lord," she said, "if you trust him, then send him to keep the Danes out of Jorvik."

"Unh," said Ethelred. His eyes went to the big northerner on his right. "There's sense in that, I suppose." The Queen sat back, satisfied.

He stood up, and the babble in the hall fell to a hush. The King lifted his hands.

"You all heard Thorkel. Our time has come. Heed me. Aethelstan, my son."

Aethelstan leaped to his feet. "Father, command me."

"Go summon up all the men you have. Sweyn will attack in the East, because Normandy and I have closed the narrow sea to him. Morcar and Sigeferth, call up the men of the Five Burhs."

There was a yell from the crowded hall, like the baying of hounds. Ethelred waved his hands to quiet them.

"Alfgar, Eadwy, bring all the men of Wessex to follow my dragon banner! Eadric Streona, bring the men of Mercia. We will gather here at Winchester at Whitsuntide, the beginning of the fighting season. And Uhtred of Bamburgh, go to Jorvik and lay it waste, so that Sweyn will find no haven there."

Again, they roared, in a high fury, all brag and bellow, so the hall boomed with their cheers. Aethelstan was already making his way out, a train of other lords close behind him. Eadric Streona and Uhtred rose, calling to their men. Through the uproar, the boy Edmund came up before the throne.

"Father, command me."

Emma laughed. Ethelred said, "Edmund, you are too young for this. Stay here and be a guard for my dear wife."

"Father, I want to fight."

Ethelred shook his head and waved him off and, turning,

bawled to the general ear, "This time we make it ours! Haste! Haste!"

Edmund was still trying to plead with him. Nobody paid any attention to him. Emma laughed again. "Silly little boy. What could you do?" Edmund turned away, his shoulders hunched.

CHAPTER TEN

At last, in the end of the winter, Raef, Laissa, and Leif forded the river and walked up through dreary, swampy flatlands to the gate of Jorvik. The wall was massively built of grey stone, but no one guarded it, and the wooden gate sagged too badly to close. Inside, the land seemed no different than outside, a broad stretch of grassy slope where sheep grazed. A path wound through it from the gate down toward the river in the distance.

Along this path stood the ruins of houses, overgrown with vines and brambles, some with walls still standing, many others no more than tumbled stones and broken wood. Sheep and goats grazed in the overgrown gardens. In the distance, the minster raised its squat block head into the sky, but they had walked down the path almost to the river before they came to a place where people lived.

This was a hovel of sticks and sod on the edge of a cluster of larger wattle and daub huts, where an old dog lay in the sun and looked up as they passed. Some rags hung on a stick to dry. A frayed red hen scuttled out of their way. They walked beneath a spreading old bare-branched oak tree, where Raef remembered a market, and stood by the riverbank.

"You said there was a city," Laissa said. "There's nobody here."

Raef put his hand out toward the water. Back at the ford he had felt the deep salt tidal tug of the river, silty and mucky and clogged, but far away, still, the sea. His sea. He felt that here too. He turned and led them back in among the houses along the river where people lived.

All that was left of Jorvik clustered around the squat, un-finished stone minster. In a yard, a man splitting wood stopped to squint at them. Smoke came from the roof holes. Two women stood beside the path talking. Their eyes followed the three, but the women chattered on.

The paths between the huts were muddy, stinking of rot, the winter's ice thawing under their top layer of filth and leaves and dirt. Raef steered to the side, out of the ditch down the center. The shadow of the minster fell over them. A man drove a pig around the corner. Dogs skulked away from them. Within a few steps they were out of the village.

Laissa leaned on him. She was round now with the baby, and her face was drawn and white. He glanced past her at Leif and saw the Icelander watching him. He had to find them somewhere to shelter. They had a little food left, but it was going to rain sometime soon. They passed along a withy fence that separated a broad yard from the street, a low three-sided barn at the far edge. The mud inside the yard was trampled and speckled with blood. The place smelled of dead animals. A shambles. He climbed the street, aimless, unwilling to stop. They passed more ruined, old, crumbling houses, what was left of the city he remembered here.

"We could stay in one of these houses," Laissa said, clinging to him.

"No," he said. He did not know what he was looking for. He could not rest here. He slid his arm around her and half carried her along. At the top of the street a big old oak tree stood. The tree looked dead, its galled branches like knobbed claws, its trunk split down the middle. Beside it was the barren hilltop, oddly flat, overgrown with weeds.

He set Laissa down under the oak tree and went out onto the flat hilltop, wading through the dead stalks of weeds. The place reached deep back into his memory. Looking up, he could see across the fields, over a little creek, down to the city wall, which was a great stone circle around the green and empty slopes, the ruins and wreckage of the overgrown city. The village was away to his left, and directly below him stretched a low meadow, what these people called a sway, crisscrossed with sheep paths. Beyond that the river ran.

He had seen that city thronged with people. That river once had dragons drawn up all along the bank. This hill had been—

He kicked at the weeds around him, scraping them back with his heel, and his foot struck something solid and even. He walked along it, here and there kicking away six inches of dirt and fallen leaves and overgrowth to expose the flagstone floor beneath. In the middle of the flat space, he came to a mounded bramble.

Heedless of the thorns, he wrenched the vines apart. Under them was a circle of set stones, two feet high, blackened, still half full of char. It was a fire pit. He cleared the rest of the vines from it. Leif and Laissa had come out after him onto the hilltop; Laissa was looking around, alarmed, and Leif had his arm around her. Raef turned back to the fire pit.

It was whole, all the stones still fitted together, except for one place, one gap, like a missing tooth. A shiver went down his spine. He stooped, groping in the weeds, and found the stone that belonged there and put it back.

Laissa said suddenly, "We could go down to one of those houses we passed before. Just for now."

Leif said, "It's going to get cold tonight if it rains."

Raef shot him a hard look. "We're staying here. We've stayed in worse places."

"Not when there was someplace better." Laissa pushed up before him, holding her belly out between them like a weapon. "Are you going to make me have my baby in the cold and the wet and the open like some kind of animal?"

"The baby won't be born for—"

"I don't care," she said, her eyes hot with temper. "I want to sleep under a roof, with walls around me and a fire to keep me warm."

"We will build a hall here, walls here, a roof here." He set himself. "I'm not going, Laissa."

Leif said, "Hold. Look."

Raef swiveled around. Laissa had begun to rail at him again, but her voice fell still. From the center of the fire pit a tendril of smoke was rising.

Laissa said, "Sweet Mother Mary."

Raef sank on his heels before it. Beneath the smoke the first few tongues of a little fire licked up from the blackened stones. He put his hands out to it, and the heat kissed his palms.

"Get wood," he said. He stood, turning to Laissa, standing there with her mouth open, staring at the fire. "Sit down here. I'll make you warm. And we have something to eat and we'll find more." He kissed her face. "Sit." He went to fetch wood for the fire.

⸻

They lay together that night under their cloaks. Raef wrapped his arms around her, his legs around her legs. Within her, between them, he could feel the baby asleep also, curled like a new leaf. The baby astonished him. Not him and yet him all through, and her too, and not her. He knew the baby was a girl; he sang to her sometimes, no words, only some old old song. His mother must have sung it to him. Or Benna. The child had no name to him yet. He longed to hold her in his arms.

As real as the baby, as unseeable, he felt the hall around them, as it had been, as it would be again, the walls, the thatch above, the beams, the high seat, the benches for their people to sleep on. He felt the people going back and forth, the haunch turning on the spit, the girls weaving, children playing, someone singing. He imagined it as if he saw it while he sat on the high seat, king of this place.

He thought he had always wanted this. He thought of the baby to be born into this hall, of his wife sitting beside him, his men around him, and his work before him, and thought, I have always wanted this.

⸻

In the morning he and Leif began uncovering the stones of the old hall's footing and putting them back into place. Many were gone; somebody would have tried to build a house out of them, which likely had not gone well. Laissa sat by the fire for a while, eating the last of their cheese. A boy bareback on a pony stopped under the dead oak tree to watch them work.

Laissa said, "I am going down to the minster."

"Go," Raef said. He was heaving a big square stone into place at the northwest corner of the footing. They were going to have to look for wood to build the walls too.

Breathless, Leif said, "Why do you let her—she's out to here, Raef—do you ever look at her—"

Raef said, "She's just going down the street." He took off his shirt and wiped his sweating face and chest. Laissa had gone away before Leif could decide to go with her. Glancing over his shoulder, Raef noticed a few more people had joined the boy under the oak tree. He thought it was a good idea to have Laissa out of the way anyway. "One of us can go get her if we have to."

"If she's even there," Leif said. He bent to another vine-covered heap of stone.

⸻

Laissa walked down the street, across a dirty little square with a heap of mossy rubble in the middle, and then around to the front of the minster. It was a tall square building made of stone, and the stone looked new, sharp edged, recently hewn. It had no bell tower. A yard full of graves stood around it, and she went up the walk and in through the front.

The inside was so big she took several steps into the middle of it, down a row of columns, before she thought to find out if there was anybody else here. She turned, looking, and straining her ears.

"Hello?"

No one answered. The place seemed empty. The air was full of dust. She went on up the main aisle of the church, which led straight from the door to a big altar of stone. Drifts of leaves lay against the altar rail. On the wall behind it a Jesus hung, made of wood, with open eyes and a thoughtful mouth. She kneeled down at the altar, crossed herself, and said some prayers; it had been a long while since she was in a church. The Jesus needed his hair painted, and his mouth was chipped. She liked his big sad eyes.

She asked him for help. She only wanted a place to live, a place she did not have to leave, where she could have her baby. All her mind was on the baby now, even Raef an annoyance, something prickly, off to one side. She needed a home for her baby.

"It's not a real church, you know," a voice said behind her. "They won't even give us a priest."

Laissa thought, Why do you need a priest? But she did not speak; she rose to face the woman behind her. Only then she realized the woman was speaking dansker.

She said, startled, "Are you a Dane?"

"No, I'm from Jorvik," said the woman, amused. "Are you a Dane? My name is Miru, I'm the wife of the butcher here, Goda. But you're a stranger. I know everybody."

"My name is Laissa," she said. "We just got here. I was expecting a city here."

"There was once." Miru's mouth turned unhappy. "The King hates us, so everybody left."

"Where did they go?"

Miru shrugged. "To London, mostly. Nottingham. Lincoln."

Laissa thought of Arre, who was from Jorvik, and swallowed. She wondered if the King's vengeance against Jorvik was over with. Miru sat down next to her. She was not tall but square and strongly made, a fit butcher's wife, with big red hands, dried blood under her fingernails, and a look straight as a knife. "With my husband's work, we can get by here. You're not alone, are you?" She put her hand on the mound of Laissa's belly. "With this baby coming?"

"No—my husband is here. And my—father." Laissa jerked her head back vaguely toward the wall. "We're staying up on the hill, by that dead oak tree. There's a ruined hall there." She stopped, startled at the sudden intensity of Miru's look.

The butcher's wife stood up. "Yes, to be sure there is. Who is your husband? Take me to him, now."

⸎

The men worked the rest of the morning until they had gone around the whole outside of the hall uncovering fallen stones and moving them back into place. Leif said, "We need to get some more footers." Straightening, he looked at the great space they had marked out and whistled under his breath.

In his mind Raef could see the hall, the walls straight and true, the door framed and hung but always open. He could feel it there, more and more, the solid shape, the strength, as if it existed whole in some space he could only reach with his mind. He glanced toward the oak tree, where a small crowd of people watched.

"Here comes Laissa," Leif said, and he turned.

Laissa was walking up the street toward them, and with her came a woman in a blood-stained apron and wooden shoes. Raef let out a yell. He took a step toward her before he even brought to his thinking mind who she was, but she had seen him too and was running toward him.

He caught her in his arms. "Miru." The name came from deep in his childhood. "Miru."

She clung to him, sobbing. "I knew you'd come back. I knew you'd come back." She stepped away, looking up into his face, her hands on his arms, and then turned and looked around. Her eyes were huge with tears. Her mouth trembled. "Where is— is—"

"Miru." He held her hands in his. "He's dead. I'm sorry. He died years ago, in the East."

"Then there's only me," she said and sat down on the ground and began to weep. "There's only me." She put her hands over her face and cried.

Laissa sat beside her and put her arms around her. Raef sat on his heels before them. "She is my foster sister," he said, to Laissa. "My cousin. Benna and Corban's daughter. We grew up together. Miru, where is Aelfu?"

The woman shook her head, streaming tears, her hands lifting and falling limp in her lap. "Dead, in the plague. She's buried in the churchyard." She raised her eyes to Laissa. "This is your wife, Raef?" She looked around, as if she were coming out of a fog, at the hall. "What are you doing here? Shouldn't you be at Corban's old house?"

Raef stood up. "Where is Corban's house?"

"Just down the street and around the corner," she said. "Behind where the old high street was." She waved her arm vaguely. She turned to Laissa. "I'm the only one left, then."

Raef went off down the street. Miru's eyes followed him. "He is so tall. Corban was never—" She was overcome again with weeping. Laissa took her in through the space where the door would be and sat her down on the heap of cloaks and dalmatics in the warmth of the fire and brought her the skin of water.

Miru said, "I knew somebody would come back." She

wiped her face on her sleeve. "The King could kill Jorvik with his taxes and blocking the river, but I knew that someday . . ." She heaved a sigh. "But I thought it would be Conn. My brother. He was sunny as a summer day, my brother; he was afraid of nothing, and I thought he would make everything good again."

Laissa took her hand. The other woman's grief tugged at her. She said, "Raef is not sunny."

"No." Miru looked at her, frowning. "He is not Corban's son, either, and that is why you are here and not at Corban's house. I understand that now." She licked her lips, and her voice sank, uneasy. "There is more going on here than I can know. My husband will be wondering where I am."

Laissa slid her arms around her own belly. "You must go home, then. Will you come back? Will I see you?"

Miru smiled at her. "We are cousins, aren't we?" She leaned forward and kissed Laissa on the cheek. Laissa smelled the strong smell of her body.

"Thank you," Laissa said, and they hugged again, their arms twining.

Miru said, "Raef was always a little strange. But now, you know, I see we all were. His mother was—" She shook her head, as if words were not enough. "My mother made things. She made drawings, and what she drew came true. Corban wasn't so strange; he was just the best man in the whole world. It was a small world, and a long time ago. I'm not especially strange now, except I'm married to Goda, which would be a strange thing for any woman. Here." Tears leaked from the corner of her eyes. She started to her feet. "I have to go. But I'll send you a joint for your fire."

She stood, shaking out her apron; turned toward the oak tree, and called, "Peter! Go down to the shambles and fetch up a haunch of mutton. Then get that pony back to its plow. The rest of you—shoo! Shoo!" She flapped her big red hands at them. Under the oak, the twenty-odd people laughed. The boy on the pony was riding away down the street, but the others stayed where they were.

Miru shrugged. "I tried. You'll have trouble with them." She dashed at her dribbling eyes with her hand. She glanced at Leif, who was clearing leaves and dirt off the floor. "He looks pretty capable. I'll see you tomorrow, Laissa, come down to the shambles." She went off; at the wall she paused a moment, as if she would step across it, but then she turned and walked down to the door and left.

⸻

Corban's old house lay in ruins, the thatch long blown off or fallen in. Mold and mushrooms grew white as cream on what remained of the walls, the broken beams. It looked dark, even in the sunlight, as if it were falling down into the center of the earth. From the street, looking in, he could see the air crinkle.

He stepped inside, and the air pressed around him as if he were under water, folding around him. He swung his leg forward to take another step, and his thigh passed through a ripple; for a long moment, his shin and his foot did not follow. Finally, he saw the foot touch the floor. He drew in a deep breath, and a shudder passed all through his body.

He stood where he was and looked slowly, carefully through the house. In the laps and coils of the air the light fell strangely sideways, crosswise, pools of shadow trapped where nothing threw a shadow.

He began to move, inch by inch. There seemed nothing left, only heaps of rotten leaves, broken timbers, dust and mold. He saw a metal rim sticking out of the rubbish, and moving slowly he reached out and pulled up an old jug.

He held that in his hands, and a stream of memory woke, old stories told a long way away, of a jug, a purse, and a coat.

He straightened, looking around the wreckage, and then he felt someone else there.

It was Corban, not in this moment but in the moment when he had lived here, long before. As if Raef were here both then and now. An instant later, in the place he shared with Corban, he sensed his mother. For the first time, he saw them for the same person, Corban and Mav, the two sides of one person, separate and yet inseparable, half flesh, half light, in and out of the world. He felt them around him; he felt them embrace him.

"Raef. Raef. Raef."

Up through the deep channel of time an exaltation welled out of him, overflowing like a fountain, enveloping the cosmos.

Dazed, trembling, he sank back into himself. They faded away, back into their time. He realized that he had found what he had come to Jorvik for. Moving slowly, he went around the hall, looking for the other pieces of Corban's magic.

He found a clot of rotten red cloth, slick with white mold, too small for a baby's coat. He found a round of leather with a drawstring through it, but the body of the purse was long gone.

Slowly he made his way back out the door and into the street. The jug was still in his hand, and he turned it over, curious: just a piece of battered brass. The purse was empty. The coat was useless.

Now that he was outside, the city around him seemed brighter, the people moving faster, their voices sharper. He walked up to the white stone outline of the hall.

⟡

Leif had gotten the boy with the pony to help him haul a slab of wood in from an abandoned house nearby, and together they set it on some stones for a table. Miru was gone, but Laissa sat by the fire turning a crackling chunk of meat on a spit. Raef put the battered jug down on the table, tossed the other things into a corner, and went to her and sat on his heels beside her.

She leaned toward him, rubbing her arm on him. This was as much as she would give him of apology for her temper. He kissed her, hoping the fight was over. She smiled at him.

"I like your sister."

"Benna's daughter," he said. "She was also quick spoken." He sat next to her, his eyes on her hands; he loved the way she did ordinary things, forking, pouring, and turning the spit.

This was her power over him, this fragile, everyday love. Her magic. Maybe the only real magic.

A few moments later, over by the table, Leif said, "Where did you get this ale?"

Raef turned, startled. The Icelander came across the long flagstone floor with the jug from Corban's house in his hand. "Best ale I've had in a long time. I wish we had a cup."

"We'll find one," Raef said. He took the jug, which was cool, full of the fragrant, heady drink. He took a long pull from the metal rim. Leif was right; it was very good—the sweetness of the barley and the bitter of the herbs nourishing as bread. He took another deep drink of it. Laissa was frowning at him.

"What have you done now?"

"One of Gunnhild's old spells, I guess, still with some juice in it." Better to lie than to fight. He handed the jug on to her, brimful.

The crowd of people by the oak grew steadily, and around sundown they started shouting. Raef went out to the door of the hall, or where the door would be. The crowd surged toward him, men and boys, yelling. Their leader was a big young man with a mop of red hair and long knives stuck through the belt of his apron. Goda, Raef thought, guessing he had not taken well what Miru told him when she got home.

"Yes," Raef said, "what is it? It's getting dark."

The young man with the butcher's knives in his belt stepped forward. His top dogteeth stuck straight out past his lips like fangs. He had sparse red hair and hundreds of freckles. "What are you doing here? Who are you to think you can just come in here like this and take over this place?"

Raef said, "It doesn't look to me as if anybody else wants it."

Behind Goda, a lanky boy called, "We know how to get rid of your kind; we did it once before." The crowd let out a chatter of agreement, and a couple of them stooped to pick up rocks. Raef folded his arms over his chest. He could tell Leif was moving up behind him.

He said, "I haven't done anything to any of you. How do you know what kind I am?" A rock sailed toward him, and he put out one hand and caught it. The crowd murmured, startled, and everybody took a step backward. "Your wife," he said to Goda, "what did she say about me?" He turned the rock in his hand.

"Leave Miru out of this," Goda snarled at him. He came forward, his chest out, defiant. "It's not what she said, anyway—it's where you are. This is the King's hall, and we don't want a king."

Raef said, "You have a king. His name is Ethelred. He's down in Wessex now, spending your wealth. This is what he's doing to you." He held his hand out and closed his hand tight on the rock and crumbled it into dust. The watchers gasped. He let the bits dribble to the ground. "He just murdered a lot of people from Jorvik. People you knew. Are you going to sit here and wait for him to decide to kill the rest of you?"

Their voices rose in a jabber of questions and names. Goda stared at Raef's hand. He looked back over his shoulder and then faced Raef again. His freckled face drew long. "It's true, then—about Saint Brice's Day?"

Raef said, "This was a great city once. I remember when there were dragons and knarre here from Hedeby, Mainland, and Dublin; when people here were rich, and the city reached out all the way to the walls. Now you live in hovels." He dusted his hands off. "You have a king. But the wrong one." He turned and went into the hall and over to the fire.

—❧—

They worked all the next day and got a good part of the front wall up, setting posts and weaving withies in between, to make an inside and an outside; they would fill the space between with turf. That night they lay in the shelter of the wall. Through the weaving of the withies the moonlight lay across the floor in streaks.

Raef and Laissa lay side by side on their cloaks. He wanted to couple with her, but Leif was too close by. She murmured something and took his hand and put it on her belly. He could feel the baby inside, turning, a tiny foot, the curve of a shoulder, and in his mind he saw her. He kissed her mother. "A little while more." He bundled the cloaks under them to soften the ground. He would build sleeping benches next. One of the old houses nearby was full of sound wood. Before she had the baby, he needed at least two stout walls up and a place where she could be away from all eyes.

He felt the beats of the hoofs in the ground under him before he heard them. Then the pony galloped up outside the wall, and the boy Peter called, "King of Jorvik! Look out—look out—"

He galloped away. Laissa sat up, and Raef put an arm around her. He said, over his shoulder, "Do you see anything?"

"Not yet," Leif said. He was at the middle of the new wall, where the door would be. "Good boy, Peter."

Raef got up and went to the doorway, looking down the street. Laissa followed him. Down near the village he could see

a faint glow. Leif muttered something under his breath. Raef
started out the door, and Laissa gripped his arm. "Stay here.
Stay here. You promised me—"

"Hush," he said.

The glow grew clearer, and closer, and shone above the bobbing heads of several people moving up the street toward them.
They were carrying torches.

"What did I promise you?" he said. He put his arm around
her and held her against him. He pursed his lips and blew a
long breath into the night. A faint whistle trailed after it.

Down there, all the torches guttered and went out.

"You promised me—" she said and stopped.

He knew what she wanted him to promise her. Down there
the mob was trying to relight the torches. He blew another long,
singing breath down the street, and the last lights died. At that
some of the people began to run, and then they were all running, pattering away down the street. He laughed after them.

He led her back to their bed and lay down again, and she lay
down beside him and was silent. She turned her back to him. He
felt her unhappiness like a wound. He kissed her shoulder, caressed her, trying to comfort her; he wasn't sure about the mob or
about him. Leif came down the hall after a while and lay down,
and they all slept.

—◦—

Laissa went down to the shambles. In the yard a flock of sheep
crowded together, and at the back, where the shed was, Miru
and the redheaded butcher, Goda, stood shouting at each other.

"God's love, woman," the butcher yelled, "I would knock
you down if you wouldn't simply get back up again. Shut up and
go gut the pig." He turned toward Laissa. "Are you bringing me
an animal to slaughter or shear? Then what are you doing here?"

Miru came nimbly through the yard toward her, pushing

sheep out of the way. "Laissa. Come on away, you should not see this, so near your time." She flung a look back at her husband, got Laissa's arm, and towed her away down the fence and around into the alleyway. Goda's voice followed them, high pitched and volleying curses. Miru took her in a door, into a small, neat room with two holes in the thatch facing south to let in good light.

"There," Miru said. "Sit down. Don't mind Goda. He listened to what Raef said the other night. We heard about Saint Brice's Day, but a lot of people didn't really believe it. We're so out of the way here now."

Laissa sank down on a stool. Miru poked up the fire. She said, her eyes on the fire, "He said folk we knew died. Was it Euan? And Arre?"

Laissa said, "Yes. I—yes."

Miru jabbed at the fire. Her voice trembled. "Arre. She cared for us after my mother died. She was the kindest woman and brave as a man." She wiped her eyes. "It just seems as if everybody is dying." She sat back, her hands in her lap, still staring at the fire. "We grew apart after I decided to marry Goda. She never liked him." She turned away, tears running down her face. "God, God, it's a wicked world."

"That's true," Laissa said.

Miru went around the room, turning up cups and filling them from a wooden keg. Laissa took one, held it cautiously to her nose, and smelled apples. Miru sat down beside her.

Laissa burst out, "I thought—when we came here—we would be safe."

Miru said, "Don't worry. I told you, Raef cooled them off. They're all saying that was a lump of mud, but nobody believes it. And I heard that the Green Stray Boys never even got close to the hall."

"It's Raef I'm not safe from," Laissa said, and put her hand over her mouth.

Miru's voice went up a notch. "What do you mean? Does he beat you?"

"No. He is good to me; he loves me. It isn't him, really." It was, but she had no way to tell Miru about Raef. She licked her lips, her eyes lowered. "He has enemies. I thought—here—"

Miru said, "If his enemies are the people who killed Arre, they are mine too. For all, I'm only a woman." She nodded toward the door. "I have to go. It's shearing time, and I have to do things like gut pigs."

Laissa was looking around the room. She had so seldom been inside a real house that it felt odd, solidly around her like a shell. Its order calmed her. I shall have a room also, a place, she thought, seeing the table, the shelf, the jugs and cups. The cloth hanging across one end must hide the bed. She said, "What is that?" pointing at a square of wood.

"Part of a loom. But I never use it. Come with me, then, and I'll get you some more meat too."

⸺⸱⸺

The men had finished the angle of the wall. The boy Peter and some other men from the village were helping them weave the last of the withies. Laissa went in by the fire. Miru had sent another big chunk of mutton along, and Leif got one of the new men to spit the meat and hang it over the coals. Laissa sat down on the fur cloaks. She had taken also some of a fleece that had not come off the sheep in one piece, which Miru seemed to think a crime fit almost for beheading.

Her swollen belly filled her lap. She spread the fleece on her knee. She had seen women spinning wool in Constantinople and in other places. This wool was not yet fit to spin, a patch of tangled dirty fibers smelling of oil, with bits of leaf and thorns and bramble twigs caught in it. Her hands were already slick with the oil. She teased out a few of the fibers, long and rippled.

Raef came over and sat next to her. She kept her eyes from him. She could not do without him. Yet what he did brought doom on them. She twisted the fibers together into a bit of string. He said nothing. She knew that he knew her thoughts, what she wanted of him, what he would not give her. Jesus would help her. As long as she was a good Christian. She pulled out more fibers and twisted them together, winding the yarn around her hand.

CHAPTER ELEVEN

The days went by, full of work. The men raised the other long wall and set the posts for benches and the roof. They built a baking oven behind the hall and a wood shed. Besides Peter and the two other men now living there, a woman came up from town and began to help Laissa cook and spin yarn. She was a widow with a toddling boy and no kin, choosing the hall over the street. Raef liked her, and Leif liked her very much.

With the widow and Miru's help, Laissa cleaned the flagstone floor of the hall and set what furnishings they could find in proper places. In one corner she came on a rotted piece of leather and a clump of old red cloth. She thought of casting them out on the midden, but she remembered that Raef had brought them there. Under the ring of leather she also found a tarnished silver penny. Maybe that was good luck. Leif had found an old chest in one of the abandoned houses, and she put the leather and the cloth into that, and they raised the new high seat on top of the chest.

Peter and his pony helped bring Miru's loom, and the women set it in one corner at the finished end of the hall. Miru brought more wool, and the widow, Edith, showed Laissa how to hang the warp from the loom's head beam, weight each thread, tie the weaver's knot, and then slip the weft in and out with the shuttle. The first piece came out like a spiderweb, all holes.

Early one morning at the beginning of summer, Laissa woke gasping in pain, and Edith ran down to get Miru, and around noon the baby was born.

Afterward, Raef took the little girl in his arms and danced up and down the hall, whirling and leaping and singing wordlessly at the top of his lungs, his new household scurrying out of his way. Miru brought Laissa a warm, smelly drink and some of the blood cake, which she ate. They watched Raef dancing with his child. Miru said, "They always act as if it were all their doing. He'll make her sick, jouncing her like that." Her voice was mild with satisfaction.

"Yes," Laissa said. "Come back here, you great fool, and give me my baby."

But when he kneeled by her, the child in his arms, she kissed him first of all.

⁓

Raef walked around the city nearly every day. The people were used to him now and hardly seemed to notice him, except to nod sometimes. He began to know more of them by name, and almost all by sight. Most of them herded sheep, kept their gardens, fished, hunted, made one another shoes or clothes. They were poor as mice. Every winter, they expected a few to die of cold or hunger.

One day, walking past the churchyard, he saw a girl in the gateway with thick curly hair like Conn's; she smiled at him, lifted her hand in a greeting, and turned back into the churchyard. He realized it was Aelfu, Miru's sister, long dead.

He walked along the river, with its fretful, uncertain flow. The banks were overgrown, and the long shelving bar along the high edge of the riverbed was clotted with weeds. Among the green tufts, chunks of wood cropped up out of the gravel, pieces of ruined boats weathered to grey planks, a thole pin trailing a few strands of hemp.

The Jorvikers still rowed little boats up and down and fished. He asked a man casting a line from the bar when there last had been seagoing ships here, and the fisherman shrugged. "Long time. When the city was bigger." He pulled on his beard. "Euan Woodwrightsson used to trade with Hedeby. Even Vinland, sometimes." He pulled in an empty hook.

Raef stood watching two boys in a round-bottomed boat trying to catch turtles on the far bank. The boat rolled over and threw them both into the water, and the boys pulled themselves nimbly back on board. They had no sail, and they used paddles, not oars. He thought the seafaring craft of these people would have rotted along with the ships.

There would be ships at Humbermouth, if he could get goods there to trade. That would bring ships back to Jorvik.

What goods? He had nothing.

He went on upstream of the village, which dumped its black water and offal into the river, and slid down the bank and waded out into the middle. The current was swift along the bottom, and he had to work to keep his feet under him. So far upstream of the village he could see down through the deepening blue-green water to the stony bottom. From the middle of the stream he looked up and saw the wooded banks, some people walking by, and the minster beyond them. The river lifted around him and fell. The pressure of the water reminded him of the air in Corban's house.

In a sudden drunken whirling of his mind, everything seemed to flip, dark for light, back for front. He felt around him the whole great light field, the real world, streaming around him. The minster shimmered, strangely shaped, the people were shadows moving through the ever-changing light, wreathed in eerie color, and the whole rang with high, keen music. Everything was present in the light field. Only time shattered it, into past and future, corruptible and material.

He realized he himself was a shadow, his body, even his mind, that only the light field was real.

Yet to know this was to yield utterly to it. He saw no way to act in it, save as he already did, sliding along on it like a wave. Slowly his mind settled back to the ordinary world, to the plain colors of the sunlight. He was standing up to his waist in the river, staring downstream.

Benna had known something. He remembered the old

stories, that Benna drew on flat stones and the things appeared, made real. Somehow Benna had known how to turn the indeterminate light into manifest things.

He remembered how he had become the wolf. Being a wolf was simpler than being a man, so it meant only being something less. He had shed something of his manness to be a wolf. He wondered if he could become something higher than a man.

He wondered where Benna was now and realized with a start that he knew: She was somewhere in the light field. They were all there, somewhere. He walked up out of the water, his clothes streaming. Maybe everywhere in the light field. Maybe they all watched him. Certainly on the bank the boy Peter on his pony was watching him, a bewildered look on his face. Raef went on up to the street that led to his hall.

⸻◦⸻

That night clouds gathered above the roofless hall, and the distant thunder rumbled nearer. Beside him on the sleeping bench Laissa crept down into the bearskins, not even waking up, the baby Gemma snug in the curve of her shoulder. He put his arm around them and pulled them close against him.

Lightning crackled. In the white instant he saw the outline of the hall, the forked flash like a hand reaching down for them. He let himself out of his body. He stretched himself over his wife and his child. At the same time, he rose up into the air above them, to the roof.

It had been here once, the roof, on his father's hall; it was still here, in the light field, and he drew those beams up again into time. He arched over the hall, the first smashing raindrops against his back, and along his spine and ribs and arms and legs he sprouted the rooflines. He pulled a lacing of branches over the beams and rafters like a blanket, bundle by heap, the straw of the thatch, thick as a man was tall, and all lashed down tight.

The furious storm broke overhead, the crackling of the lightning and the wind rushing by. Inside his hall, his wife and child and all the other people slept dry and warm. When he was done and he sank back down into his body, the roof remained. He could see through it, to the dark sky where the clouds were rapidly clearing, to the first glimpse of the moon, which was good: He liked sleeping where he could see the sky. He slipped his arms around Laissa, their child between them, and shut his eyes.

⸺⸺

With so many people around, he had been loathe to leave his body for very long; if anybody chanced on it and destroyed it, he would be stuck in the light field forever.

He realized that was what death was.

Also he knew Laissa hated his roaming, just as she feared and hated most of what he did. Even so, she would protect him. Therefore, the next night, when they were all sleeping under the new roof, the baby tucked into the crook of her mother's arm, he went.

In the blue darkness he floated down through Jorvik, over the people sleeping, past the minster, the shambles, the old abandoned Coppergate, and the gang called the Green Stray Boys— the ones whose torches he had blown out, skulking around trying to get the courage up to steal something. Down at the river, he slid into the water, into the cool and the surge of the water.

He loved the river. The tide was going out, and he ran along with it; he spun through the seething water, stroked all over, part of the fluid extension into everything, light thickened, quickened metal. He met the blockage well down the river. Before it turned toward the Humber, there was a long narrows, and the bed was packed with old tree trunks. The water ran through the chinks between the logs, but for long years anything larger had backed up and clogged. For nearly a quarter of a mile, the river was a tangle of sandbanks and rocks and branches, impassable to anything bigger than a rat.

He rose up out of the water into the night air and considered this. The rotted stumps of trees stood up in new fen on either side, where the blocked river had overflowed its banks. Stands of reeds and sedge sprouted from the swamp. Deer grazed along the high ground off to the east. There was a village down the way, on the north bank of the Humber, but it was almost deserted. Like Jorvik, it depended on the river running. The thin old moon was drooping down toward the west. Over the arch of the sky, the stars glistened like a silver mist.

At the same time, along the fringe of his awareness, he felt an intruder in the south, some lump, something otherly, that should not be there. He drifted that way. His river, the Ouse, turned eastward here, ran wide and strong into the Humber, the estuary that ran out to the sea. Where the Ouse coiled between the first sandbars and mudbanks of the estuary another river came in from the south.

He followed that other river upstream. The land was flat on either bank. To the west lay dense forest and fen, but east was farmland, villages, and, up ahead, a fair-sized town. Just above that town, in the long valley that ran toward Jorvik, he came on a camp of a few hundred men, ringed with sentries, with strings of horses, and a banner set on a pole—an army settled for the night. An army on the march.

He had been gone a long while. Laissa would have wakened at least once, feeding the baby. She might have noticed he was gone. Still, he moved closer to the camp, feeling through the tangled web of noises and smells and dreams below him until he came on a name he recognized: Uhtred.

Uhtred of Bamburgh, the overlord of Jorvik. Suddenly the clog in his river mattered much less to him than this army on its way to his city. He thought of Laissa again, who surely knew by now he had roamed away. He missed her, suddenly, and the baby, and the warmth of them together. Before he realized it he opened his eyes in the angle of the hall, to see her crooning over the baby at her breast, and dawn was breaking.

⸺⸺

When he woke again, later in the morning, she would not talk to him. He knew she was angry because he had gone roaming. He sat on his heels by the fire, watching her go around the hall pretending he wasn't there.

She was slim again, except for her milk-full breasts, and a new round beauty to her rear end; she carried the baby crooked in her arm. When she lifted her hand to brush back her hair, his heart quaked and his lust surged. But she would not even look at him.

He wondered if the time would come when she would turn her back on him forever.

He stared into the fire and thought about Uhtred. The lord of Bamburgh himself didn't worry him; he thought he could handle Uhtred. He knew who had sent Uhtred.

He went to Leif.

"Do you think we can fix that gate?"

Leif set the jug down. "What's up?" And now Laissa did look at him.

"There's trouble, isn't there?" she said. Her voice shook. "I knew this would happen. They're after you again." She turned and carried the baby away out the door. "Good-bye, Raef."

Leif looked sharply after her and back to Raef. "What is it?"

Raef bent for the jug of ale. It was always cold, no matter how near the fire, and always full. He drank a lot of it. He wondered what Laissa meant to do. She herself did not seem to know what she would do, except to go pray to her wooden god. He had to hold himself fast to keep from running after her.

He said to Leif, "We need to close the wall."

Leif was eating his bread. He chewed awhile and finally swallowed. He looked after Laissa and then back to Raef. "Something's coming?"

Raef moved his shoulders. "Nothing we can't deal with."

"Oh?"

"Just an army."

Leif gave a startled grunt. He looked after Laissa again, but she was out of his sight now, running down toward the old church. He faced Raef.

"I guess we should try to fix the gate."

——⊸⊸——

They took his two new carls with them, and Peter followed on his pony. The gateway was like a stone box, ten feet deep, its archway rising up twice as high as the wall around it and topped with a stone parapet. The wooden gate itself had been so long broken Raef could see no way to make it swing again without forging new hinges for it. The dry old wood was split down the middle in six places, but the iron crosspieces held its shape still. The old wall, three times his height, was stout as a hillside.

He caught the other men watching him as if he would some-how work magic on this gate. He thought the way to beat Uhtred was that wall, these people, and maybe a little luck.

"Where is the nearest smith?"

One of the carls said, "Harrowgate, I think. There are tin-kers. You have to wait until one comes through." They were still looking at him quizzically.

He said, "Let's just get it closed, then."

"Nobody will be able to get in." But they put their shoulders to the wood and heaved and hauled the great slab up onto the sill of the stone gate frame. The hinges groaned and shrieked, and the top one snapped free at the stone side in a shower of rust.

From inside the gate they pulled it as deep as they could into the frame. It fit loosely, but it would keep people out for a while at least.

By then a crowd had gathered on the inside of the gate, watching them. When the gate was solidly into the opening, Raef went to slide the bolt across, and Goda suddenly strode forward out of the crowd and said, "Hey, there, that's enough. What are you doing now?"

Behind him, a general yell went up, as if Goda made the rest of them brave. "Yes! How is anybody going to get in now?" An old man with white whiskers, who leaned on a stout stick, came out and shook the stick at him. "You've gone too far this time!"

Raef said, "Pretty soon you're going to be glad this gate is shut." He forced the end of the bolt into the hole in the wall. "Although it isn't much."

Goda sneered. "Nobody ever comes in here anyway."

"Uhtred is coming here," Raef said. He faced Goda, in the middle of the little crowd of onlookers: his men and Goda's. "With an army."

The crowd hushed. The old man called, "What does that mean?"

Somebody hissed, "Tem! Be quiet!" Goda glanced over his shoulder at them and faced Raef again.

"Uhtred is our lord. He can come here if he wants."

Raef said, "He is bringing an army here. Do you think he means to help you shear sheep?"

Goda looked at the gate, as if he could see through it and find Uhtred, and his red forehead wrinkled. His pale eyes in their colorless lashes looked blind. Then he burst out, "You're crazy. Miru's right. She said you were a little crazy."

Raef said, "He's coming to finish what Ethelred started on Saint Brice's Day. Can he do that if he wants? Because he's your lord?"

Someone called, "We can't stand against Uhtred." The

crowd was shrinking. Goda's face was long, drawn, his lips pulled tight over his outthrust teeth. His thin, close-cropped red hair stood on end.

He said, "We can't refuse Uhtred." But his eyes went to Raef's, questioning. "You're crazy. We owe Uhtred fealty. He's the King's man. Defying him is like defying God."

"Awhile ago you were bragging how you threw out kings. And leave God out of this," Raef said. "God is peace, and there is no peace in England. Doesn't Uhtred owe you anything? What did King Ethelred owe Arre Woodwrightsson? How did he repay it? My wife's here. My child."

Goda turned and looked at the gate, trying to see out. He said, "Nobody is coming. That will be the proof of how crazy you are. Nothing is happening." He gave Raef a furious look.

"All right," Raef said. "I'll take that bet."

Laissa went to Miru's house, which was a snug fit for three people and a baby, and Goda grumbled to his wife that she could not stay. Miru frowned at him. "She can stay as long as I can, Goda. Besides," she said, "she'll go back. She loves him. He's a strange man, but still, I think he's good enough. Just let her think it over."

"Let him come get her," Goda said. "Take his mind off this ghost army."

Raef went up on the wall and walked from riverbank to riverbank, going down only at the gate. He found several places where the stones had fallen, and it would be easy for men to come in, but only a few at a time, and they would be easy meat for anybody up there with a bow. He came around outside the gate. From here the rolling land spread away into the south, green and empty.

He stood looking out over the green land, thinking of

Laissa. He could seize her and drag her back, but she would only run away again. She would stop loving him, and he could not endure that. He felt blocked and stuffed and hampered, like his river, a singing tension through all his nerves. He could sense Uhtred drawing nearer like a black mold spreading up over the edge of his awareness.

He could not detect the Lady anywhere. He wondered if this was a trap. He caught himself longing for Uhtred to appear, to end the waiting.

When he went back to the big gate, a lot of Jorvikers were collecting on top of the wall, mostly the Green Stray Boys with rakes and withies, peering into the south, but other people too— the carpenter, some shepherds. One had a bow, and Raef sent him down the wall to the biggest gap. He sent another down to where the wall came down to the edge of the river. Nobody really seemed to be worried; they did not believe him yet. They called him King, as if it were a dog name. Leif came up with a long notched pole, lowered one end down outside the wall and tipped the other against the top, and climbed down to help Raef fit another bar across the outside of the gate, so no one could open it from within.

Goda came up above them on the top of the gate. He leaned over the top of the wall, watching them. He said, "When are you coming to take this woman back?"

"If you touch my wife I'll kick those fangs right out your backside," Raef said, heaving at the bar, which was too wide for the bracket. Goda snorted at him.

"Working hard for a wizard."

Raef ignored that. Somebody laughed. He took hold of the iron upright of the bracket in one hand and pulled with his whole weight on it. With Leif shoving, he dragged the bar down solidly inside the bracket.

"I'd get a rent if you had anything I wanted," Goda said.

Raef kept at the work, jamming the bar down into place.

Somebody yelled, "Stay on that side of the gate!" There was more laughter.

Then Goda called out, in a different voice, "King. Something is coming."

Raef stepped back. Leif went nimbly up the pole like a bird up a string. Raef looked south, folding his arms over his chest. Closer to the ground than Goda, he could not see Uhtred's army from here, but he could feel them, trampling on over the green meadows, swinging inland to avoid the low, boggy willow thickets along the river, leaving only mud behind.

He felt no trace of the Lady. He remembered what she had said, in the dream, that he could have Jorvik. He wanted too much to believe that.

"Raef," Leif said. "Do you want the pole?"

He waved his hand. "Leave it there." Leaning against the gate, he watched the first of Uhtred's army ride into sight on the open rolling ground between the tree-wrapped course of the river and the woods of the upland along the road.

He glanced up. On the wall, more and more people were lining the rampart, and a fringe of poles and shovels and pruning hooks stuck out over the edge. They called to one another, their voices shrill with excitement, and sent for others. They spread out along the wall almost to the bend, where there was the remnant of a tower. Somebody went running by, up there, with another bow and more arrows. Raef rubbed his shoulders against the gate, solid behind him. He needed these people; he hoped they were as stout as they seemed. After all that had happened, he thought, they would not still be here otherwise.

By sundown Uhtred's army had come up to fill the road and the open ground for a hundred feet on either side, all the way back to where the woods began. Most of the men were on foot, but there were about forty riders. A string of wagons was still trundling up over the rocky ground to the south. Two of the horsemen rode forward, one carrying a green banner hanging limp on a pole.

The other was Uhtred.

He was a stocky man on a barrel-chested bay horse, his leather jacket green like the banner on the pole. He wore his beard cropped short, as if he were caught halfway between a Saxon and a Norman. "Who are you? Open this gate." A helmet hung from his saddlebows, a long sword from his belt. Raef knew his reputation: hard, bad tempered, a terror of the Scots, one of the few men Ethelred actually trusted.

Raef said, "What do you intend to do here? Why are you bringing this army here?"

The Saxon lord flared white with anger, but he kept himself still. His eyes burned.

"That's my concern entirely. I am lord of Northumberland, my only liege is the King of the English." His broad face was vivid with indignation. "Who are you to stand up to me? Let me in! Jor'ck is my city."

"Your city. Then why are you bringing an army in here?" Raef looked quickly toward the army. To the people behind him, on the walls, this mass of men and pikes must look like a stubby little forest. He brought his gaze to Uhtred.

"This is a free city. Ethelred Edgarsson lost his hold here when he murdered half of Jorvik on Saint Brice's Day. See those people there?" He swung his arm up toward the wall. "They remember Euan Woodwrightsson. They remember the old days. They think you're bringing Saint Brice's Day here."

Uhtred swung his horse around. He had a heavy, sun-leathered face, narrow eyed, and he mastered the horse with a rough hand. He said, "We'll see about this. I know these people, maybe better than you. Let them think it over for a day. They'll give you to me like the Martinmas hog." He lifted his hands beside his mouth.

"You! Up there! I'll guarantee the life and holding of any-body who lets me into the city!"

Raef said, "What will you guarantee the rest?"

At that the people who could hear them let up a yell, and they repeated everything up and down the wall, so the yell spread. Uhtred mashed his lips together and gave Raef a hard stare. His cheeks flushed. He swung back toward his army. His mind was clear to Raef as a bowl of water; he was thinking of launching an attack at once, and Raef began to consider the quickest way he could get himself back over the wall. But Uhtred was a cautious man, for all his bad temper, and that slower, steadier thinking overgrew the impulse.

He said, scarcely turning around, "It's almost dark. I'll come back tomorrow. The gate had better be open. And you—" He said this to Raef— "had better be gone."

He cantered away, not waiting for an answer. Raef climbed up the pole and over the top of the wall.

If there was a battle, he thought, that would bring the Lady out. She would not be able to resist a harvest of souls. She could still be here, somehow, hidden. Yet he knew Uhtred had no magic, and there were no women with him.

He remembered how he had seen the filthy cloud boiling up out of the hole in the light field, and he thought again of the dream. Maybe she couldn't stretch this far yet from her root.

She did not belong to the light field, and he did. That heartened him. He went off across the city toward his hall.

———

In the fading daylight Uhtred set his camp up on the green meadows to either side of the road to the gate. He did not expect much trouble here. The white-haired man had stirred up the few people remaining inside the wall, but that would not last. They were peasants, shepherds and earth grubbers, not fighting men.

Once the arrows flew and the swords started swinging, they would run or beg for mercy or die. He promised himself the pleasure of spiking that white-haired head on the ruined gate of Jorvik.

He had come north with forty horsemen of his personal army, going north through Mercia; he had his own reasons for avoiding the easier road through Lindsey, east of the Trent. He had the King's writ, and as he went he collected fyrdmen from Ethelred's own lands, so well over three hundred men followed him now. He doubted there were many more people in Jorvik than followed him. He thought he would have the city in flames by the next nightfall.

He stood watching his carls throw up his tent for him. The tent was an old sail, and that reminded him of the Danes. It irked him that he had been sent up here when the Danes would surely attack in the south. He thought this was Emma's doing. She had disliked him since he had recoiled from her when she simpered up to him. He hated Emma. He thought she did much evil with Ethelred, who had always been rough and proud, but who, since his Norman marriage, had gotten savage. Now there was this ghost.

Uhtred was Ethelred's man, had been since becoming lord of Bamburgh years before. Ethelred had done some rash things, but at heart he was the same brave, hard-riding boy he had been when they were together at court. And he was Uhtred's King.

Nonetheless, when he thought of slaughtering a pack of defenseless people for the sake of the Norman Queen, it put him on edge. It would be a bloody thing if they tried to fight; his men would be hacking down women with hayforks, children with sticks. Not even Danes. Jor'ck was a good city too, or had been, sitting where it was at the center of some of the best sheep country in the North and right on a river. But the King had ordered it destroyed, and Uhtred was proud of his loyalty.

He could give the people a way out. Just before dark, with

his camp set up, he sent a messenger up to the gate to announce that they should all leave the city by the next sundown, and he would raze it then.

—◦—

He had laid out his camp on the greensward, the horses tethered where they could eat, the men where they could defend one another and the horses, and himself with his tent in the middle with the supply wagons, where he could move quickly to any part of the field. But just after dark somebody managed to get in among the horses and spook them, and the terror spread, and horses broke their tethers and ran mad through the camp, neighing and running men down and kicking over fires and gear. It took him most of the night to get his men back in order and the horses tied.

In the morning the gate was still shut. No one seemed to be leaving. The tall, stooped, white-haired man was watching him from the top of the wall. Uhtred rode away, his teeth set, to plan an attack.

—◦—

Goda had been on the wall all night, but he got back to his house to find Raef's wife in his bed. It was full daylight anyway, time to get back to work. Cursing under his breath he went around to the shambles. He had an ewe backed up against his chest, his arms around her as he scraped the long nappy wool off her belly, when he noticed that old Tem and his brother and his shepherds had come up by the withy fence and were staring at him.

Nearly everybody else was still at the wall. Goda kept on; there was no stopping in the middle of a sheep. When he had turned the sheep and cleaned her up to the neck, he clipped off the fleece, flung it white-side down on the table in the shed for Miru to pluck, and went up to the men at the fence.

Tem waved his oak walking stick at him. His white whiskers bristled. He had a big farm just beyond the old Coppergate and was always moving in on the abandoned places near him. Even before Goda reached the fence he was shouting, "It's that crazy man in the hall that's causing this. He's brought them down on us. I told you we should have run him out of there."

The other men with him grumbled in agreement. They all worked for Tem and would say whatever he wanted. Goda wondered where Miru was. Where that other woman was, Raef's wife. Tem was still shouting. "I don't like him anyway. I don't know who he is. Who he thinks he is. I say we all go up there and put him in irons—has anybody got irons?"

Nobody said anything. Miru had come out of the back shed of the shambles, her hands covered with blood and her eyes sharp.

Tem leaned on his stick, his jaw thrust out like a plowshare. Goda swung toward him.

"Listen to me, old man. I like him a lot better than I like you. And he's right. Uhtred's not here for any good of ours, and we have to stand up to him, at least long enough to get him to make some kind of agreement with us. Now get out of here."

Miru had gone, probably to tell the crazy man's wife what was happening. Tem and his men grunted a few more comments, but Goda went to work on another sheep. Then he could sleep a few hours and go back to the wall. Whatever happened, he wanted it to be out in front of him, where he could see it coming.

Raef stood in the doorway of his hall, looking off down across the town. Leif came up beside him.

"Go get her."

Raef grunted at him. "If she's not here of her own will, she's not here."

Leif grunted, his hands on his hips. He had walked down earlier and seen Laissa and the baby at Miru's, and he thought only Laissa's pride kept her away: Raef should carry her back. "You're her husband. She has to obey you."

"So I've seen."

Leif saw the flash of anger in him and hastily went on to something else. "What will happen with Uhtred?"

"He'll attack soon. He has men in the woods looking for logs to use as rams and climbing ladders. If we can keep him out for a couple of days, he'll talk."

"What will you do?"

Raef leaned on the doorframe. The missing ear made him look lopsided. "If we can keep him out, why talk?"

Leif slid his palm along the haft of his axe. He said, "It'll be a bloody mess. How long will these people follow you if they start dying?"

"I don't think it will go that far," Raef said. He raked his beard with his fingers, his eyes looking away. "I wish Laissa would come back. I can't think about everything at once."

⸺

Laissa said, "No, I have to leave your house, Miru, I'm putting you in danger. Goda is right. I'll go to the church until I find something better."

"The church," Miru said. "Anybody can jump on you there."

"Jesus will defend me," she said, and took the baby and, with Miru, went on over to the old minster.

"You're not staying here all day, are you?" Miru asked. They stood just inside the door of the shadowy stone minster. "We should clean this place up."

A few people prayed by the altar rail. Laissa did not want to go nearer them, and she went along the wall, looking for some place good to hide. By the small side altar, the basin for the water blessing stood, a round stone bowl as high as her waist and wide across as her two arms outstretched. Between the curved side of the bowl and the straight rail of the altar was a narrow space where she put her cloak and the baby's blanket and the sack of food Miru had brought. She drew back and turned to Miru.

"Let's go," she said.

"Where?"

"Up to the wall," Laissa said. "I want to see what's happening." She did not say she wanted to see Raef, if only at a distance.

Gemma on her hip, she followed Miru up the dusty street. Her mind tugged her back and forth. She missed Raef, and she wanted to go home, to her loom, her own bed, her own fire. Her husband, her husband's arms. But it was Raef who drew the evil here. Something more terrible than soldiers with swords was after him. She had to protect the baby. Gemma rode happily on her hip, unaware of any of this. She looked like Raef sometimes. It came into Laissa's mind that she had left him when he needed her.

He did not seem to need her much.

Ahead across a stretch of sheep pasture the wall rose. She gasped, amazed; it was covered with people, all carrying some stick or knife. They were all shouting and chattering at once, like a great flock of birds. The Green Stray Boys strutted by, long staves tilted on their shoulders. All along the rampart stood piles of rocks. Men talked together in groups, walked from one group to the next, rakes in their hands, their scythes silver edged from the hone. Miru turned to her and laughed.

"Yes, everybody is here. We're going to fight for Jorvik. Look, there's Raef." She gave Laissa a sly look.

Laissa had already seen him; his long white hair was like a

Raef moved down the wall, away from the thick of the crowd; trying to keep his mind on everything at once had him stretched tight as spider silk. The disorderly army in front of him was moving up for an attack. They were bringing coils of rope and limbed tree trunks to use as climbing ladders. Uhtred rode in their midst. He was the only man mounted, his green-jacketed guard walking along in a rank near the front of the army to lead the attack.

All along the wall the Jorvikers were yelling, waving their rakes and hoes. Raef thought nearly everybody left in the city was there. Even the children were here, huddled together on the stone walks, in the corners, curled in their father's coats. Then, down the wall, nearer the high frame wall of the gate, he saw Laissa.

She had come up on the wall, the baby in her arms, and was looking toward the oncoming army, and she shouted, like the others. He turned forward again. His body felt wider on that side, aching toward her. She did not come to him. Just because she was here did not mean she was coming back to him. He loved that she was here. He forced himself to pay attention to Uhtred.

The Bamburgh lord was yelling out there and waving his arm, and a string of men with bows ran past Uhtred toward the wall. From the wall a Jorviker arrow fluttered toward the army and fell short. Uhtred's archers kneeled down and bent their bows.

On the wall a shrill scream of warning rose, and the whole crowd folded at once down behind the top of the wall. Raef stayed where he was, watching Uhtred, now hustling his climbing ladders forward.

The archers shot in volleys, pelting the wall with their arrows. Uhtred was down there, yelling at them and pointing up at Raef, and two of the archers moved out of their rank. They ran down the grass, kneeled opposite Raef, and aimed at him. He leaned on the wall.

He flicked a glance toward the array of climbing ladders tilted up against the wall like tent poles. Most didn't quite reach the top of the wall, and the last few feet were going to be a hard climb for Uhtred's men. The Bamburgh lord's archers lined up below him shot.

The arrows sang toward him, well aimed; he had only to put up his hands and catch them. Seeing this, the two men with their bows startled up to their feet. One nocked another arrow, but the man beside him was already running. Raef flung his own arrow at him, and he screamed and crumpled into the grass. The other archer fired off his second shot wildly into the air and raced away. Raef threw the arrow in his hand and missed, but the archer kept on running, out of the army, down the meadow, out of sight and into the woods. The one Raef had hit was not dead. The arrow poked from the back of his thigh, and he was lying flat on his face, but he was creeping away on his belly.

The other archers were still keeping the Jorvikers huddled down behind the parapet, and Uhtred's men were swarming the ladders against the wall. Down past Laissa, Leif moved along the rampart behind the Jorvikers, talking to them, getting them ready; he walked at a squat, like a strange dwarf, to stay under the cover of the wall. Raef leaned against the wall, watching Uhtred.

⸻

Leif said, "They're coming. They're coming. As soon as they're up, throw them off. Just push them back. Laissa!"

She turned toward him; she was wedged in against the wall

with Miru on one side and Goda on the other. Leif grabbed her arm. "What are you doing here with that baby?"

"I'm fighting for Jorvik," Laissa said. "Am I supposed to hide in a hole?" A trumpet blasted.

She jerked out of his grip. Leif straightened, drawing his hand ax from his belt, and, almost at once, men with helmets and green jackets were swarming up to the top of the wall.

Laissa slid one arm around the baby, Gemma wide-eyed, both fists tight in Laissa's apron, the belt holding her fast. The people around her rose from their crouch behind the wall like a cresting wave. At the edge of the parapet, their rakes and hoes jabbed out and down into the enemy's faces. Some of the men climbing up the parapet recoiled and fell backward. Others were struggling on up, knocking aside the long poles. Laissa yelled, "Miru!"

Directly before the butcher's wife a man in a helmet was trying to swing one leg over the wall. Laissa rushed at him, her hands thrust forward, and slammed into him; she was a little behind him and she hit him on the ribs with all her weight. He swayed, half falling, clinging to the wall with his left hand, the sword in his right hand clanging off the stone. The men under him on the ladder screamed at him, pushing him back up onto the wall.

Laissa shoved him again, and beside her Miru slid her shoulder under his arm and they flung him backward. With a yell he flew off, and on the way down he hit the men on the ladder below him and brought them down too.

Panting, Laissa backed away. Gemma was shrieking on her hip, one hand fisted in Laissa's hair, and her mother put an arm around her. A horn blew. All along the wall Uhtred's men were dropping back. Miru shouted, shaking her fists. Laissa went back and looked over the top of the wall.

The ground at the foot was littered with peeled and notched tree trunks and half a dozen bodies, some trying to stand, to limp away. All up and down the wall the Jorvikers were roaring in triumph. Miru turned to her, red faced and beaming. "We beat them!" A stream of boys ran along the rampart, whooping.

"We beat them!"

The trumpet sounded again. Uhtred was galloping around back there, getting his army together.

Laissa glanced down the wall toward Raef. He had not moved. He stood in his usual stoop at the angle of the wall, looking out. He never looked at her. She turned her eyes away from him.

Leif came by her, talking to the Jorvikers lined up against the wall. "They're going to attack again. This time they'll be harder. You beat them once, you can beat them again, but it will be harder this time. Help one another. Stay together." He went past her, toward Raef. A few moments later Leif came back along the wall again, found Goda, and with him and three or four others trotted down the stairs into the city and went over to the far side of the gate.

The baby was still screaming. She had been hungry for a while, and her little fists banged in the air and her legs thrashed. Laissa sat down quickly with her back to the wall and gave her the breast while she could.

⊸⊸

Uhtred shouted, "These are peasants. Are you afraid of peasants? There are women up there. What are women good for?"

His men yelled. He had lost a dozen in the first assault, mostly wounded. His green jackets looked tough enough, ready to show the Jorvikers what fighting really was, but most of the others, especially the fyrdmen from Ethelred's lands, were common husbandmen, plowboys and reapers, and they were glum that this wasn't easier. He shouted at them, "They were lucky that time. Now we'll get them, and you'll all get yours." The men cheered.

This time he meant to come up in two waves at the stretch just right of the gate. The archers would sweep the wall clear. Then the first wave of men up the wall would push the defenders back, and the second would take control. Once he had the gate, the Jorvikers would start running.

He turned his horse; his gaze went to the tall white-haired man on the wall, a hundred feet down from the big stone box of the gate. Uhtred had sent archers to kill him. He must be wearing mail under that ragged shirt. He was watching Uhtred steadily, and his gaze unsettled the Saxon like a nettle on his skin.

He lined up his archers facing the long stretch of wall, well west of the gate, so it would look as if the attack were coming there. He nodded to his herald, who lifted the trumpet to his lips and blew.

The archers raised their bows and, with a steady rain of arrows, drove the Jorvikers down behind their parapets. The front half of the army rushed the wall, howling, and gathered the climbing logs as they got to them; then, in a mass, the men swung to their left and slammed the logs up against the stone rampart of the gate.

As they scrambled up, the archers lowered their bows for fear of hitting their own men, and the Jorvikers rose up into sight above the wall. Men and women, even children, saw the green jackets scaling up toward them by the gate; a scream went up, and they rushed to meet the attack. The crowd sprouted rakes and sticks and axes like some kind of giant hedgehog. They threw back the first few of Uhtred's men, jabbing at them with their farm tools. Uhtred nodded, and the trumpeter blew again, and the second wave went in.

The Jorvikers were crowding along the wall toward the gate, but, as Uhtred had expected, the upright wall of the gate, six feet above the rampart, gave his men some protection and kept the Jorvikers from bringing all their numbers at once. Now Uhtred's men were pouring up that narrow stretch of wall faster than the Jorvikers could stop them. Already some green jackets stood on the wall, chopping down rakes and hoes. More clambered up to join them. In a moment they could take the gate, smash it open, and let everybody in at once. Uhtred laughed. This was going to be over soon.

Then, abruptly, on top of the gate, half a dozen men appeared. Their leader waved an axe. They ran across the gate and bounded down onto the backs of the green jackets.

His men went down. Uhtred swore. A thundering cheer rose from the people on the wall, and they pushed forward again. On the ladders, suddenly his men were climbing down instead of going up. Another ladder fell. Uhtred spat, disgusted. He turned to the trumpeter again to sound retreat. He would have to think of something else.

—⟨⟩—

Gemma was screaming at the top of her lungs, her face all round, howling mouth. Laissa untied her and went to sit down and nurse her, but the baby was too angry even to take the breast. Around her the people were rushing up and down, leaping and hugging one another and screaming. Little boys were dashing all over the rampart and the ground below, picking up arrows. Miru danced around with Goda, laughing into her husband's laughing face. Laissa looked beyond them.

Someone had died, or at least was dying, and a group of quiet people sat around him. Raef was one of them. A man among them was bleeding from a gash on his face, and some others were slumped against the wall, obviously hurt. The whole side of Goda's face was purpling into a bruise. Even Leif was limping. And it wasn't over. She realized she was hungry and alone and this was not over.

She realized suddenly that it would never be over. If not Uhtred or Raef's demon, then some other evil would infest them. They would have to fight forever. She held the baby against her, warm and smelly; she had not changed her rags all day. She went down the stairs, to go find clean clothes for her child.

Miru caught up with her. "Where are you going?"

"To the church," Laissa said. They were near the foot of the stair; Gemma snuffled, her nose running, and Laissa wiped the baby's face with her sleeve.

Miru said, "You have to be careful."

Laissa wanted to be alone, to think over this whole situation. "Could you bring me some—" Her eye caught on a white head, vanishing around the corner of a building.

It was Tem, the old shepherd who had threatened her. A prickle of suspicion ran along her hands. She turned to Miru. "Come on."

"What?"

"I just saw—" She led the butcher's wife around the corner where the shepherd had gone and saw him, far ahead down the street, hurrying toward the river. She pointed. "What's he doing?"

Miru shrugged. "He's an old busybody." But she frowned. "Let's go see."

They followed Tem's white head down through the fringe of the village. On the wall even here people were laughing and dancing and celebrating, and nobody paid much heed to them. Ahead, Tem came to the bank of the little creek that ran down into the river just inside the wall.

Laissa grabbed Miru by the sleeve and held her. "Look."

Tem was climbing down into the creek. He stooped below the high bank and disappeared from sight. Laissa looked up at the wall, where nobody was paying much heed to this.

She said, "Where does that creek run?"

Miru said, "Up that way." She gestured vaguely toward the middle of the city. "It runs into the Ouse right by the foot of the wall."

Laissa looked into her eyes. "He's sneaking out of the city."

Miru's broad forehead rumpled. "Trying to escape, the miserable old coward."

Laissa said, "No—then he would go north."

The other woman's eyes widened. She swung to stare down at the creek, whose bank hid Tem from sight. "The wretch."

Laissa laid one hand on her arm. "Go down and keep watch there. See if he comes back in."

"Where are you going?"

"To tell Raef. Whatever he thinks of me, he has to know this." Laissa hitched the baby up on her hip and ran back up the slope toward the hall.

⇒

Uhtred said, "Who is this?" He stood up. The guard had come into the door of the tent. Uhtred reached for his sword, hanging in its scabbard on the tent pole.

"Some peasant, my lord," said the guard. "He's offering to hand over the city to you."

"Bring him here." He strapped the sword belt on.

"He says for you to go to the edge of the camp, my lord. By the river."

Uhtred thought this over, but he had expected something like this. It should be obvious to everybody who would win here. They had almost won that day. If he had not put his archers in the wrong place, they could have shot down the men on the gate who changed the course of the fight, and all those people would be dead now or would have given up.

It was almost sundown. He was planning to attack the next

day, in another place, so this peasant had arrived at a good time. He took the guard and another man and went down through the camp, still trampled and disorderly from the loose horses. At the edge of the willows that marked the edge of the river he left one guard, in case he needed help, and followed the one who had brought the message down a thread of a game path through the tangled thickets.

The bank here was deep, six feet down to the rushing water. Ahead the bank flattened down onto a shelving gravel bar. An old man in shepherd's boots waited there in the last sunlight. The ripples of the river glistened faintly behind him.

The old man said, "I can give you a way in without any trouble. Nobody else has to die. A key, like to the gate." He grinned.

"Good," Uhtred said. "What?" He imagined a sneaky way into the city, maybe on the far side.

"That Raef? That white-haired bastard who calls himself the King of Jorvik? I can get you his wife and child."

Uhtred clamped his mouth shut, bridling at this. It was a low evil, using a woman and a child. The old man was going on, "If you have her and the child, he will yield. I have seen him so loving with her you'd think she was his harlot. Agreed?"

Uhtred said, tight-lipped, "What do you want?"

"I will be your reeve in Jorvik—Jor'ck, as you call it. I will take the taxes and send people to you for the quarter day and keep the law."

Uhtred relaxed, pleased. When he had Jorc'k, he intended still to obey his orders: He would move out any survivors and level the place. This wicked old man would get nothing at all, not even what he had now. That evened out the dishonor of using a woman. He said, "How will you get her to me?"

"I'll bring her here, with the child, tonight at midnight. I and some of my men." The old man puffed himself a little. Uhtred thought again, grimly, This was a low business, stealing women, and in the end it might not work. But if it did work, he would have the city. He nodded.

"Midnight, then," he said. "I will be here, and with a host of my men, so don't try any tricks."

The old man leered at him and stuck his hand out, as if he thought Uhtred would shake his hand. Uhtred ignored it. Finally Tem went down the river toward Jor'ck, and Uhtred went back to his camp.

⸺

Tem poled his boat back up the riverbank; when the wall loomed up over the straggle of willows, he hid the boat under the overhang and waded the rest of the way, stooped over, until he came to the mouth of the Foss. The wall stood high over him, but the creek's bank was steep here, undercut, and he crawled along it, close to the side, where no one could see him.

The girl was staying in the church; it would be easy enough to grab her. He would bring a couple of his shepherds to do the work. If she fought, he would take the baby. She would do whatever he said for the baby's sake. Crawling along in the muck he chuckled to himself, thinking how clever he was to have thought all this out so well. He went far up the creek until he knew that an old house would hide him from anybody on the wall and stood up.

Then a hand fell hard on his shoulder. He started, his mouth going dry. A voice said in his ear, "I think the King wants to talk to you, Tem."

It was the fat man who had come here with the white-haired upstart. Tem said, "No—I have work to do—" His voice came out squeaky. "You can't give me orders!"

"Make a bet on that?" The fat man swung him up bodily off the ground and slung him over his shoulder. Tem yelled, beat his fists on the man's back, kicked uselessly. The fat man laughed; he was much stronger than he looked. He carried Tem up the hill, while Tem began to think of any lie he could tell to get out of this, any lie at all. He squeezed his eyes shut, afraid.

—⟨∘⟩—

Uhtred went down toward the river in the dark; he took along three of his men, but he left them at the edge of the willows as he had before. He could deal with a girl and her baby, and he did not think the old man was smart enough to hurt him. In any case, one shout would bring his men to his side.

He wanted to see the girl alone, first, to let her know that he would protect her. That took some of the sting out of using her. He wondered, briefly, how grateful she would be for his protection.

He found the path and threaded his way through the drooping trees to the riverbank. The moon was bright, glistening on the water, and when he walked out onto the bare pebbles of the riverbar, the girl stood there alone with her baby in her arms. He cast a quick look around and saw no one, not even the old man.

He started toward her. "Don't be afraid—" He sensed somebody behind him, and an instant later everything went away.

—⟨∘⟩—

He woke up lying on a flagstone floor, at the foot of a high seat. There the white-haired man sprawled at ease, one foot stretched out before him, and the other bent at the knee. His right ear poked through his long white braided hair, but there was no sign of the left. The girl Uhtred had seen on the riverbar came up beside the high seat and put her hand on his shoulder; so she was his wife, as the old man had said.

Uhtred cast a look around. He was in a hall, with one end wall missing and only half a roof. He realized he was in Jor'ck.

The man on the high seat said, "You have a choice, Uhtred. I can kill you, or you can go back to Bamburgh. Which is it?"

Uhtred faced him and laughed, unbelieving. He could not fathom this, any of it. He got cautiously up onto his knees. He wasn't bound. He looked around again; there were other people behind him, men and women, everybody watching. The white-haired man gestured, and a boy brought Uhtred a cup of ale. Thirsty, he took a deep draft of it.

"What is this choice?" he said. "To die or to lose nothing? What choice is that?"

The white-haired man's long mouth curled up at one corner. He had bright blue eyes, and his look made Uhtred uncomfortable, as if he saw straight through his skull.

"You go back to Bamburgh. You can play the ealdorman there all you wish. Leave me alone; leave Jorvik alone."

Uhtred said, "I am Ethelred's man." On his right, now there stood the fat, balding man with the axe, who had led the counter-charge over the gate, and on his left, the redheaded butcher, his knives in his belt and his face all black and blue. Uhtred lifted his gaze to the man on the high seat. "I swore oaths to Ethelred, true Christian vows."

Raef stirred in the high seat. "Did you swear an oath to Eadric Streona? to Emma? They're the ones ruling England. You know this. This is what you will lose, heeding me—the Queen and her knifeman. You will still have your own lands. I want only Jorvik and to make her great again. Leave Ethelred to Streona and Emma. Don't be stupid. Go along with this."

Uhtred stared at him, his mind working. He already hated Streona and Emma and what they had made of Ethelred. But Ethelred was King of the English. He looked away from the blue eyes, trying to untangle the knot.

"What is this hall?"

"This is the King of Jorvik's hall. King Eric Bloodaxe's hall."

Uhtred swallowed; he studied the white-haired man a moment. He had thought all Bloodaxe's sons were dead. He knew this hall had been rubble the last time he was here. He said, "Where are my men?"

"Outside," the King of Jorvik said. "They know we're talking things over."

Uhtred's gaze rose to him, savoring this wording, which left him a way to stand honorably with his men. "What am I supposed to tell Ethelred?"

"Don't tell him anything. Do you think this was his idea?"

Uhtred shook his head. He saw no way to go save to take this. "You're too clever for Ethelred. Maybe for Streona and Ethelred together. All right. I will go to Bamburgh. Jorvik is yours; I don't care."

"Good. And in the meantime," said the man on the high seat, "it being so near the quarter day, and your owing me a sort of ransom now, there is something you can do for me to pay it. Since you have all these men here, you can dig me a ditch. It's not a very big one. A few days' work for all these men."

⇥

Laissa sat beside him in the high seat, and they passed a cup back and forth. She had slept only a little while since she ran up here from the church, and the ale made her dizzy. Miru had taken Gemma away. The hall was full of people.

Down there Peter was playing his pipe, and the others were dancing around the fire, celebrating. Leif kicked his feet lightly with Edith, their hands joined. Goda stood clapping his hands. He was as pleased with himself as if he had fought Uhtred single-handed.

All the Jorvikers were jubilant. Through the afternoon, ever since Uhtred had packed up and ridden off south, a river of the city's people had been passing through the hall, drinking the King's ale, eating the King's roast meat, saluting Raef on his high seat, and congratulating themselves on their victory. Tem was not there. She suspected she would never see Tem again; Raef, or more likely Leif, would see to that.

Now the villagers had mostly left. Raef slipped his hand inside her gown. He had run to meet her when she came back; he had swung her up in his arms, Gemma and all, there in the middle of the street, whirled them around, carried them skipping and jumping all the way back to the hall.

"Am I Queen of Jorvik now?" she said.

"If you want." He fingered her nipple. "But you cannot go away again."

"I think I will just be Laissa," she said. She drew his hand out of her clothes. "I want you to promise me something."

He caressed her throat under her hair. She felt soft, eager for his touch. He had this way of making her forget everything bad. He said, "Whatever you want."

"Promise me you won't teach her anything. Promise me what I mean by that."

He said, slowly, "I promise it." His fingers stroked her nape. "But it will do no good to teach her anyway, if she has no gift."

Laissa took his hand. "Let's go down to the sleeping bench, where we can be alone."

He stood, following her. He said, under his breath, "Everybody has a gift." She pretended not to hear and took him away to their lair to lie together.

—❧—

Later, when they were all back home and asleep, Raef went out and walked to the wall and looked out again. The Lady had not come. She had sent Uhtred because she could not come. For the first time he had found a limit to her. She could not reach this far. He was safe in Jorvik.

He did not think that would be good enough, for him to be safe in Jorvik. There was more to come of this. And he still knew nothing of how to defeat her.

CHAPTER THIRTEEN

In the inner room, the king was screaming, not even words any-more, just a rhythmic, ringing shriek; Edmund turned away, his nerves raw. Eadric Streona was walking up and down the an-techamber, saying, over and over, "I can't talk to him. I can't talk to him." Most of the men in the crowded room were staring at the walls, their faces set.

"Where is the Queen?" Edmund said.

Archbishop Alphege stood beside him, his hands folded, and his meaty face set. They had called him in as soon as the King began to rave, but he could do nothing. In a clipped voice, he said, "The Queen is in confinement. No one gains entrance to her chambers save her closest women."

Edmund said, "When the Queen is here, he is not haunted."

Alphege said, "Yes. I've noticed that too." His lips pressed together. Edmund saw he was jealous of whatever power this was that Emma held. He said, "God acts in mysterious ways."

Streona barged up between them; he had overheard them. "But we can't wait for her to have her baby and return to the King's side. The Danes are attacking now." He faced the arch-bishop, ignoring Edmund. "Your Emminence, there must be something you can do."

Alphege lifted one hand and let it drop. "What's the latest news from the west?"

Streona shook his head. "No better."

Edmund stepped back from them. He had heard enough. The earlier news had been as bad as possible. Summer had come, the fighting season, and Sweyn Forkbeard close behind. The King of Denmark attacked in Kent and started westward across the country, and in spite of Ethelred's alliance with Richard, a Jomsviking fleet in Sweyn's pay had sailed boldly into the narrow sea. They had swept aside the few English ships that came against them and attacked Exeter on the southern coast, and the Duke of Normandy had not lifted his hand to stop them.

"Exeter has fallen," Streona said. "The Norman garrison gave in without a fight. The Jomsvikings are marching across country. They aim to meet Sweyn in the middle. Whitsuntide has come and gone, and we still have no army. Morcar and his brother have sent excuses, Uhtred isn't even answering us, the thegns in Anglia and Wessex will not leave their strongholds, and only a few of the fyrd have gathered. And when they see the King as he is—you see—" He flung his hands up, empty.

Alphege made the sign of the cross, his head turning away. Edmund went up to Streona. "Where is my brother?"

Streona glanced at him. "Aethelstan has gone away to Wessex, somewhere near Salisbury. He has all the men he could raise from his own lands. He's trying to get between the Jomsvikings and Winchester." He swung back to the archbishop, his voice pleading.

"I have sent to Morcar once more, whatever good that will do. Thurbrand Hold in Lindsey will not come. The western lords are sitting behind their walls and praying. The Jomsvikings are coming east from Exeter along the high road. They will reach Winchester in a matter of weeks, if Sweyn doesn't get here first from the other direction. You have to do something."

"I can do nothing," Alphege's voice ripped through his churchmanly calm and rose to a shout: "The King is damned!" He thrust out with one hand at Streona and walked past him toward the door. Edmund left soon after.

By noon Edmund was jogging his horse along the old road to Land's End, glad to be out of the crowded, stinking city. He had brought bread, some sausages, a cheese, a flask of ale. He passed a steady tide of people coming the other way, carrying sacks on their backs, pushing handcarts, herding a few sheep, a cow. Bringing their children by the hand. Their faces were set and grim. He did not try to talk to anybody. Nobody else was going west.

Back in Winchester he had not bothered to look for anybody to come with him. They were all blitherers. He would rather die than stand around listening to his father scream. The wind was blustery, and grey clouds rolled over the sky. The days were cold for the middle of the summer, and there was an edge to the wind. He knew there was a good chance that he would die.

There had been no rain all spring, and, as he rode, he passed fields with the crops already withered and gone, the dust blowing away, the hardscrabble showing like scabs, as if the crust wore thin over the earth. He passed through a village with doors shut-tered and no one visible, although some smoke curled up from the hearths.

But as he rode in, a half-naked man burst out of a door and ran down the street away from him. There could be others. He imagined he saw eyes in the windows; he was glad to get past the village.

It was cold, and he began to feel cold at heart. He was alone, the world huge around him, and what lay ahead, he knew, would be terrible. His food ran out. There was nothing anywhere to eat. He stayed the night in a deserted hut by the road.

In the morning, hungry, he was slow to get going. This seemed the emptiest place he had ever been, the road running west over low hills, the sky grey and low and dank. He had started this, and he would not stop now. He swung into his saddle and nudged the horse into a swinging trot, to get through it faster.

Late in the day he came up on a low rise and drew rein to

let his horse rest. His belly was cramped with hunger. A broad
valley lay below him, with a river along the near edge. On the
far side the slopes of the hills rolled up into crests of forest. The
low ground between was plowed into fields, but he saw no
people, no animals, nothing moving down there. Then his eye
caught on a thin line of smoke rising beyond the down ahead of
them.

"Aethelstan," he said, aloud. He hoped it was Aethelstan.
He wiped his face on the sleeve of his shirt and rode that way.

He left the big road behind and followed a narrow path,
which wound across the valley toward the distant down. His
horse was tired, head low, ears slack. Drifting down the western
sky, the sun fell beneath the ledge of dark cloud, and its light
came straight into his face. Then, ahead of him, Edmund heard
someone call out, not in English.

He swung his horse's head around, but, before he could get it
running, a pack of men on foot burst up along the trail, coming
toward him, yelling. Vikings. He spurred the horse into a gallop.
Where the trail curved, he left it and headed across the flat valley,
the slope of the down on his left. The dark was closing in. The
Vikings were whooping after him, and a rock sailed past him.
His horse kept wanting to stop, and he flogged it on, stumbling
and staggering along a boggy meadow. He was closing with the
hill on his left, steep and bush clogged.

Ahead part of the slope had washed out in a fan of pebbles.
Where the slope had fallen down was a deep draw, and he swung
his horse into it. The ravine pinched narrow on both sides, the
floor rising. He lashed his horse up through the clawing brush
and slippery pebble slides. He could hear men panting after him,
their voices exuberant. The draw ended in a sheer face. He was
trapped. He hauled the horse around and put it at the side of the
hill. Snorting, it bounded up, slid, lunged up again, and heaved
itself over a tumble of boulders and was suddenly staggering
onto flat ground.

He rode out on the top of the down, the brush swishing against his legs, and then from either side men sprang on him.

He reached for his sword. There were too many; he would die here. He would die here fighting. Somebody seized his horse's reins, and then he heard the voices around him speaking Saxon.

He called, "God be with all good men here. I am Edmund Aetheling—I'm looking for my brother Aethelstan."

A cheer rose. A swarm of men on foot packed around them. Edmund reached down, touching hands, greeting them in God's name. They led him to the west end of the down, where, ahead, he saw a tall shape he knew.

"Aethelstan!"

By the fire his brother turned, and he roared out Edmund's name and came running. The two embraced. Aethelstan was much the taller. "Edmund! God's love, I'm glad to see you. Did you bring—"

Edmund said, "I brought no one. I am alone."

Aethelstan looked beyond him, and then back to him, the firelight on his face. He said, "You came all this way alone? By yourself?"

"You are my king," Edmund said. "I came to help you."

Aethelstan drew a short breath. "Ethelred is gone?"

"No."

"Then Ethelred is King." He swung his arms around Edmund. "But what a man you are, for just a boy. I pray—" He looked around. It was beginning to rain. "I pray we come out of this alive. I pray we may save the kingdom."

"There are Danes below, in the valley," Edmund said.

"Yes, so we thought you were. We have been snaring them all day." Aethelstan gripped his shoulders. "You're here! What a wonder." He looked out toward the west again. "These we're seeing now are only the front edge, Edmund. I can see the smoke of the last place they burned."

"We'll be ready," Edmund said. "God save us, we are in the right here."

"I don't know if that matters to God," Aethelstan said. "You must be hungry."

"I'm starving."

"Come eat."

⟿

"Why is there no fyrd come to help us?" Aethelstan said.

"They are slow to band together. They are coming. But the King—" Edmund bit his lips. "Only the King can lead the fyrd."

"Where is the King?"

Edmund handed Reynard the jug. "He's mad, Aethelstan. He can't sleep, for fear of the ghost, and he sees her everywhere. Even old Alphege can't help him this time." He fisted his hands. "There is no king, not really."

"The Queen?"

"She is in childbed, or near to. No one sees her but her most trusted women. They say her condition is very hard."

Aethelstan grunted. His eyes shone in the fire, and he said, "The more brave, Edmund, that you came. God send us more such warriors. Let me show you something." He got up, and they walked over along the edge of the down, looking west.

The long low hill sloped away into the valley. From its edge Edmund could see only the rainswept darkness to the west and south. Yet he could hear something, off in the distance. His hair stood on end. In the dark a great mass moved along over there from the west, slipping and sliding along, coughing and breathing, laughing and shouting. It seemed one vast slow flood, louder as it came nearer, under it all a low grumble of thousands of feet.

Even the coming of night did not stop it; it spilled on across the low ground like a tide.

Edmund thought, Maybe this is the end of the world. He had seen Ethelred screaming senselessly and tearing his hair out with his fists. He had seen the land as ruined as a burned-out place. The Danes were cutting the kingdom to pieces. Now this faceless mass rumbling through the dark toward the men on this lonely little hill.

Aethelstan said, quietly, "We cannot let them get by us."

Edmund said, "Can't we strike, then?" He turned toward his brother.

Aethelstan pulled on his beard. "Spread out as they are, if all of us hit them at one place, we can punish them."

"They'll have to stop," Edmund said. "To finish us off."

For a moment Aethelstan was silent. Edmund was still hungry; he turned and looked back at the fire.

"I'm glad you came," Aethelstan said. "You bring me to the sticking point. Good. I'll find you a fresh horse. Come on."

—◦—

In the dark they slipped from the down in files, staying below the skyline. Most on foot, trampling the ground to mud, the Jomsvikings filled the narrow end of the valley. The rain fell steadily and hard. Almost at once, Aethelstan's men came up against the edge of the Viking army and charged them.

Edmund, with a shield, his old sword, and a fresh horse, lunged and struck, and when at the first shock of their charge the tall, axe-swinging men in front of him gave way, he pushed forward. His left arm began to ache. Quickly he lost all sense of where he was. His horse slipped and slithered on the mucky ground. The night was full of screaming, howls, the grunts of men falling. Aethelstan stayed hard by him; they defended each other. Something hacked across his foot.

Aethelstan had said, "Kill a few, and then back up on the down." In the driving rain they hewed and slashed at shapes in the dark, drew back, and charged in at another angle. A stew of bodies banging together. The ground was soggy. His arms were too heavy to lift, and he breathed in sobs. The shouting of men and the screams and neighs of horses sounded all around him. They were surrounded—they could not escape to the down.

A wave of men attacked them, and they wheeled and flailed around them. Edmund's horse dodged under him, and he nearly fell. The shield cracked under a blow that shivered his whole left arm. His hair was plastered to his face. His sword hit something—a tree, a body—and stuck, and he had to wrench it free. He lost the shield. A blow numbed his leg. He had no strength left, just lifting his sword took more than he had, and yet somehow he struggled it up and struck, and struck again.

Aethelstan wheeled and shouted something and Edmund turned with him. The horses were scrambling uphill. A horn blasted behind him. Blind in the rain, he fisted his hand in the horse's mane and let it carry him up. He felt the hoofs under him reach level ground again, and he slid out of his saddle and hit the grass on his back, dazed.

Aethelstan knelt beside him. "Come. Come under cover. We're safe now."

"We're never safe," Edmund mumbled, but he got to his hands and knees and followed him.

CHAPTER FOURTEEN

Raef knew that the war was blazing in the south, close enough to Winchester to draw out his enemy. When all around him in his hall the people slept, he left his body and roamed across the light field. He floated in the dark, part of everything. Going there meant only going to that part of him. Then he sensed the Lady, and he drew himself together into a single point.

The land below him broke. In the valley between the downs, the stream of light splintered, corrupted, boiling, giving up a stench of blood and filth, the music crackling into a jagged edge of shrieks. They were fighting down there. Above it, churning in the dark, was a tower of vile smoke.

He saw her as a hole in the air, a great shapeless maw. From the disintegration of the light field below rose the glimmer of the dead souls. They disappeared into her, like sparks going out. He sailed in at her. She saw him coming and rose to meet him, vast, inchoate, filthy, choked with souls. He rose up above the storm clouds, and she followed, chasing him, trying to surround him.

Frantically he struggled toward open sky. He knew if she encompassed him, she would consume him too. They spun together in a great rising spiral. He dodged her, slipped past, and turned north again, toward Jorvik. She left him and swung wide back toward the battle, a great blurred rip in the darkness.

Separate, he could feel the light field punctured and riven around him. He wondered briefly if this was why it had not rained that summer, because the sky up here was empty.

He wheeled back. He was stronger now; she no longer shattered him. But he could not hurt her, could only deflect her, and that not for long.

This time, though, when he struck at her, she seemed to yield.

It was a trap. When he pursued her, she closed on him, enveloped him.

Black stench surrounded him like a miasma. His eyes burned. He thrust his arms out, trying to find some gap, clawed for anything to hold on to. His mind shuddered. The smoke wrapped around him like a blanket, suffocating. He flung one arm over his head, and his hand slid into a cold so deep that it passed through him like an arrow. She was swallowing him.

With the last of his will he flung himself away, not backward, which seemed impossible, but ahead, which seemed like death.

For a moment he stood in a church full of men, Danes and Saxons both. There in front of them, before the altar, on a draped and cushioned throne, sat a young man he had never seen before with a gold crown on his head.

Almost at once the tidal grip of the field was drawing him backward. He slid back into the open air. She was gone. He hovered in the clear light. Dawn was coming. The battle was over. Then, a moment later, he was opening his eyes, back in his body, in his sleeping bench in his hall.

He lay still, breathing hard. Laissa lay beside him, watching him. Gemma had gone off somewhere else; he could hear her singing with Miru outside the bearskin curtain.

"You went away again," Laissa said. "I never know if you're coming back."

He wiped his face on the tail of his shirt. The reek of the Lady still in his nostrils. He had failed again. He had learned much in Jorvik and he had some strength here, but against her he could not win. Then Laissa got hold of his left hand.

"What happened to you?"

He looked down and saw that half his hand was missing. The edge of his hand was smooth as ordinary skin from the knob of his wrist to the base of his index finger, but the three fingers beyond were gone.

His guts roiled. He remembered the cold, when he thrust that hand out. He thought, That was nearly all of me.

"Where is Gemma?" he said.

She held his hand tight in both of hers. "Miru will feed her. Raef—Raef—" She clutched his hand. "You can't do this anymore. Please. Please. Promise me."

He said, "I have to sleep, Laissa. Let me sleep." He sank back onto the bench and rolled over with his back to the hall.

Yet he could not sleep, wondering what else he might do against the Lady. She was consuming the world, and in the end she would eat him too and everything he loved. He shut his eyes, rigid.

<hr/>

Edmund startled awake, hearing the shouts. "They're coming— they're coming—" He had been sleeping in his boots; all he had to do was seize his sword, and he rushed off toward his brother, at the edge of the down.

The day was breaking. The rain had stopped. Wraiths of mist rose up from the deep crevices of the sides of the down. In the cool, damp air the Danes were rolling up the steep slope of the down toward them, the front edge of a mass of bodies that filled the valley below.

They scrambled along, sometimes on all fours, always upward, clutching branches and brush and shrieking as they came. Aethelstan's little band of men lined the down's height, fighting before the Vikings reached them, hurling down rocks and chunks of dirt and screaming insults. Edmund braced himself, his sword in both hands. The first line of the ongoing round helmets rushed up toward him, and when their heads were even with his feet, he started swinging.

He hit one backward, and another went down; but still they came on. Their eyes were wild and fearless, and they clawed at him. The world narrowed to him and the gaping enemy face before him, and he fought to cleave it away. His blade slashed across an arm, blood spurted up, and when the man reeled back another leaped toward Edmund, an axe cocked in his hand.

Then below a horn blasted. And behind him, someone cheered.

"The fyrd—the fyrd has come—"

The wave of Danes was drawing back. Edmund, panting, stood where he was, wiping his hair back off his face. The slope below him was clear, the men down there rushing off to join the rest. He turned to the north.

He gave a glad yell. Down the wide end of the valley, another army was streaming, a tide of men like a river, and leading them was the great red banner of Alfred, the Dragon of Wessex.

"The fyrd!" Eadric Streona had finally brought the King's army.

The two armies streamed together, their screaming like pipes in the distance. Most of the English were on foot, like the Vikings, but the front lines were mounted men, Eadric Streona's carls. The two armies surged together on the ground between the downs, and the clash of their meeting rose, and at once men were falling and dying.

Edmund sucked in his breath; in the air above the fighting, a dark cloud was gathering, like the smoke above a raging fire. Edmund's sword slipped from his fingers. The men around him stared at him; they saw nothing. He said, "Look, look," but they saw nothing. Lightning crackled through the cloud above the battle, streaking white through its midst. There was no thunder. The cloud rose, shot through with the lightning, towering high as the sun.

Edmund rubbed his eyes, wondering if he dreamed it—if he did not imagine the terrific surge of the battle somehow reflected in the clear blue sky, in this strange titanic storm. Then a wail went up from the other men.

The fyrd was breaking. At the far end of the battle, where the English had not yet even met the Danes, men were turning, were fleeing away, and now with a roar the Danes rushed forward, and the rest of the English army staggered and reeled back and wheeled around and ran.

Aethelstan on his horse galloped along the down, shouting. "Come—help—help them—" He charged off, streaming a line of other men, snatching up their swords and flinging themselves onto horses. Edmund ran to his horse. Aethelstan was far ahead of them now, was leading his men in a rush down the slope. Edmund veered his horse around to catch up with him.

The horse stumbled; he fell off. He kept hold of the reins, and he turned to vault up onto the saddle. Then, beyond, he saw the Danes spill over the rim of the down and rush toward him, and before he could draw a breath, they were on him.

—⊶—

Edmund could barely stand. He had eaten nothing for two days and drunk only ditch water. His hands were bound behind his back. The two Danes dragged him by the arms up to a campfire in the valley, where a tall man with a hooked nose was sitting on a barrel, drinking from a horn.

Edmund had seen this man before at his father's feast in Winchester. This was Thorkel the Tall, chief of the Jomsvikings. A dozen other men stood around him, and a yellow-haired boy, no more than five or six, crouched at his feet. In dansker, the Jomsviking said, "So you are Edmund Aetheling?"

"Yes."

The tall man sipped from his horn, as if he knew that made Edmund's throat tighten, raw. In English, he said, "You father pay?"

"I don't know," Edmund said. "You'll have to ask him."

Thorkel took another pull of the ale. His eyes gleamed with pleasure at Edmund's thirst. He said, "You have pay?"

"I have nothing," Edmund said, "nothing to give to you except a sword in the belly."

Thorkel leered at him. "You talk good. I think you father pay gold for you."

He fetched the boy at his feet a kick and threw him the drinking horn. The boy gave him a black look and took the horn away. Thorkel bellowed, "Einar!"

One of the men behind him came forward, a Dane hardly older than Edmund. Thorkel jabbed his finger at Edmund. "Keep this alive until we come to Sweyn. This is money." The tall man drew a mirthless smile across his lips, his eyes on Edmund. "Talk good, you English. Always lose. Go." Edmund went away, humiliated.

Einar led him off into the camp. On the way they passed the yellow-haired boy. He had just filled Thorkel's cup from a barrel as tall as he was. The way he was standing caught Edmund's eye; the boy turned slightly away, the cup below his waist, and his free hand in his clothes. He was pissing into Thorkel's ale. Repayment for the kick. Repayment maybe for a lot of kicks. Edmund clamped his lips shut to keep from laughing and followed after Einar.

—◦—

In the days following he heard no more talk of ransom. There was little for any of them to eat. It had been a bad summer anyway, and the Danes had trampled and burned the fields as they came. In the days that followed, trudging along, Einar brought him a crust of bread, a handful of beans, a cup to scoop up water from the ground. They had taken off the rope, but Einar was always beside him. The Dane poked and slapped him at first but then left him alone. They talked in stubs of words. "Cold." "Piss." Around them, as they plodded along, the Vikings themselves complained they were hungry.

At night he slept on the ground, and Einar slept beside him, and by morning they were nestled together like puppies. He taught Einar to swear in Saxon, words he had never dared use aloud before. Einar taught him more dansker and found him a cloak.

They walked through a ruined land. After the rainless summer that had doomed the crops, now it was raining every day. The Danish army, scattered in small bands, slogged through it, foraging as they went, Edmund carried along in their midst like spindrift. He held the cup into the rain to catch something to drink and shared it with Einar. He grubbed worms from under rocks, ate leaves. One night Einar brought him a bone with some meat on it that he gnawed on all the next day as they walked.

So, step by step, day by day, they came at last to a great church. The village around it had been burned to the ground. The Jomsvikings threw up a camp on the west side of it; they meant to stay, at least for a while.

Edmund said, "What are they going to do?" He was planning ways to escape, which would be hard, but dying in the effort would be better than dying sitting down. His clothes were stiff with mud, and he had grown some scraggly hairs of a beard.

Einar gave him a withered apple and a bit of cheese and crouched there, watching him eat. Edmund ate the cheese first and then the apple, even the core. Einar said, "I'm supposed to take you in there." He jerked his head toward the big church. "Sweyn is in there. Sweyn Tjugas."

"The King," Edmund said, excited, and the Dane nodded and stood up.

"Yes. You've been ransomed. Let's go."

The great church resounded with noise. Men packed both sides of the nave, mostly sitting on the floor and eating and drinking. In a line down the center three fires burned on the flagstone floor, each with a carcass spitted over it; the smoke wreathed the air above them. The smell of roasting meat filled Edmund's nose and made his mouth water. As they walked along the nave the crowds of men on either side hooted and yelled at him.

"English! Kill him!"

"Stupid baby—learn to fight, baby!"

Edmund felt himself flush. He wanted to wheel on them and charge, but he plodded along after Einar up toward the altar. The Christ still hung on the wall behind it, looking down mildly, as if this were nothing new.

They had dragged the altar out from the wall so that half a dozen men could sit behind it. On the left was Thorkel the Tall. The little yellow-haired boy leaned against the wall behind him. At the very center of the table sat a broad-shouldered man with red-gold hair and a sweeping long, tawny moustache, and Edmund knew this was Sweyn Forkbeard, the King of Denmark.

Einar brought them up before him and bowed stiffly from the waist. Edmund stood straight where he was.

"Edmund Aetheling," Einar said, his voice shrill to clear the uproar around him. "My lord King." He turned to Edmund. "Bow."

Edmund said, in English, "I greet the King of Denmark." He bent his head to the King, as he would to his father.

Sweyn was drinking from a chalice. The bones of his dinner lay scattered before him on the gold-embroidered altar cloth, now patchy with blood and dirt. He set the cup down. He had wide-set, pale blue eyes, and when he smiled he showed his teeth.

He glanced at Thorkel. "You took this little hero? What a feat that must have been; you'll need a drapa."

Edmund had gotten enough dansker from Einar to understand this, and he heated at it; he said, "Some Jomsvikings gone too. I fight." He bit his lip, wondering if he had said what he meant. If he should have said anything.

Sweyn's eyebrows jacked up and down. His mouth turned down humorously under the luxuriant moustache. "Nothing much lost there." He turned back to English. "Aetheling, I will have of you a pledge not to fight against me."

Edmund said, "Lord, I will give you no such pledge."

The other men around the table shifted in their places, exchanged looks, and growled. Thorkel said, "Odin's balls. What a little viper. Just kill him, then, Sweyn. Ethelred will give you the money anyway."

The Danish King's smile did not waver. He said, "Are you such an iron one, then, little prince, to think you can make any difference against me?"

"No," Edmund said. "But I am an Englishman, and I will not swear away my country."

Sweyn's smile flattened. He twisted one long end of his moustache around his forefinger, and he nodded once. "I like your courage. You may look like a sparrow, but I think you are eagle-hearted. All right, iron Edmund, go sit down, and you can leave tomorrow."

Edmund's legs went wobbly with relief. He followed Einar over to the side, and they sat on the floor by the end of the altar. Nobody gave them anything to eat or drink. The roasted sheep on the fires were almost all just hulks of empty bones, anyway, and around the room, roars went up for more, for mead and ale, for blood and fighting. Sweyn's name racketed through the heights of the church in waves of sound, and then on the other side men started to call out Thorkel's name, and for a while the church resounded with waves of chanted names, like some kind of horrible false Mass.

Then up the nave came another ragged prisoner, pushed along by Vikings. Edmund saw him, and his mouth dropped; this was Alphege, the archbishop of Canterbury.

The old man was much changed. He had starved too. Barefoot, limping, he wore a tattered gown and leaned on his staff, but with the curled crozier end broken off. He had been a heavy man. Now his face was hollow, the skin hanging in empty folds below the bones, and the body under his gown looked made of twigs.

He was still fierce. His eyes blazed from the pits of his skull. He came up before Sweyn Forkbeard and banged his staff on the floor.

"You will suffer in hell for this, pagan devil!"

Sweyn glanced from side to side, and his smile came back, all teeth. He said, "Alphege, archbishop of somewhere, devil that I am, I will have a ransom of you."

The churchman banged his staff on the floor again. "I shall not! You pigs have desecrated God's house, and you will burn for it—from me you get nothing more than you have taken by force."

Thorkel muttered, "We have already eaten all of that."

Sweyn said, "A ransom, Alphege, or you die. I have nothing to feed prisoners."

"God will preserve me," the churchman shrieked. "God will send you to the deepest—"

"Preserve you from this," Thorkel shouted, standing up, and threw a bone at him. It was a shin bone, and it hit the archbishop square in the face.

Sweyn put one hand out, as if to stop him. But all over the church the Vikings howled, and they rose. Their arms cocked back and forward, and a hail of bones flew through the air. At first Alphege stood there, the blood running down his face from the first blow, his eyes furious on Sweyn, and the bones pounding down all around him. Bones smashed on the floor, struck his shoulders, his back, his round, bald head. The Vikings pressed closer, to hit him harder, and the bones became a blizzard.

Under the barrage Alphege sank slowly down onto his knees. Edmund gasped and started up, but Einar held him where he was. The archbishop crumpled to the floor. Around him on the flagstones a pool of blood widened. The bones heaped up around him. The skin of his bald head split, and streams of blood spilled down his face and cheeks. His torn robe was sodden with it. He folded forward, his mouth open, his eyes glazing.

Sweyn said something, harsh, and one of the men behind him vaulted over the table, taking an axe from his belt. The storm of bones dwindled out. The axeman went to the folded form of the churchman, lifted the axe, and cleaved the archbishop's skull with it.

Edmund groaned. Slaves dragged the body away, trailing a smear of blood all down the flagstone floor, through the heaped bones. Edmund put his hands over his eyes, shaking.

⸺∘⸺

In the morning the Danes were leaving in streams, heading for the coast. Einar told Edmund, in dansker, "There's nothing to eat, anyway. What a piss-poor little country this is; I don't know why Sweyn wants it."

"Then leave it," Edmund said. "Leave it to us."

"It's yours," the other boy said. He put his hand on Edmund's arm a moment. Then drew back. "Go." Ahead of them the road wound away over the ruined countryside. Edmund began the long trudge to London, where the King was now.

CHAPTER FIFTEEN

The long summer came to an end, and there was no harvest. The ordinary people hunted desperately through the brakes and wild places for hares and squirrels, nuts and berries, roots and mushrooms, and moss and lichen. The stormy weather raised the rivers and washed out bridges and towns. The Danes went away, since there was nothing left to steal.

Aethelstan said, "I cannot see my way in this. The kingdom is desperate, and someone must rule; but my father lives and is often times easy of mind."

Edmund sat opposite him. They had come into a tavern in Winchester, the day blowing a cold, snowy gale, and there were not many folk around. "When our father is easy of mind, he is still often cruel as an ogre."

"This is not a fit charge against a king," Aethelstan said, "who has such enemies as ours. Against the Danes, cruelty is only justice. You yourself suffered so at their hands. I hate them for it, how they treated you."

His face was riven with lines, his cheeks sunken, so he looked much older. Slowly he looked around the room and then returned his gaze to Edmund.

"And what they did to the old archbishop. How they have destroyed the kingdom. But from this hate to seizing the crown myself—that is a step longer than I can take. My father lives. My father is true King, Alfred's heir, God's champion in England."

There was a little silence. Edmund could see how this ate at Aethelstan, and he was sorry he had brought it up again, as doubtless everybody did. Finally his brother turned to him and said, "What would you do?"

Edmund said, "I have seen you do all a king should do,

when our father does none of it. To me you are the King of the English."

"Ah," Aethelstan said, looking away, "you are a child."

"So was our Lord when he spoke to the priests," Edmund said.

"I cannot decide," Aethelstan said, with a shake of his head. "It is too much for me. God keep you, Edmund. God keep you from this." He got up and went away.

⟶⟵

Edmund went out to make water in the evening, and Eadric Streona came up just beside him, as if he had been waiting for him. The Saxon said, "Let us not mince words here. I know you are inciting the prince Aethelstan against the King. Come to the King and denounce Aethelstan, and he will hear nothing of your own treasons."

Edmund turned, abruptly, his cock in his hand, and scattered piss all over Streona's shoes. "Like that," he said, and went away, pulling his clothes together.

The next day in the crowded church, someone struck at him with a knife. Edmund lost the man almost at once in the crowd, but the blade slit a long gash in his cloak.

The King still had some Normans around him. Edmund's eyes fell on their mail coats. Few Saxons wore them. Made of iron links sewn onto leather, they were heavy and awkward and made moving around hard sometimes. But he saw their value, and he went into London, to the armory there, and had one made for him.

⟶⟵

Ethelred threw his hands up. To Streona, he said, "Who can I trust, then, if not my own blood? No one!"

"My lord," Streona said, "while there are many who favor Aethelstan over you, I myself have never—"

"My own fyrd runs from the Danes," Ethelred cried. "My own son and heir plots to steal my crown! This truly is the wolf time."

Streona said, "Sir, there is an army ready to hand, who will be loyal only to you."

Ethelred wheeled. He had become much fatter, since the haunting began, as if the only comfort he could find was to eat. As if he could put a barrier of lard between the ghost and him. His cheeks were shiny and red above his curly beard. He said, "Not English, I assure you."

"No, sir," Streona said. He smiled, nodding, easing the King along into this. "These men are not English."

———⊰⊱———

"My dear one. My darling." Ethelred kissed her and took her plump white hands in his. "Mother of my true sons." He kissed her again.

Emma smiled; the Lady recoiled from him. Ethelred was chafing more and more on her. He had realized her presence kept the ghost away, and he stayed by her, day and night, insisting she sleep in the same bed, even when she complained of his snoring and thrashing. There were armed guards on all the doors. If she lay down to sleep, he lay down beside her; he woke her every few moments, starting awake, and groaning.

She could not go abroad, then, since if he found her un-tenanted body, there was no telling what he might do, especially if the ghost happened to be there. He could kill her or enough of her to make it impossible to keep on. She could distill herself into some other creature and so slip away—a fly or a bird or even a wolf, just as she had that one time—but she had noticed that most animals were even stupider than human beings, harder to manage and easily distracted. And she could not consume souls when she was in such a state, only kill, and that slowly.

It mattered little now, because after the bloody war she was replete with souls, but it annoyed her to be constrained. She began to think she might replace him. Her eye fell on Streona, who was no better. But there would be one, somewhere. She began to winnow out the possibilities, looking for the ripe kernel.

—⟨⟩—

The King pushed at the food before him. "Is there no meat in all England?"

The Queen said, "I have heard, in Jorvik, there is food aplenty."

"Jorvik." Ethelred swept that away with a wave of his hand. "There can be nothing left of Jorvik."

The Queen was silent. She knew how much there was in Jorvik, and it gnawed at her.

She had nearly devoured him once in the battle over the downs. He still had not realized that attacking her like that only made her stronger. She would take him, one time soon, and then she would have no rival anywhere in this world. She put him out of her thoughts, laying her mind instead on Aethelstan.

The Aetheling sat down the table from her, among his friends, noisy and good humored, heedlessly handsome, just the sort Emma loved, with his flowing blond hair. Like all the Saxon lords he wore his hair long, well combed, shining. She did not look at him. He would be a beautiful king, if nothing else. And he was brave, had fought hard, barely escaping, in the battle on the downs.

A page had come in and stood shifting from foot to foot, waiting for the King to beckon him forward. The Queen lowered her eyes. This was probably another of Ethelred's connivances.

He was always trying to work some little scheme, kill somebody else, steal somebody else's land. They made her angry, all these men, weaving their spidery little plots.

The urge burned in her, never quite gone now, to pack her many souls together and explode them all. She throttled it. That meant giving up everything just for a moment's unparalleled glut. She was not ready yet for that.

Ethelred said, quietly, "Wait here."

She clutched his arm. "Where are you going?" Trying to sound fretful.

"Just stay here, where I can find you at once. I have someone to meet." He kissed her and went off.

The Queen turned, looking around. With him gone she felt suddenly much larger, easier. She told herself to be patient until the war started again. For a while now she should go by sideways moves, by indirections. That meant showing them only silly, man-loving Emma.

One day she would repay them all for her humiliations, for the shrieks of the men who galloped on her flesh, the groans of labor that issued forth slick, greasy babies, the insults of womanhood among those who believed themselves made in the image of gods. Already she had much of southern England sinking. When she had taken enough, the whole kingdom would collapse, giving her more room, more reach. She smiled, thinking of it. Her gaze slid sideways, toward Aethelstan, and she caught him looking at her. She gave the smile to him.

He turned away. Handsome, brave, but innocent. Innocence was not so much what she desired.

Another innocent, his brother Edmund, sat beside him, thin as a lathe.

"So, Edmund," she called. "I heard you were a gallant knight in the battle lost." She giggled, Emma's giggle, and reached for the wine. It was fun to tease Edmund, who still blushed like a baby. "If you fought so well, why did you get captured?" His brother frowned at her. She lifted the cup again, drinking.

The Jomsviking chief Thorkel the Tall drummed his fingers impatiently on the table; he had been waiting in this cramped little room a while now, and he was a restless man by nature. He reached for the cup of ale, bitter and watery. The bread they had brought him too was coarse and poor, and there was not much of it.

Yet this was the King's own hall. The Danes had devastated England, this time perhaps too well: Sweyn had said he would not strike again until he could live off the country, and that might take years. Thorkel tapped his fingertips on the table. He needed a war to keep his men, crew his ships, push the power of the Jomsvikings into every court. Sweyn, though, had forbidden him to raid in Norway or Denmark, and east of there was nothing worth the taking. Iceland was too far, and it was poor anyway. There was Ireland, but the Irish King was throwing out the Danes. There was Orkney, but its great Jarl protected it.

The door opened, and the man he was waiting for came in.

He was alone. Thorkel stood, startled, having expected Eadric Streona again. Instead, here before him, pulling out the bench and sitting, was the King of the English himself.

Ethelred looked well fed, when his people starved. A belt of fine braided gold circled his large belly; the gold crown sat on his long, thinning hair. He settled himself on the bench, glanced quickly around the room, and said, "I am glad you have come, Thorkel. I greet you as a master warrior, chief of the Jomsvikings, a king of the sea."

His voice was too quick, his words brittle, as if he was in a haste to get through this. He gave another quick glance around the room. Thorkel said, "I greet the King of the English." I have beaten you, he thought, and you might as well admit it. He thought, I'm as good a king as you.

Ethelred was hurrying on. "Hear what I have to say to you, lord of the Jomsburg, and you will be a rich man."

Thorkel said nothing. He needed money—he always needed money—and the English King was rich. But he had something else in mind for a reward.

The King laid his hands on his belt. "My son plots against me. He is well loved among the people, and I need an army that will fight him in my name. Give me your pledge, that you and your men will come into my service when I need you, and I will pay you twenty thousand pounds of silver."

Thorkel said, slowly, "You are a generous man, my lord." He smiled.

"Is it then an agreement?" Ethelred said. "I would have you come next summer, or perhaps the summer after. When the fighting begins. By then I should know much more about Aethelstan's designs."

Thorkel said, "You think the famine will be over by next summer?"

Ethelred tossed one hand in the air. "There is no famine for kings."

Thorkel nodded, trying to look as if he were weighing this in his mind, although he had long since decided. Yet if there were no famine for kings, there was certainly hunger for their armies, and he had to make sure he could keep his men here. "How strong is Aethelstan?"

"Bah. You saw yourself, in the last war: He has no heart for a good fight. You will mow him down like a scythe."

Thorkel remembered the fighting somewhat differently than this. Aethelstan, he thought, had given the Jomsvikings the worst of it for a while in among the downs to the west. He said, "Who are his friends?"

"Morcar of the Five Burhs. Sigeferth. I don't know if

Thurbrand of Lindsey will join him. Uhtred of Bamburgh, damn him, who failed me this last time. Perhaps a few others."

"What about Jorvik?"

Ethelred's whole body moved, pushing this aside. "I said Uhtred. There is no more Jorvik." His face paled. He glanced around the room again; Thorkel wondered what he was looking for.

Thorkel said, "I have forty ships. All my men are great warriors, each one worth two ordinary men."

"Good." Ethelred smiled, stiff cheeked. He was already starting to get up. "Then it is agreed."

"Agreed," Thorkel said, and put his hand out.

Fighting for Ethelred, he could keep his men here. And he had heard the opposite of what the King told him: that Aethelstan could not bring himself to rebel. It would be easy work, then, especially if Sweyn was not coming back.

On the other hand, if Sweyn came back, they might be on opposite sides.

He cleared his throat. At least he could take this chance to rid himself of one long-standing annoyance. "I will serve you, but there is something I must do first. And in the summer I will come with forty ships." He put out his hand and clasped Ethelred's.

—⚓—

After sunrise the tide ran up the Humber, and the Jomsviking dragon left the shore. The crew had spent the night carousing in the tavern at Brough, and the men settled slowly to the work. Finally they were rowing westward along the river Ouse. The broad Humber fell into the distance behind them. Soon the big dragon glided through the channel called Uhtred's Ditch. The lift and swing of the oars and the warble of the water past the dragon's hull were like songs to the yellow-haired boy sitting in the sterncastle behind Thorkel, who was steering.

The boy had spent his life on ships or in camps—not a long life, but ever since he could remember. Ever since he could remember, he had hated Thorkel. Now he bit his lips and kept his mind fixed on hating Thorkel to keep from crying.

The pilot was also in the stern, an old man they had taken on board back at Brough. He sat on a bench with his arms folded over his chest and said, "Now steerboard," or "now backboard," here and there.

Thorkel leaned on the tiller bar. He said, "Is it true this is wizard country?"

The pilot gave him a wide-eyed look. He said, "I am native to this place, sir. I must live here. I know only what I must."

Thorkel said, "I have heard, in Jorvik, you can trust nothing. No one. Nothing will be as it seems." The tall man turned his hook-nosed face back toward the boy in the stern. He smiled, which made the boy cold. He had seen Thorkel smile so just before he beat the boy half-dead with a truncheon.

The pilot said, "Jorvik is as it has always been. Mind, the river is a little different." He got up abruptly and went forward, talking to the oarsmen.

Thorkel laughed. "Well, let's see what we find." He glanced at the boy again. "In any case, I'll be rid of one problem. Hunh. Hah? Knut! Will you be glad to be rid of me?"

The boy could not speak. Around him, gliding by, was ordinary countryside, some trees, broad meadows, sheep. The oarsmen stroked north. Ahead of them, somewhere, lay Jorvik, where he would be abandoned.

⚍

Raef sat under the oak tree, where he gave the law now, and heard people's complaints and arguments. Goda and some other men of Jorvik who cared to gave him counsel on this. On the day that Thorkel came, he was listening to the sheepmen complain that they paid too much tax to him. They paid very little, but they liked to complain, and he listened, which was all they really wanted anyway.

While they argued and wheedled, trying six different ways of saying the same thing, he watched the Jomsvikings walk up from the river. There were five men and the tall, scrawny yellow-headed boy who was their purpose here. In the lead was Thorkel the Tall. Raef folded his arms over his chest.

The Jomsviking came up before the oak tree, and the massed townspeople saw him and fell still, abashed. Thorkel looked around him and faced Raef.

"I have heard there is nothing left of Jorvik, but I see that is not the case."

"Whoever told you that is misled," Raef said. "Come into my hall, where we can talk."

He led them along the flagged path to his hall. Thorkel and his men came after him.

When they went inside, all the people there turned to see them. Leif was sitting by the fire with Gemma on his knee, playing some game with her, and down at the far end Laissa sat at her loom with Miru and Edith and another widow who had come to live there with her children. Raef's other carls were lounging around by the high seat drinking the ale, and with a jerk of his head Raef sent them off down the hall. He climbed up the step to the high seat and sat.

Thorkel stood facing him, the table between them, and his men all gawking around them. The jug was on the table, with a cup, and Raef waved his hand at it.

"Drink. You must be thirsty."

Thorkel was staring at him, unblinking. He gestured, and the boy came up and filled the cup from the jug and brought it to him. Thorkel took a long drink of it.

His eyes widened. He passed the cup to his men. "Such ale as this I have not tasted in a long while."

"Nor will you again, save here," Raef said mildly. "Drink all you wish; there is plenty of it."

The boy took the empty cup and filled it again, and it went around again, was filled again, and went around. The boy looked suspiciously at the jug, but Thorkel never stopped staring at Raef.

"We have crossed paths before."

"That is true. A long time ago," Raef said.

"Yes. I remember that. When I saw you last you had two ears."

Raef shrugged. "A man can hear as well with one as two, I suppose."

"And ten fingers."

"Eight are as good as ten."

"You are right, it was years ago. You were on a ship in the fleet my brother Sigvaldi led against Jarl Hakon, in Hjorunga Bay."

"Yes. The last I saw of you was your back, running away, and leaving the rest of us to Hakon's mercy."

Thorkel jerked his head back, annoyed at that. "Well," he said, "you are here now, and the story of that is told in every camp and hall in the world, although usually your brother is the hero."

"Conn Corbansson was the hero. Come to your business, I have much to do."

Thorkel shrugged, as much with his eyebrows as his shoulders. He said, "Well, I have come here to give you something. This you may find useful or not."

Raef already knew what he intended, but he said only, "I am listening."

"I have given my pledge and the pledge of the Jomsvikings to King Ethelred, and in the coming summer, or maybe the next, we will go into his service."

"Well," said Raef mildly, "this is a turn." Leif had sauntered up the hall and stood there to one side, watching with keen eyes.

"Fate is full of turns. Yet this puts me in somewhat of a difficult position," Thorkel said. "Since it may come of this that I must fight Sweyn Tjugas."

Raef scratched his beard. His gaze flickered toward the boy, standing there with his head hanging, his hair tangled, his face grimy. "I have no problem with Sweyn Tjugas, either for or against." On the other side of the hall, Laissa had drawn closer to listen.

"I'm glad to hear that," Thorkel said, and smiled. "Since I have stood foster father to his second son here. Therefore I am giving him to you, to get him out of the way, in case."

He put his hand on the boy's shoulder and pushed him forward. "There, Knut. I hope you find this place more to your liking than mine."

The boy mumbled something. Thorkel cuffed him again. "And perhaps learn some better manners while you're here, brat."

The boy snarled at him. Raef said, "Well, I accept, then." He was smiling at the boy, who refused to meet his eyes and kicked the straw and hunched his shoulders. "And in return I will give you two pieces of advice, Thorkel."

"Ah," Thorkel said, startled.

"The first," Raef said, "is that you stay as far as you can from the Queen of the English."

"The Queen," Thorkel said. "I have no interest in her."

"Good. Take none."

"What else, then?"

Raef said, "That you have until the sun goes down to get beyond my reach."

Thorkel's head jerked up, and his men stirred, looking with a sudden apprehension around them. The Jomsviking snorted. "I do not see you bear a sword or an axe or any weapon."

"Thorkel." Raef swiveled his gaze toward him. "You know nothing."

"Maybe. In any case I shall be gone." Thorkel reached out and smacked the boy again. "This should be interesting, Knut. Greet your new father." He strode away, out of the hall, and his men followed him, leaving the boy Knut behind.

Raef said, "Well, then, Knut Sweynsson. Welcome to my hall."

The boy looked up. He was only half-grown, and his hands and feet were too big and his neck too long, and his ears stuck out of the uncurried mane of his hair. He said, "I will not be welcome. I don't want to be here. I hate Thorkel for betraying my father, and I hate you too." Then he burst into tears.

———

Laissa said, "That is an insult, isn't it? Getting you to foster someone else's child?"

Raef was watching the boy walk away. Leif had collected him, was taking him around the hall, showing him his place there. Outside, in the city, the older Jomsvikings were all hurrying down to their ship. He had it in mind to topple a tree on them if they didn't get down the river fast enough.

He said, "Oh, he's a good boy."

Laissa grunted. "He's a nasty, bad-mannered cur—you can see that just in the way he walks." She turned back away from Raef to go to her loom again.

He followed her. She took a great pleasure in this work, in weaving together the separate strands, and he loved to watch her do it. She said, over her shoulder, "We'll see how he repays you for your kindness in taking him in." She sat down at the weaving and picked up her shuttle.

Raef fingered the stray hairs at the nape of her neck, his

gaze going to the boy, who sat by the fire, and he could not keep from smiling. He knew what Thorkel had so carelessly cast aside. He had seen this boy before, on the occasion when he lost his fingers, older by a good ten years, with Danes and Saxons all giving him homage and the crown of England on his head.

Against his will, Knut liked the hall. There were only a few people, it was warm, and it smelled good, unlike the great hall in the Jomsburg. The one end particularly was very light. He looked up and saw beams and thatch, but it was very sunny here. There were women here, and there had been none allowed in the Jomsburg.

He remembered what Thorkel had said, on the way, that the place was bewitched, and how the pilot had refused even to talk about it. Trust nothing, he thought. Believe nobody.

The fat old man showed him where to sleep, which was a fine, wide bench all to himself with a bearskin on it, and then the fat man brought him over to the fire and got him some bread and meat and another cup of the ale. The fat man's name was Leif. He told the boy some of the other people's names, but then the wizard at the other end was calling and Leif went away.

The boy sat chewing the bread and thinking about the ale. He wondered if it would put him under the wizard's spell to drink his ale, but in a moment he had found several reasons why that was probably not so and drunk a lot. A man came by him to put wood on the fire, and two women began to unhook the spit from the uprights. There were little children, who were playing a game down by the looms, and more women weaving, but he saw no warriors.

That surprised him, and he looked around more carefully. There were signs of other men—likely they were all gone now, like the king and his fat old friend—but there were not many of them. There were no weapons lying around, no shields or war chests. Neither the King nor his fat friend had worn any gold.

A little girl, not even a year old, watched Knut curiously from the other side of the fire. She smiled at him. He found himself smiling at her, but then a woman called "Gemma," and the baby turned away.

The woman gave Knut a harsh look. She was the slender, fair-haired woman who had come up beside the wizard-king: his wife, Knut supposed. She wore no crown nor coif, her yellow hair gathered up on her head in a twist of wool.

It struck him that Raef was no king at all. Thorkel had dumped him into the care of a lowborn carl with no warriors and no gold. Knut was the son of a king. That meant he did not have to obey Raef or heed him or ever call him father. That settled him. He knew his place here now. He went down to the fire to get something else to eat.

CHAPTER SIXTEEN

WINCHESTER. SOME YEARS LATER.

The white nuns had their house on the edge of Winchester. Emma went there in the spring; she had brought many more girls to take the veil. She sat watching as the long white row of women walked away, and she smiled.

The abbot came to her, bubbling her praises for giving all these brides to Christ. Emma bowed her head modestly. She wanted to rid herself also of her sons; they were growing older, unpleasantly close to her. She would get Ethelred to send them into Normandy, on pretext of educating them. She kneeled before the abbot, her hands together, to be blessed for all she had done for them.

⸺

Aethelstan sat on the long table, at an angle to the high seat. He hardly ate, his spirits low. The word had come that morning that the high reeve of Dorset had been murdered and his body dumped into a pigsty.

Everybody knew who had done this. Yet up there at the front table his father laughed full throated, his face red, and stuffed himself with meat, and around him his friends laughed too. Emma sat beside him, the wall behind her white with her women, and next to her, her older son Edward.

Edward was only seven, and he did not laugh. He was pinching bits of bread into shapes and standing them on the table. Aethelstan had made such armies when he was small and captive at his parents' feasts. Ethelred had brought Edward to court only the last winter, and the child was witnessing charters already. Ethelred meant to make Edward King after him. It was said now the boy was going to Normandy, in his father's name, and the duke, his uncle, was preparing for a royal visit.

Aethelstan saw this, and he knew that he had missed his chance to stop it. Hemming and hawing over his honor, he had let his honor dwindle away to nothing. Thorkel the Tall, who only a few years before had been burning England, now sat at the far table, already drunk; Thorkel's men stood all around the King, and he kept an army around London. He had raided all over East Anglia and Kent; it was said a dozen villages paid him tribute.

Whatever he got, it was thin on the hoof. There was no war, had been no war for years now; there was nothing to pillage or even to eat. Aethelstan himself had ridden around Wessex in the past year and seen the empty fields, the abandoned huts and villages. The wars had brought the famine; the famine had brought plagues. People were eating dirt while the Jomsvikings and his father and Eadric Streona chomped through heavy joints of meat.

He wondered if it were pork. His belly rolled over.

Beside Ethelred in the high seat, Emma was watching him, a strange little smile on her face. She had been more friendly to him lately. He thought maybe she was tired of Ethelred, who would not let her out of reach since he had discovered that she kept the ghost away. She turned and spoke to Ethelred again, leaning on him, a dumpy woman past her youth who had never been pretty. The King drained his cup and called for another. Aethelstan thought, I should have been a monk.

He should have been King, as Edmund said, and saved his kingdom. He was as guilty as the men carousing at the high table. He got up, eaten with remorse, and went before his father to take his leave. As he bowed, he saw in front of little Edward a whole host of bread people.

They were not soldiers, Aethelstan saw, surprised: They were priests, with mitres and crosses. In the middle was a little crucifixion.

His father was so drunk his eyes seemed to cross; he shouted, "Go on, Aethelstan, go to bed like the old woman you are." He roared with laughter, and along his table Thorkel laughed, and Streona. Aethelstan turned on his heels and walked out.

He went through the hall to the wide square between it and the church. The sun was going down, and a chilly wind blew in from the north. He went into the church a moment, but he could not pray. God would not forgive him for his failures.

As he left, a soft voice said his name, just inside the big carved doors of the church.

He turned, startled. It was Queen Emma, alone, her eyes shining, smiling at him. He realized she had gotten Ethelred drunk on purpose so she could get away.

He stood where he was. She held her hand out to him, the plump white palm soft and greedy. Her voice was a breathy whisper. She said, "Aethelstan, every man in England wishes you were King. I also. Please. Hear me. I have dreamed that I will lie in your arms one day." Her hand grasped at him, the fingers curling. "Whenever I see you, I want you, Aethelstan. Come to me, and you will be King."

He listened to her, gravely courteous in the face of this monstrous offer, and then he turned without a word and went away.

He started through the big double doors; behind him she gave a shriek that turned his blood to ice. He turned around. She was flying at him, furious, and for an instant he saw Emma and around her—a trick of the shadows—something else, huge and shapeless, fanged and dark. She clawed at his face with her nails, spat at him, and turned and hurried off into the shadows.

He put his hand to his cheek. Just a scratch. He struggled

with a sudden clammy fear. Just a harmless, stupid, greedy woman, willing to betray anybody. He went off to his house, down by the river.

⸺⊹⸺

Edmund muttered, "My God," under his breath.

Aethelstan laughed, or gasped something like a laugh. "Not as you remember me, ah." He lay still, panting. There was only one candle in the room, but even in the dark, he was horrible. His hair had fallen out and his beard. He lay on his back on the bed, naked, his flesh mostly gone and his body covered with sores, like holes poked through the skin with an awl, red and oozing and stinking. Thin blood dribbled from his nose, from the corners of his eyes.

Edmund had last seen him only a month before, when they had hunted together south of Winchester. Aethelstan had been hale then, strong and young and handsome. They had come on a boar, and Aethelstan had brought it down by himself with only a spear. When Edmund had heard he was sick, he had not believed it could be serious.

He said, "What happened?" He reached out as if to touch his brother's cheek, and Aethelstan shrank from him.

"Just a scratch. No, no, please, it hurts—" He began to cough. Red foam formed at corners of his lips. "God, have mercy on me, for I am a sinner—Edmund," he said, "you were right." He coughed.

Beyond the bed, the old servant said quietly, "My lord, don't make him too tired." In his hand a basin, a bloody cloth. He had been bathing his master, in spite of the prince's objections.

"No," Aethelstan said. "Tired. I am dying. Pray God take me safe away and not give me to the monsters." His head rolled toward Edmund, his eyes gleaming alive in the leprous mask of his face. "Edmund. You must go on. You must stand against the King, save England. You are . . ." He coughed. "Watch out for the Queen."

"Me," Edmund said, startled. He groped for his brother's bloody, bony hand. He began to weep. "Aethelstan."

"You must be King now," Aethelstan said. "I am leaving you the sword, and you must take it up. Be wiser than me. Take the kingdom. Save England from Ethelred."

"Aethelstan. Don't give up." He thought, suddenly, that his father had at last done away with his own son too.

Or the Queen. He wondered what monsters Aethelstan meant.

Aethelstan was charging him to the highest cause. He wondered if he were able. He had to be, he thought. For Aethelstan's sake.

"I am almost done," Aethelstan said, and his fingers tightened. "Pray for me. I waited . . . until you . . ." He began to cough again, and then was choking, his fingers stiff. "Had to . . . see . . ." He hacked up a gout of black clotted blood. Blood covered his face, seeping from his eyes, from his nose, oozing now out of his ears. After a moment Edmund realized that he was dead.

Edmund sat there a long while, holding onto Aethelstan's hand. He did not want to let go until he understood perfectly what lay ahead of him.

He had not been idle in the last few years. He wore the mail shirt whenever he went out; he had grown used to the weight. He had learned to fight. He had a good company, now, more than twenty men, and he had trained them, running down outlaws, riding with Morcar in the thegn's incessant border war with Thurbrand the Hold of Lindsey, raiding Thorkel's Jomsviking outposts in East Anglia.

He thought of his father as he had last seen him, drunken and slack, and of the greedy, scheming Queen. He remembered the Vikings jeering at him. "English. Always lose." More than anything, he wanted to redeem his kingdom's honor.

He should start with Morcar, who would surely come to his side. Gather more of the great men, each with his piece of the kingdom. He could stitch it whole again; he knew who his enemies were, and he did not fear them. He went out into the next room and told them that Aethelstan was dead, and finally he wept.

The word of Aethelstan's death spread slowly, and Raef did not hear it for over a month, until he went down on the Humber to meet with Thurbrand Hold of Lindsey.

Lindsey was the country south of the Humber and east of the Trent. Most of the people were half Danes, and they spoke dansker and favored the Danes in the wars. Their lord, Thurbrand, had hair like copper wool and too many teeth in his mouth. He picked fights with everybody, but his worst enemy was the Saxon Uhtred of Bamburgh. Jorvik lay between them, and Raef did not suffer them to reach across it. Uhtred had tried once to sneak his green jackets down to attack Thurbrand, but he would not do that again. Thurbrand was constantly wheedling Raef to join him in a war against Uhtred, but he was smart enough not to try to step north of the Humber.

Every year he and Raef met in boats in the middle of the estuary, the neutral ground between them, to talk over such matters as salvage and piracy. This time, as soon as the boats closed gunwale to gunwale, Thurbrand said, "You have heard that Aethelstan is dead."

Raef said, "I had not heard." He had seen it as soon as he saw Thurbrand close enough to read him, the prince's death being uppermost in the half Dane's shallow mind. He knew at once who had killed the Aetheling, although Thurbrand did not.

The half Dane talked about wasting disease and rebellions. Uneasy, Raef wondered if the Lady had lost her patience with Aethelstan, who would not start a war. She had been quiet a long time. He had been lulled, and he had gotten nowhere in learning how to fight her.

Thurbrand fixed him with a taut look. "I say we throw Ethelred out. Call in Sweyn Tjugas to be King."

"That's a good idea," Raef said. "Since he's coming anyway." He glanced toward Brough, on the north shore, where Leif and Sweyn's younger son were waiting for him. The boat was drifting, and he steadied it with a stroke of the oars. What Thurbrand had said about Sweyn interested him, the more because he had already heard it, in almost the same words, from Uhtred of Bamburgh, a few months before. Of course if Thurbrand had anything to do with it, Uhtred wouldn't, but still, it was interesting.

"Have you mentioned this to anybody else?"

Thurbrand cracked his knuckles. His eyes were always moving, as befit a man with so many enemies. Raef said, "Morcar, for instance?"

The redheaded half Dane snorted a laugh. "I don't talk to Morcar." He stressed the word *talk*.

Raef said, "As long as everybody in England hates everybody else in England, you could call down Jesus Christ himself and nobody would notice." But Sweyn, he thought, that would solve a lot of problems. Sweyn kept the peace very well in his own country. Sweyn was England's biggest threat anyway.

He brought his mind back to this meeting. He said, "In the meantime you keep your hands off my ships."

Thurbrand grunted at him. "If a ship sinks on my shore—"

"You towed that ship there. You're lucky I didn't burn the whole village."

"Hey," Thurbrand said. "I had nothing to do—"

"If it happens again, I'll burn out the whole place, Thur-brand. And who knows if I'll stop there."

Thurbrand glowered at him. Fear made his eyes shiny. Fi-nally, he said, "What about Sweyn?"

"Do what you want," Raef said, and lifted the oars; they had drifted far down the Humber, talking, and he turned the boat and rowed back upstream toward Brough.

Brough, which lived on the upriver trade, was a tiny village, and Knut Sweynsson had walked the length of it, bored, until he came to the meadow behind the tavern. There, half a dozen boys were kicking around a leather-covered ball, and he stood and watched a while. Leif was back in the tavern getting drunk. Raef was off doing some tiresome chore he thought meant he was really a king. Knut watched the ball bounce around the meadow, and then one of the boys called, "Want to play?"

He hopped up and down a little, eager, but he was the son of a king, and these were churls. The big boy who had spoken kicked the ball toward him.

"Come on, play. You're Jorvik's boy, right?"

"No," Knut said, but he kicked the ball, which went surpris-ingly far, and then chased it. It was a hard game, all footwork, beating the others to the ball or worming it free of a dozen legs, knocking it out to the open so they could chase it again. He and the big boy, Tomlin, stood over the ball kicking each other's shins; Tomlin backed away from the blows, and Knut blasted the ball out toward the tavern.

Leif was sitting there against the back wall of the tavern in the sun, watching. Knut burrowed into a pack of trampling boys and nudged the ball loose again.

After a while Tomlin called out, and the boys all stopped to catch their breath. The big boy came over toward Knut. His shins were turning black and blue, and his eyes had a bad glint.

"If you're not Jorvik's boy, then, who are you? You came here with him."

Knut said, "I am the son of the King of Denmark."

Tomlin guffawed. "Did you hear that? What a liar!"

The other boys roared, agreeing with him. They did not believe him. He started to insist, but they began kicking the ball again, and this time they were all kicking it at him. He jumped at Tomlin, and the ball struck him full in the stomach and knocked him flat, breathless.

A moment later Leif was in among them, and the other boys were backing quickly away. Knut was still struggling for breath. Grabbing him by the arm, Leif got him up on his feet and pulled him back toward the tavern.

"Liar," Tomlin called, after him.

Knut twisted, trying to get free and go after Tomlin, but Leif kept a good grip on him and made him sit down.

"You have to know when to fight, boy. Look how many they are, and all bigger than you. And over what?"

The boys had gone back to their game, moving a little farther out on the meadow. Raef came around the corner.

"What's going on?"

Knut hunched down on the bench. His belly hurt where the ball had struck him. Worse was Tomlin calling him a liar. "You stay out of this," he said, and darted one hand toward Leif's belt, where his axe hung. He lifted it neatly out of the slings before the fat man even turned and lunged up off the bench, starting toward Tomlin.

Raef got him by the back of the shirt with one hand, and with the other took away the axe. "Oh, no, you don't."

Down there, the boys had stopped playing, were watching this. Knut said, between clenched teeth, "They insulted me. I'm the son of a King. I have my honor. Even if you don't."

Raef held the axe out to Leif. His other hand let go of Knut's shirt. He said, "I have my law."

"Yes," Knut said, with a fine sneer. "I like my way—"

Raef fixed his blue gaze on him, and the words stopped like a plug in Knut's throat. For an instant he could not draw breath, nor could he move. Raef said, "You know, you talk too much." He stared at Knut a moment, and the boy stared back, fighting to get a word through his throat. His body loosened, but nothing came out of his mouth. Finally he looked away, giving up. Know when to fight. Raef pushed him hard toward the tavern. "Go in and pack; we're leaving."

The boy coughed up a great gout of phlegm and spat it aside. He trudged into the tavern. Tomlin had done the crime, but as usual he was being punished. He hated Raef.

⸺◦⸺

They had come down the river in an old double-ender and went back the same way; Raef steered them neatly through the snags and bends while the other two rowed. They fished as they went. At sundown they camped, made a fire, and grilled the fish. The moon rose, fat through the trees.

Knut was still brooding over Tomlin, who had escaped his revenge. He wondered if he could get away from Raef and Leif and go back to Brough. At that, he saw Raef glance at him and knew he would have to be careful. He had suspected for a while that Raef knew what he was thinking, which was why he was always ready for him, always ahead of him. Knut would not let this stop him: It just meant he had to be quicker, or better.

Raef turned to the fat man across the fire. "Do you have any new stories, now?"

Leif said, "I always have a new story."

Pleased, Knut folded his legs up and wrapped his arms around them, ready to listen. He liked the fat Icelander, who had taught him to hunt and to throw an axe. He put off thinking about running away. Leif went through the good old familiar tales, about Ragnar Ludbrok and Thorfinn Skullsplitter, Harald Fairhair and Hastein's great raid, Arrow Odd and Palnitoki, and Conn Corbansson. Knut loved this. The story poured into his ears as he stared into the fire, and a crackling army rose before him, the fluttering manes of horses, flames of swords, battling the air. At night he dreamed of fighting, but in the dream he was always carrying a stick, not a real sword.

He had never learned to wield a sword. Leif said he was good with the axe and that he could shoot a bow better than any man in Jorvik. But those were tools, not weapons. He longed to have a sword, with one use only. He thought Raef probably didn't even have a sword. Not a real king; not a real warrior.

Raef gave him a sideways look and turned to Leif. "There's a new story sometime?"

Leif replied with one of Loki and Thor and a giantess, which Knut had never heard, and which got even Raef laughing at the end. Then Leif was back to the far North, the Frost Giants, the demons howling in the wind, and then on to the distant East with its roofs of gold and great heroic deeds. Knut listened until the fire was a bed of dying coals.

"That's the way men should live. Nobody does that anymore."

Raef gave him a long look. To Leif, he said, "Does it make it easier to tell stories when you don't know anything?"

"Oh, definitely," Leif said. He glanced at Knut. "Raef and I, see, we've been all over. Raef has even been to Vinland."

"Vinland," the boy said, startled.

Raef shrugged. "Not exactly Vinland. It's gone forever now anyway." The dark was settling over them. Knut looked up at the sky, at the moon climbing up through the net of the trees. Raef said, "It was Chersonese I loved."

"Not Constantinople?" Leif said.

"Her too. But Chersonese was small, and fine, and we had won her in that bad war, and for a while . . . I thought we could keep her. That was where I realized I didn't want to be somebody else's axeman anymore. But the hawk hadn't caught up with me yet."

The words spiraled away through Knut's mind, making no sense. He said blankly, "The hawk?"

Leif said, "His godmother was a hawk. She's dead now." He was still talking to Raef. "You had that Hun woman then. She was ugly as a horse's ass."

Raef said, "Merike. She was a good woman. Don't tell Laissa I said that. Laissa is certainly a lot prettier." He pulled the edge of his cloak up over his shoulders. "I'm going to sleep. You can tell him more of your fables." He rolled himself into the cloak and lay down to sleep.

"Come on," Leif said. "I need to drain anyway."

Knut got up. He would not easily escape with Leif awake. The old Icelander's stories gripped him like a glimpse into another world. He had heard hundreds of them over the years, but Leif could find new ones every night. They stood by the riverbank and made water.

"What happened to Conn Corbansson?" he asked.

Leif got a vague look on his face. He said, "There's some that will tell you he's dead now, buried in the belly of a mountain. Some say he went on to the East and fights for the desert chieftains there, leads a thousand men, and has a great palace, all of gold, with sixty wives."

Knut liked the second story better. "Why did you leave Iceland?" He straightened his clothes. In the black dome of the night the cloudy torrent of the high road flowed from horizon to horizon. The stars danced.

"Well, hell, boy, why does anybody leave Iceland? The question is, Why does anybody stay in Iceland?" Leif smoothed the tendrils of his moustache back with his thumb. "My father used to whip me every night. One night I turned around and whipped him. Then I left. And never gone back, ever." His eyes strayed toward the camp. "I've done well enough, being Raef's axeman."

Knut didn't see he had much to do. "His godmother was a hawk?"

Leif's eyebrows jacked up and down. "You think this is a common man you're dealing with? His father was a sea wolf. His mother was an Irish shee." An owl hooted, away in the wood, and he tossed his head that way, his gaze never leaving Knut. "That could be her now. They say she can take any form. They say she still watches over him."

Knut snorted. With Leif "they say" usually meant "It sounds good to me." The fat Icelander loved Raef, so he made him great. But the one about how he had escaped his own father rang true. That was the way out, Knut saw, suddenly. He started off to walk around the camp. Leif let him go and went back to the fire, groaning about his old bones, but Knut thought best when he was walking.

⸙

Gemma went to the church with her mother, and Laissa taught her some more prayers. Miru came in with some candles, and they went to put the candles on the shelf.

Gemma kneeled down at the altar. "Mama," she said, "why does Papa not come to church?"

Miru, overhearing, gave a hoot of a laugh. "That I'd like to see."

Laissa said, quickly, "Hush, you two." She gave Gemma a sharp look and explained no further. So Gemma knew it was something bad.

But when they came back, she ran out to meet him, glad to see him. He swung her around him in a sort of dance, as he often did, and kissed her forehead, his eyes already searching behind her. "Where's your mother?" He turned away. But there before her, in his place, Knut was coming up, and he smiled at her, and her heart lifted.

⸺⸺

That night Raef lay down on his bench, his wife and his daughter beside him, and when he knew they were asleep, he left his body and floated up and through the light field.

This was home to him, more and more. He sang with the music and streamed with the light, all the gentle motion trembled in every tiny piece of him. He felt his thoughts go broad and deep; he no longer tried to understand or control what was happening; he was coming more and more to see that understanding was itself a delusion.

The holes were real.

They startled him, whenever he came on one. The light ripped apart and empty, ragged at the edges. Around it the fluid stream continued, but the farther south he flowed the more he swirled and twisted to avoid the gaps. He knew this was the Lady's doing. She had taken the souls that belonged there. The whole light field warped and ripped.

As if they sensed this, everybody in England was afraid. The King feared the ghost, many men feared the King, and everybody else feared whatever was going to happen next. Men heard of Aethelstan's death and shook their heads and crossed themselves. The ordinary folk died of plague, famine, misery, and hopelessness. Thorkel the Jomsviking was supposed to be the King's warlord and had brought his men into the country the summer before, but Thorkel did nothing but pillage the east of the country and feed his men on the King's purse. Nobody expected this to go on much longer.

Raef tried to mend one of the holes in the light field,

pulling at the edges to close it. The holes frightened him. She had made more than he could count of them. There was no music in them and no color. They rippled with a terrible cold.

He could not cover it up. It was forever.

He imagined the holes growing, more and more, until all England plunged down into the abyss, dragging the rest of the light field after.

He could do nothing. When he left the hole behind, it was the same as when he found it, fraying slightly around its edges. Daylight was coming. He slipped away through the blue predawn—past and through the trees alive with murmuring birds; the deer bedding down in the thickets; the villages and farms; the people stirring in their blankets, their sheep shaking the dew off their fleece—back to Jorvik.

For a moment he hovered above the hall. They all still slept. He could see down through the gap he had left in the manifest thatch so that the sky spread over him, down on Laissa, with Gemma next to her, their hair entwined. Across the hall Leif, now married to Edith, snored away like a bagpiper. Nearby lay the king they were nurturing, although this was proving harder than Raef had expected. He imagined them all, everyone he loved, swooped into a hole in the light field and sucked down into nothing, and the pain of thinking it was so bright he went blind a moment. Gratefully he sank down into his body, into the glistening, stinking, beautiful, loud, and impossible transient world.

CHAPTER SEVENTEEN

After Aethelstan was buried, Edmund went looking for Morcar at his stronghold of Lark Hill, near Derby. The thegn was in the middle of a feast to celebrate his brother's marriage, his hall and yard crowded with guests. In the hall the girl sat in her flowery throne, younger than Edmund, with wide, frightened black eyes, and she was shaking so that the dew flew off the blossoms in her hands.

Morcar was out meeting his guests, his long face merry from laughing. When he saw Edmund, the thegn's face fell sad again. He turned his head, looking around at the celebrating people around him, and said, "Come, there are better places to talk."

They walked down from the hall, through the courtyard, and through a gate that led into the garden. The hall stood above a river, and the outer wall ended at its bank. Behind them someone called to Morcar, and he lifted his hand. They went down past the rows of cabbages and onions to the corner of the garden wall, where the rushing of the river just beyond was louder than their talk.

Morcar said, "You wear a warrior's coat to a wedding."

Edmund had forgotten he was wearing the mail coat. He said, "I have good reason."

Morcar said, "I understand. This was ill news about your brother. Aethelstan was a great man; I loved him dearly. I shall miss him dearly."

He turned toward the water. He folded his hands before him like a priest; he rocked back and forth on his heels.

Edmund said, "He should have been a greater man. I am taking up the sword he should have drawn years ago."

Morcar swung back to him. His eyes widened, and his lips

parted. Swiftly he looked in all directions and then turned back to Edmund.

"Ah. Well, of course I am with you." Yet he sounded more startled than glad. His voice smoothed out as he mastered himself. "God, God, I have lived years despairing of hearing that." He thrust out his hand, and Edmund shook it. Then Morcar drilled him with a look, frowning.

Edmund shifted, embarrassed, knowing Morcar compared him with Aethelstan. The thegn said, ruminatively, "But it will be hard. Ethelred has murdered everyone who could stand against him. He has Thorkel the Tall now, with two thousand men, and the most I and my brother can raise is five hundred or so, and those are fyrdmen."

He cleared his throat. Alarmed, Edmund saw he was looking for excuses not to act. The oak had turned into a reed, as the proverb went.

"Hiring Thorkel to keep us down is all the more reason to oppose him," Edmund said. "I am seeking others to join us. I am going up to Thurbrand of Lindsey."

Morcar gathered his breath and then sighed it out again. "Thurbrand," he said. "You fish for allies in a cesspool." His voice changed. "It's said the King has taken Aethelstan's death very hard."

"For God's sake," Edmund said, and shut his eyes. He still dreamed of Aethelstan on the bed, bleeding to death from a thousand sores.

"They say—I have heard this—Ethelred will call a great council to make peace with everybody."

Edmund snorted. "And you believe this?"

Morcar pinched his nose. He was getting old, Edmund realized, his hair greying, his skin wrinkled. He said, "Peace here has made me rich." His dark eyes shifted toward Edmund. "You will not get much from Thurbrand, the treacherous little dog." His face brightened. "My brother has married Bramley and

Tighe, now. Thurbrand will have much less room now to be treacherous in."

Edmund thought, He has grown too long in the tooth for this. The time is past when I could rely on him. He said, "I thought he married a woman." He remembered the girl in the midst of the flowers, the big, dark, terrified eyes, her sleeves all wet with dew.

"Well. The towns are her dowry." Morcar turned, smiling. "And now we shall have justice in England and a good King." He shook Edmund's hand again. "Try Uhtred in Bamburgh and Aelfric in East Anglia. There are a batch of sons too, whose fathers Ethelred killed. Godwine of Wessex is a good one, although he's very young, only fourteen or so. If you get enough support, the King may simply yield."

Edmund doubted that. Morcar wanted anything but to fight. Edmund dreamed that night that Aethelstan's corpse lay before him, and all the sores were little red eyes that watched him.

⸺⧫⸺

The King did call a council to talk of peace, which was to meet at Oxford in the spring, when the weather made traveling easier. He gave his sworn word for the safety of everybody who came. Morcar and his brother Sigeferth went to it, along with a score of other thegns and lords; Sigeferth brought his new wife, Ealdgyth. When they reached Oxford, the first person they saw of any import was Eadric Streona, lord of Mercia.

Streona was smiling all over his face. "This is a great day," he said, "when we who have been enemies will sit down together at peace. The King awaits you even now. He is a different man since the prince died. He wants to greet you himself. Come with me, let me lead you there, rejoicing in our peace."

Morcar glanced at his brother, who was frowning. He said, low, "He gave his word." Their men were following after, and he dropped back to send most of them off with Sigeferth's wife, to Morcar's own house in Oxford, and then went back up behind Streona.

Streona took them to a hall near the middle of the old town, a small, dim place. They went in. There seemed nobody else there, the long table bare, the hangings on the walls rustling in the drafts. Streona came in after them, smiling still.

Morcar said, "Where is the King?"

Streona said, "Where he belongs. Now!"

Out from behind the hangings a dozen men leaped. Morcar shouted, angry, and then something struck him on the shoulder and knocked him down. He struggled to rise, and another blow felled him. He heard Sigeferth cry out. He pushed himself to all fours again, dazed.

In his ear came Streona's voice. "The King wanted Thorkel for this, but I said I would do it myself." He gripped Morcar by the beard. Something in his hand flashed, and a searing heat went across Morcar's throat.

———

The city of Gainsburgh lay on the river Trent, which ran through the middle of the kingdom up to the Humber. Edmund rode there with his company, left them outside the city, and went in alone, as the agreement was.

At the gate, as he paid the toll, he saw a young man in rich clothes just inside, watching him. When he rode in, the boy came forward, taking off his hat and bowing his head. Beardless, he had long, fair hair, and he was slight as a girl.

"Sir," he said, "I am Godwine of Wessex, and I have dire news for you."

Edmund rode over to a quiet place on the street by a wall and dismounted. "What is it?"

The boy had followed him. He was pale, his eyes sunken;

he looked exhausted. "My lord Morcar and his brother Sige-ferth are dead, God save them."

"Dead. God have mercy on their souls." Edmund signed himself. His horse sidestepped away, picking up his unease. "What happened?" He looked around him, his senses jangled. The bright ordinariness of the day seemed eerie. "Dead," he said, amazed. Morcar's long face swam in the air before him.

"The King swore them a safe conduct to the council at Ox-ford, only a few days ago," the boy said. Edmund realized that he must have been at the same council. Godwine was of a great old Wessex family, descended from a brother of Alfred; he was the only one left of that line. Ethelred had killed all the others. The royal blood thinned to this slender sprig. "Then Streona murdered them. And all their guards. Morcar had told me before that you were coming here. So I came."

Edmund blinked at him, his mind stalled. He turned abruptly away to hide the grief and shame on his face. "Evil, evil," he muttered. The boy was watching him but said no more, and Ed-mund crossed himself, said again, "God save them. Thank you. I have to go." He rode on into the city. A cold despair came over him.

This was his father who did this; this evil streak ran in him, this taint.

He had come to Gainsburgh because Thurbrand had finally agreed to meet him here, but he could not clear his mind of what he had been told, the sworn word crossed, the blood shed, above all that Morcar's long struggle for justice had ended like this. He thought of the frightened girl he had seen at the wed-ding. When he reached the inn, he barely paid heed to the place and settled himself only when he was climbing the stairs.

He went into the top room, which was empty, and walked around it. He wore the mail coat, and he ran his hand over the iron links. Out there somewhere another knife waited for him.

He had known the council at Oxford was a sham. He had not warned them enough. Morcar was too eager for a way out.

Ethelred would kill everybody. He wondered why the King hadn't tried to kill him yet. He realized he probably had. He sat on a bench, wondering if there were any good at all in the world. What it meant to be good in such a world.

Thurbrand came in, alone, crooked and sneaky, peering all around. He squinted at Edmund, and the prince rose, and they greeted each other, shaking hands.

Then Thurbrand said, "You have heard that Morcar and his brother are dead."

Edmund straightened, hit in the new wound. "Betrayed, murdered, the King's own safe conduct broken."

The redheaded half Dane opposite him grinned with his whole mouthful of teeth. "Yes, how unfortunate for you, though, since they made up most of your support."

Edmund said nothing. They had given him no support but words. Yet he saw how it looked to Thurbrand. To anyone else. In fact, he had no support. Thurbrand was smirking at him. He had crooked hands. He twitched his gaze here and there. He said, "So, you see, how important I could be to you."

Edmund faced him, angry. He understood why everybody hated Thurbrand. The lord of Lindsey fixed him with his glittering pale eyes. He said, "I have five hundred men. Not fyrdmen, real Vikings. I'll bring them, if you promise me that when there's a good time, you'll give me Uhtred of Bamburgh and let me kill him."

For a long while Edmund did not move. In his mind he saw Uhtred; and behind him, Morcar and Sigeferth; and behind them, other men, a line into the distance, an endless chain of murders. He stood up and said, "Get out."

Thurbrand looked shocked. "This is my room." He had paid the innkeeper for the whole room.

"Get out anyway," Edmund said.

Alone in the big room, he waited to be sure Thurbrand was gone and to settle his mind. The stinks from downstairs came up to him, the muted uproar. He had not eaten, but he was not hungry. There seemed nothing in the world save murder and treachery; wasn't it only sensible to use murder and treachery in return?

He thought, So we are a pack of snarling dogs, and the wolves come in and eat us up.

Finally, he flung his cloak over his shoulders and went down again to his horse and rode toward the gate. Gainsburgh was only one main street along the river, and with the dark coming the gate was jammed with people trying to get home. He waited awhile for the chance to go through, while people with hoes and rakes and bundles on their backs pushed in past him, and, while he sat there on his horse, Godwine of Wessex came up beside him, on foot, leading his horse by the reins.

"My lord."

The boy had taken off his hat to speak to Edmund; he seemed no more than a child. He stood by Edmund's stirrup and said, "My lord, I want to join you."

Edmund turned to him. "You are a fool, then. I have nothing. No one supports me."

"I do," Godwine said. Along his jaw the first downy red hairs of his beard sprouted. He had a wide, soft mouth. He said, "I brought some carls with me. Eight men, but good ones, I think."

Edmund had it in mind to send him off. But he had to start somewhere. The boy's direct look lifted him. Maybe he wasn't soft, so much as quick. Edmund said, "Well, then, I accept you." Then something came to him.

"What happened to Sigeferth's new wife? Ealdgyth, I think her name was."

The boy's face rumpled, puzzled. "The King had her thrown into a monastery."

"Do you know where?"

"Yes—I—yes."

Edmund said, "Then I think we should go get her out. I have twenty men waiting on the road. Where are yours?"

"I'll bring them," Godwine said. His face smoothed out at the idea of doing something, a good sign. He straightened, squaring his shoulders. "I'll meet you at the gate."

CHAPTER EIGHTEEN

Ealdgyth could get into the monastery garden, if she stayed out of the way and no one saw her, but if anyone saw her, he sent her at once back to her cell. The garden was enclosed in the cloister, and she could find no way out. Her cell was in the middle of the north wall, where the sun never reached, and its walls were green with mold. She sat there, shivering in the dark, her chamber pot already smelly, waiting for someone to take care of her.

Waiting for someone to come murder her.

A crowd of strange men had rushed in on her, back in Oxford, laid hands on her like a piece of furniture and taken her here. She had no idea what had happened to her household; her laughing little maid, Urga; good old Syme, who stood guard. Those who took her were strangers, Normans. She could not understand their speech, and they were gone anyway almost as soon as they dumped her here. She had heard the key turn behind her in the door. Before her the dank little cell, a cot, a chest, the stink of mold.

When a monk came, bringing her a jug of ale and a loaf, she had rushed at him, clung to him, her hands fisted in his cassock. "Tell me where I am. Where is my husband? Please—" He tore himself out of her grasp and fled.

The door was old, and the lock out of true. With a little jiggling, she got it open. She went around the cloister, hiding in the corners, listening, and in this way she found out her husband was dead.

She almost screamed. She was crouched behind a water barrel, close enough to hear two monks arguing about predestination on the one hand and a lay brother gossiping with the gardener on the other. Between talk of Saint Augustine she caught

Morcar's name on the gardener's lips, and the lay brother laughed.

"You see how the King deals with his enemies. Both of them dead in the same stroke."

She stuffed her hand into her mouth to shut herself up. Both of them. She struggled to find some way that could mean Morcar and anyone but his brother Sigeferth. She crept out from behind the barrel and fled back to the cell.

She sat on the cot, bundled in the blanket, her arms around her knees, and thought, This is stupid. They will find me easily here. But she could not move. She laid her head on her knees and wept. She was alone. She would die and no one would even care.

She had disliked Sigeferth before, dreaded his attentions. Now she longed for him, his braying laugh, even his big fat belly.

Only the monk came that day, bringing her bread and cheese and ale and taking away her chamber pot and returning it. She heard the bells ring; she heard streams of feet slapping by outside, but no one came to take her to Mass. She could not pray. She had to get home, even to her father's house, anywhere but here. Sigeferth must have done something wrong. She had done nothing. She would never do anything bad again. There was no one even to convince of this. They would kill her, surely, next.

She stole out again and sat in the sun in the garden, and there she could pray at least. The gardener caught her and made her go back to the cell. She bundled herself up there, cold and hungry, waiting for the monk with her supper.

Then the door opened, and strange men strode in and seized her.

———⚬———

Edmund said, "She does not belong here. Whatever the King says. The King had her husband murdered. What will happen to her here?"

The abbot said, patiently, "She is in the King's ward. I have no power to change that."

The door to his cell opened, and three men came in, the girl in their midst. She was slight as a twig, her eyes swimming with tears, and she was trembling all over. At the sight of her Edmund took a deep breath; she seemed so terrified and young. He faced the abbot again, making this short.

"I am taking her out of here."

The abbot was an old man in a long white cassock, a silver crucifix hanging from his waist. He said, "She is in the King's ward. Only he can decide about her." But he turned to her, and his pale eyes softened. "My child, have faith."

The girl was staring at the floor, her shoulders hunched, clutching her cloak tight around her. Edmund saw the best way to declare against his father's sin. "I will not wait to see what the King decides for her. God gives a wife into her husband's hands, King or no King. I will marry her."

The old man's head swung toward him, his eyes wide. "The King must—"

"Tell the King what you wish. He is far away, and I am here now. Marry us." Edmund put his hand out and took the girl's hand. Her hand was cold and lay in his like a dead thing.

The abbot looked them over, his mouth curled. His hands rubbed slowly palm against palm. He lifted his gaze and swept a look around the room at the men standing around and came up to face Edmund. Edmund drew the girl closer; she stumbled a little, as if she had no power of her own to move, and he had to hold her on her feet.

The abbot said some words in Latin, made the sign of the cross. He said, "Edmund Aetheling, do you marry this woman, Ealdgyth?"

"Yes," Edmund said.

"Who bestows her?"

Edmund said, "Godwine," and the young man stepped forward.

"Do you bestow this woman on Edmund Aetheling?"

"I do," Godwine said.

"Then you are married," the abbot said. "God bless you."

Edmund looked over the girl's head at Godwine. "All right. Let's go."

⁓

They gave her a mild little mule to ride and plunged off across the country. She was not a good rider and struggled to stay on, to keep up. Every time they stopped, she looked all around her, at the broad fields, the rolling green hills, and she breathed deeply, amazed to be outside again.

Someone had come for her. Someone cared about her.

They were riding off again. Men rode on either side of her, but not the man who had rescued her. He went in the lead, as he should.

But he never even looked at her. As they went on, and she grew more and more tired, she began to think he didn't really care about her at all. She began to wonder if she had just given up one captor for another.

⁓

They stopped before sundown at a farmstead, where Edmund's name got them in. The men all crowded into the hall, but they had a bower for the girl in the back, the farmer's wife having lately died.

They tended their horses, and Edmund saw his men fed. Godwine came up to him. Edmund liked him; he had done everything Edmund asked without question. They were all tired, and most of the men had already gone in, but Godwine was still looking for orders. He was stronger than he looked, as if a soft husk were wearing away under the pressure of necessity.

Edmund said, "We should leave early. We can reach Derby by tomorrow if we leave early."

"What do you think the King will do when he hears of this?"

"I don't know," Edmund said. "Choke on it, I hope." That reminded him of the girl. "Go to sleep, Godwine," he said. "You did two days' work in one today." He laid his hand on the boy's shoulder.

He went out of the hall. The dark was coming, the western sky a banner of red and pale blue. Circling around behind the hall he went to the bower, to make sure the girl was safe.

The door was open. Candlelight shone through it. He went to the threshold and looked in. On the far side of the little room she spun toward him, watchful, and backed a step away, putting a stool between them.

He looked around, seeing she was alone. He said, "I'm sorry for this. When we get where we're going I will find some women to attend you. Have you eaten anything?"

"Yes," she said. Her hands rose, the fingertips together. Her eyes widened. "Where are we going?"

"To Lark Hill, outside Derby," he said. "They will take us in there, for your sake. Where you were married." It occurred to him he had never heard her voice before, light and high and tinged with her northern accent. He said, "Do you want to go somewhere else?"

She stiffened. Her eyes fixed on his. Her voice came suddenly stronger. "Don't pretend to me. I will go wherever I am taken. No one asks me what I want. My father gave me to my lord Sigeferth, and he—never asked me. I will do what I am told." Her tongue slid over her lower lip. She said, "I am sorry.

That was rude. You have saved my life." She turned away from him, her head bent.

Edmund stared at her, astonished. Even in the candlelight, he saw the flush of her cheek, so she herself thought she had been bold. She was slim, but with a woman's body. What she had said about Sigeferth nudged at the edge of his mind. Until he came here he had not thought of her as more than a pawn in the game with his father.

He said, "Lady, tell me what you wish of me."

She lifted her head, her small chin set. "You should not wear a coat of mail to visit a woman's bower."

He looked down; he had forgotten, as usual, that he was wearing the mail coat. "I beg your pardon," he said, and turned and left.

━⊷━

They went on the next day through the first rocky rises of the hills and came in the late afternoon to Lark Hill. There, as Edmund had foreseen, the people had heard of their lord's death; some had run away, but most had stayed, loyal and uncertain. When he came, with Sigeferth's widow as his wife, they were glad enough to take them in. They even raised a little, tremulous cheer. He wondered how long that would last.

There were no fighting men. Morcar's carls had all gone with him to Oxford; they were all dead. Edmund made sure everyone in the hall knew this. He set Godwine to putting their men out to keep watch. The girl he sent off to another bower. He himself went around and spoke to Morcar's chief stewards here, giving them orders, so that they submitted to him without even realizing it.

Before sundown he was sure of his hold on the place. Everyone here knew him now, and all called him lord. In the hall where he would sleep among his men, he took off his mail. God-wine saw him doing this and came up to help him.

Edmund slid out of the clinking shirt. The boy grunted under the weight. "It's heavy." He hoisted it by the shoulders. "May I try it?"

"Go ahead," Edmund said. He took off the thick padding he wore beneath the mail, stiff and still damp with sweat. From his pack he got a long red coat, which he wore only at court, and shook out the creases and dust.

Godwine had wrestled himself into the mail. His head emerged from the neck, and he straightened, hauling on the sides to get the shoulders right, pushing himself up against the weight of the iron. "God's breath," he said. "I don't think I can walk."

"You get used to it," Edmund said. He put on the red coat and found a belt.

Godwine's eyes sharpened. "Where are you going?"

"Hang that up when you're done," Edmund said. He went out of the hall and around to Ealdgyth's bower.

—⁘—

The door was open, again. The sun had not yet gone down, and the warm light spilled into the little room. She was alone still. He stopped in the doorway and said, "Why do you leave the door open?"

"I never want a door shut on me again," she said. She stood in the middle of the room; she did not back away from him.

He said, "We can find some of the local girls to wait on you. Do you have friends anywhere here?"

Tears bloomed suddenly in her eyes. She twisted, turning away from him, hiding her face. "I want Urga. I want Syme—" She put her hand up to her eyes. He stood in the threshold, not knowing what to do, looking everywhere else. Then finally she said, "I'm sorry."

"No," he said, turning toward her again, glad the tears were over. "It's very sad. I'm sorry too."

She faced him again, her chin wobbling. She was so young, he thought. She straightened herself; he was minded of Godwine, standing up under the weight of the mail. She said, "Why did you do this?"

He slid his hands behind him. He said, "I will defy my father, however I can."

"Then not for my sake."

He said, "I saw you at your wedding. You looked afraid. I could not leave you to the King."

She shut her eyes and crossed herself. "I am grateful to you, then. And for bringing me here. I am—happiest here." She gave him a slight look and turned away.

There was a little silence. "I shall take my leave," he said, disappointed.

She turned toward him again. "No, come sit down."

Their eyes met. He swallowed, excited. This was another kind of game, in which she set the rules. His hands at his sides, he came into the bower and sat on the stool by the bed.

She said, "I don't want to be alone. Stay with me. I have nightmares." She put her hands to her face. "They burst in on me, then I heard my husband was dead. I thought any moment they would kill me too."

He said, "I would say you are safe here, my lady, but there is nowhere safe, really."

"So I have learned."

She got up and moved around the room, putting out some of the candles; she poured water into a basin and washed her face. He realized she was getting ready to go to sleep. He swallowed again. He did not look at the bed. She turned, a cup in her hand.

"I will have a drink of this cider before I go to rest," she said. "Will you?"

"Yes," he said. The word came out like something he had to hawk up from his throat. "Thank you."

She brought him the cup. He held it in both hands. She was so close he could smell the scents of her body. He said, "The abbot took your side also. He could have made it much harder. I had no wish to attack the monastery." He sipped the heady drink.

"It's a good idea, don't you think, to go along with what's going to happen anyway."

He laughed. Their eyes met again, just a glance, and a shock went through him. They were married, after all, an unintended consequence of snapping his fingers in his father's face. He drank more cider.

She said, "Will the King come?" She sat down on the bed, so near their knees almost touched.

Edmund stared at her thigh, curving the stuff of her gown. "I don't know. From here, though, I am in a good position; I can watch the whole south—the King in Winchester and Thorkel in East Anglia—and I can move wherever I want."

She put her cup down, stood again, and began to fold back the coverlet on the bed. Edmund jerked his gaze toward the door, putting the back of his head to her. Maybe he should have thought this over more. She brought the last candle to the bedside and put it down. He heard the crinkle of the rushes in the mattress as she slid down onto the bed and every nerve in his body quivered.

"There are servants in the hall I know," she said. "They will attend me until we know what became of my old household. Do you think—What do you think could have happened to them?"

Edmund said, "I will find out. They were in Oxford?"

"At Morcar's house."

Edmund gave a little shake of his head. But ordinary people might have escaped, like mice, hiding in holes. He said, "I will find out."

She sighed. She was lying down, just behind him, her body inches from him. Her knees softly rounding the bedclothes. Between her knees, the hollow. She reached out and pinched the candle.

In the abrupt descent of darkness he almost seized her. He mastered himself. This was her game, he thought, and better that way. He could wait. Give her that power, since she had asked for it.

She said, "You need not sit up all night. Come lie down on top of the cover."

He turned toward her. Faintly in the dark he could make out her shape in the bed. He ached with expectations. Let her lead him. Delicious, how she led him on. He went carefully around and lay down on the other side, as far from her as he could, with the heavy coverlet between them. In the dark they lay quiet a moment.

She said, "Do you rebel against the King for my husband's sake?"

"No," he said. "For England's sake. They were murdered because of my rebellion."

"Edmund, what do you want, then?"

He lay still, breathless. His head felt light. He said, "For you to say my name again. You have never said it before."

"Edmund," she said, and laughed. "Is that all it takes? Edmund. Edmund."

He said nothing. In the dark her hand grazed his face, and he started from head to foot. She laid her hand against his cheek. She said, "Will you come under the covers, my husband?" He slid out of his coat and in beside her.

⚬

He had been right to come here. In the morning the commander of the garrison in Derby rode in with thirty men behind him and swore himself Edmund's man; he was Morcar's cousin. In the day after that others appeared, a steady stream of kindred and bound men. Edmund met them in the hall, and they talked reverently of Morcar and Sigeferth and the evils of the King, and every night he lay rejoicing in the arms of Sigeferth's wife.

⸙

Godwine remembered the weight of the mail shirt; he admired Edmund for that more than anything else, for wearing that iron. Getting the girl out, that had been good too, although it meant now Edmund spent much time with her and less with Godwine himself, Edmund's friend. But now they had gone on a patrol. The hard riding was a relief, being with Edmund a pleasure. Godwine drew back with the other carls, watching Edmund ride forward to meet the little group of villagers.

The prince and his men had ridden over thirty miles east of Lark Hill to Ermine Street for this meeting. The great road stretched from London to the Humber, sometimes broad and straight, sometimes narrow, through the forests and the lowlands and the fens and now and then a village. Edmund was looking for spies among the local people to keep watch on Thorkel the Tall, who had an army somewhere farther on. So far, little had come of this, but Edmund was patient. Godwine hooked one leg around the pommel of his saddle, his horse shifting under him.

He was not patient. He did not want to attack Thorkel; he wanted to go after Ethelred. Ethelred had outlawed his father, had seized his inheritance and driven him into the forest. Edmund had this big, vague notion of England and of saving the country's honor. Godwine just wanted revenge. And the lands restored, of course. He liked the feel of this, the balance of it: revenge for wrongs, the world made right again.

Edmund had turned up there, was beckoning him, and Godwine straightened his leg down to the stirrup and, leading the four other carls, went out after the prince, on south down Ermine Street.

"They say—" As they left the village, Edmund turned, looking back, and with his voice and his look brought Godwine up beside him, stirrup to stirrup. Godwine wished briefly he were as good a rider as Edmund. "The villagers have seen sign of the Jomsvikings within a day's ride of here." He shook his head. "I think. They spoke such rude Saxon, I could barely understand—and they me too, of course."

Godwine said, "Did they know who you are?"

"They know of Alfred. Of the Aethelings." Edmund said. He reined in so that all the carls came up around him. He gave Godwine a sideways look. "Do you mean, would they say the same things to anybody, including Thorkel? Yes, likely, what choice do they have? Thorkel is supposed to be my father's man. But he seems to be operating pretty much on his own." He turned to the other carls. "Someone needs to ride scout. Warn us of anything ahead."

The other men all called out, asking to be chosen, and Edmund took two of them and sent them up front. The other two he set out to ride off to either side of the road, as much as possible. Godwine could see he was trying to figure this out even as he gave the orders. He was learning how to command even as he commanded them. They started off again at the center of the broad wedge of the scouts.

They moved on through the forest. Godwine thought again of the evils done him and his family. Maybe being with Edmund was taking him out of his proper course. He meant to kill Ethelred himself if he could. He imagined this often, standing face-to-face with the King, swords drawn. This would not only avenge him but also settle the balance of the world. Whatever happened was either right or wrong: you did the one and avenged the other. He glanced at Edmund. The heavy mail made him look bigger, and he rode a stout horse to carry the weight.

Godwine thought, I will get a mail coat.

They went on through deep oak woods, the trees so thick overhead there seemed no daylight, only a pattern of shadow. The old road was thick in leaf drift and dirt, rutted here and there, but under it was stone, like all these roads. He let his mind wander into his one-sided argument with Edmund again.

The trouble was, Edmund was too high thinking. He had never been run out, homeless, afraid. Godwine still remembered when the decree against his father came. His foster father had sent him off at once. No one would take him in; he had gone up to the ancient manor of his house and lived with the crofters in a mud hut.

Edmund had never really been on the outside. Godwine wanted only to be back in the middle, safe again. For that he needed to belong to some power, and so far Edmund was all he had. And there was the mail shirt. He would stay with Edmund until something better appeared. Maybe he would stay with Edmund forever.

⸺⸺

Ealdgyth watched the old steward turn the key; she was reminded uneasily of the monastery. The old man said, "There is no barley now, but soon." He pushed the door open. A stale, sweet aroma gusted out at her. She looked into the broad, dim room. The vats where the barley would be soaked until it sprouted lay on their sides along the walls. She wondered how it was dried. She backed up, let him shut the door again, and took the key.

Every key was more control. She hung it on her big hoop of a ring.

"The barley is green now," the steward said. "We shall see a good harvest in June, God willing." He crossed himself.

She copied him. They were going along the top row of the

gardens, where the onions and cabbages grew. She looked all around the place. People went about their chores, sweeping and cleaning and paring and chopping. The maids were out spreading bedclothes to air on the bushes around the hall. At the gate two men were bringing in a cartload of wood. She said, "Pray God my lord will soon come home."

The steward said, "Amen." His voice was intense. "God bless our good prince Edmund."

She felt light with satisfaction at that. Edmund, her prince, her husband. They loved him, these people, another key for her ring. She let him show her ricks of hay, saddle rooms, even the dung heap. She thought, I am Edmund's wife.

She had done some thinking about this, now that she was in a safe place and was calmer. He was the Aetheling. Of this she knew only what the old tales told her, but it was enough: when his father died, he would be King. She saw no reason for his rebellion. He talked to her sometimes of England and of honor and of justice, but these were phantoms.

Now he was gone, off on one of his long, searching rides. Soon he would be back, and, when he was, she would give him such reasons he might never leave. She would make him love her. She would make him happier with her than his dreams, and he would defend her, not the phantoms.

—⸙—

Half a day's ride south on Ermine Street the broad-standing oaks gave way to more open ground, and the road went down a slope onto the edge of a long stretch of bog, green as a meadow in the open sun. The scouts had to come into the road, because the only way across the bog was an old causeway. They slowed their horses, watching for holes, but the long, thin corridor was stout enough. The berm of the causeway was stone, and Edmund guessed the work was very old. Roman. He thought of Aethel-stan and crossed himself. O Lord, keep him from the monsters. The bog stretched off on either side into the distance, islands of grass in the still water scattered with half-dead pine trees and scrawny birch. At the far end of the causeway the road climbed another short, easy slope into an open stand of trees, and there, by the road, was a building.

Or the beginning of one. A pile of stones stood beside a square marked out with wooden posts, and more stones stood in two sides of a footing. But one post had fallen down out of its hole, and the stones were knocked out of line; whoever had been making this had given up. Edmund dismounted and went to where the ground had been turned and touched it, trying to make a good guess how long ago it had been broken.

Godwine said, "Jomsvikings?"

"Maybe." Edmund straightened and walked up the road to look back at the causeway. "This is a good place to hold; everybody has to come down the road there." He frowned, won-dering if Thorkel had begun this, and, if so, why he had given it up.

Godwine said, "Maybe we could build it, then. This is the road to London."

Edmund knew Godwine wanted only to get at Ethelred; he had no good idea of the whole of this. They certainly could hold no place so far from Lark Hill, not with the men he had now. If Thorkel had begun it, then maybe something had hap-pened to cause him to give this place up, something Edmund should know of. He turned to his horse and gathered his reins.

He thought of Ealdgyth. His wife was always at the edge of his mind now, always a dream of her. As an excuse to go back he thought also of the men he had sent out to scout in other di-rections.

"Let's get home," he said to Godwine.

CHAPTER NINETEEN

Knut had been in Jorvik for years, and he was still finding new things: the stone rings of ancient towers, old money, wild things. Snakes lived along the foot of the wall, and lizards in its cracks. Parts of the walls themselves were so old they seemed to have grown there. In the sway behind the hall where Raef kept his horses, tall, slender mushrooms sprouted after the rain that made him drunken when he ate them. Nut trees and apples dotted the higher ground. He found the rusted flake of a spearhead on the hillside, so old it crumbled in his hands. He thought sometimes of running away from the hall and living as an outlaw, pillaging these people.

He liked going into the old, empty houses, although new people were always moving in and rebuilding them, which annoyed him. He sneaked into houses with people in them too, like Goda's new house by the river; he liked the risk of being caught. The only place in Jorvik he could not go was the old ruined hall behind the high street.

The one time he got courage to go in, he took three strides into the thick dark, turned, and rushed out. His top half outran his legs somehow, and he toppled into the street and ate a mouthful of dust. In the moment he had stood there lapped in the churning of the air, he had felt something wrapping around his ankles and dragging him down.

Otherwise he went everywhere, as he willed. He did nothing he was told to do. Raef tried to make him sit under the oak tree, where he gave law to the ordinary people, but Knut argued with everybody, and Raef was glad to see him go. When he refused to fetch and carry for her, Laissa railed at him that he was useless. Leif took him out hunting and sometimes fishing, but

Leif was Raef's man and showed it. Only Gemma loved him, his little sister, and he loved only her.

Raef had learned how to get him to work. "Go to the woodshed; don't come out until you've cut and stacked all that wood." Knut had given up refusing this when he saw that starving himself to death in defiance would serve Raef just as well.

He chopped wood; he hunted; otherwise, he ran loose. He had collected eight or ten boys his age, showed them how to fight, and led them around the streets at night attacking the other gangs in Jorvik, the Green Stray Boys and the Cross River Boys. This often got him hauled up in front of the oak tree for Raef to rail at; this was why he was in the woodshed now. This time, he thought, he might have gone too far.

—§—

Gemma sat on the bottom step that led down into the woodshed, watching Knut with the axe. She loved him. She had told him so and made him promise to marry her when she grew up. She loved how tall he was and his yellow hair, darker than hers, and how he faced her father, straight on, brave as a hero.

She said, "I hate Papa when he's like that to you."

Knut drove the axe down through a log and the halves bounced onto the ground. "He's a slow, soft old slug. He's not even a real King." He put another log on the block and hoisted the axe. "Be careful, Gemma. These things fly."

She said, "If you run away, will you take me with you?"

He laughed. He lowered the axe against the block and came up to her and took her face between his two hands.

"You are a dear one, Gemma. But I couldn't take you with me. You're too young yet. You need your mother." He kissed her forehead and went back to the axe.

Gemma sat with her forehead glowing, her cheeks warm

from the touch of his hands, and in her mind lopped off most of what he had said. She sat watching him split wood. She thought, I am the princess, you must save me from the demon. The idea was so intense she found herself turning her head slightly to be kissed.

Then she heard someone call her name, up in the hall.

"That's supper," she said. "I'll bring you some." She sprang up the steps and in through the door.

⸺⸺⸺

A little while later the door opened, and his foster father came in. Knut straightened, the axehead on the floor and his hands crossed on the butt, and waited. Raef sat down on the steps, just as Gemma had. Sitting down, he folded like a stork, a long, skinny, white-haired man, homely as the log butt. His lone ear jutted out of his hair like a sail.

He looked nothing like a king. He had no crown, no ceremony. He wore no gold, no mail, no emblems, only clothes his wife patched, baggy hose, and a faded, long shirt he had gotten years before in some far eastern city of myth, where he had learned his magic. Knut stirred, uneasy. Or whatever it was he had learned.

Raef said, "He broke your bow."

"He did it on purpose," Knut said hotly. "He waited until I was in the sweathouse and chopped it in half with an axe."

"So you dragged him outside the walls and nailed him naked to a tree."

"I wanted to hurt him." Knut remembered the other boy's screams with some pleasure.

"He may still die. Then you'll have to pay wergeld. You'll be chopping wood all winter." The blazing blue eyes pierced him.

"Wergeld!" Knut said. "He's a common churl, and I'm the son of a King—"

"Yes," Raef said. "That's always your excuse. You don't see there's something going the other way. If you had brought this to the oak tree, you'd have gotten a new bow, and the right man would be punished, but you're too damn dumb to see that."

Knut glared at him. "That's not honor. The law's just what you say it is, anyway, since you're King."

"Kings go in and out with the tide," Raef said. "The law is what matters. And if he dies, you're no better than an outlaw that anybody can kill. What's so kingly in that?" He said, deliberately, "You'd be no better than Thorkel."

Knut jerked all over; to seem anything like Thorkel stung him to the marrow. Raef's eyes glittered with amusement. Knut knew that Raef had used Thorkel's name just to taunt him, this so-called King who talked so much about justice and then turned Knut's own mind against him.

"Listen, Raef," he said. "There is nothing good between us. There never will be. I want to go. Let me go, with my war band, and we can find glory and gold, as men should, and not rot here."

Raef snorted. He was sitting on the top step so that they were eye to eye. His long arms hung over his knees, his hands slack; the fingers of his bad hand curved like a hook. He said, "Your war band. You mean those rag boys you lead around the streets here?"

Knut said, "You don't fight wars. You don't even have warriors. How am I to make a name for myself? I'm a younger son."

Raef shook his head. "Who knows? Why do you think you and your gang—I'm sorry, your war band—would even make it as far as the Humber?"

Knut swelled at this, as if at the stroke of a whip. Raef stood up. "Get this wood cut. Hope that fool doesn't die." He went on out of the woodshed. Knut turned back to the next log, and hit it as hard as he could.

—◦—

Laissa and Miru had made the church beautiful, Gemma thought. They had cleaned and swept it, gotten Leif and some other men to repair the altars, and woven new clothes for the altars and to hang on the walls. Now they were fixing the Jesus, painting his eyes with a goo made of egg white and chalk. Gemma kneeled down behind them, crossed herself, and prayed to God to love her and to let her marry Knut.

Laissa had taught her the Great Prayer, and she said that over and over, because Miru had said the more times God heard it, the happier He was. When she came to the place about forgiving trespass, she said it slowly and carefully. She thought that was the important thing. As long as she forgave everybody else, God would forgive her.

She wondered if God would ever forgive her father.

She sat with her mother in the back of the church; the other women were talking about bringing in a priest. Gemma did not understand where some stranger priest fit into this. She said, "Mama, all power comes from God, doesn't it?"

"Everything comes from God, dear one." Laissa put an arm around her and told her the story of the beginning, how God made the world and everything in it, but when He made Adam, some of his angels were angry, and He had to throw them out of heaven, and they fell all the way to hell, where they became devils.

"Some of them," she said. "Some made it only as far as Jorvik." She and Miru both laughed. Gemma knew what they meant.

When they went back, she sat by the fire, playing with

Edith's baby. She glanced continually up at her father, on his high seat.

She knew he was watching her. He had always watched her from somewhere inside her own head, and at first she had not minded, but now she saw this was wicked. Only God should watch her like that. In her mind she made a wall, smooth and round against him. After a while she looked toward the high seat, and he was looking in the other direction.

⸻

It was not so much what she thought she had done as that she wanted to do it that made Raef low; he avoided the girl now, where before he had always been dancing with her or playing the riddle games she loved. She spent all the day with Laissa, helping with the hall work or at the church, and at night she slept on her mother's side of the bed.

⸻

Leif had gone to Mainland and bought two keels, both from ships that had traveled to Vinland, and he brought them back to Jorvik lashed to either side of a knarr. He was standing there on the gravel bar watching the shoremen carry them up to the shipworks when Raef found him.

He had brought Knut with him, and for once the boy had come, because he loved ships. Raef looked over the long oak keels, pleased.

"You did well. They're very sound and they feel lucky. The shipbuilders will be here by summer."

They talked about Leif's journey. Knut hung by—as always, drawn to stories. The old Icelander's eyes snapped, talking about struggles with the wind and the tide. His sunburned nose was peeling. He still loved to sail, even if only up to Mainland.

On the way back, Knut said, "Those are knarr keels."

"Yes," Raef said, short. He knew where this was going. "Goda is paying for them. They'll carry wool to Hedeby."

Knut strode beside him. Raef gave him a quick look. The boy had grown almost visibly every day he had been here, all of it up. His arms and shoulders were stout with muscle from chopping wood. When he was full grown he would be as tall as Raef himself. Raef remembered being glad he had come here. Now he wished he had never seen him. He had taught him nothing. Knut had defied him from the start and now gotten Gemma to defy him.

Two girls with bundles of laundry on their heads came by from upriver, their bodies lithe under their burdens, and Knut looked at them and they looked slantwise at him.

He turned back to Raef. "You should build a dragon."

"I have no use for a dragon," Raef said. "I have no crew." They had come back to the hall, and Raef went in. Knut pursued him.

"If you had a dragon, I could raid along the coast. We could start the slave trade here."

In the middle of the hall Raef turned and backhanded him so hard the boy stumbled and fell full length on the floor. Without a pause he launched himself head first at Raef, his fists cocked.

Raef sidestepped his rush. "What makes you think—" He grabbed the boy's nose as he passed. "You could make your own way in the world—" He pulled the nose around, and when the rest of Knut followed, helpless, yelling, the wild fists milling the air, Raef led him across his outstretched foot. "When you can't even take a slow, soft old slug like me?" Knut went sprawling flat on his face on the ground.

Gemma had watched this, and she ran forward. "Papa!" Knut rolled over and sat up, his face glum, blood trickling from his nose. Gemma sank down beside him, her arm out across him to protect him, and looked angrily at her father.

"Papa!"

"Not yet," Raef said to Knut, and went off down toward the looms.

Laissa was watching him. She said, "What was that about?"

Raef shook his head. "I lost my temper."

"He's a foul, wicked boy. I've told Gemma to stay away from him, and she does not heed me."

Raef looked toward the fire. There Gemma sat side by side with Knut, the firelight glowing on them. She had Edith's little girl on her lap, her arms around the child. "She doesn't heed anybody. Especially about Knut."

He lowered his eyes, sore of mind. He knew there would be no more children born here of his making, that something in Laissa's womb resisted his seed. Gemma was the only one.

She was perfect. He knew the power of the manifest world when he saw her before him, every look and gesture wonderful and new. Yet she had turned away from him. He lowered his eyes to his wife's hands, his heart aching.

Laissa said, "I want you to do something for me. Find us a priest."

"A priest. Why will I do that? A priest will only burn me, or try. Next you'll want that archbishop back."

"I may," she said. She glanced up at him. "Well," she said, "maybe we'll talk about it later." She took him by the bad hand and kissed him.

CHAPTER TWENTY

Knut came in through the big gate, leading his horse with the quarters of the deer hung across the saddle. On his way to the hall, he came on Gemma, walking along the top of a stone wall by a field. Her long, uncombed hair was a cloud of white gold in the sun.

She said, "My father is waiting for you." She put her hand on the haunch of the deer. "Poor thing."

Knut said, "You won't think of that when you're eating it. What does he want?"

She went along the wall beside him, her arms out, dancing from rock to rock. "I don't know. He says I'm not to marry you."

Knut almost laughed; he had forgotten this daydream of hers. "That's probably for the best, Gemma."

She said, "Well, I will always love you, Knut."

The way she looked at him startled him. He said, "What is it?"

She turned her eyes on him, damp with tears, and suddenly flung herself into his arms, clutching him, her cheek against his chest. He dropped the reins, his arms around her to keep her from falling. She smelled like a little girl, sweet young female mixed with smoke and sweat. He said, "What's wrong, baby?"

She tore herself free and fled, back over the wall, into the town. Knut took the deer up to the hall, around to the kitchen in the back.

———

Two days later he was moving down the Ouse with Raef in a borrowed two-man boat. He fished much of the time, and Raef rowed. After the tide changed, they raised the sail and swept with the wind toward the Humber. By the next sundown they were pulling out into the braided streams and shoals at the neck of the great estuary.

Knut stood up in the boat, his breath gripped in his chest. His eyes flew over the shores and the sandbars. Everywhere along the water lay ships, dragons, long bodied, high necked, some with their sails still up, around each one a busy troop of men. He let out his breath in a sigh. He had not seen such a fleet in a long time, and he felt this like a homecoming. His heart raced.

Raef was watching him. Knut said, "What is this?" He searched the fleet with his eyes; he saw none of the red sails of the Jomsvikings but many sails with the crisscross markings of Tronde ships and red Danish checks.

Some of the red-checked sails had stitched crowns in the middle. His heart began to gallop.

"Come with me," Raef said.

They drew the little boat up on the end of a sandbar and walked along the northern bank of the estuary through the camps of the fleet. Knut followed close on his foster father's heels. They passed campfires crowded with men; no one stopped them or challenged them.

The fires came closer together, more men sitting around them, the talk and laughter louder. Then Raef was walking into a great knot of men.

They parted for him, although Knut could not see why. Jostled somehow out of the way, they turned and stared at Raef, tall and stooped, who ignored them as he went by. Knut kept at his elbow, but he could not keep from gawking. Everywhere he saw men with gold rings on their arms and in their ears, swords in their belts, cloaks lined with fur and clasped with gold. Then Raef had stopped, and Knut stopped with him and looked forward.

They had come to the center of the crowd. Several men were sitting on the ground there, and in their midst, on a rough-made chair of stones and planks, was a big, red-headed man with a long moustache that swept back over his shoulders. A tingle went up Knut's back. This was Sweyn Tjugas.

"I greet you, King of Denmark," Raef said.

Knut clamped his jaw shut. He had not seen his father for years; suddenly he was shy, a child again, as if Sweyn would not know him, and yet he was full of pleasure at simply being in his presence.

Sweyn said, "Well, I greet you, King of Jorvik. You come unannounced." Behind him, one of the other men had stood up, a short dark man in a rich coat; several of the other men stood then too.

"I am here," Raef said. "What warning do you need?"

Sweyn smiled. "You know, when I knew you last, it was your brother everybody remarked on."

Raef said, "Conn Corbansson is far famed, and justly, much more than I."

Sweyn leaned his forearm on his knee. Knut could not look from him. He seemed hardly older, his father, than the last time he had seen him, in Canterbury, when they boned the archbishop. The King gave off a scent of power, just the way he sat while everybody else stood, the way one turn of his head brought the other men around him instantly a step closer. His gaze flicked by Raef toward Knut and turned to Raef again.

"I am going to Gainsburgh," he said, "to claim the crown of England. I have reason to believe this is no surprise to you. I am glad you of all men in England should come first to give me homage. You may attend me there, if you wish, and sit at my right hand."

"I do not wish," Raef said, "nor am I giving you homage. It was Thurbrand's idea that you come to England, and I agree with that, but that's England, not Jorvik. I came here to suggest you stay out of my kingdom. And to bring you a fighter." He turned toward Knut. "You can take this one. He's yours, anyway."

Knut trembled with eagerness. He took a step forward, farther into the light of the fire, and said, "I greet my father, King of England and Denmark."

Sweyn gave a harsh grunt, and his eyes widened. So he had not known him until now. He said, slow voiced, "Knut, by Thor-blast. Grown like a beanstalk. I wondered what Thorkel had done with you." His gaze ran up and down Knut's length, measuring him, and Sweyn smiled. He showed his teeth when he smiled.

"I will fight for you now, Father," Knut said. He shot a hard look at Raef. "Whatever he does."

Sweyn said, "Come, then." His eyes had gone back to Raef. He said, "I am taking hostages of all the nobles here."

Raef made a gesture with his bad hand. "That's wise. None of them are worth much, though, except a few of those with the prince. Edmund's down near Derby, but he can't let you get close to him. His war band is only a few hundred men. Thorkel must have heard you were coming. He has pulled the Jomsvikings all back into London. If you can, take the Queen prisoner, never let her touch you, and burrow her away."

As he spoke he was withdrawing out of the light, leaving Knut alone there. Knut could not keep the smile from his face; he looked around, at the men around him, scarred and muscular from fighting, their arms burdened with gold, their hands callused from swords. Already he belonged here. He was his father's son at last. He would have a sword. He would fight.

He brought his gaze back to his father. Sweyn Tjugas was still staring after Raef. He said sharply, "I want a hostage of you."

Raef said, "Oh, consider him a hostage." He had drifted back almost out of the reach of the fire, and then, in a moment, he was gone. Someone called out a question. Everybody looked around.

It didn't matter. Knut stepped in among the men around his father, who ran their eyes over him, frowning. Sweyn turned and looked at the short dark man behind him.

"Maybe we should bring him down. He is overweening."

"Don't get distracted," said the other man. "Thurbrand is more important to you."

Sweyn shrugged, saying, "Jorvik has no fleet. No army. He is no danger."

The short man said, "Sweyn, he is the most dangerous man in England. But you have no way to attack him. The thing here, as he said, is the crown. You. Knut? Come sit down with us, we'll soon find out if you're worth having."

The short man, he learned at once, was Eric Hakonsson of Lade, the Trondejarl, who ruled Norway in Sweyn's name. He was supposed to be descended from the Frost Giants; there was something eldritch in his looks: slanted eyes, slanted brows, slanted mouth, dark skin. His coat was deep in marten's fur, and he wore a gold chain around his neck with links an inch thick. He jabbed a thumb at the ground, and Knut sat there. This put him side-by-side with a boy his own age.

"I am Odd Ericsson," the other boy said, and they shook hands. Knut guessed he was a son of the Trondejarl; he had the same dark skin and slanted eyes.

Knut said, "Does he still have the iron ship?"

Odd gave him a quick, surprised look. "Shipbiter. He'd not bring her here, she's not a river ship. How did you hear of her?"

"Stories," Knut said. He thought of Leif. "I have a friend who loves to tell stories." Had. He wondered at the little pang that gave him.

Odd was leaning forward, watching him. "You lived with the wizard of Jorvik?"

"A while."

"Can he fly? Does he make potions?"

Knut laughed. "No, he does nothing so interesting." Eric had turned around to hear him, and Knut said, "Shouldn't somebody see if he has really gone?"

The Trondejarl's dark eyes poked sharp at him. "Go, then. Odd, you too." Knut got up; he knew they would be watching him for a while, to see if he was a spy.

He didn't care. He was back in a war camp, familiar to him from his cradle and simpler than the King's hall at Jorvik. Here all he had to do was fight. Whatever enemy appeared, he should mow down. Anyone the King aimed him at, he should strike. He thought again that he had to get a sword, or something, anyway, bigger than his belt knife. He and Odd went back along the riverbank, toward where Raef had left the boat.

The tide was ebbing out of the river, but the boat was gone nonetheless. Knut stood with his feet on the little trench the forefoot of the double-ender had left in the sandbank, the only proof that Raef had ever been here.

Odd said, "Are you sure this was where you hauled out?" With the tide going out it was well up the bank.

"I'm sure." He stood watching the water ripple in the dark, winding on down from the north. The night wind blew softly into his face. He thought of Jorvik, suddenly a little sorry to be gone. He remembered the last time he had seen Gemma. She had known he was going away forever; she had wept for losing him. But he was free of Raef at last.

He said, out loud, to make it so, "I hope I never set eyes on him again."

Odd said, under his breath, "Watch out."

That brought him back to the moment. Up the bar toward

them several men were coming. Their leader was tall and stringy and was trying to grow his moustache long; he was older than Knut by ten years but no taller. All of them, the three men with him also, wore the dirty shirts and loose leggings of oarsmen. Somebody's crew. He saw a shadow of his father's face in the leader's face and guessed whose.

He stopped, Odd staying well behind him. He knew Odd was out of this. The leader of this pack sauntered up to him, his hands on his belt, and said, "So you're the little brother."

"Hello, Harald," Knut said. He knew him only by name; Harald Sweynsson had already gone to the Tronde for Eric Hakonsson to foster when Knut was born.

"That's *Prince* Harald." The tall skinny man reached out and brushed his hand at Knut, as if he were knocking off a fly. "I just wanted to give you some warning. It's Prince Harald, always. And a low, humble bow. And stay out of my way. All right? I go first. Always." His hand flicked at Knut again. "Now bow."

Knut gave no thought to this; he just dropped his shoulder and pumped his right fist as hard as he could into Harald's gut. Harald doubled over, the breath exploding out of him, but the other three men leaped all together on Knut. For a while, because of the confusion, he could hold them off. He hit each of them hard; he kicked and felt something break, but then a blow pushed his nose back past his eyes, his side stabbed with pain, and he lowered his head and just tried to get away. They kicked him and thumped him, but finally he broke free and shambled off into the brush behind the camp.

Odd found him there a few moments later. "You're good," he said. "You're really quick. I think you hurt Harald."

Knut sat trying to push his nose into a reasonable shape. He said, "Thanks for all your help." It hurt to talk.

"I could see from the beginning you were going to get

thrashed. What was there for me in that?" Odd shrugged. "Father told me to get you back down to camp. The King is wondering what happened to you."

—⚬—

They stayed in the throat of the Humber for another day while more ships came in. With horns blowing and loud talk, another man arrived to give the King homage. Knut stood behind the King when this one came ashore, a short, knobby-looking man with spiky red hair.

A herald came rushing in with a short staff. "Thurbrand Hold of Lindsey," he shouted, and banged his staff down, which had no effect since the ground was sand.

Knut almost laughed. Thurbrand, though, was making a speech.

"Great King of Denmark, I am here to lay my sword at your feet and join you in your righteous war against the wicked Ethelred." He repeated this in other words for a while, saying he had five hundred men on the ground across the river from Gainsburgh, real fighters, true Vikings. Then he said, "And all I ask is that you let me take Uhtred of Bamburgh, when the moment comes."

Sweyn did not stir where he sat on the big chair; perhaps he had dozed off. From the semicircle of men around him, Eric of Lade stepped forward, bent, and whispered into the King's ear, "Uhtred of Bamburgh, the one who beat up the Scots."

"I called you in," Thurbrand said. His eyes darted from one man to the other. His toothy smile sagged. "You owe me this."

"But I'm here now," Sweyn said, with a laugh. His merry blue eyes were pitiless. "Do you submit, or no? These are your choices." He said, smoothly, "You are not first. I have already seen Jorvik."

Thurbrand's face settled. Knut nudged Odd with his elbow,

pleased with how Sweyn handled this. Odd whispered, "Ssssh," although Knut had said nothing.

Sweyn said, "I will have your answer. Obey me, or go to Ethelred."

The wiry-haired thegn of Lindsey kneeled down. "You are my King." He put his hands between Sweyn's.

Sweyn clasped his hands and said, "This whole kingdom is mine, and I will not suffer you to attack any part of it."

Thurbrand's head bobbed. Knut went away thinking his father was a great man, who had made Raef seem to pay homage even when he hadn't.

In the morning Knut walked up the river to fish, and his brother and his gang set on him again.

He remembered what Odd had said; he worked on marking Harald up before he yielded to the agony in his side and the pounding of their fists and knees and feet and scrambled for cover. They did not chase him. He lay under a driftwood log and grit his teeth together until the fiery pain in his side died down. He thought one of his ribs was broken; it hurt to breathe. He foraged among the ships and found some rope and tied it around his chest, under his shirt, as a kind of armor. That helped him breathe better. They had left his fishing line on the bank, and he went up the Ouse a long way to fish.

On the way back, they fell on him a third time. This time there were only three of them. He got Harald by the hair, and, even with the other two banging and kicking at him, he ground his brother's face into the gravel. They smashed his nose in again and left him sprawled on the riverbank, his fish trampled around him, and ran off. He went back to Sweyn's camp empty-handed.

Sweyn sat on a log among several men, Thurbrand beside him and just behind him the Trondejarl; they all watched him trudge to the fire. The sun was just going down. Sweyn said, "What is this, are you running into trees?"

Knut stood stiffly, favoring his side. He looked straight into his father's face. "Oh, bad ones, Father. Such a place as this is." Beyond Thurbrand, Eric Hakonsson sat in his glossy fur coat, a drinking horn on his knee, a broad smile on his face. Knut sank down, clenching his teeth at the pain. There was blood all over his shirt.

Sweyn turned back to Thurbrand. "Did you actually see Thorkel, or is this rumor?"

The thegn squirmed a little. "I heard it from a man who saw it."

Sweyn's eyebrows jigged up and down. "Then the rumor is he has lost most of his men?"

"The Jomsvikings fight for loot. Thorkel is running out of money. Now they know you're coming." Thurbrand rubbed his hand over his head, making his wiry red hair stand up. He liked being important; he was casting around obviously for more to say, to keep the King's interest. "But Thorkel still has a lot of good fighters, hungry too."

Knut grunted. His old hatred of Thorkel at least did not change. He hoped to be in the fight that killed Thorkel. He wanted to kill Thorkel himself. Of course nothing Thurbrand said was trustworthy. Knut glanced at his father, who was so cunning in his questions.

Raef had not been so cunning. Then he realized that the wizard had already known, in his own way, what people thought. He had been just ahead of Sweyn too, as he had always been a step ahead of Knut.

Knut had no gift like that. He had no idea now where Harald was, which he thought Raef would have known. When Odd got up to fetch firewood, he went with him and looked around for Harald but didn't see him. He realized the prince had his own fire, his own camp—a mark of his rank. Or maybe Sweyn and Eric did not like him enough to keep him around. He thought, I could think more broadly, anyway. As if he were

Raef. Noticing everything, looking for the sense of everything, seeing outside of himself. There were other ways people gave away what they were thinking than in words.

The sun set. They ate fish and drank bad ale. Knut silently took the place of serving his father. When he filled Sweyn's cup the second time, the big red-gold head turned toward him, glint eyed.

"We are going on up the Trent tomorrow, with the tide," he said. "Did you row much, up in Jorvik?"

"Around the river," Knut said. He had preferred horses.

"You will row with us tomorrow. We'll see how good you are with an oar."

Knut said nothing. He knew Harald also rowed in the King's ship. He hoped his bad rib would let him draw a full, hard stroke.

The next day, they caught the tide up the Trent, going south toward Gainsburgh. Thurbrand's ships led the way, since Thurbrand said he knew the river's course. Knut rowed in the aft steerboard quarter, Harald in the fore backboard of Sweyn's dragon. Someone else, Knut heard quickly, had been sent off to a lesser ship so he could take the oar, and he had better be good at it or they'd get Einar back.

But he had no chance to prove anything. Thurbrand did not know the channel, and, with the thick press of ships and the tide and the current, the fleet moved slowly when it wasn't stopped altogether. They sat, the oars shipped, and passed cups of water up and down the benches. For a while his ship was close enough to Odd's that they could call back and forth.

Knut caught sight once of Harald, when his brother got up on a shift change, ahead of him and across the way, but there were too many backs between them to start anything, and he was still on oar. Anyhow, Harald went the other way.

Sweyn was always there. He walked up and down the ship, talking to everybody, keeping them in rhythm when they actually got to row. He had a joke often, asked questions, heard a story. He gave Knut no special interest.

At night when they pulled off on the shore Sweyn sat twisting one tendril of his moustache around his forefinger and staring into the fire. Knut stood behind him. Thurbrand came up and sat beside the King, and Sweyn told him he knew nothing about the river. Thurbrand went on for a while about how it changed with every tide. Then Harald walked up and bowed to his father.

"You sent for me, Father." His gaze stabbed at Knut, over their father's shoulder. His face was scraped and scabbed from his chin to his hairline.

"Yes," Sweyn said. "You two—" He pointed to Harald in front of him and jabbed his thumb back over his shoulder at Knut, not even turning to look. "Stop fighting."

Knut said, "Yes, sir."

Harald said, "Then tell him I come first."

Sweyn bounded up on his feet, his teeth showing, and not in a smile. "No, I am first. Only I command here. Only I give orders. Even though you be son and heir you obey me."

Knut said, "Yes, sir," again. Harald had been staring at Sweyn, but now he dropped his gaze.

"Yes, Father," he said.

"Good," Sweyn said. "Go."

Harald went away. Sweyn crooked one finger over his shoulder, and Knut came around in front of him. Sweyn measured him with a look. Then he turned to Eric.

"Get him a sword." He lifted the cup, and the firelight gilded his hand, his arm, the cup, his face. "I think he's going to need one." He smiled, his teeth white, and drank.

CHAPTER TWENTY-ONE

Gemma went with her mother down to the church in Jorvik. She missed Knut, and it made her angry that Raef had sent him away. When she kneeled down at the altar and said her prayers, she made one especially for him.

Her mother said, "Not Knut. I'm so glad to be rid of him."

Gemma said, "But Knut is one of us too, isn't he?"

Her mother was busy. She and Miru and Edith were planning a procession, carrying the little stone Virgin from the baptismal altar all through Jorvik, to celebrate the coming of spring. Laissa said, "You'll forget about Knut, Gemma."

Gemma didn't want to forget about Knut. Every night she remembered the last time she had seen him, when he had held her against him, tender with her as he was with no one else. She hated her father; she thought he had driven Knut away because of her, and she brooded on it.

At night Laissa told her stories about Jesus, how he was the light of the world and the hope of all good men. She told her about the great Flood that wiped out all the wicked people, but then they came back again and were turned into salt and set on fire; but still, they came back, and so Jesus was born to save all mankind and bring peace to the world.

Raef said, "Why do you tell her that? There's no peace in this world."

Gemma turned on him; she and her mother had been sitting by the fire, and he had come up behind her. She said, "Keep still, Papa, this is about God, and you are not godly."

Laissa gasped and all around the hall people turned. Raef jerked his head up. He said, "Well, it all depends, I guess, on the disciple." He glanced at Laissa. "Where is she getting this, now?"

Gemma leaped to her feet, her arms out, defending her mother. "Will you beat her, like poor Knut?"

Raef turned on his heels and walked away. Laissa gripped her daughter's gown and pulled her down again.

"How dare you speak to your father so. Jesus would not want this of you."

Gemma hunched her shoulders, her eyes following her father away down the hall. She wanted suddenly to run after him, to tell him she was sorry. And she didn't want Jesus angry with her. Certainly the right deed was to speak the truth. Her father was a demon, even her mother said so. She turned her gaze to the fire. When she thought of Knut she felt him close again, his arm around her, comforting. Her eyes burned. She was suddenly exhausted.

She could not see Raef now without running away; she could not speak to him without fighting with him. It was as if to keep something of Knut there she filled Knut's place as his adversary.

"What's the matter with her?" Raef asked. "She used to love me."

Laissa said, "Oh, it will pass. She misses Knut. She blames you for that. Keep out of her way for a while." But he looked so grim about it that she put her arms around him and kissed him until he seemed better.

Raef did not sleep, even when Laissa slept. He would keep Jorvik out of Sweyn's reach, but the coming of the Danish King would shake the rest of England. He wondered how it would sit with the Lady, down in Winchester; what Ethelred would do; which way Thorkel would jump; and how Edmund would go.

They would find out, soon enough, as the word of Sweyn's passage went on before him; the word itself would change everything, even before the Danish King arrived.

Ealdgyth slid her hands down her husband's back, arched herself under him, whispered, "My lord. My King." His thrusting body rocked her back and forth. She cried out, which he liked. He shuddered, gasping to a close, and lay on her, breathing hard. He was covered with sweat.

She said, "I missed you very much, my lord."

He laughed, still slightly out of breath. "Well, you don't know." He rolled onto his side. "Are you happy here? I saw you had found some women." He reached out and stroked his hand down her hip. His hands, rough with callus, still gentle on her. His eyes warm on her.

She laid her head down on her arm. Everything about him absorbed her. His body was white as cream, his neck and face brown as his beard. "I have been making the place ready for you." She reached out to touch him again, to draw him to her again. There was a knock on the door.

"Go away," Edmund called, and his hand reached out for her.

"My lord." It was his second in command, Godwine, calling through the door. "This is important."

Edmund lay still a moment, his hands on her, his eyes looking into her face. She pressed herself toward him. She had to gather him in before they took him away again. Then he was saying, "I'm sorry." He slid back, off the bed.

She cried, "Edmund, stay. It can wait." She sat up, her whole body bare to him.

"No," he said, and went out. She turned and beat her fists on the bed, furious.

He came back, a little while later, but he had changed. He explained nothing. His eyes were different, distant, harder. She was afraid to speak to him, afraid of what he might say. He kissed her, and that night again he held her in his arms, but that was all. In the dark she clutched him as if she could keep him, but she fell asleep and in the morning woke alone in the bed.

She sat bolt upright. He stood in the middle of the room. The first daylight was just coming in. He came toward her, his hand out.

He wore the mail coat. He said, "I have to go. I'll come back when I can. I'm leaving you a guard. Tell no one who you are."

She grasped his hand in both of hers. "No, Edmund—stay. What is it? Please—stay—" He pulled out of her grip and walked out the door.

Finally the King of Denmark's fleet reached Gainsburgh on the Trent. Almost at once, Uhtred of Bamburgh came with forty horsemen in their green jackets; and gritting his teeth he swore himself into Sweyn's service. Thurbrand Hold stood there leering at him the while.

Knut realized they had already agreed to all this somehow. Everything that happened now had been crafted beforehand, planned and built like a ship, and now launched, ship tight. He saw that Uhtred dared not stay out of his father's court. Every day more of the thegns of Mercia came in, gave over hostages as surety, kneeled down, and put their hands between Sweyn's. Without a battle, without an argument, half of England was going over to Sweyn, and Uhtred had to join them or be cut off.

That night, Sweyn sat at a table with Thurbrand on one

hand and Uhtred of Bamburgh on the other. The two English lords sat like rocks, not looking at each other, saying nothing to anybody. Eric of Lade was on Uhtred's far side, and he and Sweyn talked back and forth at the shout, while the Saxon and the half Dane stared woodenly forward.

Sweyn gave Uhtred gold rings and named him lord of Northumberland and also to Thurbrand, as lord of Lindsey, he gave some gold. He beckoned to Knut to serve them all, and Knut brought the ewer. Harald was sitting at the side table—not a place of honor, but better than the wall. Knut kept his gaze on the ewer. As long as Harald was around, he was just the younger son. This burned unbearably in him.

Eric of Lade called out something across the room, pointing, and laughter erupted. They were talking about horses. Sweyn made some joking response, and the laughter doubled, the listeners roaring except for Uhtred, who obviously did not understand the dansker wordplay. Watching him, Knut thought, He's not like us. This alliance all rests on something that may not be there. He switched his gaze to Thurbrand as he sat picking at his meat, his eyes constantly moving, the rat brain inside his skull watching for some opening.

Sweyn, in a high good humor, traded quips about horses with Eric of Lade that were really jokes about women, drawing the rest of the hall hilariously into the quick-minded twists of meaning. Keeping everything under his eyes. Over at the side table Harald was shouting with laughter, his scabby face red with drink and mirth. Knut settled against the wall, folding his arms over his chest.

⚊⚌⚊

The whole fleet was drawn up on either bank of the river. Eric called Knut over to his ship. He dragged a big chest out from the forecastle and tipped the lid back.

It was full of weapons, swords, axes, knives, a big club with spikes. Eric reached in and took out a long, plain sword.

"Here. This is a good one. See there, that's old Finnleigh's mark. Bad Irish curses worked into every inch of steel, and they never break." Eric laughed. "You've used a sword?"

Knut felt ashamed, as if caught in a lie. "They taught me to use an axe. And I'm good with a bow."

"The sword is different." The Trondejarl ran his fingers along the blade, and Knut for an instant thought he saw the steel glow at his touch. Son of the Frost Giants. "Hold it low, the point higher than your hands. Use the heavy part up here for defense. Strike at arm's length, use your weight, put everything you've got into every blow. Know the counterstroke to every stroke you use." Eric held the sword out to him. "Odd can likely show you more. Odd's a fair hand with a sword."

"Thank you, sir."

Eric gave him an intent look, as if he knew something he did not tell. He said, mildly, "Oh, you'll pay me back, sometime." A moment later he was doing something else, and Knut went to find Odd.

Although only a handful of Gainsburghers still lived in the town, during the day men came in from the country driving flocks and herds and wagons full of turnips and cabbages, which they sold on the street at outrageous prices. Sweyn sent men down to keep the peace, and in this service Knut and Odd wandered all day long up and down through the market on the street along the river. They had no money and could buy nothing. The baskets of turnips and onions could as well have been the golden apples of the sun.

Instead they had to keep the market, tedious work, which was mostly just being there for hours and hours; Harald and his friends escaped this somehow, but the rest of Sweyn's crew also trudged back and forth through the busy place. Even when something happened it was boring.

"This one says you didn't pay."

"Did I not, now? His word against mine, I guess."

"Pay him."

"Come on, son, I'm one of you. He's a fucking Saxon."

"Sweyn says pay him."

"Now, come on."

"Is Sweyn your King?"

By then they had always paid, usually before. Not often enough he got the fleeting excitement of a real fight, where he could knock somebody down. Even then, it was Sweyn's name that ended it. Knut thought his father was the greatest King in all the world.

As they walked along, they talked about fighting and women. There were very few women in Gainsburgh, and none who would consort with a Dane.

Odd was full of quick talk. He said, "I've heard girls like men with big noses."

"Why?"

"They think they have bigger swangs."

Knut barked a laugh. "Then Thorkel the Tall's fathered half of England." He reached up to his own nose. Odd laughed.

———

As Eric had told him, he got Odd to practice with him, out in the woodlot behind the hall, first hacking with his new sword at logs, to get used to the edge, and then sparring with sticks.

Odd was quick and sure with every stroke and battered Knut back and forth across the yard, grinning widely, until Knut was bruised all over his arms and legs. Taking twice the blows he gave, he struggled to drive the staff through Odd's guard, strike low at his legs, high at his arms. Finally Odd himself stepped back.

"Stop. I'm out of breath." He sat down on a log butt.

Knut dropped the staff and doubled over, his hands on his knees. "You're good," he said.

"Sweyn taught me," Odd said proudly. "When he fostered me in Roskilde. Didn't the wizard teach you anything?"

Knut said, "I'm not sure what he taught me. Nothing about swords." He thought Leif had taught him more, with the axe, with the stories. He was jealous of Odd, fostered at Knut's own father's knee.

Odd stood up again, picking up his staff. "You take too much of a backswing. There are strokes where you've got to start with the sword behind you, but that's when you're plainly winning. Mostly keep the blade in front of you. You want to drive the other man back. And don't look where you're going to strike. Watch my eyes. Keep your knees bent. Here, let's try it again."

⸺◦⸺

One day Sweyn called Knut up beside him in the high end of the hall. He and Eric and Thurbrand sat at the table, half-eaten food strewn around them. Uhtred had gone down to take Lincoln, which Edmund Aetheling had abandoned when Sweyn came to Gainsburgh. Knut had been standing on the wall all evening, filling his father's cup and starving, and his father gestured at the meaty bone in front of him.

"Here, take that. Sit."

"Thank you," Knut said. He seized the bone and, sitting on the bench, began to tear off the shreds of meat with his teeth.

Sweyn laid his right arm on the table. "I am going into the West, to a place called Bath, to take the homage of some important men there. While I am gone, you will have Gainsburgh in your keeping."

Knut shot up straight, dropping the bone. "Yes, sir!" He fumbled for sufficient thanks, but Sweyn was talking on, twisting his right moustache tendril with his forefinger. His shrewd blue eyes glittered.

"Eric is going back to Norway and taking half the ships with him. Thurbrand here is going with me, and his carls, and most of the rest also, so there will be few men under you."

"Yes, sir," Knut said. He didn't care if it was one ship, if he was in command.

"Good. Keep order. If these local people want to come back, sort that out. Make sure the market's safe for the merchants. Tell them what to do when they need it. You're captain." The pale blue eyes narrowed, mirthful. "You and Harald."

Knut lost his breath. He felt as if a treasure had been snatched from his hands. He kept his face still, hiding the first flash of anger; his gaze shifted slightly, looking over Sweyn's shoulder. His temper cooled, and he saw this in another way.

He met Sweyn's eyes again. "Yes, sir," he said.

"Good," Sweyn said, and clapped him on the arm. "I like you, boy. I'll see you when I get back."

CHAPTER TWENTY-TWO

Sweyn left almost at once, taking much of the fleet; ships could travel the Trent as far south as Nottingham. Thurbrand and the other carls marched overland. The city was quieter, and some of the people who had lived here before moved back.

Eric and his ships lingered. Then one morning Odd said, "My father is going back to Norway tomorrow or the next day. Somebody named Olaf is trying to take the throne there." He and Knut were watching the smith, who had started up his forge again and was banging out a horseshoe.

"Are you going with him?" Knut thought he would miss Odd. "Don't. There'll be better fighting here."

Odd said, "So far, there's been none. But I'm staying." He said, "You know, once my father's gone, Harald's going to start something with you."

Knut began walking along the market street again, restless. "You think he'll wait until Eric is gone?" He had already considered this.

"Oh, certainly. My father fostered him; what Sweyn says goes with him too."

"I had the feeling Eric didn't like Harald much."

"Nobody likes Harald," Odd said.

On the side of the market street the tradespeople had their baskets and casks lined up for nearly half a mile. Knut walked along, looking everything over. Looking the people over. One of the women selling bread was a girl a few years older than he was, with long brown hair hanging loose. That meant they were unmarried. He stopped, gathering his Saxon.

"You live here?"

The girl looked up, flushed, and looked away. "Once. We

lived up there." She pointed with a quick jerk of her head along the street.

Knut wished he had some coin to buy the round, crusty loaves of her bread. He said, "Come back."

The women on either side of him were listening, and they laughed and lifted their hands, as if they pushed against him. "When you're gone," one said. The girl was looking down, carefully stacking her loaves, not talking anymore.

"We take—" He lost the words. "Peace. We keep peace. Sweyn is King here now. We not go."

But they were shaking their heads. Sweyn's name did not have its magic with them. One of the women held out her hand, palm cupped, and rattled off Saxon so fast he caught only the gist of it: Buy something or move on. He moved on.

Odd said, "What was that about?" He knew no Saxon at all.

"Practicing," Knut said. They walked up slowly along the market street, turned, and walked down again.

At night they slept in the hall, where Eric took the high seat with the other royal carls. Harald stayed with his three friends in a house he had taken over down by the river. Knut suspected some advantage lay in this, but he could not figure how to use it. Anyhow, Odd had said that nothing would happen until Eric had left.

This made him careless. Late that night he went out to the privy, and after he stood up from the hole and pushed the door open, two men closed on him, one on either side, and poked knives in his ribs.

"Move, and we'll stick you right now and throw you in the cesspit." The tall one snatched Knut's belt knife out of its scabbard. "You won't need this."

If he hit either of them, both would stab him. He knew them: Harald's friends, whom he had beaten a couple of times. They had reason to hate him. One was already pulling his hands behind him, looping a cord around his wrists and yanking it tight.

A bowstring, he thought. He tried to keep his hands apart, to get some slack. They took him off down to Harald's house, by the river.

Harald was there, sitting in a big chair in the one room of the house. There was a sleeping bench against one wall, but from the blankets strewn around Knut guessed most of them slept on the floor near the fire. Harald was drunk. He smirked and lounged around his chair, gloating.

He said, "Well, well. It's the little brother. And not looking so tough, is he? Sweyn's gone now, brat. I've seen how you suck up to him, little no-name, but I am the prince and the heir to Denmark, sworn so, and that's how it's staying." His smile widened. "Especially now, since I'm getting rid of you."

The man behind him moved, and Knut knew something was coming; he yielded with the blow but it still knocked him cold.

—⚬—

He woke in total darkness from a dream of smothering. He was upside down, his legs doubled up to his chest and his arms behind him, and everything wrapped round and round in rope. His head was splitting. For a while all he could think of was the pain.

There was a wad of cloth stuffed into his mouth, so he could barely breathe. The space around him was close enough that he touched wood on three sides, and it tipped slightly when his weight shifted. He could see nothing. The close air smelled sweet, yeasty, like ale. He was inside a barrel.

His mind went white. In a panic he struggled violently against his bounds, gasping for air, and almost sucked the gag down into his throat. Hacking it back out again settled him. He forced himself still, to listen, to pay attention, understand.

Wherever he was, he was not moving. As he shifted his

weight the barrel tipped back and forth on some uneven surface, but it was mostly level, so he was not on a beached ship. He could not hear the sound of the river. Nearby a nightjar began to chur, and faintly came the sound of the wind in the trees.

He was on the land, in Gainsburgh still. He suspected he was just outside Harald's house.

He began chewing at the gag, wadding it up with his tongue, tearing it with his teeth. He swallowed some and spat the rest. He drew a deep breath of yeasty air. That made him feel better, although he was still upside down and his head was pounding. His pulse was hammering in his ears. His body ached all over, his legs cramped, and his neck kinked. He could barely move his hands. Stretching out his fingers, he felt as well as he could along the curved stave wall behind him.

The staves fit perfectly together: a well-toasted barrel. He was still breathing hard. He wiggled, trying to get the pressure off his neck, and his shoulder scraped against the insloping side of the barrel and the rope around his arms slipped.

That was something. He twisted, pinning the rope again between his shoulder and the barrel. His neck twinged, but, shrugging and heaving, he dragged the rope a little higher on his shoulder. He slumped, exhausted, panting. For a moment he could not think, and he could not catch his breath. One loop of the rope came down and slapped him in the face.

He pulled and wiggled, but the rope was just as tight as before. Pushing with his head he forced his body up again toward the wider part of the barrel and jammed his arm against the side and twisted, and another loop came off, and then another, and then suddenly he was buried headfirst in a pile of rope and his legs were free.

He groaned with relief, pushing his feet up; his leg muscles were clenched, and it hurt to stretch them. His knee banged the incurving top of the barrel, and, before his legs were halfway straight, his feet came up against the lid.

He pushed as hard as he could, although it made his neck throb. The lid yielded only a little.

He paused a moment, forcing his mind to work. The rope was all over him. He was still breathing hard. The air inside the barrel was going bad. His heart began to pound.

He wondered if they had put a guard on him. He listened, but he heard nothing. He banged with his foot on the lid of the barrel and waited, and nothing happened. Nobody could hear him.

He smashed his feet against the lid; each time he struck it gave a hairsbreadth but then stopped, held fast. He kicked it again and again. Cramped in the barrel, he could not get a good angle on it. He was tired, his head muzzy. He kicked again, and something up there cracked.

At that, he pounded on the lid until his ankles were sore, but the wood held. Then in one desperate kick his heel skidded to the edge, and there was another crack, and bits of wood sprinkled down on him.

He blinked. Before him in the dark a ribbon of pale light shone down to a spot on the stave wall the size of his palm. He twisted his neck painfully and up there in the blackness saw a faint, ragged little hole, full of moonlight.

With all his strength he hammered his feet on the lid, which still did not move.

He had to get up there. For one thing, he could breathe up there. He began to work the rope down under him, rolling a little, shoving with his elbows, his shoulders, until most of it lay beneath him, cushioning his head. He rested again. His neck felt better. His head felt as if someone were pounding nails into it.

He began to work his way around upright, wedging himself against the barrel with his shoulders and feet and sliding upward, his head tucked down almost to his chest. His strength paid out and his muscles began to burn, but he could not stop. He wiggled and pushed himself around into the fat part of the barrel. The bowstring was still fast around his wrists, and there was no give to it; they had snugged it up again. The rope got wrapped around his neck and leashed him like a dog for a while until he worried it loose. He was trembling all over, gasping for breath. Twisting, he got one leg down, braced himself, and pulled his head around, scraping hard, bent forward under the lid. With a wrench he forced the other foot down also.

He squirmed sideways, his head jammed against the underside of the lid, found the little hole at the edge, and pressed his face to it. The sweet, pure air flooded into him. The pounding in his head eased. He took in a long deep breath and held it. He felt the cool air run all through him.

He was still pent in the barrel. He could neither sit down nor stand up, his hands bound behind him, his neck bent. His knees, jammed against the barrel's side, already ached. When he shifted, the barrel tipped slightly under him. He was on the ground, on a rock.

He hunched there for a moment. A thin flag of moonlight came down through the hole; he could see the ragged edge, where the stave had rotted. That was why it had broken. The rest was not rotted and would not break. Suddenly he was worn out. The urge came over him to scream for help. He bit his lips. Harald had him well tucked away. Nobody would hear him who would help him. Tomorrow, in the daylight, he could scream then, and someone might find him. It would be a huge joke, the kind of story he would hear everywhere the rest of his life. Barrel Knut. He knew of a man at Jomsburg called Oink Gorm because, when he was dead drunk once, somebody had thrown him in to sleep with the pigs.

If they even let him live that long. They could just haul the barrel downstream, after Eric had gone, and throw him into the river.

His knees and thighs were throbbing with pain. He twisted, trying to get the pressure off. The barrel rocked in its little tilt, and he banged his head on the lid. He thought of his belt. He wrenched his bound hands around and gripped it. With his fingers he worked the belt around until the buckle was in the small of his back.

It was a plain brass half circle, common as a rock. The flat was smooth, but the edge had a little tang from the mold. He wedged his hands down, one inside and one outside the buckle, and began to saw back and forth against the rough place.

It was hard. The brass was dull even along the edge. His arms ached. He stopped once, thinking this was useless; he was getting nowhere. He smelled wax: It was a bowstring. Twisting his hand around he got his fingers on the cord.

It was fraying. Wisps of fibers fuzzed it. Encouraged, he began sawing at it again. He was tired; his muscles burned and cramped. In a fury he banged his hands down, as if he could break the cord on the buckle, which did nothing. He tried to drive the buckle between the strands of hemp and got nowhere with that either.

He collected himself. He put his mouth to the hole in the lid and sucked in the air like food. He opened the belt by two notches, careful not to drop it out of reach, and went back to the steady sawing. Now he had more room. His eyes closed, his head nodded, and he jerked himself awake again. He told himself: Barrel Knut. Or you're dead. He wondered which was worse. Furiously, he sawed and hacked at the rope. His mind went grey with exhaustion. His legs were numb. He could not stop. He forced his hands to jerk back and forth, side to side.

Then his hands slipped and separated, and he brought them out in front of him and pressed them to his face and groaned.

He raised his hands up flat to the lid. This was not as well made as the rest of the barrel: a quick rig, the staves not even tongued together. On one he touched a flat metal ridge. He felt along the next stave and found another, and on the stave beside that another: crimped nails. A few inches beyond another row of them, two inches apart, ran edge to edge across the staves like the first. There was something nailed to the outside, holding the staves of the lid together. A handle.

He could fit two fingers through the little hole where the stave had broken. On the inside of the hole, on top of the lid, his fingertips grazed a stout piece of wood. The piece he had broken out had rotted along the edge of this crossbar. The staves on either side of the hole were solid, and he could get no purchase on them anyway.

He pushed the whole lid up again. It lifted slightly off the groove it sat on, but he could not budge it farther. He jammed his fingers into the hole and tried to turn the barrelhead in place.

It moved a few inches and then stopped. When he turned it back, it moved on about the same distance in the other direction and stopped again.

He let his hands rest. He thought of Raef, his broadmindedness, seeing this all around. He imagined what the barrel looked like, the lid on its groove, its top flush with the upper edge of the barrel, the crosspiece. He thought of every water barrel he had ever seen, tucked in by the mast of the ship, the lids held down with rocks, with axes, missing entirely. The barrel tipped under him again.

Then in his mind, as if the barrel had talked to him, a rope appeared, wrapping around it lengthwise. At the top the one crossbar became two, and the rope ran between them, down again the other side and under the barrel. That was why the barrel was tipping back and forth: it was resting on the rope. The rope crossed the top between the two lid braces, which kept the lid from turning any farther.

He rocked the barrel back in one direction and wedged his fingers into the hole in the lid and pushed sideways. If he could move the rope along the edge of the barrel, it would slacken. His fingers hurt, and he jammed his fist as much as he could into the hole and leaned on it.

The lid jerked an inch under the pressure. He grunted with

the effort of forcing it on, another inch, another, and then abruptly the lid popped up and slid sideways. Through the opening he saw the wash of the moonlight over the sky.

He pushed the lid off and stood up. The sky above him was creamy with the moonlight, more beautiful than anything he had ever known. The barrel was sitting with three others in a wagon, waiting to be loaded onto a ship. The other barrels probably had water in them and not men. He climbed out of the barrel and down to the ground and tightened his belt again.

He was behind Harald's house, far from the street. Night lay heavy on the town. The full moon was an arrow's length above the western horizon. He wiped his hand over his mouth. He had about two hours of darkness left. Eric was supposed to leave early, and these barrels would have to be on board by sunrise. He got up onto the wagon again to get the loose rope inside the barrel and went toward Harald's house.

——⚬——

Just before dawn the bore came up the Trent from the sea, a growling, muttering wall of water like an ocean wave that had gotten lost. When it ebbed back, Eric of Lade started off down the river, and as the sun rose dragon after dragon slid back off the riverbar and followed him. Knut stood on the bank watching. He loved to see this: the glide of each ship onto the flow of the river, the call of the helmsman, and then all the oars rising at once.

Eric's ship stroked away up the Trent. Just aft of its mast the water barrel was still packed in tightly, its lid roped down. Knut turned away, pleased.

——⚬——

That night in the hall, with Eric gone, no one sat in the high seat. There was still meat hanging in the cold house, but Knut could see he would have to get more. He sat on his bench eating when three men he knew came up to him.

"Well," he said. "Looking for someone?" They were Harald's friends.

The one in the middle, the tallest, glanced at the others and turned back to him. His name was Broom-Orm. "Where's Prince Harald?"

Knut swallowed a mouthful of roasted goat and tossed the bone down on the floor. He looked up at the tall man. "Weren't you going to throw me in a cesspit?"

The three shifted around, uneasy, and the man on the left nudged Broom-Orm, who said, "Look, we want to stay here."

"All right," Knut said. "Stay. I'm in command now."

"Is Harald gone?"

"He's not dead. If you owe him anything you still do."

"Is he in Gainsburgh?"

Knut drank the last of the ale in his cup. It was thick with sediment; he had to get some more of that too. He looked from one to the other of the three men.

"Harald is on his way to Denmark."

They looked at one another. Knut watched them; they were better fighters than Harald. Broom-Orm turned to him and said, with some urgency, "Look, what I did, I'm sorry."

Knut said, "Yes. I'm sure." He waved at them. "Go on, you can stay. Live up here from now on. Do what I say."

One of the others broke into a wide smile and came at him with an open hand, saying, "I'd like to tell you—" Knut frowned at him, drawing his head back, and his friends dragged him off. Knut went for another cup of ale.

CHAPTER TWENTY-THREE

Where the road from Derby met Ermine Street the great old road ran straight off through the forest, a long, shadowy cavern under the trees. The village was a mile away, but the spy had come down to meet Edmund here. Edmund's men were waiting in the trees, and Edmund stood with his back to his men so he could watch both ways of the road.

Being this close to Gainsburgh made him uneasy. He had already heard more than he wanted to know. He poked for anything else, anything that might come in useful.

"So you think Sweyn is on his way back to Gainsburgh?"

"He was coming into Nottingham when I left, sir."

That meant the Viking fleet was only days away. "Who are his closest men?"

The spy chewed his fingernails. "Eric of Lade, but he's left. Thurbrand Hold, the half Dane from Lindsey. Uhtred of Bamburgh. They went with him into the West. And his son. Sweyn's son. He's at Gainsburgh."

"Harald."

"No, he went back to Denmark. The younger son. Knut."

"I never knew there was such a one." He had heard Harald was a layabout.

"It's said they fought, the brothers, and the younger won."

"Knut," Edmund said, to remember the name. He nodded to the spy. "That's enough. Stay down and quiet. Thank God for your help, which I will not forget. You'll be well rewarded when the Danes are beaten."

"Pray God," the spy said, and, hurrying off, shied from the riders in the woods and plunged around them into the forest. Edmund went back to his horse.

They went back along the old Roman road, straight as an arrow shot. Edmund let Godwine lead the way. The road stretched south through the forest, shadowy even in daylight, the old broad-headed trees broken only by stretches of fen, broad, quaking green bogs. The summer was coming to an end. On the bogs the grass was blazing gold. Ahead was a village, where Edmund intended to spend the night. After that he did not know what to do.

He brooded on what he had learned. Sweyn had come into the North and brought his fleet up to Gainsburgh without a single man standing against him. Bath and Oxford had submitted. They had planned this, he supposed, or at least had known of it—all the Saxon thegns, whispering in corners, weighing each advantage, probably for years. All this while he had thought only Morcar spoke out against Ethelred, but now he knew they all had, in other ways, turned against the King.

In his mind he saw England like a chessboard, on which Sweyn's pieces filled one side and moved down along the left onto the other. Edmund's piece, one piece only, was in the middle. The King's pieces were in the right-hand side behind Edmund, Thorkel's Jomsvikings were around the castle of London, and Ethelred himself was the castle of Winchester, already in peril of check.

He saw no way out of this. He thought he would have to make peace with his father. The idea left a sour taste in his mouth. He could not bear to see his father again after Morcar's murder. He knew Godwine also would not endure it.

Then, ahead of them, a horse neighed.

He flung his hand up, jerking his horse to a stop, and swung down fast enough to get his hand on the horse's muzzle and pull its head down so it could not neigh back. He looked up at Godwine, who had wheeled around on the road, his eyes sharp, looking for orders. Edmund said, "Off the road," and led his horse quickly into the forest.

The other men followed. Back among the trees, knee-deep in mast, they stood by their horses and watched a stream of horsemen pass along the road they had just left. The riders up there were strung out for over a mile and moving fast, and Edmund could not keep count of them. Every time he thought they had all passed by, another group came along. He got close enough to hear them calling to one another in dansker.

His hair prickled up. This was a lot of men, but not really an army. A raiding army: the Jomsvikings. Going north. Going, he thought, to Gainsburgh. Just as Sweyn was to arrive in Gainsburgh.

There was only one way to understand this. He went back to Godwine, waiting nervously with the rest of the men in the woods. "Come on," he said. "I think this is Thorkel the Tall, abandoning my father for Sweyn."

Godwine said, "We could ambush them."

Edmund laughed. "No, much better. We can get London from them. Let's go, we haven't much time."

⟶⟵

In Winchester, even the oak leaves were changing color, and the days were shorter and colder. The news from the north was worse every day. Emma slept, but the Lady could not leave her to forage or to hunt. If Ethelred found her body empty, he might run mad; he could do anything.

There was no prey anyway. Sweyn was taking England without any fighting. The Lady was baffled. So many people around her, coming in and out all the time, tiptoeing around the chamber behind the curtains, kept her jittery and scattered. Now they were moving. The slaves were packing up chests and baskets. She had not been paying much attention. Ethelred was so annoying, a fat old man, grey faced, his hands on her constantly.

She had made a mistake being a Christian. She could not be a woman on her own; she needed this man, and now he was failing.

"We're going to Normandy," he said to her in the morning. He sat down heavily on the bed, breathing hard. "I've decided. My lord Eadric here will make the final arrangements. Get your whole household down with us, dear, never fear."

Eadric Streona, lord of Mercia, stood twisted by the wall, his hands wringing. Clearly he was less than happy with this. The Queen straightened, paying more attention.

"You're fleeing? You'll leave England to the Danes?"

Streona oozed his way forward, his knees bending as if he bowed and walked at the same time. "Sir, if you leave, that will be the end of it. Sweyn will be King of the English."

Ethelred lurched in his place, like a rock shifting in the rain. "God's eyes, it's just to Normandy. I will get Richard to help me. He will, for Emma's sake." He smiled at his wife.

"Sir—" Streona came up and kneeled before him. "You are leaving us all to Sweyn. Me, your son Edmund, all your people—"

The King's face did not change. The skin of his cheeks was thick and grainy. His eyes were red veined, yellowish, his mouth damp in the great, stained thicket of his whiskers. She shuddered when she imagined that mouth pressed to her face.

He said, "Let that traitor Edmund try to be King. The Normans are sending me a ship. It will arrive in Portsmouth in a week or so. My sons are already across the sea. My real sons." He turned again to Emma; he never took his eyes from her for long, and he leaned out to kiss her cheek.

The Lady slid away out of his reach. The boys were good currency. She was glad to have gotten them to Normandy. Emma said, "We shall go to Rouen. It's very pretty there."

Streona stood up, summoning more arguments. The Lady

watched him from the corner of her eye while Emma told Ethelred the glories of Rouen. She knew why Streona was so itchy. If the King left, he was thrown down. He was close to Thorkel, but Edmund mistrusted him, everybody else in England hated him, and Sweyn knew nothing of him save what the gossips said, and he had been involved anyway in Saint Brice's Day.

The Lady turned her attention away. Emma was uncomfortable, and that made her balky and whiny. All the household was jumbled, and their coarse, noisy feelings clogged the Lady's senses. She could rest until they reached Normandy, where new possibilities would unfold. She turned her back on Streona and Emma and Ethelred and their jabber.

—◦—

Streona paced back and forth, back and forth, his arms swinging. He had given everything for Ethelred, and now the King was letting him down, and it made him angry, the more angry because he was panicking, the ground under him suddenly steep and slippery. He could go to Normandy, but he had no friends there. Emma was not smiling on him anymore. He looked around the hall: the fire banked, the torches put down, except for one at the far end near the piss pot. People slept on the floor, on the benches, making the air foul with their breath.

He had worked so hard to make himself great, done such things for Ethelred that might damn his soul, and now it was all tipping into the hands of Sweyn Tjugas. He went up and down the floor again. With each step this grew clearer. If everything he had was going to Sweyn, then he should go there also.

In fact, he realized that, for a while anyway, he had something valuable to offer Sweyn. But he had to hurry.

He went out and found himself a horse. Before the sun rose, he was on his way to Gainsburgh.

—⚬—

Knut said, "Just down street. Just walk." He had bought one of the bread girl's loaves and was tossing it from hand to hand. "You, me, walk, street to end."

She giggled at him. She gave him a look from under her eyelashes, and he smiled at her.

She said, "I can't walk with you."

Then the two women on either side were gabbling at her in Saxon and shooing at him. He stood his ground, ready to argue. The girl gave him another look through her lashes, and he almost climbed out of his drawers. He wanted to bury his hands in that long brown hair. The thought itself was giving him a long sword. Then one of the women pushing at him was shouting, "Drake! Drake!" and pointing behind him.

He twisted around. A big dragon was coming down the river from the south. The girl went out of his mind like a dream, and he strode down to the riverbank. As he ate the loaf he watched them come in, first the one ship, and then three hard after, and then a long wait, and finally a steady stream of them. By noon all the bank was thick with ships and people.

Sweyn Tjugas's ship rowed in with pennants floating from the mast and a crown on the dragon's head, and when everybody let out his name in a bellow the King stood and waved his hand in greeting.

His ship was led into the bar, and he came up the bank. He saw Knut at once and looked around.

"Where is Harald?"

Knut said, "He went with Eric." That seemed too blank. "Something about somebody named Olaf."

Sweyn gave him a keen look and a smile. "Well, then, I'm glad to see you, as I said before." He stretched out his arm and laid his hand on Knut's shoulder.

Knut swelled, pleased, but before he could enjoy this, Sweyn said, "And see who has come with me." He waved behind him.

Knut saw, and his face stiffened. Thurbrand had gotten off the King's ship too, the moth-eaten gnome, but now coming ashore was another man.

Older, tall and dark, eyes still small and mean behind the axe blade of his nose. The Jomsviking Thorkel the Tall.

Knut gave the Jomsviking one furious glare and swung in behind the King as Sweyn climbed up the last of the bank onto the market street. The rest of his men streamed after him. The King came out into the middle of the street and looked around, unpinning his cloak in the sun. He said, "It looks well-kept here."

Knut glanced over his shoulder. Thorkel had stopped in the crowd behind them. He spoke to his father's ear. "So what is he here for, then? Has he sold Ethelred to you? Are you hiring him on?"

Sweyn stopped and faced him, his eyes cold. "What are you asking me? This is nothing you have a voice in, anyway. Who do you think you've become here?"

"Are you hiring him?"

"He has wisely come to submit to me, bringing London with him, which he holds."

Knut said, "He betrayed you to Ethelred, and Ethelred to you, and now you're giving him another round."

The King shot a sideways look at him and made a shake of his head. Beside him, Thurbrand was smiling through his thicket of teeth. Sweyn said, "He is a Jomsviking. They fight for money. Very well." Something struck him with amusement, the big golden head tossing with a quirky laugh, and he flipped back a long part of his moustache. "Then you can go with him, Knut, to take control of the garrisons there in London. To keep watch on him for me."

Knut was too angry to think. His cheeks were stiff. He

remembered being little and frightened and kicked around in the Jomsburg and still little and frightened going up a strange river to be abandoned to an even stranger man. Now here was Thorkel again.

And worse, this put battling Harald in a different light. He began to see his father juggling this, as he had played Jorvik against Thurbrand, Thurbrand against Uhtred, Harald against him, now him against Thorkel.

He had to say something. He said, "Yes, sir."

Sweyn was watching him steadily. "Good. That's more what I want to hear from you." To Thurbrand, he said, "I forgot what a green stick he is."

"They're all honor ridden at that age," Thurbrand said. "A few more years on him, he'll season." Knut simmered behind them, humiliated, fighting down his temper. Anger just got in the way, but it was hard.

He had stopped being angry, except at Thorkel, by the next dawn, when he and the Jomsviking chief started south on horseback toward London. Thorkel had brought a good four hundred men of his army with him, which slowed them down. Knut rode near the front, out of the dust, and as fast as he could without distancing Thorkel. They went straight down Ermine Street, the old Roman road, and in a few days they met the first Jomsvikings coming north.

"Edmund has London."

Thorkel's jaw dropped; he turned and stared ahead of them as if he could raise up the city out of the air. "He hasn't got enough men."

"He came in gate by gate and took each garrison piecemeal. Except most of us escaped."

Fled—when they saw they were being cut down, while their leader collected the fees, which they would be paid whether they fought or not. Knut turned and glared at Thorkel.

Boiling words seethed in his throat, and he was ready to pour them all over his one-time foster father when another horseman galloped up with word even more important: King Ethelred had deserted his throne and fled the kingdom.

CHAPTER TWENTY-FOUR

Ethelred had lied; when they swept out of Winchester onto the road south, the Lady discovered he had not brought all her women; he had brought only three, the rest to come later, he said. So far from their bodies, their souls were feeble, and so she was enfeebled too: She hated him for this. In Portsmouth they went to a townhouse, and, just as they were dismounting in the courtyard, armed men surrounded them. Still furious, buried deep in Emma, she chose not to help him.

"Sir! You are to come with us now, sir, you and your lady-wife."

There followed several moments of Ethelred offering the leader various bribes.

The leader was a scrawny-looking man with hair like red wool and awful teeth. Who took none of the bribes.

Then, from among the soldiers, a dark-eyed woman stepped forward in a dirty coif and a stained apron. Still sulking and inward, the Lady took no notice, until Ethelred screamed.

Then coming all awake she rose up through Emma and saw Arre, her soul naked before her, that sweet, glowing light. A rush of greed went through her, and she rushed to sup, but Ethelred seized hold of her.

"Save me! Save me—"

Without all her power, she could not fling him off. His weight dragged her down, his flesh, his carcass. And she could not save him. His face was green-white, mottled, sparkling with sweat, his eyes bulging from his sockets. She gripped him to keep him from pulling her off her feet. He wrestled with death only for a moment. She saw the life die in his eyes. She bent and pressed her mouth against his and drew out of him all that was left, heavy and coarse as it was, still life food. But when she straightened, the ghost was gone.

———

So, suddenly, she was alone, confined in a body no longer as important as before, at the mercy of these dull strangers. The Dane with the wooly hair, who turned out to be the notorious Thurbrand Hold of Lindsey, took her to Sweyn, who had come into Winchester since the King left it. Fortunately that was closer to where her women were, and she felt stronger with every step.

In Winchester Emma learned quickly what was going on. All of England but London was under Sweyn. Ethelred's son Edmund had seized London and still defied the Danes from there, but it was said everywhere that Sweyn would not wait for the city to fall. He would summon his own council and have himself crowned by Christmas.

Emma asked for a hearing and was called at once, as fit her rank. The Danish King was a fine, strapping man, with a splendid moustache, gold rings on his arms, and a gold belt. He laughed a lot. A translator carried their words back and forth. She kneeled down before him and asked him for leave to go to Normandy, where her sons were.

"I am alone now. You have taken away even my household." She wept, and patted the ground before his feet. "I have only my two baby boys. Let me go to them." She laid her head at his feet. She kept low, humble, meek. Best not to help him remember that, in Normandy, her sons were now the real Kings of England.

Sweyn stood and went behind his chair, leaning on it. "Lady," he said, "I shall take this in mind. Tomorrow I shall answer your plea. In the meantime, you will be comfortable in your own bower here in Winchester. I have restored your whole household, and I shall see you have everything you want."

This satisfied her. Now she had her women back too, almost without effort. She gave him Emma's sweetest smile and left.

—⊷—

Sweyn said, "We need to move quickly now. Most of these English lords hated Ethelred himself. Since he is gone, everything will change."

He misliked being so far from the sea. It was the overland trek, exposed on the road, that had made it impossible for Ethelred to escape. He thought about what Thurbrand had told him of the death of the King. Some violent spasm, he had heard of such things, especially among fat men. Still, the mark of fate was on it.

The Queen was yielding enough and seemed fluffy headed. The wizard's advice with her had a broad wisdom: Hold her against her brother, Normandy. But it might be good to put her under him, to take full possession.

He remembered that the wizard had said not to let her touch him. A warning shudder passed through him. She was ugly anyway. He gave orders for her to be kept in close confinement, always under guard.

—⊷—

The next morning the Queen said, "I will go abroad today."

Her women said nothing, having no power of independence. One went to fetch the man outside. The guard came to the door, a bony Danish face, young, with a pike in his hand.

She said, "I will need an escort. I will go to church."

The Dane said, "The King has said you are not to leave this place."

She flared at him. "Church! I want to go to church!" Her

voice rose to a shrill whistle; she gave off a rush of heat. She was too wild: She sent him off; he fled, and when she went to the door, the latch was pulled and fixed. She leaned her back against the door. The bower was a jail.

Inside Emma's body she roiled like a gathering wind. As if these puny things could hold her. Around her the accidental matter dissolved into a pulse of color and heat. She could blast everything apart and escape. Fly wild again. An ancient passion quivered in her. Once she had rushed out boundless over the void, her own skin the edge of everything—

Something cool formed in the red bloom. Patience. The old, raw lust faded. She built herself around that blue cold, crystalline, a still place, a center.

There were guards everywhere. They would kill Emma to defend themselves. If she had to leave Emma—if the stupid woman died—she would lose all her powers; she might even dissipate if she could not quickly find a new host. She composed herself of the blue cool patience, she made a castle of it. She saw there would be a better way out of this.

But surely this was a warning. Emma was no longer useful. She should shift again before Emma was too old. She began to think of transferring everything into a new body—younger, fresh.

She remembered taking Emma. She had been housed then in the nursemaid, attending the little girl for years, making possible the long, slow crushing of the child's mind to make room.

So she began to plan. There would be some way to escape Sweyn. She thought first that she would go to Normandy. Maybe she could go into a nunnery. One that took in foundlings. Then she remembered that Raef Corbansson had a daughter.

She savored that a while. There was something elegant in that, a symmetry, a triumph. Maybe after all this time here, she was becoming too human. Besides, the girl was tucked away in Jorvik. And first she had to get rid of Sweyn.

⸺⸺

Uhtred of Bamburgh stood with his face stiff and his hands together in prayer, watching the crowning of the New King. This was like a sword through his belly. He had been among the men at the council that declared Sweyn their King a few days before, when their voices had come out of them as if the Danes put them there, Danes at their backs. All this, the end of the long earth slide that began far back when somebody had said, "We should call in Sweyn Tjugas."

Now Ethelred was gone. And Uhtred was witnessing the crowning of a Dane in his place. Worse, he himself had helped it happen.

He had thought, once, that this was the only thing to do. It seemed much different, from this side of it, watching the crown settle onto Sweyn Forkbeard's great golden head. Uhtred had the taste of dirt in his mouth.

He glanced around at the other Saxon thegns, watching, lined up there before the new King. Half of them were heirs to Ethelred's victims. They stood looking at the ground or staring away into the distance, their faces grim. Uhtred thought he saw in them the same unease and rancor.

Up there, Sweyn sat in his fine, fur-lined robes, smiling, his eyes narrow. Probably he was seeing this too. Now up before him came the thegn of Lindsey, Thurbrand, to give homage— Thurbrand, who loved this day. Thurbrand with his hundreds of men. The half Dane kneeled before Sweyn and, in a loud screech, proclaimed himself into Sweyn's service.

Uhtred thought, I will not swear. Though they kill me. But even as he thought it, he shrank as if from an icy coat. He raised his eyes to Sweyn again and found the King watching him, smiling. Uhtred straightened up, squaring his shoulders.

They spoke his name. He could defy them now. He could stand here like a man and say, "You are not my King." Let them strike him down for it. The others were all watching him. Thurbrand, up at the foot of the King. The other, younger Saxons. The Danes, all around, all armed. Beyond them the ordinary people who had squeezed into this hall. Above all Sweyn watched him, with that smile, as if he knew everything already. Uhtred went up there, kneeled down, put his hands between Sweyn's hands, and swore the oath.

—⚬—

Edmund kneeled at the altar of the little old church, Saint Mary's, the oldest church in London. He was trying to pray for his father, but he could not. He thought his father had somehow worked his brother's murder. He hoped Ethelred was in hell.

To the left of the crucifix hung an old banner, a long blue strip of cloth figured with a yellow lance. He thought of the great banner of the Wessex dragon, hanging in his father's hall in Winchester. Probably the Danes would haul it down. He realized that there was no banner for England.

There might never be. He thought he should pray for more than his father now, with the kingdom all but gone.

"My lord?"

"Come up, Godwine."

The Saxon came forward; with his shoulders hunched, he looked even younger than he was. The news of the King's death had stunned him. Still more, the crowning of Sweyn Forkbeard. He said, "My lord, I need to ask something."

"You wonder why do we not give up," Edmund said calmly. He crossed himself, to end his hearing with God, and turned to Godwine. "Let Sweyn have England, since he already does."

Everybody would have heard by now that he was to meet the Vikings outside London, under a truce, in the afternoon. Most of them would be expecting him to surrender London to Sweyn.

"My lord, he holds all the country." Godwine swayed from foot to foot. "We are all that's left. How can we stand against them?"

Edmund said, "So you think we should give in. Go to him and kneel. He will treat us honorably; we have done nothing to disquiet him. We can go home, learn to speak dansker, and live in peace."

Godwine licked his lips. His eyes were hollow; Edmund saw he had not slept for brooding on this.

Edmund said, gently, "Go home, then, Godwine."

The boy was still a long while. At last, he said, "I don't want to."

"Why not?"

"I don't know," Godwine said. "My lord, why do you fight still?"

Edmund said, "Because if I don't keep fighting, there is no chance at all of winning."

Godwine's eyes widened. Someone had come into the back of the church and was waiting for them there. It was almost time to go meet the Vikings outside Bishopsgate. Godwine said, "Do you think we can win?"

"Yes," Edmund said, although he did not see how. "Yes, I do." He pointed up at the old standard on the wall. "Bring that, Godwine. Hook it to a banner staff so we can carry it."

—⊷—

"My lord, remember, they are treacherous." Godwine held the staff of the new banner with the butt wedged in his stirrup. He had shaken the dust off the long blue cloth and hung a pennant from the top to make it fancier. But he thought the yellow lance was brave. He was sorry he had spoken so to Edmund that morning. Edmund's courage buoyed him. His horse was eager and pushed on the bit. He glanced at Edmund, proud to be side by side with him.

"I want to see them closer," Edmund said. He wore his mail coat, his sword at his waist. He had no helmet on, nor the hood of the mail, and his long brown hair hung down over his shoulders. Godwine held himself that straight. What Edmund could do, he could do.

They rode together through the cavern of the Bishopsgate and onto the road outside. Godwine kept his horse to a jittery walk.

In spite of the bright sun, the air stung with cold. Below, the road ran off through trampled fields, blotchy with old snow. The Viking army was spread out on either side of the road. He wondered if they were trying to look like more than they were. On the road ahead of the rest, waiting for Edmund, were half a dozen men on horseback.

"Thorkel," Edmund said quietly. "And I have seen that yellow-headed man before. I don't remember where." He stared as they rode along, and said, "I think that's Knut Sweynsson, the King's son."

Godwine said nothing. The herald had said that name, along with Thorkel's, when he appeared the day before to ask for the meeting. None of the six Vikings in front of him looked like a King's son. The yellow head belonged to someone only a few years older than Godwine himself, although the boy was much taller, his sleeveless leather jerkin showing long arms ropy with muscle.

As Edmund came down the road toward them, Thorkel held his hand up, signaling that he should come no closer. The prince let his horse go on a few steps, to show what he thought of Thorkel, and reined in. Godwine nudged his horse off to one side. The banner flapped in the wind.

"So," Edmund said, "what do you have to say, pirate?"

Beside Thorkel, the yellow-haired Viking scowled and folded his arms over his chest. Thorkel spoke Saxon. He said, "You took the city. Meanwhile, Sweyn took the kingdom. Your father the King is dead. Sweyn is the King now. Give up, and we'll see to your safety. And that of your men."

Godwine grunted. Jomsviking promises were legendary, especially in another language. But he remembered what Edmund had said: They could go home and be at peace, and he wondered if he should want that. Ethelred, his enemy, was dead. He had not killed him, which left him unsatisfied. He fixed his gaze on Edmund. He would follow Edmund.

He thought, suddenly, What is the worst? I could lose. I could die. He flexed his hand around the banner staff. He would follow Edmund.

Edmund said, "I heard Sweyn Haraldsson was crowned in Winchester. But he may find the crown harder to keep than to win. I swear to you I will not cease until I have won my kingdom back again."

Thorkel said, with a cold laugh, "We can just sit here and wait until Sweyn comes."

Godwine raised his head. He thought, They think so little of us, then. He clenched his jaw, wanting to show them differently.

Knut Sweynsson spoke. His voice was harsh, and his Saxon wasn't as good as Thorkel's. "If we break in, we sack the city."

At this Godwine said, "You'll try," and Edmund flung one hand out, to quiet him. He bit his lips, embarrassed.

Edmund said, "Yes, as this boy says, you may try. I promise you, you will lose. There aren't enough of you to take London. You make a soldier of every soul inside, and we shall fight you street by street. You may win the city a while, but we will never stop fighting, and in the end you will always lose."

He gave them no more chance to talk. With a tap of his heel he spun his horse around, and Godwine wheeled to follow him. He thought Edmund was brave as a lion. Maybe it was better to fight, even if they could not win. They galloped up the hill to make the banner fly.

On the wall of the city, as they approached, cheers went up, people waving their arms at Edmund, calling his name and God's name and whooping. The gate was still open, and he and Godwine galloped through it with the banner and the cheers doubled. All along the street inside, people were gathered to see them come in. Behind them, the great gate creaked shut.

Edmund turned his horse around and raised his arm. "Godwine. Put the banner on the gate."

This much pleased the whole crowd, which roared and chanted and clapped. Godwine dismounted, gathering the banner in his arms.

"What did they say, my lord?" someone in the crowd called. Godwine hauled the banner up the steps to the rampart above the gate.

"That they will sack London," Edmund said, his voice ringing. "What we said was, they could try."

A roar of a cheer greeted them. At the top of the gate, Godwine found a socket for the banner pole and sank it in. The cloth furled in the wind, its bright blue rippling, and the yellow lance shining. Out there, the Vikings were riding back to their camp. He stood there beside the banner, hoping they would turn and see him, there beside it. He felt a quaver in his belly, a last uncertainty, and thrust it away.

—⚬—

Edmund thought of stealing out of London, which would be easy enough; boats came up and down the river every day. He could sneak away and go to see Ealdgyth.

He had seen her only a few times since he had left her at Lark Hill. Derby had given homage, and Sweyn had kept the peace there. She fared well there. Every time he went back, she wept and begged him to stay.

He wanted less to go because she wept. But he craved the sweet release in her arms.

He wondered, at night, when he should have been sleeping, if she was right, if he was chasing a phantom. He was the Aetheling and now tried in battle; by all the old rules, he should have been elected to follow his father. Instead, Sweyn wore the crown, and all England bowed to him save this one city.

Yet he felt himself the King. He lusted for Ealdgyth, but he loved his kingdom, and he alone fought for England. Sweyn was seizing something to add to the realm he had already. The rebels who had called in the Dane were fighting for their own strongholds, their revenge, their hatred of Ethelred. Now that Ethelred was gone, what kept them together? Edmund alone saw it one, the kingdom, the country, the people. If he gave up, would that not die too?

He shivered. His father's being dead made him feel as if some skin he had never noticed had been suddenly peeled off, and now he felt the cold. He thought again of his brother, his brother's murder, his father the murderer, the blood fouled, denied. How was he King, if not by blood?

In any case, Sweyn had the whole kingdom, and all Edmund could do was defend this one place. He couldn't leave to play with Ealdgyth, even though in the grey gloom before dawn he saw no hope in what he was doing here, whatever he said to hearten Godwine. He had to keep going, fight every day's little fight, even though he saw it narrowing before him to his doom. He rose from his bed, then, for fear that, if he stayed down, he might never get up.

CHAPTER TWENTY-FIVE

Knut kept his camp and his twenty-odd men separate from Thorkel's, a little to the east. The Jomsvikings spread out before the big north gate of the city. But then they did not attack, only went around the countryside in packs, stripping away all the food and driving off most of the people. Knut went to Thorkel's fire one sundown; the long city wall stood over them, and beyond rose the smokes and clamor of a lively place.

He said, "This is no siege. We should get ships, to attack up the river. Cut them off. Make them starve."

Thorkel was playing bones with two of his men. He jiggled the little white knobs in his hand. "We have no engines, boy. Sieges need engines." He glanced at the men around him, who grumbled in agreement. "Just sit tight. Sweyn will get to this in his own time. Meanwhile, we need to eat."

"Well, then," Knut said, "since I plan on attacking this place, you can supply me."

Thorkel's eyes blinked, his forehead creased. "What are you, not listening to me? That time with the wizard did your manners no good, I see. Sit tight and raid on your own."

"I am the son of the King," Knut said, and used the magic word again. "Sweyn's orders."

Too far from Gainsburgh. Thorkel's creased and bony face almost smiled. "Well. We'll see." He glanced at the men around him, smiling.

None of them were smiling. They were Jomsvikings and far from their ships, with no sign of plunder anywhere. That was why he would not attack. They were not land fighters. Their ships were all beached at Sandwich, far away.

Knut said, "Come when I call you, then." He turned and walked off, not waiting for anything from Thorkel.

—❦—

That afternoon they attacked the small gate, and with axes and sheer weight they beat it down and swarmed into the narrow gateway and drove the English back into the street. Knut led them to make sure they went the right way, hacking down two men who tried to hold the passage and then charging into the little square beyond, where the English were jamming together to make a stand.

Here the stair went up to the gate tower. If he could take that tower he could bring in the whole Danish army, whatever Thorkel did, and he bellowed to the rest to follow and rushed the stairs.

The English met him in a solid wall. He planted himself, slashing and swinging around him. Odd was at his shoulder, a long shield on one arm, an axe in the other. But steadily more English were pouring down on them, and he had to back up.

He gave the whistle signal. Step by step they drew down into the gate; they gathered up their wounded as they went, and then they turned in the outside gateway and ran down the long slope toward the camp, with the English jeering behind them.

Knut ran only a few steps from the English. His back to them, he walked up to his camp, three fire rings on the trampled grass with a litter of gear all around. Five hundred yards west, by the road, lay Thorkel's bigger camp, quiet as always.

Knut's sword was in his hand, the hot temper still coursed in his blood, and he slashed at the nearest bush.

"If he gave me more men. If I had enough men." He cleaved the bush in half and stuck the sword hard into the ground. The

others were scattering around the place, looking for drink, sitting down. He shot a look at Odd.

"Thanks. I'd have gotten killed without you."

Odd said, "Maybe. We nearly had it. You're right. Twice as
many men, we take the tower." He nodded, smiling. "You did
well. I could hardly keep up with you. You must have had a good
teacher."

Knut snorted at him. He turned, looking over his band; some
were lying flat on their backs, but they were just resting. He had
lost nobody; there were only two wounded men, hunched over
by the fire. He went over and squatted down beside them.

"What happened to you?"

"Something landed on my back, and then Ketil damn near
cut my head off."

"It was a mistake," Ketil said. He came up with a bucket of
water and some ale. The nick on the wounded man's neck did not
look serious. Knut went off to the edge of his camp and looked
toward London.

The city's old overgrown wall stood at the top of a slight
rise, the tower of the gate rising straight in front of him. He
meant to keep hammering that gate until he took it—and to hell
with Thorkel, sitting on his backside.

"Altar boy!"

He looked over his shoulder. This was the name they had
given him after the argument with Sweyn about Thorkel. In fact
it was Thurbrand, who had been there, riding up toward him,
trailing a string of his own fighters. Knut put his hands on his
hips.

"I hope my father's sending you with more men."

Thurbrand reined down, swung his leg over the pommel of
his saddle, and slid to the ground. He had gotten a lot of gold
since this started, rings and chains and earbobs. "No, in fact the
King wants you in Winchester for a council."

Knut crooked his finger at somebody to bring by a jug

of watery ale. "Take Thorkel. I'm close to breaking through here."

Thurbrand drank deep of the ale, his throat moving under the wiry flare of his beard, and lowered the jug. A rim of foam clung to his moustache. He said, "This is the King, commanding," his voice a little testy. He held the jug back to the man behind him. "Kings Day. In Winchester."

Knut still stood with his hands on his hips. He looked up toward the long spine of the wall, and the gate he was trying to capture. "Kings Day. What's that?"

"A Christian feast. Three days from now."

Then he had to leave at once; he could not mount another attack. He gritted his teeth. They would think, in there, he had given up. He began to argue with Thurbrand, who was pulling him away from this. Before the words came, it occurred to him that if they thought he had given up, they would be softer when he came back.

He said, "All right. Odd—"

The Trondejarl's son walked up to him, eager. "I'll go with you."

"No, you won't; you'll keep the place. I can go by myself. Move along this wall. Let the English see you. Try to get them to raid out. Pound them if they do."

Odd's face fell. Knut laughed at him. "What, you think this will be fun, sitting at tables listening to people talk? I'll be back. Keep them working." He turned toward Thurbrand again. The thegn of Lindsey was watching him, smiling. "Did you bring me a horse?" Knut said. "Good. Let's go."

—◦—

He had never been to Winchester before. The size of the buildings amazed him, the hall of the King stretching its great roof back among the old oak trees and, across the broad open square, the church soaring vastly up. The people all seemed to wear gold, rich velvets, and laces. Even the horses were more richly dressed than he was. Thurbrand took him to the King's hall; said, "Go in and wait"; and rode off.

Knut dismounted. His eyes turned after a pretty girl walking by; he thought he might as well make some use of being here. He remembered to keep his eyes wide, looking at everything. People were walking up and down the long, flat step to the hall, and he hitched his horse to a pole and went inside.

The room was high ceiled, dim after the bright sun, and half full of people, all talking. The space cupped the dozens of voices into a single blur of noise. Knut went along the wall, wondering what he should do. He kept a sharp watch around him, saw men he recognized: Uhtred of Bamburgh in his green jacket, some of the thegns of the Five Burhs—all surrounded by servants, floppy hats, gold badges. A wasp buzzed by him, humming in the dusty air. In the back of the room the high seat stood on a box. There was a big pale square on the wall behind it, as if some hanging had been taken down.

People went to and fro in crowds and singly. Most of them were Englishmen. He marked a few Danes here and there, but they all seemed to be on guard. He stood near the wall, considering how to find something to eat, and then saw Thurbrand walking across the hall toward him.

Other people saw Thurbrand; they turned and swept him bows, in the English way, very wide and deep. The thegn paid them no heed, came straight to Knut, and said, "The King wants to see you. Come along."

He followed Thurbrand down the length of the hall to a little door, and through, and stood in a small chamber. This was some kind of closet, small, with a big padded stool and a bench and a small door out the back. In the door was a round window, its shutter open. The room was empty: Sweyn was not there.

Thurbrand huffed, surprised, and went out, and then the King came in through the back door. He was pulling his clothes together. He had gone out to make water. Knut felt suddenly much easier, his father somehow smaller, manageable, if he had to piss like any ordinary man. He said, "Hello, Father, do you want to talk to me?"

Sweyn sat down on the stool. "Knut," he said. He planted his fists on his knees and stared at him. "What is this I hear of you?"

Knut jerked, his mouth falling open; he thought suddenly, wildly, that Thorkel had sent foul stories about him, that he had done something ill without even knowing. Sweyn watched him with narrow eyes, his constant, meaningless smile on his lips.

"So London is a tough nut."

Knut wondered if he were in trouble. Thorkel could be blaming everything on him. He thought of Thorkel again, with a brimming rage; if Thorkel would attack, they could take the city. He held this in. It did nothing to talk about a man behind his back, even as shiftless a man as Thorkel. Whatever Thorkel said behind his back.

He said, "We'll get it. I need more men."

Sweyn said, "I'm thinking to give you the whole command and send Thorkel on his way. What do you think of that?"

Knut was still. His father confused him; in a flash, he knew that was Sweyn's whole intent, that he never feel certain. But to command the whole army against London. He warned himself not to rejoice in this; Sweyn had done this before. There would be somebody else to knock against, some new rival in Sweyn's eternal balancing game. He said, "Yes, sir."

The King's smile widened, and he leaned forward a little. "What I've heard of you, you are the only one doing anything there, and your men would follow you into the abyss for the sake of a good word."

Knut swallowed, wary of believing it, yet he was childishly pleased at this. "Thank you, sir."

The door into the hall opened, and Thurbrand came in. "They're here, Sweyn."

He held the door open as he spoke, and Knut saw something moving toward them through the light there: the wasp. It was late in the year for a wasp. He watched the thing buzz into the room. It circled around the room and landed somewhere, out of his sight, and the buzzing stopped.

"Send them." Sweyn nodded to Knut. "We'll talk about this later."

"Father," Knut said, moving sideways, looking for the wasp. Thurbrand went out.

"Go, Knut," Sweyn said. "I have much to do. You can sit at my table tonight; I will have some presents for you." He leaned back on the stool, and then he let out a yell, slapped his neck, and swore.

Knut shouted; he plunged across the room, his eyes following the sudden zigzag course of the wasp rising into the air. Sweyn reeled up onto his feet, brought his hand from his neck, and looked at his fingers.

"Something bit me."

"I saw it," Knut said. The wasp went out the round, unshuttered window, and he followed it out the small door.

The door opened on a garden, tucked for the winter under heaps of grey straw, with leafless little trees around the edge. He saw the wasp flying off toward the far end and ran after it. The wasp flew over a hedgerow, and he scrambled through the thorns, got stuck, and lost it, until he heard the buzz.

He turned. The wasp was landing on the wall of a little octagonal building behind the hall. As he watched, it crept up in under the eave. He ran around the building, looking for the door, and found two English guards dozing there.

He kicked the nearer one. "Let me in here."

The Englishman twitched up onto his feet. "Hey, who are you?"

Knut gathered his Saxon. "Let me in; I am from the King."

The other man said, "She's foul when she's disturbed." But he turned and unlatched the door and opened it.

Knut shoved his way in through the door, into a beautiful, crowded room. The walls were white, hung with flowered cloth; scented rushes covered the floor. It was the Queen's bower. Her women in their white gowns were doing chores: brushing, cleaning, sorting. They seemed unsurprised to see him. They said nothing to him. None of them looked like a Queen. He strode across the room to a curtain and pulled it back.

Behind the curtain was an alcove. There on a cushiony bed a plump woman in a silken robe was just yawning awake. Her white moon face turned toward him, and she started in fear at the sight of him. "Who is this? Help!" He threw the curtain back in place. He wondered if he imagined that her voice buzzed.

He went out again through the listless women. On the floor among them a brown wasp was lying on its back, its legs wiggling in the air. Emma's shrieks sounded behind him. He crushed the wasp under his foot and left.

—◦—

He could not explain to Sweyn what he suspected. He wasn't even sure himself what had happened. For a few days anyway the King seemed no different. He was hearing men's complaints and granting charters, and he wanted Knut there to witness them. Then, on the third day, he fell sick.

He was a big, strong man; at first he was only tired, and there was a sore on his neck. He went on with the work of being King: seeing men and hearing petitions, sending men here and there to speak for him. There was to be a council in two days, when he would declare a full attack on London, which Knut would lead.

He gave Knut a gold arm ring, and they talked over storming the city.

In two days Sweyn was lying in his bed, covered with tiny open wounds that oozed and bubbled blood. Knut hung by him. He kept watch out for more wasps; he made sure the guards kept the Queen always under their eyes. He himself gave his father sips of ale and bits of bread and cheese and helped the servants who changed the soaked bloody bedclothes. He watched Sweyn's face for the first sign he was getting better.

He was not getting better. Thurbrand, Uhtred, even Eadric Streona stood around the hall muttering, their eyes white. In the town the streets were quiet. To get his father away from the Queen, Knut took him in a wagon up to Gainsburgh. By the time they reached the little city on the Trent, Sweyn was dying.

Knut felt stupid with grief and fear. In spite of everything, he loved his father. He could not leave his side, and after a few days Odd and the rest of his men showed up from London. Half the fleet was already at Gainsburgh; on the beach, around the fires, men talked of nothing but the dying King.

Thorkel came, and Thurbrand, and stood beside the King's bed. Uhtred did not come. Nor did any of the other Saxon lords. Knut noticed this; he sent all the men out to the hall and sat alone with his father.

The King lay on his back, his flesh raw and oozing, and his breath rasping in and out. He said, "Knut."

Knut moved up nearer; he could not speak. He knew the King was near his death.

In the rotten mess of his face Sweyn's lips moved. "Take . . . me back to Denmark. To be howed. Not here. My son. My son. I leave this work to you. But I tell you . . . the crown of England is a curse." His eyes gleamed in the bloody ruin and then closed.

Knut sat there, hunched forward and in a long daze. He became aware again, trying to understand why it seemed so still, until he realized his father had stopped breathing. He slid abruptly down off the stool and sat on the floor. Tears squirted down his face. He ground the heels of his hands against his eyes.

He sat in the hall with a cup and a loaf of bread, and people came up and spoke to him, but he hardly heard them. For the first few days, he did nothing but see that Sweyn's body was washed, dressed, and then packed in salt to be taken back to Denmark. The salt, strangely, made him look better, the sores paler. Odd helped him.

Knut remembered what else Sweyn had said before he died. "What do I do now?" he asked, and Odd shrugged.

"I have no idea. If I were you, I'd be scared."

He was not scared, just stupid.

Thorkel came to him and said, "You must drink the arvel-ale. As your foster father I will sit beside you at the rite."

After Winchester the hall at Gainsburgh seemed small and mean. As many as could crowd into it, that many were left outside. Knut sat at the head of the table. He still could think only of Sweyn. The high seat had been taken away and a bench put in its place. Thorkel came and sat beside him, and they poured the ale.

"Sweyn Haraldsson," Knut said. "King of Denmark, King of Norway, King of England. Of all the Vikings he was greatest. Those who did not bow to him were those he did not fight. He closed the ring." He raised the cup at arm's length and lowered it to drink.

The hall thundered with voices: "Sweyn. Sweyn."

Knut put the cup down, and beside him Thorkel raised his cup and drank. "One king falls, another rises." He looked out over the hall. "For Denmark, there is Harald Sweynsson, but for England—let the swords choose!"

The roar went up again, like some beast, and then all around the hall men were shouting, "Thorkel! Thorkel! Thorkel!"

Startled, Knut lifted his head. At once he saw what the Jomsviking had done, and he wheeled around to face him. Too late. Thorkel's lips thinned in a smile, his little eyes gleaming. He was stealing the crown of England.

Then, in the crowd, other voices were shouting.

"Knut! Knut!"

Thorkel's face stiffened. Twisting, Knut looked out over the hall. Men from outside were pushing in at the back, and the sound of his name grew to a thunder, and Thorkel's faded away. They were all shouting his name now. Thurbrand stood in front of the table, bellowing. Odd came up beside him.

"Knut! Knut! Knut!"

He got up onto the table and stood before them. The whole hall thundered with his name. This was, he thought, their last salute to Sweyn. They lifted him up; for Sweyn's sake, he was their King now. But these were Danes, not English. And this was England, not Denmark.

CHAPTER TWENTY-SIX

"The King is dead."

Uhtred startled all over, as if a cold hand touched him. He said, "Where?"

"In Gainsburgh," Thorkel said. He leaned his back against the door; he wanted this kept quiet as long as possible. "His body's being taken to Denmark. His son is up there seeing to the proper rites. Uhtred, hear me. This is in our hands. We have to call the council together. We can make the next King."

The Saxon straightened; his eyes went blank. He looked around; they were in the back of the great hall in Winchester, in the little room with the circular window in the door. "The next King. Did Sweyn lay his hand on anyone in particular?"

"The fleet shouted for Knut," Thorkel said. There was no way to keep that hidden: better to admit it right away, although he still had hopes of getting in there himself. Even if he could only maneuver this for Knut, there would still be some edge in it for him. "But he's not here. We can call a council. Most of the thegns must still be here, aren't they—waiting for Sweyn to come back?" He nodded to Uhtred. "Then you and I can talk them into anything." His voice fell. "You can make yourself great with this, Uhtred."

"Yes," Uhtred said, and his face twisted. "Greatly evil, I think." But he shrugged. "We can get enough thegns together to call it a council." He crossed himself. "God have mercy on King Sweyn. He did not look good when he left here."

Thorkel said, "He looked a lot worse when he died." He slid away from the door. "You summon the council. As soon as we can, get them in here."

"Yes," Uhtred said. "I will." He thought of someone else he would summon, as well, and with what.

     —❧—

Edmund said, "You're sure?" He held the folded cloth in his arms and stroked his hand over it. The red was faded but still lovely. He could see just the tip of a wing of the golden dragon sewn onto it.

"They are calling a council tomorrow to announce it. In Winchester, at the Great Hall there."

"The King is dead." Edmund turned to Godwine. "That's what it meant, when the armies withdrew." Suddenly, almost overnight, a few weeks before, both the little Danish forces opposite the walls of London had drifted away.

Godwine said, "This could be a trap, Edmund."

Edmund turned back to the boatman who had brought the news and the banner itself down the river. "Who sent you here?"

"I cannot tell you. But he means you well, sir, or I wouldn't have brought it." He straightened, leaning on his boat pole. "You can trust this, sir."

Edmund's blood coursed with excitement, and his skin tingled with the urge to act. He felt as if he had been let out of his coffin, his life begun again. King Sweyn was dead. What had seemed an impossible task now was within his reach. His gaze fell again to the red banner, the Wessex dragon, the standard of Alfred, who had thrown out the Danes a hundred years before. Edmund was called to this, and he would answer. He turned to Godwine: "We're going to Winchester. Send for horses."

     —❧—

As Thorkel had foreseen, many of the thegns and lords who had sworn their oaths to King Sweyn were still around Winchester, expecting to be summoned back into council anyway. When the call went out, they gathered swiftly, pouring into the city and coming at once to the great hall.

Few knew yet of the death of the King, but rumors swept them. Uhtred, as he greeted them, turned aside their questions—Sweyn is not here, he said, truthfully. No, Sweyn is not here. Thorkel, the Jomsviking chief, is here.

One of the Wessex thegns frowned at him. "The last I heard, the King was deathly ill. What's going on?"

"Wait," Uhtred said. "He was sick, yes." He went on to meet a swarm of men from Wessex, surrounded by their underlings, coming in the door.

He went up to the high table, where Thorkel stood before the empty high seat. The Jomsviking chief was looking out over the hall, his brow rumpled. Uhtred said, "There's many of them, see, and all the important ones."

"Thurbrand isn't here."

Uhtred snorted. "Did you ever think Thurbrand was coming?" When Thorkel shrugged, frowning a little, Uhtred turned away, altering his judgment of Thorkel's wit. Then his gaze caught on another parade of men coming in the door.

"God have mercy on us," he said. "The vultures are coming in to roost."

"What?" Thorkel said, and turned. When he saw who had come in, he muttered a nasty Danish oath.

"Eadric Streona," he said. "That snake. You know he betrayed Ethelred to Sweyn."

Uhtred grunted. He had not known, but he had suspected this. "Whatever he did, he's here now. I think we have a full hall, here, don't you? Let's get started."

Thorkel said, "No, wait, we have to—"

Uhtred brushed past him, moved up by the high seat, in front of the wall. He threw a look over his shoulder at the wall. Where the Wessex dragon had hung was a patch of lighter wood. Sweyn had taken it down when he came, but Uhtred had kept it, and now he wondered if the banner had gotten where he had sent it.

He turned toward the crowd again and raised his arms. "God's peace to all men here," he said, and the place quieted. "Christ have mercy on us." He crossed himself.

The prayer rumbled back through the hall toward him. Now they were all watching, even Thorkel. Uhtred licked his lips. He had no notion what this could come to, but he knew where he wanted to go.

He said, "I am to tell you all that King Sweyn is dead."

For an instant, the whole hall fell silent. Then, like a pot full of noise, it boiled over, everybody turning and speaking, a foam of white faces. Thorkel came up beside Uhtred; he had finally caught on.

"The King named his son as his heir, his son Knut," the Jomsviking chief called. "The Danish army hailed him King. Now we are here to recognize him as the King of England."

Uhtred said, "Knut. Who is this? A boy, a greenling."

Thorkel's face flushed dark. "King Sweyn named him—"

"And he is not English," Uhtred said.

A roar went up from the crowd. In the hall, men were pushing closer to the front, climbing over the tables, filling up the space before the high seat.

"Uhtred, speak!"

"We are Englishmen—"

Thorkel bellowed, "You all swore to obey Sweyn's will, and his will is that Knut follow him, King of England." His voice carried over the clamor in the hall. A tall man in a long green coat rushed up across the table from Uhtred.

"We're with you, Uhtred. Keep on." He banged his fist on the table.

On the far side, Streona, still wearing his short black Norman coat, thrust up his arm into the air. His waxy voice rolled out. "Sweyn's gone. England's free again. We shall not follow this stripling boy!"

Thorkel shouted, "If you defy him, this will bring war, and war, and more war—"

Then, in the back of the hall, the doors flew open. The great crowd swayed, hushing. Thorkel fell still, his mouth open. The crowd yielded, half to one side, half to the other of the hall, and down the aisle they left rode a file of horsemen.

Their leader was Edmund Aetheling.

He wore the heavy mail coat he had put on when he began his rebellion against Ethelred. The sword at his side had been Aethelstan's. After him came another man with a staff, and on it, the Wessex dragon.

As Edmund passed through the crowd, the men stilled and stood to face him; many bowed, and many more kneeled. He and the man with his banner rode straight up the hall to the high seat. Uhtred glanced at Thorkel. The Jomsviking had clamped his face shut. The lord of Bamburgh faced Prince Edmund.

"Welcome, my lord Prince."

"I have brought this," Edmund said, in a voice that carried through the hall, "to put it back where it belongs." He waved his hand at the great red banner above him, and the watching men burst into a bellowing, jubilant applause.

"My lord," Uhtred said, "it is your honor to put Alfred's banner back in Alfred's hall." He hesitated a moment, to give weight to this next. "My honor is to greet you first as King of England."

A roar went up from the surrounding men. Thorkel stood still, his shoulders hunched. Edmund waved to the rider behind him, and he and others took the great banner of Wessex up, climbed up behind the high seat, and shook it out, red as blood, the winged dragon flying on it as if alive. They hung it on the wall where it belonged. Then Edmund turned and stood before his father's high seat, looking out at the crowded Saxon nobles.

Thorkel was sidling away. Uhtred kneeled. Everybody was

kneeling, paying homage to their new King. Some wound had been healed that Uhtred had carried since Sweyn's crowning. England, he thought. We English have made the King of England. He bowed his head, grateful that at last he had done something good.

━━◦━━

Edmund went to Lark Hill a day later. They rode in the gate to the courtyard and dismounted, and Godwine took their horses away. Edmund went around to the bower behind the hall, but he met her on the way there, coming up from the garden.

She startled, seeing him. He stopped, wondering again if he should have come. She was older. Not as pretty as he remembered. He wished her well away from the court, anyway; he had much business there and could only stay here a day, even less. But his body was already quickening; she came toward him with her hands out, and he went into her embrace with delight.

━━◦━━

In Gainsburgh, Knut said, "They elected Edmund."

Thorkel said, "It was Uhtred of Bamburgh, that lying dog. He got them to throw aside their oaths."

Knut gave him a hard look. He blamed Thorkel too, mostly because it pleased him to do so. He paced away from Thorkel, remembering to keep his temper, to see this wide and deep. In the bottom of his mind, he realized, he had been expecting this.

But it was his kingdom. He wanted it, whatever his father had said, dying. The fleet had shouted it to him. He stood at the door of the hall, looking out over Gainsburgh, down toward the river. Only two days before, Sweyn's gilt-headed dragon had sailed away down that river, taking the dead King home.

He had done this, a son's duty. Served his father's wishes, honored him as the mighty man he was. What to do next was more of a problem.

Thorkel said, "They swore sacred oaths and broke them. I've got five hundred men. Call back Thurbrand, and, with the crews here, we can go down there and raid the whole of Wessex. Wipe out Edmund. Sack all those cities, the churches, the monasteries, the manors. Whatever's left, you can be King of."

Knut said, "I saw how your men fought at London." He said nothing about Thurbrand, who had gathered his horsemen right after the King's ship sailed and ridden back home to Lindsey, across the river. Thurbrand had been Sweyn's man. Knut doubted Thurbrand was his.

"Damn Uhtred," Knut said. "Where are those hostages?"

"I sent them down to Sandwich, with the rest of my men," Thorkel said. "Where did it get you to fight so hard at London? Each Jomsviking is worth ten of the Saxons." He crept closer, whispering into Knut's ear. "Now, you know, we could take fat places: Glouchester, Glastonbury, Bath, the places Sweyn left alone for the sake of their homage. You saw Winchester. You can strip enough gold off the walls in Winchester to make a crofter rich."

Odd had come out of the hall and stood listening to them. He said, "I told you that you were going to have to fight for this. Go to the Tronders. My father will give you an army."

Knut looked into the street. People moved briskly along, the market wives with their baskets and a man leading a goat. A dog went loping down the street. On the thatch above his head, a cock crowed. A shutter opened in the row of little houses across the way, and a woman leaned out to flap a dusty cloth. All this was Saxon, he thought. They would always outnumber him.

He had to decide what to do. There were fifteen dragons down on the beach. Thurbrand's men were better off back in

Lindsey. With a force this size, he could not take a city, much less the whole kingdom. He said to Thorkel, "Where are your ships?"

Thorkel said, "Sandwich. We beached them proper too; they're kept."

"Then I will meet you there," Knut said. He turned to Odd: "We will go with the tide, on down to the Humber."

Odd's head bobbed. He glanced at Thorkel; like Knut, he probably wondered whether Thorkel would be in Sandwich when they got there. It mattered little to Knut, one way or the other. He went out into the street to walk around, restless.

He stood on the river street and watched the brown water roll by. Where the Trent met the top of the Humber was the mouth of the Ouse, and thus he would be two days from Jorvik. He thought of Raef, up there, and wondered what he would say about all this.

In Jorvik, under the stars, Raef knew that ships crowded into the wide estuary at the southern edge of his kingdom. Although Laissa slept close enough by to realize he was gone if she woke, he let his mind rise out of his manifest self and floated down the light field to watch.

Especially near Brough, the little village where they could get pilots, the ships were knarre, laden with iron and glass and fine goods to trade for the wool of Jorvik. But it was the lone dragon ship that drew his interest. This ship's dragon head was sheathed in gold, and in its belly it carried a dead man.

It was anchored, not beached for the night, out away from any mischief. He floated around it awhile. Sweyn's soul was gone, only the eaten and moldering body left. Yet it was clear to Raef what had happened. He rose into the air again.

As he did this, he realized Knut was thinking of him, which surprised him. But he went back to Laissa, who still slept.

He lay beside her, wakeful, cursing himself. He had let himself expect that Sweyn would be King here awhile and that he would keep the peace. Do Raef's work for him. Raef knew himself for a willful fool. He had taken this easy way, all this while that the Lady was hindered and cooped up, thinking that he could somehow teach the bloody-minded Knut to be a good king and keep her quiet forever.

She had not stayed quiet. Sweyn had her pent up tight, but she had killed him anyway. Now there would be another war. His skin crept. Like a beast rousing hungry from a long sleep, she was returning to the hunt.

He thought back over every time they had fought. When he attacked her the only way it seemed he could, while they were both in their elemental form, he had no impact on her. He wondered if he could attack her in his manifest body. He saw no way to do that, except to kill her host, but it was not Emma who was evil. The Lady would escape anyway, probably lessened, but not for long.

He remembered the hole he had seen in the light field and her fumes boiling forth. It came to him that he had never even seen her. The stinking, filthy smoke was not her—was, he thought, the mark of her passage through the world, like the wake of a ship. Calling her "she" was false too; it could be she needed a female body because of what she lacked, not what she was.

He touched the edge of his bad hand. He put his good hand up to his ear—where his ear had been. Piece by piece, he was disappearing. She would finish him someday, unless he found some way to destroy her. She would finish the world. He had to find another way to battle her.

He thought of Knut, sailing up the Trent. Maybe Knut was not such a waste after all.

A few days later, he said to Laissa, "I have to go. You must keep the bearskin closed over the sleeping bench and let no one near my body."

Her eyes opened wide with shock. She glanced quickly around them. "Now? You must not. What if she—This is why she thinks you are demonic." She clutched his arms. "Raef. No. Do you want her to hate you?"

"I am going," he said. "Keep her away." Gemma was off in the city, helping the sheepmen with the new lambs; she loved all baby creatures. "Keep the bearskin down." He turned toward the bench.

She grabbed him by the arm. "Come, at least. When I call you. Come."

He went into the bench. He knew she would protect him, whatever she said. Gemma hated him already. He was not used to doing this in the daytime, and the light was bright. He rolled over facing the wall. In a moment he was going down the river toward Brough, on the north bank of the Humber.

———

As Knut's ships rowed, picking their way down the Trent, Knut said, suddenly, "My foster father sailed these rivers like a long drink of ale."

Odd said, surprised, "Thorkel?"

Knut said, "No, the wizard, Jorvik. He knew the water like his own blood. He had better ale too."

He could taste the ale, brewed somewhere they were always turning out the first clean new batch. It nagged him that they were going so close by Jorvik. He saw nothing in what he was doing that would lead Raef to help him. Yet now he wanted Raef's advice as keenly as he remembered the ale. Odd started to say something and stopped, seeing him deep in thought.

Ahead lay the broad white shoals along the neck of the

Humber. Jorvik would be two days away if he could find a horse at Brough. He had sworn he would never see Raef again. He thought anyway Raef did not want him.

They came in by Brough at midafternoon. His men beached their ships, and many went to the tavern that was the village's only large building. The hovels around it were no bigger than their villagers' fishing boats. He let Odd handle the ordinary work of settling the crews. He walked along the riverbank, still wondering what to do. He could take his ships and Thorkel's and try to overthrow Edmund in one great strike. That would put him in Thorkel's debt. He could go back to Denmark, to Norway as Odd said, and raise another army. He hated to leave England.

He remembered when he had come here and met Sweyn, and then through his mind unfolded all his life with Sweyn, the greatest of the Vikings. He remembered his father's hand on his shoulder. Sweyn's laughter, telling jokes. He strode along the bank of the river. There, on that meadow, he had played ball once. Here, where the brush grew down, he had beaten Harald with his fists. Up ahead, past the bend of the river, he had gone to fish.

He went around the bend, through a stand of willows, and came on Raef, sitting on a stump.

Knut stood, his mind frozen. He met the other man's blazing blue eyes. It was Raef, tall and stooped, with his strange left hand and the waist-long, white-blond hair that Laissa kept neatly braided. Knut gathered himself.

He said, "Did you call me here?"

Raef said, "The King is dead. I saw his ship pass. How did he die?"

"A wasp stung him. I think." He half shook his head. "I might be wrong." He stroked his hand over his hair. His voice burst out, "I never thought I would be glad to see you, but I am. I need your advice. Everybody talks to me from some narrow view. You alone, I think, sees this broadly enough to know what I should do."

Raef said, "You want to be King."

Knut's hands fisted. "I am the King. The army acclaimed me. My father left it to me—but Uhtred betrayed me."

"Uhtred has his own mind and his own fate. Take what you want," Raef said. "I saw you the crowned King of England before I ever met you or knew who you were; it was foretold before you were ever born. For how long, I cannot say."

These words hit him like gold hammers. He felt a shock down his backbone, a new will, a sudden soaring triumph. Fate, he thought. It is my fate to wear the crown.

"My father said it was a curse."

"If he called it so, it was, for him. Be careful what you call it."

He said, "My brother Harald will already be the Danish King."

Raef shrugged. "You don't need Harald's help. Tell him to give you an army or you will fight him for Denmark. Get the Trondejarl to give you men and ships. There's always Thurbrand. Don't trust Thorkel."

Knut raised his head. His skin tingled, eager. "I will deal with Thorkel."

"To me, frankly, it makes no difference who is King. My concern is the Queen."

"The council freed her." The council had freed all Ethelred's prisoners also.

"That was ill done. You must capture her. Keep her in England."

"The wasp that bit my father," Knut said. "I saw it go into her bower. Did she murder my father?"

"Not Emma," Raef said. "But she is possessed, and the evil that owns her killed him. You remember how Aethelstan died. Take her and keep her close, watch her always, and never let her touch you."

"I want revenge," Knut said. His hands fisted. Sweyn's

death burned in his heart like a coal, and now here was some balm for it. "I am his son; it is mine to avenge him."

"That," Raef said, "may take some doing. Seizing Emma will be the easy part. I'll help you." His head turned, as if someone called him. "Go, they're looking for you, back at your ships." He stood up.

Knut said, "Are you out here alone? Come to Brough—they'll have bread and meat. Where is your boat?"

"No, no," Raef said, already walking away. "I can't, goodbye." On the third stride he vanished in front of Knut's eyes.

Knut stood a moment where he was, gaping at the empty air. The feeling swept over him that he had never been talking to Raef at all. Was any of it true, then? He started back toward his camp. Someone up ahead was calling for him. That much was so. Therefore, he would trust all of it—the promise, the knowledge that he would be King. He shouted back and went on.

———

In the morning Knut went down along the coast to Sandwich. When he arrived, to his surprise, Thorkel was waiting, his ships lined up on the beach, in order and ready.

Knut had been stocking up all the way down the coast for the short cross-water to Denmark. He moved in beside the Jomsvikings on the pale, sandy shore. It was a cold, windy day.

When he walked up on the beach, Thorkel came to meet him. They talked over some small things, neither saying much. There was still the matter of the hostages. Thorkel was dragging around more than thirty Saxons given as pledges for the oaths sworn and broken, and he wanted to hold them for ransom.

Knut said, "You mean, stay here and wait for somebody to pay up." They were standing in front of the row of dragons, and he swept his gaze along them. He had thought Thorkel was lying about having five hundred men, and now he saw how bad

the lie had been. With his ships, there were twenty-one altogether; he would need many more than this.

But he would win if he didn't give up. He was almost sure
that had been Raef he spoke to. He did not think he had such a
gift as that, to invent a whole man, even to tell him what he
wanted to hear.

The sun was just rising. The tide was still wrong, but Knut
was itching to set sail. If he raised the call soon enough in the
North, he could bring an army back here by next summer, the
fighting season, when he could keep a lot of men on the country. But he had to leave now.

Thorkel was squinting at him around his bony nose. "Thirty
ransoms. There will be gold enough for every man on the fleet.
Some left over for us." His eyes shimmered like coins.

Knut realized his fist was clenched. He said, "All you think
about is gold, Thorkel. Get those hostages out here."

Thorkel said, "Now, listen, boy—"

Knut said, "No, you listen to me." He lunged at Thorkel
and grabbed hold of his shirt, and, although Thorkel was two
fingers taller, Knut forced him back on his heels in a rush. Into
the harp nose, Knut said, "I am King. You are almost useless,
Thorkel, except when you do exactly as I say." He shoved
Thorkel away and punched him in the chest, not hard. "You understand that? And you call me boy once more, I'll kill you."

Thorkel shoved back at him. "Don't talk to me like that."
He looked quickly around, to see who was nearby. There were
a lot of people nearby, all watching, hands at their sides. Nobody was coming to help him.

Knut went at him again, furious, shouting into his face.
"You lost London, you bungled the siege, you let Edmund get
to Winchester, you let him become King, you are a shiftless,
worthless fool. It's a puzzle to me how you ever got command
of the Jomsburg. Get those hostages out here." The words came

out with some spittle, and Thorkel stepped back, daubing at his beard.

Knut leaned toward him still, hoping he would pull a knife, or at least say something. His hot, surging temper wanted blows, wanted blood. A murmur went through the men watching them. Thorkel did nothing; something in Knut's face forestalled him. He licked his lips and then turned and walked off. Raw with unfed anger, Knut lowered his eyes. Odd walked up to him. "When are we leaving?"

"In a little while," Knut said.

"You've got him by the balls."

"I wish I didn't have him at all."

Odd said, "Tronde ships are bigger. Get my father's fleet."

"I hope I can." He looked around, trying to see things broadly. That meant cooling down. He took a deep breath. It was, as Sweyn had said, something of a curse. Hastily, he backed off that word. A burden, anyway. To win this crown now, he had to lead this army, show each his place in it, and keep each one going.

I am the King, he thought. That much was true. For how long I cannot foretell.

The hostages had been scattered among the ships, like ballast. They gathered on the grey beach in a huddle, cold and wretched. Somebody built a fire. Thorkel came toward him. "Now, what? You're going to let them go, is that it? Just dump them here?"

Knut said, "They betrayed me. They betrayed Sweyn. Cut off something, from each one—a hand, an ear—slit their noses. I want everybody to know what liars those people are."

Thorkel grunted, surprised. This, though, he understood, and he turned and called up some of his Jomsvikings, and they tramped over toward the miserable hostages crowded on the beach. Knut turned to Odd. "We'll leave when we're done here."

Odd said, "Where are we going?"

"To Denmark, first," Knut said.

From down on the beach came a chorus of wails and screams. Odd looked the other way. He said, "I could take my ship straight up to Lade. Talk to my father. Meet you, say, in the Limfjord."

"That would make it quicker," Knut said. "We should try to get back here this summer. We'll miss a whole year if we don't hurry."

He looked down the beach. The screaming was still going on, but Thorkel and his men were walking away, axes and swords in their hands. Behind them they left a churning, sobbing crowd of people. Knut lifted his arm, and all along the row of dragons, men turned, and everybody watched him.

"Let's get these ships out there." He started toward his own, a big stout dragon from his father's fleet, shining in the new daylight.

CHAPTER TWENTY-SEVEN

Raef thought much about the Lady without coming to any conclusion. He felt his mind locked in an endless circle of doubt and fear. He lost interest in everything else. Laissa took care of his household without needing anything from him, and now that Gemma hated him he took no pleasure in the everyday things. He stopped going to the oak tree for his councils; Goda was sensible, the others respected him, and as long as the city was prosperous everybody was willing to get along. He had always meant to let them go on their own eventually anyway.

Another thing he did not think about was something that had been there all the while before him but that foolishly he did not take the time to foresee.

At last, on a warm spring day, he went down through Jorvik. There were new houses on the streets and more people he didn't know, and he went slowly to catch their voices. Two women talking over a fence. A tinker, a cobbler. Somebody went by him speaking Saxon. He walked into the midst of a crowd of children at some game, and they shrieked and dodged around him until he was past. Nobody paid much heed to him. He turned the corner at the old street by Corban's house.

The dust of the street before it lay thick and undisturbed; not even birds landed there. He went up to the front door and stepped inside.

For an instant his head whirled. He gulped. His stomach rose. Then he got himself straight again. The air around him seemed thick, like water he could breathe. He felt everything subtly shifting around him. When he moved, ripples spread out away from him. He went slowly, to keep himself together, and still had to wait for his foot to catch up to his leg once, and his whole elbow another time. Around him he could see nothing, only the ancient, moldering, empty house. For a long while he stood there, waiting.

Then he began to feel Corban's presence in the thick air around him, slow, deep, layered in echoes. Like the waves of air against his ears, he sensed his uncle's breathing next to him. A sudden excitement stirred him. He felt himself open like a flower in the sun, and then Corban was all around him and within him, as if they stood in the same place, shared the same body, soul on soul.

In his mind, Corban said, "Raef. Raef. Son of my heart."

"I need your help," Raef thought. "Help me."

"The Lady."

"Yes. Help me. I can't do this alone."

"Only you can do it."

"How? Nothing I have done makes any difference."

"Only you can do this."

"How?"

"Force her out of her host body. And stay inside yours. Make her come to you and take her in."

"How?"

"Use the coat."

"The coat," he said, aloud, astonished.

The air rippled around him, broken into waves by the sound of his voice. In his mind, Corban said, "Take her in. You are greater than she is."

"I don't understand." He said this in his mind again.

"You just took me in," Corban said.

"I'm not afraid of you. I love you."

"You must not be afraid of her. Take her in. She does not belong here. You do. You belong to this being; you are stronger than she is. All this being dwells in you."

The coat, he thought, in a wild panic; he had forgotten about the coat.

"Take her in," Corban said. He was fading; Raef's fear was driving him out. In a moment he was gone, and Raef stood alone in the house, empty as a shell.

Take me with you, he thought. Uncle, take me with you.

No one answered. After a while he turned slowly to the door and made his way out.

⚘

Laissa was at the church with Gemma; often they slept there after they had worked. The hall was empty except for a couple of the men sitting around the fire. Raef remembered finding the coat, years before, but he could not remember what he had done with it. He went around the hall, looking, but he saw nothing and could not remember. Finally he went up to the high seat and sat down.

He was afraid; the fear held him rigid, like an iron skin.

It was fear that would ruin him. That would ruin the world in him. He remembered Gunnhild slapping him. "Raef. You are such a coward." He made himself calm. He thought of Corban, his mother, Conn, Laissa, Gunnhild, Gemma, everyone he had ever loved, and the love settled him. Love drove out his fear. He sat there for a while thinking of nothing but how he loved them, and then slowly he came to realize where the coat was.

He stood up, pulled the old chest out from under the high seat, and tipped the lid back. He plunged his hand down into the dark hollow and felt a ring of leather and a great heap of coins. And beside it was a dank, moldy mass of cloth.

He took it out, sat down again, and set it on his knees. It was rotten and crumpled, too small to fit even a child. He remembered the old story, how the Lady had given this to Corban to keep him bound to her will and how he had flung it off and freed himself. He spread it out, and it crumbled in his hands— filthy, useless. He still did not understand. He put his hand to his bad ear, afraid again.

―⚬―

Laissa knelt at the altar and prayed a few moments; she tried to find words to speak to God for her husband, whose strange grief was locking him away from her, but she knew no god for Raef. Gemma came up beside her and crossed herself.

"Mama. What's wrong?"

"Nothing," she said, which was not true. What was wrong had too much to do with Gemma to disclose it to her. She looked up at the long Jesus on his tree, wondering why she could not find peace here.

She heard footsteps behind her; she signed herself and stood up. An old man leaning on a stick was trudging up the aisle toward them. When she turned, he stopped, spread his arms out, and smiled.

"My children," he said. "God bless you. God bless you for being here, and for this church."

Laissa said, puzzled, "Welcome, sir, whoever you are." He wore a ragged dark robe with a rope for a belt, his feet bare; she had never seen him before.

He said, "For your welcome, I thank you, most humbly." He looked up at the Jesus and then around at the whole church. "I am home," he said. "God have mercy on me, at last I am home."

"Home," Gemma said, bewildered.

Laissa said, "Home?"

"Yes." He sat down on the ground before them. "I am Wulfstan. Once I was archbishop of this place, but the wicked King Ethelred cast me into prison for telling him his sins. But now the new King has set me free, and I have come back."

Gemma let out a cry. "Mama!" She wheeled toward her mother. "It's our priest."

Laissa went down on her knees by the old man and seized his hands, her heart galloping. "You have come. We prayed for you to come." She looked into his clear, pale eyes, and, when he smiled, she saw the light in his eyes and could not but smile back. He was good. She could see the faith and joy in him. She clutched his hands. "All this time, we have been keeping the church. Making it ready—" She began to cry. "We never really knew if—but you have come back. God has sent you back to us."

"Ah, child." He patted her hands. "All this while, you have kept the church? How good, how good. Your faith is like a fire to me. God bless you." He kissed her forehead and got himself crookedly up onto his feet; he was very old. He said, "Let us then pray together."

At the far end of the aisle the door creaked open. "Laissa? Is that you?"

"Miru," Laissa called. She danced down the aisle a few steps. "Miru, come, it's the priest! The priest has come at last!"

She reached back and caught old Wulfstan by the hand again. "Here he is—our priest! All our prayers have come true."

"Come," old Wulfstan called, in a strong, high voice. "Come and let us give thanks to God Almighty, who has preserved us through the darkness."

Miru gave a whoop of joy. "Wait—wait—I shall bring others—" She ran out of the church, shouting.

⸻

Wulfstan went up before the altar and raised his hands. It had been years since he had done this, but the words rose from his memory as if God spoke them into his ear.

"I will go into the altar of the Lord."

Behind him, the few voices said, "Amen," and the hollow of the church echoed the voices back like sacred music.

Wulfstan thought he would burst with happiness. He had walked all this way, not knowing what he would find, and what he had found passed all his hopes. The church was clean, and the people faithful. Now the word of God came from him like cool, pure water to wash away the sins of the world. He had his church back. He had the first of his flock here.

Someone had brought him bread, and he laid it on the altar and made the sign of the cross over it. Someone had brought wine, and he poured it into the chalice. He raised the blood and body of the Lord, tears on his cheeks, grateful for Jesus, whose love filled the cosmos, and behind him, the faithful cried out, "Amen."

⌒

Raef was sitting in his high seat, and Gemma flew in the door and rushed up before him in an attitude of great bravery. She said, "Papa, you cannot be false anymore. The priest has come. God is back in Jorvik. You must get down on your knees and pray to Jesus to save you."

He lifted his head. She was like a young tree, all straight and clean and golden leaved, and yet she stood against him like an enemy and said this ridiculous thing. He said, "Why have you turned on me?"

"You must be saved, Papa." She leaned intently toward him. Laissa had come in behind her; she would not meet his eyes. "Jesus loves you, but he cannot save you unless—"

"Jesus," he said, his voice harsh, "I have seen men in Jesus's name stick pikes through other men like a second backbone, girl. You are a fool if you believe—"

She flew at him. "You can't say that! It's sinful!" Her little hands slapped at him; he reared back, his arms up, but he did not fight her, only let the painless blows bounce off him. She cried, "I cannot live here—not until you kneel!" She flung herself down on her knees, her hands clasped, her eyes lifted toward the sky. "Dear God, help him."

Laissa said, "Gemma. Stop. He is your father."

Gemma got up and backed away. Her face was flushed. Her hair seemed to crackle with her righteous fire. She said, "My real father is God Almighty. You told me this. You tell me one thing in the church and another thing here. Only Father Wulfstan tells me the truth."

"Wulfstan," Raef said. "Who's that?"

Laissa came up beside him. "The archbishop has come back. He is at the church." She passed one hand over her face. "I did not see—until now—what this means."

Raef leaned past her toward Gemma. She had been wild against him before the priest came. "What do you know about truth?" he said. "What did your mother tell you?" He gave Laissa a sideways look.

Gemma cried, "Mama and I know Jesus. But she is two-faced." Her head swiveled, and she gave Laissa a serpent's glare. Then she whipped back to her father. Her cheeks shone red. "I am not. I will not live here until you kneel to Jesus and accept him as your Lord!" She turned and ran out the door, into the sunlight beyond.

Laissa wheeled after her, crying her name. Raef leaped down from the high seat. "You did this. You started this with her. Where did this priest come from? How did you get him here?"

She faced him, her mouth set and her eyes angry. "I know Jesus and did not leave you. This two-faced idea is just something new. She needs only to—to—see that Jesus loves everybody. And such talk as this will not bring her back. You know her mind; you can sway her, if you'd bend your stiff, kingly neck."

"I don't know her," he said. "She's shut herself off from me. Long ago. Now she's gone. Because of this priest. Because of you." Laissa turned and went out the door, stiff backed, after Gemma.

———

When Wulfstan came into the church on the Sabbath day, the long hall was only partly filled. The women he knew already stood at the front, but rapidly the rows behind them thinned until a long, open stretch lay before the door. Wulfstan said his homily, that certain signs portended the coming end of the world, and gave the message of the Mass, of hope and salvation and love.

The child Gemma especially moved him to a fatherly tenderness. She was pretty as a golden-headed dandelion. He would baptize her soon and give her a Christian name. After the Mass, she sat at his knee and soaked up the stories he told her. He began teaching her prayers, psalms, chants. He thought he would name her Maria, after the mother of God.

She opened her heart to him. She told him of her wicked, pagan father and of how he had kept her from her love, her foster brother, whom she had decided was a secret Christian, beat him, and then sent him away. Wulfstan told her of the higher marriage of the soul to Jesus and how she might become the bride of Christ.

He had not known there were many pagans in Jor'ck. It seemed the worst was this very father of his dandelion child.

Wulfstan was sweeping the little room behind the church where he lived when a man in a fine coat and a hat with fur trim came in. He took the hat off. He had thin red hair, and his front dogteeth stuck straight out. "Father," he said, "welcome home to your church."

His name was Goda; he was a butcher, but also a wool trader, and he sat on the town's council. He had come from the council to swear their faith in God to him. Most of their faith. It took Wulfstan only a few minutes to discover the girl's pagan father sat on this council too, and many thought he was some kind of wizard.

"He hasn't been coming, though," Goda said, "since the girl left. We've been doing it all. We're all good Christian men. The sheepmen have formed a kind of company, and they—we—are talking about building a big hall in the town so we don't have to sit under the oak tree and can keep out those we want out. I don't think he'd come to that at all."

"Are there other pagans in Jor'ck?"

"Maybe. A few, here and there. The church was long quiet here; many lost faith. They will come back. There's no harm." Goda crossed himself, looking around the walls, where ivy grew in through the corners. "It's time to finish this church, anyway. Build a bell tower and a proper house for the priests. I've heard that the archbishop before you scratched out the plans somewhere."

Wulfstan was thinking of the pagan, but Goda had cleverly led the talk away from him, and the idea of a bell tower seized him. "Bells call more people to Christ even than priests and monks."

"Yes," Goda said. "Yes. Many have long prayed for a true church here. We could lay aside some money. The city. And the sheepmen's company." Goda's face was red, his blue eyes worried.

Wulfstan said, "It would take a quantity of money." He crossed himself. This was the oldest church in England, but the one at Winchester was bigger. Even the one at Canterbury. He would build the finest church in England here. He wondered how much money the sheepmen of Jor'ck could give him.

More, he thought, if he cleansed them of this pagan wizard. Although it did seem Goda had brought the whole thing up to steer him off that track.

The next Sunday, there were more people at the Mass, and

he preached another homily, this one about evil close at hand and the need to be on guard against the wiles of the devil.

⸻

Gemma said, "No, Mother, I am staying here. Or I will go with Miru." She smiled at Miru, who shrugged; she had been putting up Raef's strays for a long time. Laissa held the girl's hands.

"You must see your father cannot be other than what he is."

"Which is sinful and damned," Gemma said, precisely. The priest's very words. "How he treated Knut—I should have known then. I did know. I am never going home, Mama, until he has accepted Jesus and healed himself."

Laissa flung her hands down and stalked away. Up by the altar Wulfstan had come out to pray. She almost started toward him. The little old man delighted her; his happy, wizened face; his wisps of white hair and broad, bare, horny feet; his kindness and love of God; and his learnedness—he had all the books in his head and knew all she had to know to become a perfect Christian. In him she loved all but this, how he turned Gemma against Raef.

How he and Gemma turned her against Raef.

She went around the corner of the altar rail and sat down on the step at the side, behind the stone bowl for the water blessing, where no one would see her. She shrank from thinking about this, but she had to do it. She caught herself starting to cross herself, and her hand froze.

She had been going to sign herself in the western way. She remembered, though, the other way, the way the Greeks did it, as she had grown up. How in Italy she had worked to change that habit, doing it over and over and over, lest she be stoned for a heretic.

Something was going on here that ran back past the archbishop. Always before, though, she had kept the cracks from showing.

She thought of Raef, sunk in thought, as he battled his demon, and of Gemma, gone down this flower path to Jesus. She missed them. She could not be with both of them. She turned her head against the hard wood of the altar rail and thought she must choose, and soon.

—⚬—

Leif came back and said, "They are both in the church."

"Yes, yes," Raef said. He was standing in the doorway, his shoulder against the frame. Leif put his hand on his arm and went past into the hall. Raef looked down into the city, grown so big now, that had eaten up his wife and daughter, and wondered if his time were passing, with his task undone.

—⚬—

The next Sunday, Wulfstan preached against the wizard directly. There were many more people in the church now, and he felt himself lifted by the spirit, his arms swaying as he talked of the devil's tempting that had taken root here in Jor'ck, and of how the pagan had to be driven away or converted. The crowd surged up, agreeing, but then a woman in the front took a step forward.

"I will not hear this. I prayed you would come, but I regret that you did. My husband is not evil. This is evil, that you see as sin everything you did not already know."

It was Laissa, who had so welcomed him. She turned and walked out, but the crowd pressed in close behind her, as if she had not been there. He stumbled only a moment in the homily. She had been one of his first, his dearest flock. And her friend Miru also was leaving. He saw with gladness that the girl Gemma stayed, her eyes shining at him, her hands clasped in prayer.

She cried, "I will pray for his conversion, Father."

"Yes," Wulfstan said. "Let us pray for the pagan to be saved." His voice rose again, confident.

—⚬—

In the twilight Raef stood in the doorway to his hall, looking out, his arms folded, hiding his bad hand. People walked by in the street, men going home from the fields with their hoes and rakes, their dogs at their heels. Now and then, an older man nodded to him as he went past, but most ignored him.

He saw Leif coming toward him, smiling wide, but the fat old Icelander went by him without a word.

After him came Laissa. She walked slowly toward him up the road, her eyes on his face. As if she was uncertain how he would welcome her. He would have fallen at her feet if he had not been propped up against the hall. He saw in her the beautiful wild child she had been and the woman she was, more beautiful, still wild, and true. She came up to him, and he bent and kissed her, and they went into the hall together.

—⚬—

Every day Wulfstan preached against the pagan. He called the city back to Christ and reminded the flock that here was the oldest church in England and that it had to be made pure after long years unkempt. More people came to his sermons. Most of these, it seemed, were newcomers to Jor'ck; the older people stayed away. But there were many more newcomers, especially young people. And the girl Gemma was fiercest of them all.

"We must save the world, all the world, if it is to end so quickly," she said once, and he pressed her hand, moved by her stout spirit and her love for all.

From the crowds came voices. "Tell us what to do. Tell us. Tell us."

So he called them to witness with him. Easter was coming; he brought them all before the altar of his church, to swear that Jor'ck would be cleansed of pagans before the rising of the Lord. He said, "We will start with the man in the old King's hall. He will convert—" he smiled at Gemma, "for the sake of love. Come."

He took holy water and a cross and walked up the road toward the pagan's hall. Some called this the King's hall, but he knew that the last King of Jorvik had died years before. As he went up the stony hill, other people fell in around him and came after him.

The man Goda came rushing up, saying, "This is no good. This will do no good." Wulfstan brushed by him.

"If you love this city you will join us."

Goda dropped back. Wulfstan marched toward the hall, the great thatch looming up ahead and the oak tree beside it. Without looking back he knew a crowd followed him. And he had the Lord's blessed water and the cross. When the door opened and the pagan came out, he did not falter.

He raised the cross. "What gods do you profess? Speak true!"

The pagan stood, his arms folded. He was missing an ear. His hands were strange. He looked not at Wulfstan but at the people behind him.

He said, "You ask this to trick me. You want only one answer."

"You confess by your very refusal to confess. Choose Christ instead, I beg you. Now—become one of us, in the true Church." Wulfstan took some of the water and sprinkled it on him. "Join us, in the true faith." The water sparkled, but Wulfstan wasn't sure if that was only because of the sunlight. The pagan ignored him, anyway, was looking at the people behind him.

"So," the pagan said. "I see how it is. You've forgotten who did this for you. You've forgotten who opened the river, and made Uhtred kneel, and brought the trade back and the law, and raised Jorvik up again. Thus it goes. Do it yourselves. If you don't want me, I don't need you."

He lifted his maimed left hand, as if he saluted them, and turned and went back inside the hall. The door shut. Wulfstan wondered what to do next. Before him the hall stood there, solid against the edge of the sky, closed against him.

Then the stone walls began to waver, like something seen through fire, and fade away.

The crowd let up a collective gasp. Wulfstan crossed himself; he spilled his holy water. Now before him on the hilltop where the hall had stood was nothing but a crumbled ruin, no two stones on top of one another, the grass blowing. Wulfstan gaped at this. The child Gemma screamed. The wind gusted, and the branches of the oak tree creaked as if dead.

⚬

The crowd drifted away, and after thoroughly dampening everything with holy water Wulfstan went home to his church. Gemma went back and forth around the ruin, climbing over rocks. She could find the hearth, even the ruin of a loom. She began to cry.

She had always thought she was running away from them. She had never imagined they would not be here when she wanted to come back. She could not find the way in; she felt the magic gone out of the world, the ordinariness gathering around her, the dull rocks and weeds and decaying wood. She went back out to the street. She remembered the shield she had made around herself. She had broken what bound her to this place. She had built some wall against that greater world. She did not deserve it anymore. She crossed herself and went down to the church, praying again to be allowed to be a nun.

—⸰—

Laissa said, "Can we go out?"

"Yes, do as you please. It's just a little later. You can even—" he smiled, "go to church. Wulfstan won't be there. Just remember where the door is; it may be hard to see from outside." He flung himself down on the high seat, his long body awkward, all angles. "I need to think."

She said, "What do you mean, later?"

"Never mind." He looked down the hall.

Laissa could hear them, talking down there, as if nothing had happened: Leif, Edith, and a few others. She heard little Simon laugh, Edith's son. Maybe nothing had really happened.

Raef blurted, "I don't know what to do now."

Laissa did not see this was too much different than before either. He was always blundering along. She shrugged. Giving up the church made her see him clearly, and she felt nothing lost. Whatever he was, she loved him; she had faith in him. She needed something strong, and alive, not a wooden doll. When she went to the table and got him some ale, she saw the clump of red cloth on the floor by the high seat.

"What is this?"

"I don't know," he said. "There was an old story. Corban had a coat."

She sat on the edge of the high seat beside him and laid the red coat on her knees. Nothing had changed in here; they were "later" outside than in here, she thought. He had taken the hall back to the time before they came. She ran her hands over the red coat. The fiber was rotten and crumbling; as she stroked it, more of it shredded into fluff and dirt. Raef leaned on the arm of the high seat, watching her. Then she suddenly swung the coat up in the air, shook it hard, and showed it to him.

"Look."

The coat was in separate pieces, but they did not fall away. Even when she shook it again the red patches, seeming unconnected, stayed in the form of a coat. She spread it on her knees.

"What kind of enchantment is this?"

"I don't know," he said. He was staring at the cloth in her hands, his face intent.

She ran her hands over the coat, slowly, feeling its surface with the pads of her fingers. After a while she took it down to her loom. The thatch overhead was gone now, leaving only the open sky, as if moving the hall out of the present had made the pretense unnecessary. The sun shone in: a little crooked, an older sun.

Shutting her eyes, she turned the coat over and over, wearing off the outer stuff, until she could feel the thread underneath. This was as fine as the breath of a fish, the footfall of a cat, as the old poem went, but when to keep it fast she wound a little around her finger, it tightened suddenly as if to bite her finger off.

She unwound it swiftly, her eyes opening. She could not see the thread, but she could see the red gash around her finger. She found a stick and wound the thread around that. It seemed not to tighten on the wood. Maybe it needed living flesh. Drank blood. Snake thread. She began to unravel the whole coat onto the bit of wood.

⟜

Raef lay wrapped in his bearskins, his wife in his arms, and wondered what he had done now.

It had been easier than he expected to hide the hall. He had only had to take it forward by two years, and it was gone.

He was running out of time, and he had no idea what to do next.

He drew slowly, softly, away from Laissa so she wouldn't

waken and lay still, and shutting his eyes drifted into the light field. The deep blue surrounded him, rising and falling; he could not tell if the color was the music or the music was the color. He lay still in it, longing to let himself go into it forever.

It would not be forever. The Lady would end it, and soon.

He did what he had done before to know the future: he gathered and flung himself forward, deeper into the field.

Instantly his mouth, eyes, and ears were stuffed with stinking, foul, unbreathable smoke, and the shrieks of the Lady pierced him like needles; he could not move, as if he lay under a thousand feet of rock. The tidal draw of the light field pulled him back, and he opened his eyes, lying beside Laissa again, shaking.

He turned toward her; she had not roused but lay with one arm flung up beside her head, her hair all around her. He bent and kissed the place where her neck joined her shoulder, and she stirred, smiling, murmuring his name. He slid close to her, his arms around her, and buried his face in her hair.

Do not be afraid, Corban had said. You cannot be afraid. But he did not know how else to be.

⟶⟵

Laissa sat at her loom and hung a warp of white wool, and then wove across it with grey wool, carrying along with this weft the invisible thread from Corban's coat. Raef stood there watching her. Steadily the piece grew longer and very beautiful, but no matter what yarn she wove on, the color always came out red.

CHAPTER TWENTY-EIGHT

"There she is," said the helmsman.

Knut said nothing. Under him the ship rocked easily along a wave. He stood by the mast crutch, staring west at the narrow shoreline, the faint blue rise of hills behind it. Something in him came unbound and flew: He had come back. It startled him how good that felt.

Getting this far had taken longer than he had expected. All the while the doubts had grown on him like moss: that he would never see England again, never wear his crown, never rule, that Raef had been a trick of his mind, his promises lies.

Twisting around, he looked behind him at the great fleet scattered across his wake. Odd had brought half his father's fleet, the big Tronde ships streaming after Knut's. Beyond them, the Swedish ships sailed all together, led by his cousin Ulf Thorleifs-son; in the North, it seemed everybody was his cousin. Around them the rest of the Danes kept no particular order. Thorkel had stayed in the Jomsburg, where Knut preferred him anyway.

There were three ships from East Anglia also, which Eadric Streona had sent, with an offer that Knut had ignored. The ships belonged to danskermen, and he gathered them in.

Bringing this fleet together had been hard, and keeping it together harder still. Of the two hundred ships he had been promised, at one time or another, fewer than one hundred and thirty followed him now. His brother had worked against him, and the weather had gone bad for months. He kept running out of stores. People got bored and went home. People got in fights and went home.

But now he had come again to England—that long, flat beach there was England. On either side of him, his own crewmen sat on their benches, talking, passing skins of water, and pointing toward the land. All the men who had been with him at the siege of London had followed him here. Broom-Orm had decided he would rather be Knut's man than Harald's. Some of his father's own oarsmen had joined him. He was getting something of a name, although he wasn't sure what he had done to earn it.

The ship slipped along the waves, her checked sail full, the slipped water chuckling along her hull. The wind was driving her into the narrow sea. In another day, they would have to start rowing again. In less than a month, he would reach the Severn and attack.

He had planned this for months, every night, storying out to himself what might happen—this unforeseen obstacle, that fatal disaster. He had only been a boy when Sweyn's and Thorkel's great armies had burned the whole place and starved themselves out of the war, but he remembered it. To avoid that he wanted to take everything in one quick fight.

Raiding the southern coast might bring Edmund out. If not, coming ashore through the Severn, into the heart of Wessex, certainly would. If Knut could force him to battle, he could take the kingdom into his hands in a few months.

Unless Edmund beat him. He made himself consider that, but then his mind always leaned on what Raef had said. He would win. It might take longer. But he would win. Across the glittering water the pale sand shone, behind it, the green meadows and the distant forest. England—his kingdom, his fate. He felt suddenly light and high with love.

—⊰—

Edmund reined in his horse at the edge of the cliff, shading his eyes with his free hand. "Sweet Jesus. There are so many."

Uhtred hurried in importantly. "Danes, mostly, my lord. There are a lot of Tronde ships. You can always tell them, they're bigger and their hulls are black. No Jomsvikings. No red sails. A lot of smaller ships. Not the big royal fleet. No crowns on the sails, no gilded dragonheads."

Edmund made a soft sound in his throat. He watched the parade of the dragons glide past Dover into the narrows. France was close here; a keen-eyed man could see it on the far side, the first rise of land out of the sea, the gnawed beach of Normandy. He knew Richard of Normandy would do nothing to stop the Danes.

At least he would not help them. Edmund had refused to let Emma leave England. The boys were in Normandy, but as long as Edmund held his sister, the duke would likely keep out of this.

"Is it Knut?"

"There's no way to tell, my lord." Uhtred's horse pawed the ground, catching its rider's eagerness. Streona was coming up to them, trailing some carls and a few other lords. Uhtred said quickly, "Will you summon the fyrd, my lord?"

Edmund knew the lord of Northumberland wanted to keep Streona and the others out of this. Everybody wanted to be first with Edmund. All the great men loved him now, fawned and begged for orders—even those who, when Ethelred was still alive, had fawned and begged for orders from Sweyn. Edmund said, "No. It's too soon." He glanced over his shoulder toward Godwine, waiting behind him.

The other men rode up among them, shouted, called, pointed out at the distant, shadowy stream of ships. Edmund turned his horse and went off through them, back down to the road.

Godwine followed him and their train of pages and guards. The younger man's face was stiff, his lips thin, but, when Edmund looked at him, his gaze was direct.

"A lot of ships," Edmund said. "More than a hundred, I think."

"Yes, my lord," Godwine said. "There are a lot of them, the Danes. What do you think they will do?"

"Burn up the coast for a while," Edmund said. "I've sent off warnings." He doubted the little villages along the coast, harried for years, would put up any resistance, even forewarned. Likely they would just all retreat inland. Godwine's gaze stayed on him.

"You want to know why I don't call out the fyrd," Edmund said. "As Uhtred says."

Godwine said, mildly, "It had passed through my mind."

"The trouble with the fyrd is they're always counting their days. They are farmers, tough and strong; they can fight; and there are a great many of them, a lot more than there are Danes, if I can get them all together. But they only serve for two or three months. We have to start gathering them right when we can use them, which means when he comes to land. I don't think he will do that soon. I think he'll raid, where he can, and try to draw me out that way first."

Godwine was nodding. He said, "That sounds good to me, then. You're sure it's Knut Sweynsson? Here comes the lord Uhtred."

Edmund shrugged. "It doesn't matter. Knut or someone else, it's all the same." The lord Uhtred galloped up beside them.

"My King, let me be of some use here." Uhtred was aging, but he was still broad-shouldered, square-chested, and hard-eyed, his long hair grey and his eyes deep in wrinkles. Over his green jacket he wore crossed baldrics and a cloak pinned up in the new fashion at the shoulder. He said, "I have an army in the South. I can attack the damned Danes while you raise the fyrd. I'm ready to snip some Viking noses." He had brought three hundred of his green jackets down from Northumberland; he was still burning over the damage done to cousins who had been among the hostages at Sandwich. "Give me the honor of an order, King Edmund."

"Go, then. But you cannot take your army out to sea, and I don't think he will put into land just yet. You can watch him along, and when he does land, hit him. Be careful. I'll catch up with you with the main army."

Uhtred's eyes flashed. "I shall, my lord. Thank you." He maneuvered his horse out of the pack forming around Edmund and called for his second in command. Into the space he left, another Saxon pushed, another eager face, mouth open, well-groomed head bobbing up and down. Everybody would have a suggestion, an opinion, a comment, a scheme. Every man would want Edmund to listen only to him. Edmund wished he could get off by himself. Godwine rode up on his left side, fencing him off that much at least from the nattering mob. Godwine never had any schemes. That made him more useful than anybody else. Edmund lifted his horse into a lope, toward the road.

—❧—

Emma lay in her bower, and day by day went by. The summer withered away. As the days shortened and the news came of the approach of the Danes, the Lady knew that the war was upon them again. She would feed again. She stirred, hungry, and Emma grew restless and chattered about going to Normandy, but the Lady had no interest in Normandy.

—❧—

At the end of the summer Knut led his fleet into the Severn toward Avonmouth. Along the shore the little fishing villages looked empty, their boats hauled in and turned over, no smoke rising from the hovels. There was a bigger village with a stone church, just up the river from the estuary, and the men swarmed off the ships and attacked it, stealing everything they could lift and killing some pigs and cattle. Knut ran with the rest, wild to be off the ship, looking for somebody to fight, but all the people were gone.

In the church they turned over the altar and found beneath it the little gold cups and plates, the fancy cloths and books the Christians treasured. Somebody else had already put the torch to the village, and they carried the loot back to the ships and rowed on upstream.

A few miles inland, where the river narrowed down into a gorge through the hills, they came on a farmstead by the water. This too was deserted; the people had left in a hurry, running off their beasts into the forest, and Knut's men managed to round up several horses. They camped there overnight, roasting the pigs and cattle they had killed.

In the morning they hauled the ships out and packed up what gear they needed. Knut put Odd and some of his men on the horses and sent them out ahead to scout, and then they set fire to the village and walked off into the hilly country to the east.

The high bluffs along the river forced them south. On the shrubby hillsides the leaves were already turning orange. Where the forest began, the oaks were still dark and thick. They saw no fresh sign of people. They came on cattle wandering loose and gathered them and drove them along ahead of them; they caught more horses. Knut found one with a broad, flat back; made a bridle of rope; and rode up in front, where everybody could see him. The horse was a big black, a cart horse, not used to being ridden or going fast, and Knut whacked it a few times with the rope end to make it trot. When it kicked out, wanting to go faster, he patted its neck.

Odd went off again in the morning to ride scout, and Knut followed along a worn rutted road in toward a pass through the hills. Midway through the morning, somebody shouted, and he looked up ahead and saw a single horseman on the saddle of the pass, waving his arms wildly.

"Go!" Knut reined his horse around and charged up the overgrown road. The rest of the army streamed after him, yelling.

They flooded along the rutted stony track and into the pass, and as he came down the other side, Knut saw a wide, dark plain spreading out before him. A river wound, gleaming in the distance. Down there, his back to a wind-fallen tree, a single Dane on foot was fighting three horsemen.

The Dane was Odd. Knut bellowed and sent his horse at a dead gallop down the hill. The big black stretched out. Knut drew his sword. The rest of the Danes roared down from the pass after him.

The horsemen attacking Odd looked up, saw the Danes coming, and turned to run. As they fled, Odd stepped forward from the shelter of the fallen tree, gripped his sword backward, and hurled it flat through the air like a knife, straight into the back of the last rider.

The man slumped off his horse. The others raced on, down toward the river. Knut galloped up beside Odd and jumped down.

"Good throw," he said.

"I need the horse," Odd said. His own horse lay dead on the grass near the fallen tree.

"What happened?" The other Danes were swarming down around them.

Odd went over toward the fallen man, sprawled on the ground with the sword sticking straight up from his back. "There's an army down across the river. Couple of hundred men. We were looking it over, and then some of them saw us. I sent Grim on and tried to hold them off until you came." Odd put his foot on the corpse and drew his sword out.

The sword came out in a gush of blood all over the dead man's green jacket. Knut hissed through his teeth. "It's Uhtred's army." His heart began to gallop. He had hated Uhtred for a long time. "Is Edmund with him?"

Odd shook his head. "It's only a few hundred men—there's no sign of anything bigger for miles."

"Good," Knut said. He was rethinking his plans. Uhtred had betrayed Sweyn and given the kingdom to Edmund, and Knut was going to pay him back. Odd was off catching the loose horse, which spooked away from him, wary. A couple of the others went to help him. Knut turned to the big black and vaulted onto it. Odd rode up alongside him.

"Where are we going now?"

"If Uhtred is down here," Knut said, "then who's keeping Bamburgh? We're going north."

——

From the cover of the trees along the river, Uhtred watched the Danish army coming down out of the pass. He had thought that they would keep on straight down into Wessex and that he could raid their flank.

But they were turning. The whole long flow of men, some mounted, most on foot, with herds of cattle and sheep among them, reached the bottom of the pass and swung to the north. Uhtred pressed his lips together. He twisted his head toward the horseman beside him.

"How far off is Edmund?"

"We will be here within three weeks," said Godwine of Wessex. He was a reedy boy, son of an outlawed thegn, who had been Edmund's shadow since before Uhtred had begun paying attention. It infuriated Uhtred that this somehow made Edmund warmer to Godwine than to him, the lord of the North, especially when Uhtred had made Edmund King.

"Three weeks," Uhtred said. "That's not soon enough." In three weeks Knut would be halfway to Bamburgh. He turned to his horse. His second in command, his son Eadred, was just behind him, and he jerked his head at him. "Get the men ready to march."

Godwine said, "My lord, the King wants you to stay here until he joins you."

Uhtred lurched toward him, suddenly angry, the more angry because he was afraid. "He's going north, do you see that? He's going to attack Northumberland. That's my country. You tell Edmund to come after me as fast as he can move." He vaulted into his saddle, yanking his horse around. "Come, Eadred."

———

Edmund rode along into the west, sending the heralds ahead of him to call each company of the fyrd to their meeting places. In crossroads, churchyards, village commons, and open fields he told the crowds of men who met him always the same thing.

"The Danes are fighting for vainglory, for bloodlust, and for loot. We are fighting for our land, our fathers' graves, our wives and children, our homes, our hearths. We are fighting for England. We cannot lose. But we must all strive, or we cannot win."

They answered him, cheering and yelling, and they followed him, first scores, then hundreds of men, all armed, most in leather armor, many mounted. They poured on down the high road into the west, every day gathering more.

Godwine said, "Edmund, nobody thinks of England but you."

Edmund said, "What are you carrying that for?" He was staring down the road ahead of them. He never stopped looking forward.

Godwine lifted his eyes to the banner above them. The Wessex dragon still hung in the hall in Winchester. It was the long blue pennant that fluttered out above them, bright in the sun, the yellow lance on it rippling. Godwine had brought it from London. He held the butt of the staff firm in his stirrup, his hand on the haft. He said, "I like it."

Edmund was smiling. "So you think of England too." He nudged his horse on.

⸺⸎⸺

Moving north, Knut crossed a river he thought might be the one that ran through London. There he sent half his army off under their own captains to raid the villages and farms along the riverbank, and then to follow him to the north to come together at the full moon.

With the rest of his men he went quickly across the flat midcountry, chasing the people into the few little cities, and stealing everything the men could carry, and burning what they could torch. They ate roasted meat and drank good ale every night. He found himself a saddle and got more and more of his men on horseback. He found some bows and a large cache of arrows.

He had left two men back at the river to keep watch, and after a few days they caught up to him with news: Uhtred was marching on their trail. Knut slowed down so that Uhtred would keep coming.

They rode into the first broken shoulders of the hills. He sent most of the men still with him to push on north another few days and then stop, west of the hilltops, and wait for Uhtred to catch up. With Ulf Thorleifsson and Odd and their crews, Knut himself went east through the wild country. It was starting to rain. Already, at night, the wind blew sharp and cold.

⸺⸎⸺

Uhtred went gratefully into the lean-to. The rain thundered on the roof above him. He rubbed his hands together to get them warm. Some shepherd had built this shelter, up here on the tree-covered rise, overlooking the broad sweep of the meadow below. More even than the roof, the hillside behind kept the rain off. He turned to the man beside him.

"The scouts should be coming in. There's a higher valley, just north of here—that's where we should spend the night. Go get me something to drink. God knows how a man goes thirsty when the rain falls."

The man saluted and left. Uhtred turned his gaze back to the sweep of old grass below him. It stood waist high, all the sheep gone, driven off well ahead of the coming of the Danes.

Damn him, he thought. He knew Knut was attacking him because of what he had done in Winchester. He was glad of that. He was glad of Edmund being King. But in the cold and the rain he knew he had to get to Northumberland before Knut did, call out his people, and defend his country, or he would lose everything.

Uhtred's horse lifted its head, looking out into the rain. Sheets of water dripped off the edges of the lean-to. Uhtred knew he should get moving, but he was tired. It was a long way on to Bamburgh, a long way in fact to anyplace he could fort up. He thought of the valley where he had sent the scouts. An old road ran south through there. If he swung toward it—if he got Knut going north, and then he and his army turned south— he might be able to meet up with Edmund and hit the Danes from behind.

Down the meadow, through the silver rain, he saw a horse-man come out of the woods, and then another.

His scalp prickled up. Not Saxons. He could tell even this far away that they weren't practiced riders. They were Knut's advance scouts.

He drew back from the edge. He had to get moving. His man came up with a cup, and the first of his own scouts appeared behind him, soaking wet.

"My lord—my lord, there are Danes north of us."

Uhtred swore. He drank the sour ale his man had brought,

stirred from riding. Now he had no choice; he had to swing to-ward the old road to the east.

Even as he thought that, he had the feeling he was doing what Knut intended. Still, he could think of nothing else. He said, "Let's go."

⁜

The rain let up. As the moon waxed toward full, Knut reached the old road west of the Trent. With his men he found a good place to camp on the high ground, where he could see every-thing, and he was putting out his sentries when Broom-Orm brought him a man on foot, at sword's point.

"Now, now," this man said, hopping along ahead of the sword. "That's not necessary." He blinked at Knut, who did not know him, and scowled at him. "This is outrageous."

Knut ignored him. Ulf Thorleifsson tramped up. His Swedish cousin was fair as flax, with frizzy hair all over him, shaggy brows, a beard that grew in tufts along his jaws. He was always smiling. "Where's the meat? We've got a fire going."

"Is there anything to drink but water?" Knut turned back to the stranger. "Who are you?"

"I'm glad you got to that," the stranger said, sharp. "You're Knut Sweynsson, now? I'm talking to the right man?"

Knut folded his arms over his chest. "That depends on what you have to say. I'm Knut Sweynsson."

"Well, then. I'm from Thurbrand Hold, the lord of Lindsey. He says to meet him in Gainsburgh, one week from now." The man stood straight, his hands behind him, as if he thought that was enough to get him an act of homage.

Knut snorted at him. "I'm not going to Gainsburgh."

The other man's face altered, puzzled, and he started, "Thurbrand Hold, you know—" Knut turned away from him; Odd was handing him a sack of ale.

"By the bones, this is awful." He lowered the sack. "Get away from me," he said to the man from Thurbrand. "I'm not going to Gainsburgh now."

He looked down toward the road. Behind the rain the air was cold and harsh, which meant the storm was over. The light was fading. Somewhere up there he hoped Uhtred was beginning to realize that, if he kept going north, the Danes would close on him from two sides. East was the Trent and Thurbrand Hold. The only way for Uhtred to go was south, along this road where Knut waited.

Uhtred would not come within his reach for a few more days. Knut saw to his horse and made sure of his sentries. When he came back to the fire, Odd was already directing the skewering of meat.

Knut sat down by the fire. "I get some of that."

Odd said, "You should get your own meat. You eat more than any two of us."

"When we have the kingdom, I'll pile you with meat," Knut said.

Thurbrand's man had followed him to the fire. Stood stooped a little, twisting his hands together. "My lord—"

"I don't want to hear this." Knut shrugged him off. Broom-Orm gave him more ale, in a smaller sack, much better. Knut said to Thurbrand's man, "Sit down and shut up." Knut gulped the ale. Everything in him ached to run down Uhtred and walk on his face.

But he made himself think over this about Thurbrand. The half Dane wanted to talk, to bargain some advantage for coming in on his side. Thurbrand had five hundred men, just the other side of the Trent. Wherever Edmund was, he was every day closer, and he had probably twice the men of Knut's army and Thurbrand's together.

Farmers. Not Vikings. It wasn't safe to reckon on that. But

they were well south of him now. He wouldn't need more than his own men to take Uhtred.

In the growing darkness the men sat around the fire. They began to tear chunks from the roasted meat; for a while they were silent, except for the grinding and chewing. Thurbrand's man sat among them. Ulf Thorleifsson leaned back, his hands shining with grease.

"Now all we need are some women." The fire made his pale eyes look colorless.

"No women," Thurbrand's man said. "Plenty of sheep." The other men all laughed.

"There have to be some women around here," Broom-Orm said. "One or two would be enough for all of us."

Odd had cracked a bone and was digging out marrow with his knife. "I'd sooner have one all to myself."

Knut said, "I'd rather six or seven." He had not lain with a woman since they left Denmark. He shifted his weight, thinking of the last, her long fair hair, the fair curly hair in her crotch.

Odd said, "The same one, all the time, is better. That way she gets to like you and wants to make you happy." He shoveled a knife blade of blood-red mush into his mouth.

The others hooted at him. Ulf's voice boomed. "Do it fast, get it over with, on to the next!"

Knut stood up, hitching his sword belt on his shoulder. They would go on talking about women all night. "We're not looking for hole anyway. We need more meat, and we're going to fight in a couple of days, so get ready." He went to walk around the camp.

Then, two days later, there came a horseman down the road, a single rider in a green jacket, carrying a white flag. It was obvious he knew where Knut's camp was, and he reined in his horse on the road and waited.

Knut sent Broom-Orm down to talk to him; the tall man sauntered down the hillside on foot, in no hurry.

Odd stood beside Knut at the top of the slope. "Uhtred wants to change sides again. Maybe he'll give you some more hostages."

Knut gritted his teeth. Down there the two men talked, and then Broom-Orm came back.

"Uhtred of Bamburgh sends his greetings. He wants to submit. There's a hall off by the river, in a place called Weal. He'll meet you there in two days. He'll give you his word if you give him yours."

Knut lowered his eyes. His temper churned. Uhtred knew he was surrounded, knew he had no chance, and now he was following the English way of war. He wouldn't even give them a good fight. He would submit, weasel through this, pay some ransoms, maybe even join Knut's army. Knut would never be able to trust him. Worse: He would never get his revenge.

He turned to Broom-Orm. "Go down, tell him he has my word: I won't touch him."

He watched the lanky Dane go down the hill. Odd was watching him, frowning. Odd knew something was up, but this wasn't a matter for him. Knut sauntered over to someone else. And sent him to find the messenger from Thurbrand.

—⋄—

Later, he leaned against the back wall of the house in Weal, his arms folded over his chest, watching Thurbrand's men lug the last bodies out. They had dug a hole in the woods behind the privy and were throwing them all in there. It was a big hole. Knut thought, I have avenged his betrayal of my father. But he was uneasy.

He was beginning to regret this. Seeing this broadly, he realized this was something Ethelred might do, Thorkel, or Eadric Streona, luring a man with false promises into a trap and loosing that man's worst enemy on him. In fact, he knew those three had done this very thing. He saw himself no better than they were. At that, he pushed away from the wall and strode out, hurrying.

Uhtred's army scattered. Knut moved on east, crossed the Trent north of Nottingham, and picked up the ancient road called Ermine Street that ran down straight as a bowstring to London. Thurbrand's army had joined his, the rest of Knut's men had caught up, and the Viking army crowded the road. They crossed another river, where they stormed a little city.

There, he heard rumors that Edmund was marching up from the south with an army larger than his and was gaining more men every day.

The open country fell behind them. The road led down into the great forest, stands of oak trees and beech on the higher ground, long stretches of fen and quaking bog, shrub and brambles. It was late, cold at night, the year dying. Only the oaks were still heavy with leaves. Knut could not shake his foul mood. Thurbrand was high hearted with his murders, but Knut spoke to nobody, not even Odd, who seemed content with that. Day on day, he sent out scouts, but they brought him no sign of Edmund.

Deep in the forest, still well north of London, the road ran onto an old causeway across a bog, a narrow passage of split logs with berms of stone. On the far side the ground rose into a stand of trees. Knut sent Thurbrand on to scout it. The bog stretched off a good way on either side, brown in the autumn frosts, stands here and there of reeds and sedge sticking up like clumps of sword blades. A few half-dead pine trees rose like wet feathers. Along the edges black tangles of willow grew. Thurbrand went slowly on across, rode up onto the hillock beyond, and turned to signal that the way was clear.

Knut galloped his horse out onto the causeway. It was too narrow here, and he saw the dangers in it, so he wanted the army across as quickly as it could go. He lashed the horse into a flat run, his men and the rest of the army hurtling along after him, and then from either side a storm of arrows tore into them.

Knut's horse slammed headfirst into the ground. Knut flew forward and tumbled over and over until he came up against a stone post. Dazed, he uncoiled himself, looked down the long, narrow passage, and saw his men screaming, helpless, dying, falling, arrows jutting from them. Some leaped out into the bog, wobbled a few strides, and then sank down through the mosses as the bog ate them. More horses galloped past him, some riderless. Another wave of arrows stabbed down into the crush of bodies on the causeway.

Then, behind him, on the hill, he heard shouts and the clash of weapons. They were attacking Thurbrand too. The main army was still fighting its way across the causeway, but from the bog the Saxon bowmen were cutting them down.

He turned his eyes on the bog. Now he saw that every sharp-bladed clump of reeds held an archer, a darker mass in the heavy dark spikes. He got up and, stooping, ran back to his dead horse. His sword lay under it, but he pulled a bow and some arrows out of the pack on the saddle. Lying by the horse for cover, he picked out the man in the nearest clump, only fifty feet away, and shot.

This wasn't Raef's great Welsh bow, so he needed two arrows to figure the drift, but then the third knocked the Saxon sprawling on the bog. From the other end of the causeway somebody else began shooting back at the Saxons. The army kept on. Some others stopped, took shelter among the dead, and started shooting the Saxons. In a constant stream his men pounded past him, stumbling and staggering over the bodies, trying to hide between dead horses and men, hauling each other along by the arms, carrying wounded on their backs.

They staggered up onto the hill, and now from the hilltop there was a sudden dansker roar of triumph.

Knut crawled up to the milepost. Two arrows struck it as he crouched behind it. Knowing what to look for now, he found the Saxons easily, kept the bow low, and took out two more. A horn blew.

Odd rode up, lying low over his horse's neck, and slid down next to him. Knut waved a hand at him.

"Go on—Thurbrand's attacked—on the hill—" He stared at Odd. "Are you all right?"

Odd pawed at the side of his head. Something had hit him, maybe an arrow, tearing close to his eye. Half of his head was slick with blood, and the white of his eye was red. "I'm all right." He waved his men on and vaulted back into his saddle.

The Saxon bowmen had stopped shooting. They had faded away. Even in the meadow now he heard no signs of fighting, only the yells of dansker men. Knut stood up, daring a shot, but none came. They were gone. He went wearily up the road onto the hillock.

An open grove of trees crowned it, deep in mast, their high canopies like a roof. The road arched up across it and down the other side; near the top somebody had put some posts in the ground, but they were rotting out and falling over. He saw only Danes around the hilltop. Bodies lay along the road. Thurbrand, on the far side, was shouting as if he had won a great victory.

Knut's belly hurt. He turned back to the causeway. The long track was covered with the dead, horses, men, arrows sticking out of them like thorns. He had lost. This was how it felt to be beaten, this dank black grief. The tail end of his army was streaming off past him. The last was his cousin Ulf, on foot again, a bow in his hand.

"Good work," Knut said. He knew Ulf had managed things at the far end of the causeway.

Ulf shrugged, smiling. "Glad you're still upright, anyway. Quite a dive you took. You making a camp here?"

"Yes," Knut said. "Up on the hill." He felt leaden, cold and thick and stupid. "Get out the sentries." His shoulder was aching where he had hit the ground. He wiped his face, exhausted.

———⚬———

In under the tall trees they made a strong camp. Knut sent Odd and Ulf and their men out to find any wounded men among the bodies on the causeway and to start burying the dead. He himself went to find Thurbrand, who had built his own camp at the far side of the hill. Thurbrand saw him coming, moved in among his Lindsey men, turned to face him, and swelled out his chest, his wooly red hair standing on end.

Knut walked up to him. "What happened?"

Thurbrand stuck his thumbs in his belt. His eyes went back and forth. "I rode over, looked clear, the hill looked clear, so I told you to come on. Then they came barreling up the road."

"How many?"

"A lot more than me. But the road's narrow; they couldn't get at me all at once. I held them until your men caught up there, then they left."

"Why didn't you see the archers out on the bog?"

Thurbrand's jaw fell. "You know, I can't do everything—"

Knut roared at him, "You could do as I tell you, which was to scout." Thurbrand backed away from him, and Knut stalked after. The Lindsey men gathered behind Thurbrand. He remembered unwillingly how Thurbrand had helped him with Uhtred. Knut bit his lips. He thought suddenly, I have killed the wrong man. Thurbrand was hunching away from him, his hands like claws, looking at him through the corner of his eye.

Knut said, "Keep watch. They'll be back." He turned and tramped across the meadow again. Dark was falling. He felt the evil of the night, a dank mist seeping from the ground.

—⚬—

Above the murky glitter of the battlefield, newly freed in their numbers, the souls rose in wisps and tendrils of light, dazed and dismayed, many struggling still to be alive. While they floated lost, waiting for the light to come to show them the way home, the Lady devoured them, one at a time and severally.

She rolled and stretched around them, luxuriating in her appetite. They realized she was there, and they tried to escape, poor blind, dumb sparks. She hunted them in the trees when they tried to flee back to the mundane world, in the stinking swamps, along the causeway, in the air as they rose, mistaking the stars for the true light. But the light did not break for them; night went on forever for them. Raef did not come. She turned and spread herself thin, fearless, and sucked in soul upon soul, each a snap of pure sweet light, and gloried in her triumph that Raef did not come to disturb her.

—⚬—

Odd's eye hurt, and he daubed at the blood leaking down his cheek. Knut's army filled the meadow, their fires pushing back the dark. Knut himself sat with his back to a log by the campfire, Ulf beside him, across the fire ring from Odd.

Ulf said, "You look pretty bad, Odd."

"I can see," Odd said. "It'll mend."

They were all banged up. Odd glanced toward his left, where Knut sat. Knut's face was scraped down to meat along one side from falling on the road. He said nothing, brooding, staring into the fire while he chewed. They were eating the last of the beef they had picked up in the North, which Odd was glad of, since the meat was turning.

He thought over the ambush on the causeway. Any way he looked at it, that was a loss. A lot more Danes had died than Saxons. They were lucky it hadn't been worse. If not for Knut with a bow at one end and Ulf at the other, it might well have been much worse. Odd was glad he was alive; the arrow had flicked into the corner of his eye, torn along the side of his head, and clipped his ear. Now they had nothing left to eat, and they were in the middle of the hostile forest.

Even so, he knew Knut would lead them out of this. He had seen Knut now beat everybody he came against, and he thought Knut would eventually take Edmund too. He tossed a piece of gristle into the fire, which burst in a flare of sparks. Ulf, beside him, had the ale sack upended, the firelight glinting in his shaggy, pale hair; Knut was still staring into the flames.

Odd leaned back against the log, looking up at the sky, depthless black behind the wispy light of the fires. From nowhere, an old wonder came to him, and he said, "Do you ever think if there's someplace else?"

Ulf goggled at him. "What?" Knut lifted his head. His black mood was all over him like a haunting.

Odd folded his arms behind his head, leaning back against the log. "The Christians say there's a whole world out there, behind the stars. That's where their God lives."

Ulf said, "Oh. Asgard. That's at the top of the Tree."

Knut said, "How would they know?"

"Well—" Odd shrugged. "They have this book."

Knut lowered his gaze to the fire again. His voice rasped. "I don't think anybody knows much of anything. And the worst thing is what you don't know until it's too late."

He got up and walked off. Ulf said, under his breath, "What's got its hooks in him?"

Odd shrugged. He had a guess, but he would not venture it. Knut had gone off to the next campfire, talked a little to those men, and moved on. He would do this for hours, going around the camp. Odd said, "Get some sleep, Ulf." Rising, he went after his chief.

CHAPTER TWENTY-NINE

Eadric Streona said, "My lord, we should get back to London before the winter comes."

Edmund said, "We are beating them here." He was sitting on the wall at the end of the village, watching as the people and his soldiers carried out everything the Vikings could use. The village had been full of its harvest, and this was taking longer than he wished. Knut was less than half a day behind him to the north. The battle on the causeway had bled him but not stopped him. Edmund had underestimated him; he had expected to smash him on the causeway and break his army in half, to finish off the pieces one at a time. Now he was hoping to starve him to death.

Godwine came up to him. "My lord, I think the place is stripped."

"Good," Edmund said, and slid down from the wall.

Streona said, in a stout, resigned voice, "Then, my lord, I ask your leave to go back to London myself."

Edmund swiveled toward him. "I refuse it. Go back to your men and get them ready to follow me."

"My lord—"

Edmund stared at him. Streona had grown his hair long, like a Saxon, but he was still clean shaven, and his face was pinched with lines. His gaze shifted away from Edmund's. He was sweating in spite of the cold. Edmund knew if he sent him back, Streona would make trouble for him. If he kept him here, probably Streona would make trouble for him. Edmund said, "My lord, go back to your men and get them ready to move out."

Streona faced him a moment, his mouth working. He blinked a few times. Abruptly he turned and walked away.

Godwine came up, and he and Edmund watched him go down the street toward his men.

Edmund said, "He does not know what to do. He has never given his faith to anything, and so now he has no guide."

Godwine said, "Oh, you'll make heroes of us all eventually, Edmund."

"I will make you Englishmen," Edmund said. "I don't know about him." He led the way on down to their horses.

Godwine rode beside Edmund, silent, the banner staff in his hand. His blood was full of a wild singing. They had nearly won back there. For a while, at least, they had been beating the Vikings. When he charged them, they had fallen. He had struck down many of them.

He realized he had thought, somehow, they were made of tougher flesh than his, that if he hit them, they would not die. But they had died under his blade. He felt like an angel, invincible.

He had led the charge with his carls. He claimed this now as a right, because he was Edmund's first warrior, his standard-bearer. He remembered the attack like a pattern on his skin, his horse flying up the road, his arm cocking back his sword. When he saw the Vikings there, coming up through the trees, he let out a yell that still sang somewhere in his heart. He and his carls had plowed into the first few men there and threshed them like wheat under their horses' hoofs.

In among the trees, the Danes had slowed them. Godwine had hacked and chopped down at them, cut his way forward. But more Danes rushed up from the causeway, and the fyrdmen, behind him, were slow to come on. Then Edmund's trumpet had called them back.

Now, as they rode along, Edmund said, "You heard Streona?"

Godwine glanced at him. "He wants to go back to London." Streona had been noising this around for two days. He had many of the fyrdmen itchy with it.

"We need to force a battle."

"That won't be hard," Godwine said. "He's coming." He wanted another chance at the Vikings. "We need to get all our numbers to bear at once, Edmund. All the carls in the front."

"Yes," Edmund said. "The problem is to choose the ground. Find me somebody who knows this part of the road well."

Godwine nudged his horse into a jog up past the marching army, the blue banner fluttering over his head. He watched them as he went. They were trudging along, even the mounted men, their heads down. Some of them were wounded. Uneasy, he wondered how much more they had in them—if they had another battle in them.

Then as Godwine passed, the banner drew their eyes, someone shouted out his name, and he saluted him. He called, "For Edmund and for England!" and a cheer rose. They cheered the banner. Then someone else began to sing. Gradually other voices picked it up.

Heigh ho, heigh ho
Off to war a man must go
Until it cease
There is no peace
Heigh ho, heigh ho

The singing made them walk faster. He saw their heads come up. He thought, They are good men, these, all good men. His spirits rose.

Asking around, he found someone who knew this stretch of the old road and took him back to Edmund. This was a man on foot, in a ragged coat and baggy leggings, carrying a staff in his hand and a short sword in his belt. When he saw Edmund, he gabbled like a goose, bobbing up and down.

Edmund dismounted. "That's enough. Face me, I have questions of you."

The man clung to his staff with both hands, as if he needed it to stand up. "Ask me, my King."

"What lies ahead of us, on this road? More bogs?"

"No, my lord." The fyrdman began to bob down again, and Edmund got his shoulder and straightened him. "Mostly it's just forest, sir. And then there's a village, sir, a couple days on, maybe, at the Cambridge crossroads."

"How big a village?"

"A good size, sir. Eight, ten families, sir."

Edmund nodded to him. "You go with Godwine here and tell the people there they have to leave. We're going to fight there." His eyes swiveled to Godwine. "You know what to do."

"Yes," Godwine said. "I will."

⸺⸻

Thurbrand scrubbed his tangled beard with one hand. He had his horse by the reins. "There's another old road, east of here. Cambridge is out there somewhere."

Knut stood with him by the well, looking around the deserted village. He had hoped to find food here, but Edmund had already been here and cleaned it out. The Danes were poking into every house and coming out empty-handed. Ulf came up to him.

"There's nothing here. Nothing. They're talking about killing horses to eat."

Knut said, "Kill horses, then. I'm walking." He turned to Thurbrand. "Why should I listen to you?"

The half Dane scowled at him. His cheeks were red as his

bristly hair. "I know what I'm talking about. There's another
road, out to the east. There's even a cute way to get to it."

Knut walked around, his hands on his hips and his head
down, thinking. If there was another road, Edmund was unlikely
to have cleaned out any farms or villages on that one too. And it
had cost Edmund time to do this; he could not be far ahead. He
circled around to Thurbrand again.

"How long a ride?" He turned and sent a man for Odd, who
came over.

Thurbrand said, "If I can find the way, half a day, maybe."

"If you can find the way."

"I can find it."

Knut balanced this in his mind for a moment; he did not
like Thurbrand, but he liked the idea of the other road.

He turned to Odd. "Take your men, and Thurbrand take
yours. Go find this Cambridge road. Go south a day, as fast as
you can, pick up anything you find, and cut back to this road
again. The day after tomorrow, sundown, be back on this road.
Then come north."

Odd said, "I didn't want to eat my horse anyway." He turned
and whistled up his men. Knut went down through the village.
The rest of the army, smaller, might be easier to feed. At the end
of the village he stood looking into the darkening forest.

He turned. "Camp here. I'll eat horsemeat." He saw Ulf, behind him, his cousin's speculative, pale eyes above his bemused
smile.

"Still no women," Ulf said.

Knut batted Ulf on the chest. "Keep it in your drawers. Get
some sentries out."

＝⊶＝

Even the oaks now were turning, their leaves glowing in the
naked branches of the lesser trees. The day was breaking, and

the first light spread through the squat trunks in rays and streamers. Godwine hurried the last of the villagers south down the road, three old men and a woman, carrying packs. He had promised them they had only to go into the woods, that they could come back in a few days, but they did not believe him. They couldn't stay, whatever they believed, and they were running as they left.

He jogged his horse back up the common. Most of the houses were built against the south foot of the little hill, under its crown of ash trees. The road ran across the west edge of the common, meadows on the far side. The crossroads was a quarter mile on.

On either side of him, in among the houses, were Edmund's fyrdmen on the one hand, and Streona's Mercians on the other, the two sides of the trap. Godwine wondered if the Vikings would walk into the same setup twice. He wondered what else they could do, especially if the trap was well baited.

He was the bait. Along the old road Godwine's own men were gathered, the carls who had followed him and Edmund from Lincoln long ago, the first and best of the English army. He dismounted from his horse and walked along, looking from face to face—common, battered men, tired, dirty.

He said, "The King wants this of us. So we do it."

"We do it," they said, in one voice, and swung in around him. He mounted up and led them north. He pulled his cloak around him. The sun was rising, but it was still cold. After they had cleared the village he spread his men out in a single rank, edging into the forest, and they moved on north along the road.

He had left the banner behind; he missed carrying it. He was thinking again he should get a mail coat like Edmund's when ahead of him something moved fast across the road.

He shouted, calling his men together, and plunged forward. The road here dipped, and as he slowed his horse on the descent five Danes sprang on him from either side.

He hauled the horse back on its hocks, his sword in his hand, hacked once on his right and then wheeled, striking on his left. Somebody whistled. His men swarmed on the Danes, driving them back along the road, and then from the north there was an answering whistle.

Godwine shouted. The four remaining Danes were backing fast up the road; he called his men off and gathered them.

For a moment they were alone on the road. The full light of day was blooming through the oak trees to the east, golden on the mast and leaves that covered the ground, barred with the shadows of the trees. Then up the slope and through the shadows and down the road between them a tide of Danes rushed on him.

Godwine raised his arm with his sword and led his men in one short charge toward them. The Danes turned toward him, coming on three sides, and he turned.

"Back! Back—"

For an instant he held his horse short, making sure all his men were in front of him. "Back—" They rushed off down the road south again, as if they were retreating. The Vikings were almost all on foot; Godwine slowed again, making sure he did not outrun them. They were streaming down the road after him, spilling off into the forest. His men were running at full stride back into the village, yelling. Godwine galloped down the road to the edge of the houses.

The hill still blocked the sunlight. His men were scattering into the empty houses. Godwine swiveled his horse to look up the road. The Danes had slowed, or stopped. Up the shadowy road nothing moved, the long, blank, straight gash through the woods empty. He had failed. The bait had failed. The sun broke over the top of the hill and spread across the road and the woods, and then, almost in the corners of his eyes, he saw, all around him, men creeping in through the forest.

A whistle sounded. Godwine spun his horse around,

shouting a warning, and from either side of the road the Vikings attacked.

He backed up fast into the village and bounded off his horse. Easier to fight on foot here. His men were waiting, packed onto the common, shoulder to shoulder, each guarding the other. Down into the village the Danes roared like a wave.

Godwine raised his sword in both hands; the first lines of the Danes rushed down on him, and he stood square against them, hacking broadly from right to left. His men were screaming and fighting around him, so close they banged together. He bellowed, "Back! Back!" All at once, as they had planned, they backed up into the common.

The Danes shrieked and pressed after them. Godwine flung up his sword to fend off an axe, and then stood toe-to-toe a moment, trading blows. His men were falling back still. Suddenly there were Danes all around him; he leaped and whirled and hacked the sword desperately to fight them off.

A trumpet blasted, Edmund's trumpet, and out of the houses below the hill the rest of the English army poured, taking the Vikings without warning from the side.

The man in front of Godwine jerked toward the sound, and Godwine stabbed in finally past his elbow, deep into his chest. He dodged another blow, turned on his heels, and cut back, feeling the blade slide into flesh. He roared. On either side now were English, and he had to run forward to find a Dane to fight.

The Vikings were swarming up the road again, trying to get out of the trap. Godwine strode after them; the strength surged through his arms as if the earth itself fought through him. A bushy-bearded man stood against him, and he hacked him down. They were thrusting the Vikings back. They were winning. The hot triumph forced a yell out of him.

"Edmund! Edmund and England!"

Around him the other Saxons bellowed. He battered down another Dane who dared stand against him. The forest loomed around him; he was north of the village. The Vikings packed the road ahead of him from trees to trees. He called on the English behind him to charge. One charge to break them. He called again. No one charged. Behind him, someone cried, "Watch out!"

He realized he could hear men fighting behind him. There were Danes behind him too.

In front of him suddenly an axeman rushed at him. He fended off two strokes, and then knocked the Dane flat, rushing toward the nearest of the houses.

From the shelter of the wall he looked quickly around. There was no Danish side, no English side, just hundreds of men fighting hand to hand all through the common, in and out of the houses. The Danes somehow had come in from the south too. They had set their own trap. Another Viking rushed at him, glanced a stroke off his sword, and ran on down the alley between the houses. Suddenly two of Godwine's carls ran up to him.

"My lord—My lord—"

"Come with me!"

He led them farther into the village, looking for Edmund. They had to gather, to make a strong point, so they could fight together. More of his carls saw him and followed.

Between two of the houses he and his men came suddenly on a band of Danes, their leader a short, ugly man with wooly red hair. They stood a moment trading blows, but Godwine had more men, and the redheaded man abruptly rushed off. Ahead was the common, and Godwine strode out across it. His men scattered behind him into separate fights. His sword in both hands, he turned in a circle, trying to make sense of this. Men ran past him, screaming, Danes and English. A horn was blowing, somewhere, over and over.

He lifted his head, and on the hillside above him he saw the blue banner. He shouted his men together again and struggled up the hill. That was Edmund. He gave a glad cry. Edmund, with his banner, calling his men together. Godwine staggered toward him, the steep slope slippery with the long-fingered ash leaves.

Edmund stood square, watching the fighting before him, his face gleaming with sweat, the banner staff in one hand and his horn in the other. With Godwine only steps below him, Eadric Streona came running at him from one side.

"My lord!" Streona cried. "Yield! Yield!"

Edmund hardly looked at him. "I'll never yield."

Somebody shouted, "They're coming!"

Godwine wheeled. Pushing, shouting encouragement and threats, he got his men into a wall before the King, facing the Danes. A long wavering rank of Vikings was scrambling up the hill toward them. Godwine hewed away at the first, dodged a flailing axe, and knocked the man behind it backward.

Then, up the hill, he heard a savage cry.

He jerked his head around. Streona was leaping on Edmund from behind. In his hand a long blade stabbed in through the open underarm of the mail coat.

Godwine shrieked. Edmund staggered, went to his knees. The banner fell to the ground by him. Above him on the slope Streona was screaming, "The King is dead! The King is dead! Escape—flee—" Godwine ran to Edmund, who was wobbling, upright on his knees, blood running down his side.

Godwine clutched Edmund by the arm. With that help the King pulled himself up onto his feet again. The blood was soaking out of his side. He shoved his left hand against the wound and held it. "I'm here—" It took all his breath to say that.

Godwine turned, and shouted, "The King lives! The King lives!" The men around him closed tight around him, their backs to him, a Saxon wall. He wrapped one arm around Edmund and half lifted him backward, step-by-step up the hill behind them. Another man turned and gripped Edmund from the far side. "Here, help me," Godwine said. "Take him up the hill." They hurried up the slope, their feet skidding on the loose ground, the King between them, his feet dragging.

They reached the high ground, and Edmund steadied. He was still clutching the wound closed with one hand; but he stood by himself. Godwine turned, looking down.

They were near the top of the hill, a knot of Englishmen all around them, five men thick. The long slope stretched down, and at its foot the Danes were gathering. As he watched, they circled the whole hill. There were far more of them now than the English. Their heads tipped up, their looks turned on one place, on Edmund, and he thought he saw their eyes glow hot.

Godwine gripped his sword. He thought all his life came down to this moment, when he stood beside his King, about to die with him. Then one of the men in front of him turned and held out the blue banner to him, coiled on its staff.

"God be with us." Godwine took the staff and planted it, and the wind opened the long blue pennant. "For Edmund and England!"

The English gave up a single roar that deafened him, jubilant, in the teeth of death. "Edmund! England! England!"

Edmund said, "If we all die here, yet we have won, for this moment." He was breathing hard. The blood seeped between his fingers. "That's Knut Sweynsson, there." Godwine put the staff into his left hand and drew his sword again. Down there the Danes were circling closer. He watched that yellow head. He would take Danes with him. He was not afraid. The honor of this was greater than any man, greater even than Edmund. He planted himself, ready.

⟞⟊⟝

Knut saw the banner on the hill and shouted, fighting his way toward it. He was cutting his way through the space between two houses when he looked up and saw a Saxon in a black coat strike the King down from behind.

He gave a yell, as if the blow pierced him too. A wail went up. "The King! The King is dead—" In front of him the English scattered away like leaves.

Knut raced out toward the hillside. Up there a hundred Saxons had closed around their wounded King like a shield and got him up the hill, but the rest of Edmund's army was fleeing into the woods. The Danes swept around the hillside, howling. Ulf ran by him, his pale eyes glaring, his sword cocked over his shoulder.

Knut stopped, lowering his sword, and looked around. His men circled the hill, many more than the Saxons packed together up there. But now suddenly the Saxons had raised their banner. They were cheering. He saw Edmund standing in their midst. He was alive, and he was going to fight.

Knut looked right and left along the circle of his men. Ulf had stopped a little way away and was watching him. Beyond him Odd, with Tronders all around him, watched him, waiting for orders. Knut turned his gaze back to the men on the hill. The Saxons who had run off could come back at any time; he had to get this done with. Edmund and his carls up there could not escape, and right now he outnumbered them. He still held his sword in his hand. But he needed to think wider now.

He lifted his left hand up. He called out in Saxon.

"Edmund, listen to me. I will end this. I don't want to kill you or your noble men. Let there be no victor between us. Be King with me."

Around him there was a sudden blank silence. Ulf's mouth dropped open. For a moment the Saxons up there did not move. Among the Danes a low buzz went up. Then among the Saxons Edmund moved down hill, his blue banner following after.

The King was unsteady, his face sleek with pain. He let no

one help him. Still wearing his mail shirt, his standard-bearer behind him, he came down onto the slope before his men. Blood dripped from the mail. He stood straight as the banner staff.

He said, "I doubt I will wear an earthly crown much longer, Knut. But what you offer me is noble." He looked across the space between them, square and straight, and held out his hand. "I accept this. May you be as great a King as you are a fighter."

Knut went up to him and gripped his hand. "Let there be nothing between us from now on but honor."

Edmund said, "Honor. England's honor. I am—I am—" His eyes rolled up and he collapsed.

Knut caught him before he hit the ground. He turned, Edmund's body in his arms, and called, "Come bear the King of England away."

The Saxons were already pouring in around him. They took Edmund from him; he was still breathing; he would live a while longer. Knut backed up out of their midst. His arms were smeared with blood. Odd walked up beside him. They watched the Saxons carry their King away down the road.

"God save our good King Edmund."

Odd said, under his breath, "Iron Edmund." Knut grunted, remembering who had called him that, what seemed a hundred years before. He lowered his eyes.

The Danes had gone back into the village, were breaking into houses, looking for food and loot. Odd turned to Knut. His eyes shone. He had sheathed his sword. "I have seen today what will be storied around fires for the rest of time. Let me give the order to camp."

Knut took him by the arm and towed him out of the way. "Ulf can do that. Do this yourself. Go to Winchester and take the Queen of England prisoner. Throw her in a sack if you have to, but don't let her get away. Don't let her lay her hands on you. Keep her under constant guard."

Odd said, "How long before you are sole King of England?"

He struck Knut companionably on the chest. "What you did—that was King's work, as he himself said—they fought too well to die."

Knut said, "He's dying anyway. Go do as I say." He gripped Odd's arm to give this weight. "You alone I trust with this."

"I will do it." The other man went off.

Knut went outside, into the street. The Saxons were moving away in a mass, bearing Edmund home. Their voices rose in a chant. Already it looked like a funeral procession. In the gathering dusk, Ulf stood there, smiling, his frizzy hair matted with blood. Broom-Orm called, and Knut waved, and he came walking across the street.

He said, "Do you have any orders?"

Knut said, "Wait," looking past him.

Ulf said, "What's going on?"

All the Saxons had not gone with their King. A little train of them was walking up the street. Knut recognized the black coat of the leader before he saw the man who wore it: It was Eadric Streona.

The Danes were moving around in the nearby houses. The wind was rising, and they were building a fire in the middle of the village and gathering around it. Knut said, his eyes on the men coming toward him, "We need to put out sentries."

Ulf said, "I have done so. But the war is over, isn't it? Honor, you said." He slapped Knut's arm. "That was well said. You've got a way about you, boy."

Knut said, "Between me and Edmund the war is over. There's more to this than us." Eadric Streona was striding up to him, his face straining to smile. The Mercians had fallen behind him.

"Well done, my lord, well done." He put out his hand to shake Knut's. "But you could not have won here without me, my lord. May I be bold enough to say so." His hand waggled out there between them. His voice babbled on. "If you but confirm me lord of Mercia, that shall be enough for me. And with my troops—"

Knut glanced at Ulf. "Hold him."

Ulf leaped forward, and Broom-Orm also, and they seized Streona by the arms. The Mercians behind him turned on their heels and walked away. Knut drew his sword. The Saxon flung himself backward against the hold and cried out, "Now, wait, I've been—" Knut ran him through the body.

The Saxon slumped down and died. Ulf said, "I like your decision here."

Knut said, "It's the country's evil that no man knows what side he's on." He wiped the blood off his sword on Streona's shoulder and thrust it back into its sheath.

CHAPTER THIRTY

Edmund lay dying in London, and Knut went there to see him. All around the hall of the Saxon King, people were gathered, praying and weeping. He went in among them, and they hardly saw him. He walked into the long hall.

Edmund lay at the back of it on a pallet, under a cross. Knut thought at first he slept, but then he said, "Knut. I am glad you came. Sit."

There was a stool by the bed. Knut waved back the servants who came sprinting forward and sat on it, stretching out his legs. Edmund was flat under the blankets, his face pale as wax. He said nothing for a while.

Finally Knut said, "I am here."

"Yes. I heard you killed Streona."

"Yes."

"Good." Edmund lay still a moment, but Knut could see he was not done talking. He said, "You will be King of it all, when I am dead."

Knut said nothing; he knew this.

"You must honor the Saxons."

"I will not be here long if I honor only Danes." He studied the pale face on the bed. Iron Edmund, he thought. You should have been a Viking. He blurted out, "I will be such a king to England as you would have been, Edmund. I swear this."

Edmund's eyes moved, just his eyes turning, as if he had no strength to move his head. "God keep you as you keep that promise." He smiled, and he let his eyes close. "God keep England." He was falling asleep, his wrecked body slack. Knut looked for the servant, got him back to the bed, and went out.

Edmund waited until Knut had gone and opened his eyes again.
The quiet space of the hall comforted him. He was glad to have
seen Knut but glad also he was gone. He was too alive, and Edmund was almost dead now. He looked around toward the far
corner.

She was there, as she had been since he came here, in her
dirty coif, her wooden shoes, her dark eyes fixed on him. She
smiled at him, her eyes warm. No one else could see her. He understood now why only he could see her and why she was waiting for him. The servant murmured and drew his blanket up.

Knut got on his horse and rode back down toward the river. Edmund, he thought, might not live through the night. Everybody
died. But some died better than others. Edmund had given his
life for England. Who even knew what England was—Saxon,
Dane, and in between? Yet Edmund had seen something and
followed it. Now Knut had pledged to follow it also, when he
scarcely knew what it was.

First he had to deal with his enemies.

There was his brother Harald, King of Denmark, but he
had his own plans for Harald. Thorkel was nothing. Good men
Knut would keep fast beside him: Odd; the Trondejarl, Odd's
father; Ulf Thorleifsson; Broom-Orm and the rest he would
bind to him, tight as iron hoops. And Saxons too, the men who
had stood with Edmund. He saw now he should have done this
with Uhtred and let Thurbrand go by. Godwine, for one, he
would make his man. If he gave the Saxons peace and justice,
they would follow him as they had followed Edmund.

There was Richard of Normandy.

Of them all Normandy was the most dangerous, with his mailed and mounted thousands. Horse Vikings. His sister, Queen of England, and her sons, the Aethelings, gave him any excuse he needed.

His sister, Queen Emma.

Now Knut brought into his mind everything that Raef had spoken to him about the Queen and her demon. His belly tightened; he had to do this, although he quailed from it. He had grown up in an eldritch house. He knew he had no power there.

He rode down toward the river. Emma was held fast in a tower near the bridge, and there he went to see her.

They had made the big, shadowy room softer for her, with hangings on the walls and fresh rushes, but it was a prison still. The air felt raw. He saw her, and he almost stopped in his tracks.

She was years older than he was, fat, not pretty, already the mother of two sons. She flew at him when he came in, and at once he saw the demon in her eyes.

She said, "I will not be treated so. I demand you let me go to Normandy." Her voice crackled. She swayed when she walked, as if she were much taller. "At least, give me my whole household, as your father did."

He kept out of her reach, circling past her into the middle of the room. Some of her women hovered in the corners, all in pale gowns, like seashells hollow to the wind. He said, "My lady, hear first what I intend for you." He could not let her go to Normandy.

She wheeled toward him. Pudgy and plain, yet she gave off a ruddy flash now and then, like small lightning, as if she could not quite keep herself down, and for an instant he thought he saw something, a vast shadow around her. Her eyes glimmered, red; he imagined something he could not see reaching toward him with open claws.

He had trapped himself. She was between him and the only

door. His skin tingled. He saw his death in her eyes. But he knew what he could offer to both of them, the woman and the power that possessed her, what would keep her here, and him alive, and maybe solve the whole problem.

She said, "What then do you intend for me?"

Knut said, slowly, "I want to marry you."

That struck her all at once: so she had no gift such as Raef's of knowing minds. She faced him, calmer. The long reaching claws drew back. He saw in her face, around her like a shimmer of light, the demon in her, calculating, hungry.

She clasped her hands together, holding all this close. It was not Emma who spoke to him now. The voice deeper, harsher. "I will marry you. But I will have one gift of you."

He said, "What?"

"I want your foster sister for my maid of waiting," she said.

Knut lifted his head, surprised. The woman before him went on. "Jorvik's daughter. He fostered you. He will do this for you. And it is an honor; make him see that. It will heal the rift between us." The voice smooth as butter. The eyes slick as oil.

He said, "I will ask him."

"Insist on it," she said. "There is some rumor she may be turned against him. That should make it easier." She stepped aside. "You may leave me now." She sank down into a Norman bow. "My husband and my King." She simpered, rising, Emma herself again, the shadow deep, hidden away. Knut went by her, almost fleeing.

⸎

Godwine stepped down from his horse; he had left his men behind in Derby and come out alone to Lark Hill. He looked around the little cobbled courtyard, uncertain, and then the door from the hall opened, and Ealdgyth came out.

She was taller than he remembered, her hair hidden under a

coif and her cloak clasped in gold. She said, "Godwine. I dread what you have come to tell me."

He took his hat off and faced her in the doorway. "Edmund is dying," he said. He kept his voice steady. He had rehearsed this all the way here. "He told me to bid you stay here. Better not to remind people about you."

Her face was pale as wax. Her eyes swam suddenly with tears. She jerked her head to one side. "I knew this would happen. He gave me up for a dream. I should have realized that things you can't see are impossible to fight." She laid her hand on her belly. "What will become of this?"

Godwine lowered his eyes; he thought, Ah, God, I would you had not told me that. He said, "Pray it is a girl."

"Oh, well," she said, "so that's how it is." She was turning to go inside again, her body stiff; she put one hand out to the doorjamb, blindly, as if to hold herself up. She said, "I always knew better than to love him." The tears spilled down her cheeks. The door shut between her and Godwine. He put on his hat and mounted and rode back to London.

⎯⎯⎯

Laissa never left the hall anymore, and Edith seldom, since Miru could come in and out as she pleased and bring them what they wished, but Leif walked abroad nearly every day, wandered around Jorvik, and saw his friends in the crowds. At first they looked a little different and stared at him oddly, which he expected, but that passed. Day to day, the time went by inside the same as it did outside. Nobody said anything about the priest, and he avoided seeing Gemma.

On the river bar three ships were already being caulked that he remembered only as frames, keels just laid, and men then still hunting the right shapes in the trees for the strakes and ribs. He skipped over what this meant.

He met Goda on the river bar, the townsman looking very well in a nice coat, but his face seamed with discontent. He said, "Leif. For God's sake. When is he coming back?"

"I don't know," Leif said. "You're doing well enough without him, it seems to me." The council had its new hall, and the harbor was very orderly.

"It doesn't feel like it." Goda bit his fingernails. "It's hard; he always knew who was lying, who was telling the truth. He always knew what was right. There are so many more people now."

"He only did what you would have done, really," Leif said.

Goda laughed, unbelieving. Then, both at once, they saw the ship coming up the river.

Everybody turned and watched. The big golden-headed dragon rowed neatly up the channel, turned, and tucked into the river bar. Half a dozen men there ran to help them beach her. Leif stood back a step. It was Knut getting off.

Leif had not seen him in more than two years. He was still lanky, big boned, but he had grown into his size. He had his hair braided up Viking wise, but his wispy young beard grew long like an Englishman's. On his arms he wore golden rings, and his belt was of gold, as was the clasp of his cloak. He walked with a longer stride. He walked as if no power on earth could stop him. He tramped up the bar toward Leif and Goda. His eyes were sharp; he saw everything.

"What are you doing here?" Leif asked.

"I'm the King of England now," Knut said. "I go where I please."

Goda said, "If you're looking for the King of Jorvik, he's gone."

"Gone," Knut said, startled.

"Maybe he never existed."

Knut turned to Leif. "I need him. He promised me." His voice was keen. "He has cursed me, if he is gone."

Goda said, "Well, he's gone."

Leif said, "Let's go talk this over." He jerked his head at Knut and started off up the river bar. Goda watched them go, frowning.

⟐

Knut followed the fat Icelander. He was fumbling out ways to take back his promise to the demon, but there were all sorts of stories about doing that, and none of them ended well. The fat man led Knut on up through the Coppergate, past the shambles, and up the slope toward the hall. Knut strode beside him.

"This is bad, if he is truly gone."

Leif said, "He's still here. But they've disowned him, and you know how he is. Even Gemma." Then they came up toward the top of the hill and the oak tree, where the hall should have been, and Knut stopped and let out an oath.

"Where is it?"

Leif said, "No, come on. Follow me, on the flags, step in step. He'll let you in." He gave Knut a curious, amused look. "Are you afraid? Let your breath out, all the way, before you come in. Don't breathe until you're inside. Otherwise you can get really sick." He turned and went up through the grass; onto the bare, windswept crown of the hill there beside the oak tree; and in midstep he vanished into the air.

Knut marked exactly where he had walked, and he put his feet down in those steps. He felt slate under the grass. His heart was pounding. But he needed Raef, and he let out all his breath and went on. One step he was in the grass, and the next in the hall.

He drew in a breath, had a moment of terrific nausea, and steadied. The hall stretched long and dim around him. From the far end came the clatter of the looms. Two men were mounting meat on the spit. Raef, sprawled on the high seat, looked half-asleep. Leif stood across the room at the table, pouring a cup of ale.

Knut went up before the high seat, and Raef raised his head. Several other men came up the hall also; Laissa was there. He did not see Gemma anywhere. He turned to face Raef.

"Well, King of England," Raef said.

"King of Jorvik," Knut said. "You told me you would help me. I have got the Queen in Winchester."

"Keep her in England," Raef said.

"Oh, she'll stay in England," Knut said. "I told her I would marry her."

Laissa gave a soft, amazed sound. Leif had turned to listen. Raef's eyes opened, direct.

He said, "Did she agree?"

"Yes," Knut said. "But she wants Gemma."

Laissa said, "No."

"You promised her my daughter?" Raef said.

"Yes. But not until after we are married. We have to banish the demon, then, before she actually gets her," Knut said. He had thought this out. "At the wedding. You said you would help me. Otherwise—"

Raef said, "If we fail she will have my daughter."

Knut said, "Then we can't fail."

Leif said, "She can't have Gemma. No matter what she's done."

Knut looked around again. "Where is she? What's she done?"

"Cast me out," Raef said. "Lacking a convenient swine, she has thrown me into an old man with many bad thoughts."

Laissa came up beside him. "What have you sworn to him?" She laid her hand on his arm. "I fear the cost of this."

Raef touched his ear—where his left ear had been. "I fear more myself, that I can't do it." He nodded at Knut. "Let Gemma say if she will go. I can't say for her."

Knut said, "I will, if I can. If you help me."

"If she will go, you must swear to me you will protect her."

"I swear it," Knut said. He cast around for something strong enough and said, "I swear as a son to a father."

Raef smiled at him. "I will do all I can, then. As a father to a son."

Laissa said, "Raef."

Knut said, "The wedding is in Winchester, in a month."

"We will be there," Raef said. "Go talk to Gemma."

⁂

When Knut had left, he turned to Laissa. "She cannot go alone. They are young, and they love each other. You must go with them and keep them out of trouble."

She said, "But not you?"

"I'll go with Leif," he said. He took her hand and kissed the palm and closed her fingers over it. He smiled at her. "Don't be afraid, Laissa. I will not suffer my daughter to be attacked. Go with her and keep her safe."

She looked into his eyes; something had happened in him. All the years she had known him he had been edgy, inward, uncertain; part of his brilliance had been his constant shifting nerve. Now he was calm. His eyes were still as blue as the deepest sky, but she saw only peace in him. She took his hand to her lips. She said, "Good-bye, then." The words resounded in her mind, more meaningful than she had intended. She went out after Knut.

⁂

Knut went to Gemma, who was living in the garret of Miru's new house. The girl came down into the hall in her simple dress and made him a bow.

"Sit," Knut said, and made her perch on a stool. He sank down on his heels before her, his eyes on her face; he had not remembered how beautiful she was, but she looked sad, and older.

She said, "Why have you come? Have you seen my mother and father?"

"Yes," he said.

To his surprise, she put her hands up over her face. She sat still awhile, her face hidden, and then she looked up.

"They're here? They are in Jorvik? I cannot—I have not seen them it seems for years. I betrayed them. I have lost them."

"I don't think so," he said. "They still love you."

"Yes," she said. "And I them, but that doesn't always matter." She turned her gaze on him. "You are King now. This is such a marvel."

He said, "You know, I cannot marry you, even so."

"Oh, well." She laughed, not happily. "I'm not sure anybody will ever want to marry me anyway."

He said, "I am to marry the old queen. Emma."

"Oh," Gemma said. "She's much older than you. Is she pretty?"

"No. But she's Queen, which is what matters. She wants you among her household."

Her face changed. The smile disappeared. "She is my father's enemy. Isn't that so? My mother told me once how she harried them out of London."

"Yes."

"That's why you came here. To get my father's help. And that's why she wants me, to ruin him."

"Yes."

Her face crumpled. Her tongue ran over her lower lip and she looked elsewhere a moment. Then her gaze came back to his. "What does he say?"

He shrugged. "That you should decide for yourself if you will come."

She gave a shiver. "What will happen?"

"I don't know." He thought of the long, reaching claws, the black shadow of the demon.

"If I do this, will they take me back?"

"I will make them take you back."

She gave the short, unhappy laugh again. "You have never understood my father." She lifted her eyes to him. "If this will help him, I will do it, whatever comes of it."

He said, "I will take care of you." Although he did not know if he could.

Then, in the door, Laissa came. Gemma cried out, leaped up, and ran into her mother's arms. Laissa began to weep, her hand on her daughter's hair. Knut went by them to leave them alone; he was thinking he had at least kept some of the promise.

⸺◦⸺

They went south on his ship. They did not go directly; he stopped along the coast, in several places, to take homages, so that the moon was almost gone when they came to Sandwich. It amazed Gemma how people treated him, bowing and fawning on him. He ignored it. He hardly spoke to her and Laissa either; he was thinking about something else. Laissa never let her be alone with him.

At Sandwich they left the ship and went overland to Winchester on horseback. They came into the city in the afternoon and went to his hall.

There a man came up to meet them, young as Knut, with tilted eyes and dark skin. He saw the two women and said, "Well, I see you used your time there wisely."

Knut said, sharply, "Odd, this is my sister and her mother." He took hold of Gemma's hand.

The dark man smiled at Gemma, merry. "That's even better."

Laissa said, suddenly, "Leif." She pushed past them, down the great torchlit hall, her arms out.

The Icelander had been standing there by the wall, waiting, and now he took her into his embrace. For a moment they were silent, holding each other. The old man laid his cheek against her hair and shut his eyes. He had always loved her. Gemma went toward them, looking all around them.

"Where is—"

Laissa stepped back. Tears spangled her cheeks. Leif turned to Gemma and took her hands.

"He's here." He looked beyond her, to Knut. "He thought he should stay out of sight." He turned back to Gemma, smiling. "Ah, but I've missed you, little one."

She flung herself into his arms. "I missed you." She rubbed her face against his shoulder. "I want my father back."

"That's all right," he said. "Don't cry." He did not say: Yes, he will come back.

Behind her, Laissa said, "When will she meet the Queen?"

Knut said, "I will present her tonight, but only for a moment. The wedding is tomorrow. After that, Gemma will go into the Queen's household."

Gemma turned toward him. "You made it close," she said. Her heart pounded.

"I meant to."

She said, "My father—"

Knut shrugged. Leif said, "He's here somewhere."

She said, "Will I ever see him again?" She turned toward her mother, but Laissa said nothing. "Please," Gemma said. "When can I see him?" And still no one spoke. She laid her head on Laissa's shoulder. She had been happy for a moment, seeing Leif. Now she was cold with dread. Something terrible was going to happen now. She buried her face against her mother.

Knut had made sure that several other girls were being put forward into Emma's eye on this evening, so that when Gemma
came up and made the sweeping bow he had taught her, there
were many other people around.

Nonetheless, Emma lurched toward her, for an instant un-
gainly in her lust. Knut saw the Queen wanted to gather the girl
up at once, but another maid was coming forward, bowing, the
herald saying another name. Knut got Gemma by the arm and
drew her away. He saw the avid look on Emma's face and turned
his back.

⸙

Emma thought, She is perfect. Young, pretty, and clever, and
with some small gift of sight. She thought, I will have her by me
always. And my new husband has brought her to me as a wedding gift.

That made her laugh. She wondered if she were becoming
too human: laughing. But it was an elegant circle: Mav's grand-
daughter would become the Lady of Hedeby. She hoped Raef
knew this, wherever he was, and took it like a knife in the heart.

⸙

Before he said the vows with Emma, Knut wore his crown
before the gathered lords of England.

It was different than he expected, sitting there with all his
sworn men before him, Saxon and Dane together. The crown
was heavy. It drove his mind deeper. He remembered again
what he had promised Edmund. He would be a good King. He
would not take England to himself but give himself to England.
Around him the great church hummed with the singing of the
monks, the charges of the bishop. He thought how many kings

there had been in so short a time—Ethelred, Sweyn, Edmund, him. In and out like the tide, as Raef had said. The kingdom needed peace, and peace meant evenhanded law.

Now this thing with Emma.

They were married by a Christian rite, which didn't bother him. He had taken the water blessing once, a long time before, when his father had, to get some advantage with the Germans. It was just a word, anyway, *god*, for that beyond words, as irreducible as the ocean or a star. He stood before the altar and put a ring on her hand while the bishop recited. They did not kiss.

Turning, they went down the aisle of the church toward the door, his men packed in on either side. She was smiling. Her greying, dark hair was smooth under a gold-embroidered coif. Her feet walked smoothly in Eastern slippers. He saw she was pleased with all this, and he turned and bent to her, husbandlike.

"Take my arm. Here." They walked out through the deep door of the church, the big wooden doorways cast wide open on either side. Emma leaned on him, delighting in his solicitude. Gemma had come out behind them. On the threshold, he said, the words ringing in his ears, "It's cool, my wife, you will need a cloak."

Gemma brought up the red cloak, collared with soft marten fur, and he himself helped swing it around Emma's shoulders. His heart thundered. She would know it instantly by the color. She would fling it off. But she gathered it around her, smiling, flattered. She turned to him, her face shining with pleasure. "Your arm, my King." Knut put his hand back and pushed Gemma hard away, back over the threshold and into the church. Side-by-side with his new wife, he walked out to the sunlight, where her women waited in two long rows. Laissa and Leif waited just beyond, the first of a crowd, which let up a cheer at the sight of the King and Queen.

Before the King and his Queen had gone three steps, a shriek pealed out of her. She looked down at the cloak around her. With one hand she flung Knut aside as if he were a rag. She tore at the cloak, trying to rip it away. From her eyes, her ears, her mouth, suddenly, there leaked wisps of filthy smoke.

She wheeled and she lunged for Gemma, standing there on the threshold of the church. From her reaching arms the black claws of the demon stretched out for the girl.

The church door slammed closed between them, and Raef leaped forth to meet the Lady.

His eyes blazed. His hair was white as the sunlight. His face glowed. He flung himself at her as if he would swallow her up. She recoiled, the black, smoky miasma spinning around, trying to get back to Emma, who was still screaming, still wrapped in the red cloak, and Raef closed in and enveloped them both.

He gathered Emma into his arms, her head clasped in his bad hand and her whole body pressed against him. The whirling, gritty smoke rose out of her in a stinking cloud. From it screeches rang, as if from a hundred mouths. Knut staggered backward, thrown by the whirling air, and fell.

An intense cold rolled over him. Lying flat, he gaped at Raef, standing with Emma in his arms, almost hidden in the stinking smoke. Around them her women in their white dresses were scattered like eggshells. Laissa had gone down on her knees, halfway between Knut and her husband, the blast of the air taking her long hair out straight as a banner.

The crowd was shrieking in terror, trying to run. Many had collapsed. The church doors banged open and flew off. A child's body sailed through the air, becoming only pieces as it flew. Laissa was trying to get up, and Knut bellowed to her to lie down, the roar drowning his voice. Leif was beside her, his scanty hair aflutter; he forced his way against the terrible wind, flung himself over Laissa, and held her down, his body shielding her.

Gemma had fallen to her knees on the threshold behind her father. She was trying to reach him, but the blast of the wind tumbled her backward, into the church. The church itself was shaking. The wind howled, and the stout tree beside it bent like a bow. A roof slate struck the ground a foot from Knut and shattered into pieces. A tree across the yard cracked down the middle. Out there in the crowd huddled on the ground, a man tried to stand and fell back, blood spurting from his cheeks, his lips.

The center of the whirling stink of smoke grew brighter, shedding rays of light in all directions. Outlined in the light, Raef appeared, Emma held hard against him, his arms wrapped around her, as if he could press her into him. The smoke was vanishing into him. As the light around him swelled, the boiling, dirty smoke sank into him through his eyes, his mouth, his skin. The last tendril vanished. The air stopped moving. The noise faded. The air lightened.

In the ringing silence, Emma slid from Raef's arms down onto the porch. Raef stood straight, his feet spread wide thrust his arms out, tipped his head back. He gave a howl of triumph. All around him the light streamed in ripples of unnameable color.

The light flowed back into Raef, and he burst into flame.

His hair burned up in an instant, and then his shirt. His skin bubbled up, the muscle underneath, the bone thrusting out white against the red for an instant before it too blackened and was gone. The throbbing red fist in the middle of his chest exploded into a golden jewel. The great blood sacks of his lungs. His belly, his man's parts. Above Emma, sprawled senseless on the red cloak, the white bones of his face gleamed like a reflection in the air, the long white bone of his left arm, the fingers of his maimed hand. They melted into nothing. There was silence.

Laissa was pushing up, trying to get out from under Leif. The fat Icelander's body was sprawled over her, limp. His head was covered with blood; a slate from the roof had dashed his skull in.

Gemma staggered to the door of the church and stood gaping there. Knut got up, shaking, and went toward the red puddle of the cloak on the ground, toward his new wife. Laissa got to her feet, her arms out to steady herself.

Knut kneeled by Emma and lifted her in his arms. She was soft, dazed, her coif gone and her hair wild. The red cloak had left welts around her neck, her wrists. She raised her eyes to him, bewildered. He saw at once the demon was gone. He said her name, and her brown eyes blinked up at him as if she had never seen him before. He lifted her like a child and turned to Laissa, beside him.

Laissa had dropped down on all fours where her husband had been. But of Raef there was nothing left.

⁓

They buried Leif in the graveyard behind the church. After the priests had gone, Laissa went around picking up stones and began to lay them down in the outline of a ship. She wept as she did this.

Gemma came and put her arms around her mother and sobbed.

"Was this me? Did I make this happen?"

"No, no," Laissa said. "He was always meant to do this. It was for your sake that he could. He loved you more than he feared her." She held the girl tightly. "Come back to Jorvik with me."

Gemma shook her head. She stood back, wiping her hand over her tears. "I am staying here, Mama. The Queen is not what she was. She doesn't even remember. She needs me." She wiped her eyes again. "And Knut is here, you know, and . . . I could not bear to go back and have it all be different."

Laissa said, "I have to go back to Jorvik."

"Mama, I love you. Knut will care for you, for the sake of what Papa did." She began to cry again. "What Papa did. I was a fool, Mama. Please stay with us."

Laissa said, "Here? He isn't here. If he's anywhere, he'll be in Jorvik."

Gemma gave her a wild look and said nothing more. She went away to her new place, in the Queen's court. She would be great there. She would marry one of Knut's friends. Her sons would be princes. None of them would have the sight.

Laissa felt nowhere, suddenly disjointed, as if something had changed fundamentally and she had just noticed. She missed Raef with an inconsolable ache, and yet he seemed to be all around her. In crowds, near the river, at night when the wind blew hard, she heard his voice speaking, too low to catch the words. She felt the touch of his lips on the places he loved to kiss: her throat, her hair, her palms. She woke one morning drenched with sweat from a dream where they coupled in a wild lust.

Knut came to her.

"I did not intend this."

"Ah," she said, "don't talk to me like that. It happened." She had always hated him, but it was not his fault.

He said, "When you get to Jorvik, if there is no hall, if nothing is left, send to Odd. He will be the jarl in Northumberland. He will provide for you all the rest of your life."

Laissa shrugged, indifferent. She knew there would be no hall in Jorvik. That was what he had meant, "later." She was beginning to wonder if Raef was calling her.

She went back to Jorvik. She had a token from the King that made everybody along the way give her anything she asked for. Raef tormented her, a glimpse, a touch, a whisper, the dreams of rollicking as merrily as bears in heat. She came into Jorvik and saw how different it was, how much bigger. They called it Jor'ck now. They admitted her at the gate with many bows for the favor of the King. She went along toward the hall and out on the low hilltop there, the stones tumbled around and the grass blowing in the wind. In one corner the brass jug lay on its side, full of dead leaves. The fire ring was there also, cold as the dirt.

Now she knew that he was calling her.

She went down into the city, finding her way through a new close, across a wide new street with a fountain. Down the next alley she came out before Corban's house.

The ruin still stood in the row of well-built houses around it. She walked in over the threshold. At first, she felt nothing. Her heart sank; it had gone with him too. Then she took another step, and she felt the air thicken around her, folding, bending, opening into a field of light.

Voices sounded around her, deeper than human. Slower. Old, mellow, like bits of a strange, pure music. She went farther into the house, into the curved and folded space. Nearby Raef was saying, "Come home. Come home." She looked down and saw her body floating off in pieces, like spindrift carried by lapping waves. It was warm. His hands touched her. She lay back, spread her arms out, and let herself go, bit by bit, into the endless stream.

Devotees of the reign of Ethelred the Redeless, or Unready, will see what liberties I've taken with the historical facts here. This would pain me more if the facts about this bloody and vicious reign weren't so sparse and unreliable. I've left out a lot of what seems redundant. Ethelred was murderous and inept, and various Viking armies marched back and forth through the country for years, hacking and hewing and destroying everything. It seems unnecessary to untangle this very much. On Saint Brice's Day 1002, Ethelred engineered a massacre of all the Danes and Danish sympathizers he could get his hands on, which wasn't enough to do more than make everybody really angry. The Vikings were no less vicious. In the following war the archbishop of Canterbury was beaten to death with bones in his own cathedral.

Nonetheless, Sweyn Forkbeard was apparently summoned to England by the northern lords in 1015, who submitted to him in bulk at Gainsburgh, handing him the kingdom. At this time Ethelred did actually escape to Normandy. When Sweyn died, less than six weeks later, probably not from a wasp bite, Ethelred crossed the Channel and claimed the crown again, and then he died within a few weeks. All this while, Edmund Ironside was conducting operations against Sweyn and was functionally king. Excising Ethelred a little early seems merciful.

Emma was probably not possessed. Jorvik, or York, did not go through a major decline during Ethelred's reign. Archbishop Wulfstan was much different than I have made him. Knut's war actually lasted fourteen months and involved an inconclusive siege of London that I have not inflicted on you; so the last campaign, on Ermine Street, the great old Roman road, moved north instead of south. Thorkel the Tall was there for part of Knut's war, although they didn't get along; Knut's thorny relationship with the Jomsviking is part of the lore, as is the suggestion that Thorkel fostered him. How old Knut actually was is one of those wild guesses. He first shows up with Sweyn at Gainsburgh, and the sagas say he went young to war—and certainly if he was fostered by Thorkel, he couldn't have been much more than a teenager in 1014.

Thurbrand Hold's murder of Uhtred of Bamburgh, with Knut's connivance, is well documented. Several stories suggest that Eadric Streona murdered King Edmund, either at the Battle of Assundun or later, and that Knut had him killed because of it. Knut's offer to Edmund to share the kingdom rather than fight on is also well attested. Edmund's wife, Ealdgyth, bore him two sons who wound up in Hungary. That tidal bore on the Trent in Gainsburgh is the tide Knut allegedly commanded to stop.

Greatest of the Viking kings, Knut reigned for twenty years over England, Denmark, Norway, and part of Sweden; he was so powerful and successful that some modern writers call him the Emperor of the North. But he left no dynasty. Both his sons were inept. After the death of Harthacanute, his son by Emma, the English high council called in Edward Aetheling, Emma's son by Ethelred, who reigned for the next twenty-odd years. He was called Edward the Confessor for his piety. Knut's real heirs were Godwine of Wessex, who married Knut's sister, and his son Harold Godwinesson, who effectively ruled England through the reign of the mild and unworldly Edward.

What happened after the death of Edward the Confessor in 1066, everybody used to know, and that so many people don't anymore is a puzzle to me.